Crowned By Love

Crowned By Love

The Yorkist Saga Book 1

Diana Rubino

Chapter One

Westminster Palace, London, April, 1471

Denys Woodville hiked up her skirts and hopped onto the palace gate. The crowd cheered as King Edward led his Yorkist army into the outer court, fresh from another defeat of the Lancastrians. The scene evoked mixed feelings as despair overtook her joy. How she longed for a soldier of her own to welcome home.

Mounted on his white stallion, the king waved to adoring subjects as if today were any other. Trumpets and clarions blasted a sprightly tune. Knights unhorsed and removed their helmets as families and lady loves flocked to them. Richard, the king's brother, leapt off his mount into his sweetheart Anne's open arms. The king led the stream of squires and grooms into the palace to greet his pregnant Queen Elizabeth. Amidst all this embracing and kissing, Denys stepped down from her perch and stood alone.

Only one knight remained mounted. He didn't rush into the arms of an ardent maiden. Instead, he halted his gray stallion directly in front of Denys.

"Good morrow, my lady!" His tone, clear and confident, boomed from his slatted visor.

Her eyes locked on the proud figure, its regal bearing a portrait of chivalry. The sun's rays blocked all but the outline of his pointed helmet. With one graceful move, he threw back his visor. Her gaze lingered on his face, shadowed with stubble, a cut on his chin his only physical mar. The sun's rays glinted in his sky-blue eyes.

"Welcome home, my lord," she greeted him. "We are all very proud of you."

He plucked a white rose from the vine behind him, leaned over and handed it to her. The striking contrast twixt delicate rose and hard plate armor sent a

1

thrill through her. She longed to clasp his fingers under those gauntlets. "Why, thank you, my lord."

He gazed at her with such longing, she knew he shared her loneliness, her displacement.

He also needed a special someone to come home to; she knew it in her heart.

The revelers converged, pushing them apart, yet their eyes still locked. The press of people and horses drove him away, only helmet and gauntlet visible as he waved. She waved back, but for certes he could no longer see her.

"Farewell, Sir—"

Sir—who? As he vanished, she caressed the rose petals and her imagination soared.

She never had a sweetheart or a romantic liaison. She cherished her childhood friend Richard, but that was childhood. This soldier made her feel like a woman for the first time in her life.

She nudged her way through the crowded palace grounds. No sight of him. "I shall find him," she vowed out loud.

* * *

Valentine Starbury guided his mount around the outer court's perimeter, trampled flowers and handkerchiefs the only remnants of the joyous parade. He glanced over his shoulder but couldn't find her, the only maiden without a steepled headdress. Only an elegant pearl circlet graced her silver hair. Standing alone when he entered, neither welcoming nor embracing a special soldier, eyes downcast, she'd looked so despondent. But they brightened like jewels when he approached, his own heartache reflected in those eyes. She was the maiden he'd envisioned all those lonely nights in France—the maiden he always knew he'd find.

And in a moment, he'd lost her.

Swearing, he shook his head in despair—*you lost her, you fool, you can't even do that right.*

He couldn't bear another loss.

* * *

Alone in her chambers after the feast, Denys stroked the fragrant rose he'd given her. After her Aunt Elizabeth adopted her, she passionately pursued Edward, England's future king. Edward fell hard, and they married. The new bride had no need of a child, so she sent Denys to Yorkshire, far out of the way.

The childless duke and duchess of Scarborough raised her as the daughter they never had. When the duchess died, the duke sent Denys back to court, unwanted again. Despite having a king and queen for an uncle and aunt, Denys languished, a lost soul. Today, as reunited lovers surrounded her, she stood alone, unwanted. To add to her misery, the knight of her dreams appeared, only to vanish. Such was her life as an outsider.

Her lady-in-waiting entered, curtsied, and held out a folded parchment embossed with the royal seal. "A page delivered this from her highness the queen, my lady."

She dismissed the maid. "It can wait." Probably a summons to one of the queen's silly musicales, an excuse for court ladies to gossip.

She put the message out of her mind till that eve as her tiring woman stood behind her brushing her hair.

"Jane, please fetch me that royal parchment." She waved in the direction of her writing table.

Denys broke the seal and unfolded it—a summons, all right—but not to a giddy musicale.

It was a summons to a wedding—her own. Her heart took a sickening lurch.

Her intended was Richard, duke of Gloucester, the king's youngest brother, her childhood companion. Queen Elizabeth always married relatives off to the cream of nobility, and Richard was the highest ranking bachelor in the kingdom.

Far from her idea of a husband. A brother, yes. A husband—never!

A fastidious prude, he intended to wed his sweetheart Anne Neville.

Denys and Richard played together as children, and renewed their friendship when she returned to court. They played tennis, chess, cards—but play ended at games. Just the thought of kissing him made her shudder.

Now the queen wanted them wed on Christmas Day.

Seething with fury, she strode to the hearth and flung the parchment into the flames. They licked and charred it beyond recognition. She crawled into bed for a long, hard think.

By the time she fell asleep, she'd already thought of several ways out.

* * *

King Edward stood to bid his queen good eve; she left the dais and her bevy of maids followed her out of the great hall. Denys climbed the dais steps and approached her uncle with a curtsy. "Uncle Ned, I need speak with you."

"Denys, my dear, come, sit by me!" His beefy hand wrapped hers in comforting warmth. "I hardly see you, what with all the battles and council meetings—you must let me get my revenge on the chessboard!"

She smiled at the memory of their last match—she captured Uncle Ned's own king with no more than rook and pawn. "I would much enjoy that, Uncle." She sat beside him and kissed his ruby coronation ring.

He motioned a passing steward to bring Denys a cup of wine. "Are you happy at court, my dear? Or would you rather stay up Yorkshire way where it's quiet at least?"

"Oh, I felt especially misty today, the first anniversary of the duchess's death. I miss Castle Howard so much." Ah, Castle Howard—where warmth and love surrounded her, embracing her childhood with rocking cradles, a lullaby every night and the duchess's soft breast to rest her head on. "I had my studies, gave alms to the poor, read to the urchins ... they devoured King Arthur tales." Her tone lightened as she recalled the joy of bringing brief happiness to bleak lives.

"I know how much the folk and the duchess adored you." King Edward gazed into the distance. "In the years my brothers, sisters and I lived at Castle Howard, the duchess was a mother to all of us."

Denys nodded. Her eyes caught the blur of lights glinting off her goblet. "Duchess used to spend hours fussing over my hair, especially when the sun bleached it white. 'How pretty you are, like a little Dove!' she said to me one day." Her pet name was Dove from that day on. But her halcyon childhood met an abrupt end.

A playful grin frolicked on King Edward's lips. "She had pet names for us all. I was Knobby, for my big knees and elbows. But I've grown into them." He splayed his fingers, rough and calloused from wielding sword and mace.

"I'm lost here, with the constant buzz of court affairs and trappings of royalty. I just don't fit in here." She could talk to him this way; his was the most sympathetic ear at court. He shared her love for the Yorkshire countryside: lush green fields, gentle dales, moors purple with heather. She hated London, a filthy, crowded stinkhole. Most of all, she despised the queen's greedy family. "How I wish I can find my true origins. I'll never believe I'm the queen's niece."

"Have you appealed to her since your return to court?" He took a swig of wine. "She may accommodate you now that you're older."

"Aye, the day I arrived from Castle Howard. She dismissed me with 'your father never married my sister, they died of the sweat, and be grateful I adopted a bastard like you.'" She looked her uncle in the eye. "She hides something, I know it."

With her first spoken words, she began asking her aunt—"Who were my lord father and ma mere?" Elizabeth either slapped or shooed her away, and when the questioning became too annoying for the queen-to-be, with coronation jewels and feasts on her mind, she cast Denys off to faraway Yorkshire.

But Denys never stopped wondering. *What does Elizabeth hide? Who are my parents? Who am I?*

Edward nodded, a dimple in his cheek punctuating his frown. Oh, he knew his conniving wife, all right.

Denys took a deep breath and squared her shoulders. "Uncle, last eve, the queen dispatched me a most preposterous demand. I must appeal to you about it."

"Oh, no, what does she want this time?" His tone weary, Edward motioned one of the servers for a refill. "Shall I fetch a pitcher for this?"

"I would fetch a cask." Denys gripped her goblet. "She wants me to marry Richard. On Christmas Day."

"Richard? My brother Richard?" Edward rolled his eyes and took a long pull of wine. She read his thoughts: "High time we married the urchin off." But not to Richard!

"I knew it was just a matter of time before she betrothed me. But I cannot marry Richard. He's a brother to me. Besides, he's intended to wed Anne for years as the queen well knows." She took a much-needed gulp of wine, draining the goblet. "Elizabeth pushed me round since infancy, shunting me out of the way, then dragging me back. But she cannot marry me to Richard on Christmas Day or any other day. Uncle, please, deny permission."

"So that's the urgency." He chuckled, swinging his goblet twixt thumb and forefinger.

"Urgency?" She sat upright.

Edward nodded. "Richard already cornered—" He twirled his goblet. "I mean requested that I grant him permission to marry Anne at dawn tomorrow. I've seen men anxious to get unmarried, but not the other way round."

"Oh, thank heaven." She sighed with relief. "They should be wed. They're ever so fond of each other. They are to wed tomorrow, then?"

"Aye, but not at dawn as he requested. He was ready to hunt down any priest he could drag out of bed, but I thought it wise to inform the bride first." He gave a smile and a playful wink. "I promised to post the banns twixt council meetings tomorrow, so he can't enter wedded bliss at least until after vespers." He glanced round the noisy great hall. "Now I've got that dreaded funeral mass to attend, so I must be gone, my child. But we shall have that chess game, I promise."

"Whose funeral?" She stood as he did.

"The earl of Desmond. He was executed as were his two small sons." He tugged on his doublet.

"Desmond? Executed? Why, he was a most loyal Yorkist. What was his crime?" Denys shuddered at the thought of this latest execution. "This court is a bloodbath," she muttered.

"There was no crime. Not on his part, but on the part of my wrathful queen." Edward spoke as if resigned to the steady flow of executions Elizabeth instigated. "When Desmond first arrived from Ireland, we went hunting. I lightly solicited his opinion of my marriage to Bess. Desmond replied in all honesty that it was better to marry into a foreign alliance. Thinking no more of it, I made the mistake of casually mentioning the conversation to Bess. She flew into a rage, and cajoled the earl of Worcester into devising a trumped-up charge against poor old Desmond. He was arrested a week ago and brought to the block yestermorn."

"But why could you not stop it?" Denys insisted, following him down the two steps of the dais.

"I intended to grant him pardon. Whilst in the council chambers, I led a futile search for the royal signet, and discovered my queen pilfered it in order to seal the death warrant." He stifled a yawn. "Desmond was ever so faithful. Wish I could say the same for—others here." She knew exactly whom he referred to.

Denys frowned in disgust, knowing she didn't have to hide it from her uncle. "Whenever will your rope snap?"

"No need, lass." The king displayed a rare frown. "The queen's about to birth now, and I'll keep her breeding the rest of her days. She's bound to bring forth a prince fit to be king, or at least as robust as the two wags she whelped by that other canker."

That 'other canker' was her first husband, John Grey.

"We shall hope that's where the similarity ends." Uncle and niece exchanged amused glances.

Edward waved to courtiers as they exited the great hall. Several of his retinue followed him out.

"I must change into black raiment." He bent and hugged her. She felt so safe encircled in his warmth.

"Thank you, sire." She tightened her embrace.

"Sometimes I wonder why I bother to change out of black. One would think I was a widower."

"Be careful what you ask for, Uncle." She nudged him in the ribs. "You may get it."

They shared a more secret exchange of smiles this time.

She loved Uncle Ned with all her heart. He was father, brother, and friend to her—she trusted him with her every problem. He was the only good thing to come out of this twist of fate. She missed him so when away to battle or on progress. But why had he fallen under Elizabeth's spell? She'd heard many tales, most of them outright bawdy, about maidens Uncle Ned courted. He nearly married one of them.

But Elizabeth fixed all that.

And many thought it witchcraft.

Elizabeth Woodville first met Edward Plantagenet under an oak tree. The eve before their wedding, thirtieth of April, was a sabbath in the witches' year. Witches always held their sabbaths beneath oak trees. Elizabeth's neighbor publicly accused her of witchcraft, producing two small leaden figures representing king and queen. Edward took the charge seriously and investigated it himself. But hopelessly smitten with the Grey Mare, as she was known, he married her. Was it because she wouldn't give him what he wanted till the wedding night? Denys always wondered.

* * *

All throughout Mass the next morn, Denys observed Richard fidgeting, glancing everywhere, ignoring the priest at the pulpit. He toyed with his rings, smoothed his tabard till she thought he would wear the fabric out, and spent the latter half of the service hunched over, head in hands. His mind was not on worship.

No, the queen could not be so cruel as to deprive him of happiness with his true love. *We shall find a way out of it,* she swore before God.

As the chapel emptied out after Mass, Richard tugged on Denys's sleeve and motioned for her to follow him. But he made an abrupt twirlabout and strode back down the aisle. "No. Let's sit in the back instead." He added, muttering, "the farther from the altar the better."

Denys gathered her skirts and sat in the last pew. Richard paced back and forth, hands clasped behind his back. "Richard, please sit. You're making me dizzy."

"I cannot sit. I can only think on my feet—moving feet." His voice echoed through the empty chapel. "The blasted queen is up to her usual tricks. And this one might even work." He drove a fist into his palm.

"What has she done now?" Her voice rose with alarm. "I thought Uncle Ned gave you permission to wed Anne today."

"He did. So, after securing permission and summoning Father Farley, all in the space of an hour, I went to fetch my bride, but her sheep-biting father already sequestered her." His voice dripped bitterness.

"Why would he do that?" She got to her feet and stood next to him.

"Oh, it wasn't entirely his doing. He had help." He emphasized the last word with a sneer.

"Oh, no." She clenched her teeth, blood growing hotter with each breath.

"Oh, yes. Queen Elizabitch at it again." He threw his hands up. "I'm trying to find Anne, sent out a search party, but they do sod all. I'm chasing my tail all over England." He pounded his fist on the edge of the pew. "Oh, we should have eloped!"

A heavy pall descended upon her spirit. "Even Uncle Ned said you should secure your bride in place first."

"But is it not like me to overlook the most easily recognized?" He rubbed his eyes. "Holy hell knows where she is and we're back to square one."

She held up her pointer finger. "Not yet. I'll depart court disguised as a maid and take up residence in the north, near Castle Howard. I'm familiar with those parts, I know trustworthy folk, and can pursue my quest for my family from there. Bess can't marry us if she cannot find the bride."

He shook his head as she spoke. "Far too dangerous to sneak away from court in disguises, wandering Britain dressed like a bloody fishwife."

"Very well, then, ponder my next idea. It hit me like a flash of light in the night."

His eyes lit up and fixed on hers. "Carry on."

"You can marry someone else," she offered a simple solution.

"Me marry someone else? Pray why me?" He fixed his fist on his hip. "You're the one your aunt wants to marry off. I'm just the hare caught in the hound's ugly jaws."

"Well, I shan't marry someone of the queen's choosing. I want to find my parentage first. When I do marry, it will be a man of my own choosing who's courtly, handsome, and—virile. Not that you're not all those things, surely," she added.

He nodded, egging her on. "Carry on, let's see you wriggle your arse out of this one." His grin spread, yet aslant. He liked making people squirm.

"Oh, you know what I mean." Her heart leapt at the memory of yesterday. "I want someone like the knight who pranced up to me in the outer court yesterday."

"What knight?" He raised a brow.

"We exchanged nowt but a hello. The crowd forced us apart. He was come and gone in a twinkling. But oh, he made me feel so special, so wanted, so—" She released a longing sigh. "So womanly. No man ever looked at me like that before. The outer court filled with maidens, yet he chose me. I always dreamed of a fairy-tale wedding—to someone just like him." She lowered her eyes. Richard was right. She was dreaming again, out loud this time. "But what good could it do you, or anyone else, to marry the queen's orphaned illegitimate niece anyway? I don't even have a dowry."

"Oh, you do now." Richard chucked her under the chin. "The old witch covered her corybungo, as usual."

"She furnished a dowry?" Denys's eyes widened. "Of what?"

"In noticeably larger lettering than the rest of the message, and underscored no less, she tried to prey on my sense of greed using Foxley Manor for bait."

"Foxley Manor?" She shook her head. "Never heard of it."

"Tis some property she claims is substantial. As if a poxy manor house can compare to what Anne brings to the table. With all due respect, Denys—" Richard paused. "Anne's dowry is vast, and she stands to inherit half her mother's estates."

"I know of no Foxley Manor." She shook her head. "I never had any form of dowry. How can I, being an orphaned bastard?"

"I thought it part of the queen's own dowry, but her dower lands were in Northamptonshire, where Edward first fell under her spell. Her family home in Grafton Regis became Edward's after their wedding in the chapel there," he explained. "But I know not where she came up with this Foxley Manor. Nor do I care. Sounds like an old cow shed to me. Utterly useless." He waved the idea away like a housefly.

"Well, I care." She folded her arms across her chest. "Did she say where this place is?"

"Somewhere in Wiltshire—oh, what was the name of the town?" He tapped the side of his head. "It sounded like a kind of wine—oh, yes. Malmesbury."

Denys gasped and clasped her Book of Hours, its spine digging into her palms. "Malmesbury! God's truth!"

"You've heard of it?" Richard tilted his head.

"Divers times!" She couldn't seem to catch her breath. "Richard—" Her heart pounded. "Divers times before she sent me to live at Castle Howard, I heard her all over court speaking of Malmesbury, followed by my name, in muffled voice. But I was never able to make out the words through the palace walls, with servers clattering about. Thinking there must be some connection, I wrote it in my journal immediately after hearing it so there would be no mistake. I even found it on the mappa."

"Mayhap that's where your father hails from," Richard ventured.

"Well, I never believed I was her sister's child. I don't even look like a Woodville, and by the grace of God, I possess nary a characteristic in common with any of them."

"So there may be a connection with your family to this Foxley Manor." Richard drummed his fingers on the pew. "Hmmm."

"Richard, I must depart for Malmesbury to find Foxley Manor, and God willing I'll find what I look for." She pumped her clenched fists. "Whilst I'm journeying, you carry on your search for Anne."

She struggled to breathe evenly and stay calm, when she really wanted to storm into the queen's chambers and throttle her.

Richard tapped his foot. "Well, whether you find what you seek at Foxley Manor, we just might find a way to make your other fairy tale fancy come true."

Denys gazed up into the vaulted recesses of the chapel ceiling and conjured the image of that knight, so vivid in her mind. If Richard could find someone remotely resembling him…

"I call it a fairy tale because that's all it is, Richard." She plummeted back down to earth. "I should wake up."

"Mayhap not. The realm has its fair sprinkling of courtly—" He waved his hand. "Whatever you said. There are divers more where he came from. Trust me to help procure you one. Then get Edward's permission to wed and be done with it. The Grey Mare need not know a thing."

A spark of excitement spiked her pulse. "I'll consider this if you dip into that fair sprinkling and retrieve a gem—but he must fit the description of what I want. First, go find Anne and I shall go to Malmesbury to seek my family. At least one of us should find what we seek. Now I'm off for a word with the queen—and there's nowt less courtly than she."

He shook his head with a smirk. "Not outside the privies, anyway."

"Oh, how I wish to sprout wings and fly to Malmesbury," she fancied out loud. "Another link in the mystery within reach, finally. I shall go there and God willing that's where my true beginnings lie."

Please let it be the place I've wondered about through all those nights in the drafty chamber as a child, every time Elizabeth shooed me away, she begged God above. It made her more determined to defeat the queen at her own cruel game. Now she had purpose—somewhere to go—the first step in the journey to her heritage. And if Richard found the knight of her fancy, life would be complete. Was that too much to ask? Finding family *and* true love?

"For now, let's keep that in the mists of dreamworld whilst I go on my quest." She clasped his hand and led him to the chapel door. "I need to know who I am and where I belong. Then my life will have meaning. I'm not royal. I don't belong here nor do I deserve all these royal trappings. Even if they're peasant crofters working the soil, they're my family. Oh, how I long to find them! Then I'll be worthy of a knight's love." She paused. "Mayhap he sensed my loss and displacement and that made him go away. He saw sadness and anguish in my eyes. Who wants to share such misery?" She pushed the door open.

"But something brought him to you in the first place." He followed her out. "The crowd separated you. You did not drive him away. I know how those victory celebrations are. Chaos prevails—especially once wine starts flowing. People get pushed apart, and I daresay even more often, pushed together. Many a maiden is shoved into the arms of an eager knight, who takes every opportunity to celebrate with her, in more ways than one, into the wee hours before finding out her name."

"Oh, and how do you know this? Experience?" She smiled, knowing it wasn't.

"Nay, I couldn't trick a maiden even if I wanted to. Everyone knows my distinctive countenance." He licked a forefinger and ran it over his brow. "But it's happened to mates of mine. Sometimes I think they're out there fighting in anticipation of the celebrations rather than the survival of the kingdom."

"We all live for something, Richard." She ran her finger down his cheek. They parted and she removed to her chambers to rehearse her dialogue with the queen.

Chapter Two

Denys entered Queen Elizabeth's audience chamber as the church bells clanged thrice. A lady-in-waiting went to inform the queen. Denys prepared for a long wait: her highness always made her grand entrances when good and ready.

As she paced the floor, three serving women scrubbed the woodwork with red, raw hands. Two more servers beat tapestries and polished furniture. A maid wobbled atop a rickety ladder, straining to fan dust webs from a ledge.

Queen Elizabeth entered, swept past Denys without acknowledging her, and headed straight for the maid polishing her writing table. Denys had seen that poor lass on many a dark morning scrubbing the floor, pushing a candle along to light her way.

The queen flattened her palm on the table. "This is not warm, you are not rubbing hard enough. And it is streaked!" she bellowed. The lass cringed in fright. "You rub that till it's warm, or you shall hit your pallet every night for a week sans supper!"

She glanced at Denys and her smile did not reach her eyes, enhancing its falseness. "Do sit, they just aired out the receiving chamber." The queen snapped her fingers twice and the servers vanished.

She settled her swollen-with-child figure into the oversized chair across from Denys, a bit too far away for normal conversation, but distance seemed to boost the queen's sense of superiority. Her pointed headdress cast an ominous shadow over the painting of London behind her. Denys sat across from her in a velvet chair and toyed with its braided trim.

"Now what is it that you would tell me, dear?" The endearment tagged at the end was clearly an afterthought. "I meet with kitchen staff shortly to command the evening meal. So have your say quickly."

Denys cleared her throat for the carefully rehearsed words: "Aunt Bess, you know I like to distribute alms to poor children. Since I'm back in London, I've observed the wretched condition of our poor here, and want to arrange progresses through the city. I would do this on a regular basis."

She smoothed her skirts over her middle. "You ask for a royal stipend?"

Denys nodded. "That and a guide, mayhap a fit mount to carry me on my travels."

A frown etched deep lines around her mouth. "The royal treasure is strained, financing these incessant battles with Lancastrians. 'Twould be a great burden."

"I shall cut back on my own expenses." Her words rushed out. "For instance, I needn't be waited on by the maids I've got here. I shall dismiss four of them."

Elizabeth looked at Denys with a mixture of begrudging and wide-eyed awe. "To live with fewer than six maids?"

"I need but one." She gripped the chair arms. "My heavens, at Castle Howard, I had a lady-in-waiting and a chambermaid, and that was more than enough. I'd much rather give the money to poor orphans. The maids can work elsewhere."

"You've a big heart," she remarked as if it were a fault.

"Aunt Bess, you're a well-traveled woman. You've been on progress with the king to the far reaches of the Scots border—I've never taken a goodwill trip quite like that, being so isolated up at Castle Howard. I would arrange for a traveling party to go on seasonal progress, to distribute alms, and read to the children of their good queen, even outside London. I hoped you would tell me of villages where local folk would most welcome a Woodville family member."

Elizabeth, admiring her fingernails, finally looked up, but didn't meet Denys's eyes. She never looked anyone straight in the eye. "I do like the New Forest, and Devon and Cornwall's rugged beauty. Some poor wretches may dwell there, I know not. Those local folk do admire the Woodvilles. Then, of course, there is East Anglia. I always did enjoy Colchester, although the castle is not to my standards."

"I wonder what Wiltshire is like," Denys mused.

"Why Wiltshire?" Her eyes narrowed as she tilted her head. When she saw Denys staring, it unnerved her.

"Oh, I would like to see a few towns there. Malmesbury…" Still staring, she managed to keep her voice level.

Elizabeth's hands fluttered and she cleared her throat. "Now why would you want to go there?"

"Why not?" she challenged.

"Just tell me, of all the places in this kingdom, you specifically single out a poxy hamlet in Wiltshire." The queen's stern tone intensified.

"Whilst I help the poor, there are things there I'm interested in visiting." Denys kept her voice level.

"Such as?"

"Oh, the Abbey has a rich history. Then there's the eleventh-century Three Bells Inn, and Foxley Manor." Keeping her tone as innocent as a saint's, still she stared.

"Foxley Manor?" The queen's tone deadened, like an untuned string.

Aha!

Elizabeth Woodville could never succeed as a stage player.

"Aye, Foxley Manor." She nodded, her tone wistful. "I read about it whilst a child. 'Tis quite charming, dating back to Arthur's time. As such, it spurs my curiosity."

"I've never heard of it. I've never even heard of Malmesbury." The queen's fingers strummed the strands of pearls about her neck. Denys knew she was lying. "St. Giles right here in London is much more practical. They don't come poorer than that. Toss a farthing to that piteous rabble and they fight to the death to catch it. 'Tis more amusing than bear-baiting." She gave a sadistic cackle.

"You're sure you've not heard of Malmesbury?" Denys prodded. "Dig into your memory, mayhap you can recall something. After all, you're as well read in British history as you are well traveled."

Red blotches spread across the queen's cheeks. Her chest rose with the deep intake of air she held for a beat. "Nay, I haven't. Goodness knows where the Godforsaken place is." She exhaled and her breath hissed like a snake as she waved her other hand.

"A stone's throw from Swindon, actually," Denys informed her. "I read that Foxley Manor has some connection to the Woodvilles. A remote ancestor, a distant relative of Ethelred the Unready, built it."

"Mayhap I do recall hearing about it." She tapped the side of her head. "Aye, it was King Edward's father spinning one of his tall tales."

Codswallop, Denys scoffed. If Richard never heard of it, it was never in Plantagenet possession. If anyone knew every scrap of property the Plantagenets ever owned or seized, it was Richard. But her aunt was falling into step as plotted.

"Then I should be happy to visit there and to have them receive me as a royal niece," Denys declared.

"N—nay—" the queen stuttered. "There's no one about. It burnt down."

"An entire town?" Denys inquired.

"Nay, Foxley Manor, you dolt. Burnt down ages ago." She gave a dismissive wave.

"A stone keep isn't easily burned down," Denys challenged.

"'Twas a timber-framed cottage, nowt more. A pile of rot. It no longer exists." The queen's eyes darted round the chamber.

"Ah. Very well then." The truth was within reach, though she didn't quite know how. Elizabeth's weak attempt to cover her lies gave her away. It convinced Denys that she had some family connection in Malmesbury. The possibility of not being a Woodville was akin to rebirth.

She stood to take her leave.

The queen looked up to face the sunlight, all the misery of a raging storm condensed within those eyes. She struggled to her feet, brushing away Denys's attempt to assist her. "Foxley Manor no longer exists. 'Tis a myth now, like Camelot, reduced to sketchy legend. If you care to go on progress for the poor, do so, but not to Malmesbury. 'Tis a wealthy town, they've no need of alms there. You waste your time. Stay in London. I order you."

A myth. Indeed. The prattle about it burning was more believable. The truth was barely beyond her reach.

"Ah, then I shall, Aunt Bess. As long as you command. Do I get the stipend?" She crossed the chamber and grasped the door knob.

"Aye, I grant you ten pounds per annum. And if you insist your maids be dismissed, so be it. I shall add them to my personal staff. I am short of help."

Oh, but of course. Denys his a sneer behind her hand. The queen barely lifted a finger even to attend to her most basic privy needs. Forcing a curtsy, she backed out of the chamber, her mind whirring with plots.

"I know she lies!" she spat out loud. She didn't expect the truth, she just wanted her aunt to know that she had some information. She strode down the corridor, head high, shoulders square. It was that knight—he'd made her feel so worthy of attention. As much as Uncle Ned adored her, she was still a child in his eyes. But that knight, whoever he was, changed the way she now saw herself, because of the way he'd looked at her. And she may never see him again.

* * *

Graveyard of All Saint's Church, Surrey

Having returned from warfare training in France straight into battle at Barnet, Valentine now basked in respite at his family estate, Fiddleford Manor, beyond the City gates. How lovely to be back in Surrey, with no talk of court affairs or enemies. He beamed, so happy to be reunited with his dearest friend, visiting for the day. But why did Richard find churchyards so comforting? Valentine relished peace and quiet, but his own grounds would suffice. He didn't need *this* much quiet.

He reclined against a tombstone. Its coolness soothed him, as did the grave-yard in a strange way, shaded with aged trees, leaves rustling in the breeze. Headstones stood in eternal testament to crofters who'd toiled their lives away, the etchings worn smooth by the ravages of time.

Leaning forward, he wrapped an arm round Richard's shoulders and gave him an affectionate squeeze. "A pity you never visited France, Richard. The French have words to describe every conceivable fancy for which there is no English equivalent."

Richard scowled. "No wonder we beat them at every turn. They're too busy carousing to defend their own land. When it comes to the art of war, they reek."

"War isn't everything." Valentine gazed out over his birthplace. "We must love, too. "From atop the knoll where the graveyard lay, he gazed across rolling dales where he'd frolicked as a child, the landscape rich with cultivated strips of land. The village of Twickenham lay in the distance, the church steeple reaching toward heaven, circled with wattle-and-daub cottages. Horses grazed alongside a flock of sheep fluffy as the clouds above. The hills met the sky on the wispy horizon, surrounded by lush forest, where he learned hawking and hunting, and shared his first kiss.

In the thick of the last battle, a Lancastrian soldier struck out at Valentine with a poleaxe and clipped his arm. He managed to hold out and helped smash the center of the enemy line. He could barely move his arm till yesterday when he picked up his sword and cautiously swung it. He shifted position to ease the discomfort. He didn't want Richard to know he was injured. It was a matter of pride; they'd always been friendly rivals.

"God's truth, Val, your stay in France has brought out the romantic in you." Richard cast him a sly grin.

Valentine's hair blew into his eyes and he brushed it away. "Ah, yes, nowt matches the passion of a man and woman whose hearts are one."

Richard glanced round. "A pleasurable enough pastime twixt battles, I reckon."

How Valentine wished Richard had gone to France with him! Mayhap he would stop obsessing about war.

Richard's grin widened. "Pray do you compose love sonnets in your head during Mass?"

"Aye, but just the words, not the music," Valentine replied. "How about you? Any maidens catch your fancy?"

"Just one." Richard's expression hardened, the smile gone, lips pulled taut.

"Why but one?" Valentine shifted his arm, trying to ignore the pain.

Richard shrugged. "I only hunt one at a time, friend."

"Who is she?" Curiosity got the best of him.

"Anne Neville." Richard's smile returned. "My Annie."

"Little Annie? You're still smitten? Why, that's marvelous!" He clapped his friend on the shoulder. "You make a fitting couple."

"Aye, we do. Edward granted us permission to marry. But by the time I called on her with a priest in tow, her father had her sequestered so tightly, we could not even elope. That blasted Warwick—" he muttered. "I should have known."

"Why would Warwick keep you apart?" Valentine probed.

"'Tis a conspiracy twixt him and the queen of the witches." Richard cleared his throat and released a resigned sigh. "She wants to snare me into a union to advance her own tribe, as usual."

"To whom?" Valentine's eyes widened. Curiosity burned now.

"To her orphaned illegitimate niece."

Valentine's jaw dropped. "God's foot!"

"Marrying me is as high as her niece can aspire, but her dowry isn't more than an afterthought Elizabeth tossed into the bargain, and a right piddly one at that. A bloody insult, compared to Anne's worth. 'Who better for my niece than the king's own brother? Yakity yakity yak!'" he mimicked Elizabeth's nerve-grating tone.

"Is the niece as versed in trickery as the rest of the lot?" Valentine asked.

"Nay, not at all." He shook his head. "She's a most trusted confidante. She promptly tells me of every happening with the Woodvilles."

He blanched in disbelief. "Why betray her own family to you?"

"She doesn't believe she's a Woodville. There's no resemblance in any way. Moreover, for good reason, she's ashamed of Elizabeth and her relations clawing their way through court, like vultures swooping on prey. She wants no part of it. Their values are worlds apart, the Woodvilles value nowt but titles and riches. Look how they manage to cajole Edward into ennobling them and giving them court appointments. Then they got him to finance that poxy navy of theirs. All with help from the queen, of course. And I need not explain how."

Valentine was tempted to probe his prudish friend with, "Oh, please, Richard, tell me exactly how," to indulge in a moment of amusement. But the conversation had captured his fancy. "So, the niece—what are her flaws? Besides the taint of her name."

"There's nowt about her that puts me off. Unlike her pomp-gobbling relatives, she prefers bucolic pleasures. Court life holds no allure for her. I relish her company, but nowt else. My humours, if you will, lie stagnant when she's near. I feel no..." Richard's tilted his head and drummed his fingers on his chin.

"Desire?" Valentine suggested.

Richard shrugged.

"Passion?" he ventured.

Richard looked away and yanked on a blade of grass.

"Rapture?" he tried.

"Something like that," he muttered, with a toss of his head. He turned to face Valentine. "How do you know about those things? Have you felt the intensity of any of those feelings you mention? Or do you draw on what you witnessed at the French court?"

"Oh, I've been smitten, but not the deep-seated emotional pangs of a man for a woman, the way my father and mother were. When I was barely old enough to talk, I sensed all the amour they had for each other." His eyes slid shut as he evoked the memory of his parents.

"Well, I certainly don't feel French when I'm with her." Richard frowned. "'Twould be like marrying my sister. I've barely seven months to escape the travesty."

"There must be a way to duck this marriage." Valentine held up a finger. "A-ha! Tell the queen you prefer men."

The lines twixt Richard's brows deepened. "What bloody good would that do? She knows I'm a soldier and prefer the company of men, I—"

"Nay, Richard," Valentine cut him off. "I don't mean just their company. I mean—you know—" He gave Richard a wink. "Tell her you're one of *them*."

"You mean—" Richard flicked his wrist.

"Aye!" He nodded. "She wouldn't want her niece wed to a sodomite, would she?"

Richard pondered that and shook his head. "Nay. I'd have to play the part, and swishing round court would get me into more trouble than I'm in now." He brushed an ant off his arm. "She'd see that and try to marry me off to one of her whoopsie brothers."

Valentine sought another solution. "How about taking sacred vows?"

Richard expelled a whoosh of breath. "I've no inclination to be a priest, Valentine. God will have me for the rest of eternity. As long as I live, the kingdom needs me more. No, I must find Anne and get her out of blasted Warwick's clutches. Or else I must find—" His eyes lit up and sparkled. "Val…" He laid his hand on Valentine's arm. "You and I are closer than brothers, and I must discuss something with you. About—female response, to put it delicately."

"Pray tell why you chose a graveyard for the subject. Do females play dead when you make advances?" Valentine, rather pleased with his friendly taunt, chuckled. Mocking each other good-naturedly was a favorite pastime.

"Will you do something for me?" Richard's fingers tightened on Valentine's arm. "Since you're so very capable."

"What something is that?" Valentine eyed the picnic basket, hoping it wasn't empty.

Richard relaxed his grip and took his hand away. "Seduce Elizabeth's niece for me."

Valentine's hand froze on its way to the basket. "For you? You mean pretend I'm you and steal into her chambers after the candles are snuffed? I daresay she'll notice the difference after a stroke or two."

"Nay, I mean instead of me! God's truth, you know what I mean. That is my contingency if other plots fall through. She wants someone out of King Arthur tales. Care to have a go at it, Lancelot?" He raised a brow.

"Oh, grand. So now I'm a bloomin' scheme." Valentine shook his head. "When I said I'd do anything for you, I didn't mean seduce away your betrothed's maidenhead."

"We're hardly betrothed. One of her plots was to flee court in disguise. I couldn't let her wander the realm, 'tis much too dangerous. Better to carry out my plot. And you fit her description of a courtly—oh, what did she call it, her fancy one—handsome, virile, and some such—"

Valentine lowered his head to hide his smile and rummaged through the picnic basket.

"You inherited your father's title, you possess lands and plate," Richard carried on. "You are just what she fancies. You'll be perfect together. Just make her acquaintance, will you not?"

"Richard, I'll not create a rift in your family. You assume the queen would approve. You assume the niece will swoon at my feet. You assume too much." He found a cold chicken leg, pulled it out and took a bite.

"The queen will know nowt. Now is no time for doubt, Val. You'll have no trouble capturing her heart. Look at you. Tall, charming, and an accomplished soldier. Everything I'm not."

"Now, I agree with almost everything you said, my friend. But you are the true soldier," Valentine countered in mid-chew.

"That is expected of me. Just as statesmanship is your strength. But the kingdom will always need a brilliant leader. Couple that with the art of statesmanship and you have an invincible kingdom!"

Valentine cast a glance at his tireless friend. "Do you suggest that should you become king I would make a fitting chief councilor?"

"Mayhap. I hope you would consider the appointment." Richard's reply sounded much too casual for such a serious subject.

Taking another bite, Valentine wondered if Richard entertained thoughts of being king. With Edward now siring heirs, Richard's claim to the throne was farther removed.

"You've had barely a morsel of this repast." Valentine tossed the chicken bone aside, found stewed lampreys at the bottom of the basket, slid one into his mouth and savored its sumptuous texture.

"Extra weight would throw me off balance." Richard smoothed down his doublet.

"You never had an appetite for pleasure, except ghoulish ones, like graveyard picnicking. How can you spend so much time in bone orchards like this?" Valentine suppressed a shudder as a hare scampered by.

"'Tis the only place one can be truly alone." Richard lay on his side. "There is no better sanctuary. You must admit, 'tis rather peaceful here. Its dwellers are unlikely to rise up for a chat."

"You don't fear wraiths rising from these ancient graves?" Valentine's voice took on mock spectral tones as he wiggled his fingers in a gesture of eeriness.

"Bah! I have never seen a spectre, nor do I expect to. They do not exist."

"But you believe Elizabeth Woodville is a witch." Valentine tilted his head.

Richard's lips compressed into a thin line and he turned away. "We were discussing not the queen of the witches, but her niece."

"I hoped you'd forgotten," Valentine muttered. "Why did I never meet her?"

"Elizabeth sent her to Castle Howard when she was a child, and she returned only last year, whilst you were in France." Richard brushed a fallen leaf off his leg.

"Lucky me," Valentine muttered.

Richard sat up. "Shall I arrange for you to make her acquaintance?"

Another rustling noise made Valentine jump. "I cannot take advantage of this waif, especially since I met the most enchanting lass the day we returned from battle, and though we merely traded pleasantries, I'm on a campaign to find her again."

"Until that momentous event takes place, offer her your companionship. Do that much for me," he pleaded, hands clasped. "You'll arrive at court on the morrow. If she repulses you that much, you can at least say you tried. It can be practice for you, if nowt else. By God, you may even find yourselves carried away on the wings of Pegasus!"

Valentine's eyes grew wide. He'd never known Richard to allude to mythology. He *must* be desperate.

"She will cherish the flowers you bestow upon her and memorize every line of your ardent poetry," Richard continued in an eager pitch.

"Poetry? In French, I expect."

"Her French is so flawless she practically sings it!" Richard's lips spread in a wide grin.

"So what of her countenance? I admit she sounds rather intriguing, if she likes French poetry. Mayhap I'll introduce her to other French delights..." He left the rest of that thought hanging in the air, but Richard didn't catch on.

"Her looks? I never noticed. I suppose she's..." Richard stumbled over his words, eyes wandering. "...normal, I suppose."

Valentine leaned forward. "A garden slug is normal, Richard ... to another garden slug. What color is her hair? Her eyes? What of her stature?"

"Well, she's ... her hair is ... now, let me see, what color is her hair? It's very light and pale, so since childhood they've called her Dove. Her eyes are rather ... well, have you ever seen bat guano?"

"Cor, she sounds a right abomination!" Stewed lampreys weren't so appetizing now.

"What do you want me to say? That is how I see her, like my own dear sisters, whom I do not think of as women. They're sisters. You must see for yourself," Richard insisted.

He held up his hand in a halting gesture. "I think not, Richard, we don't sound at all compatible."

"I wouldn't ask you to meet her if I thought you incompatible. I must consider every option, should I be unable to rescue Anne." Richard's unblinking stare burned into Valentine. "This is a very special favor I ask of you, dearest friend."

"Oh, God's truth—" He couldn't refuse Richard. He could load up on malmsey and she'd look better with every gobletful. "I tell you what." Valentine sat straight up. "Let us play our favorite game, that we always enjoyed as lads. I've practiced my battle skills religiously. I daresay I'm now quite adept. Let us cross swords, blunted of course. If I lose, I shall honor your request. But if I win..." He held his hands out in a giving gesture. "She's all yours, at least until you rescue Anne from her father's clutches and marry her." Valentine knew his sword-wielding skills would earn him a dukedom someday; this was much-needed practice. He stood and brushed himself off, flexing his bad arm. Giving him only twinges of pain, it felt recovered enough.

"Challenge accepted, my friend. Right here on this spot on the morrow at dawn." Richard's lip eased into a wily curl. "Retrieve your weapon and say your prayers."

* * *

Richard unsheathed his sword and raised it. "You shall pay for this, my friend. Prepare to lose every vestige of your dignity."

"There's no shortage of dignity in this world, Richard. I shall simply collect more." Spasms of agony speared Valentine's bicep; his tight grip on the sword's hilt caused rods of fire to shoot up to his shoulder. But he couldn't back down now.

The verbal sparring ended, the two soldiers circled each other, closer, and closer still, till their gleaming weapons clashed with a ringing of metal. The sun cast a blinding ray of brilliance off the swords' sharp edges. Dodging tombstones, the they entered the heat of the blazing duel, equally matched in strength, agility, and desire to win. Valentine knew that, despite his injury, they matched each other fittingly, as did their fathers, who perished together in battle. Valentine's movements had just a bit more fluidity, his split-second timing catching his opponent out. Richard swore under his breath in frustration. Valentine took pride in his deft footwork. He darted to the left, feinted to the right, causing Richard further vexation. The shorter and leaner Richard fumbled, parried, then regained his timing, only to falter again.

Valentine's lips twisted into a grimace of determination and pain, his gaze piercing the slits of his helmet, sweat stinging his eyes. "Richard!" he panted as their swords clashed, slid, and clashed again. "We needn't spar over this wench any longer!" Valentine rasped, his voice hoarse with distress. Every clatter of his sword ripped straight through his arm. "I yield! I'll help you find someone else for her!"

"'Tis too late now. The best man has to win!" Richard called out confidently as Valentine's sword slipped in his weakened hand. Richard's gleaming blade slashed the air within inches of Valentine's throat.

But Valentine's expert maneuvers finally outfoxed his opponent. Richard lost his balance, slipped and crashed into a slanted headstone. Valentine moved in on the faltering duke and let out a cry of victory. But a searing stab of agony shot through his arm. He stumbled, allowing Richard to regain his footing.

Valentine's arm went limp, his knees buckled under him, and his sword slid to the ground as he fell like a swooning maiden. Richard stood over him, raised his weapon and aimed for Valentine's heart...

Then laughing heartily, he tossed his weapon aside.

Richard bent over to help Valentine to his feet. Valentine stood wearily, arm hanging at his side like dead weight. He moaned aloud, trying to bend his elbow, clutching it with his good hand.

"Val, are you fey? Here, lean on me." Richard held out his arms.

Valentine leaned on his sturdy friend. "Just a slight injury. 'Tis nowt, really."

"From our jousting?" Richard cupped Valentine's elbow.

"Nay, a minor collision with a poleaxe at Barnet." Valentine shut his eyes as the pain subsided to a throb.

"Why did you not say so?" Richard led him to a stone bench. "I never would have let you raise a sword, you puddin'!"

"Nay, I lost fairly. I shall court your cow," Valentine surrendered.

"Only if you're physically able."

"'Tis my arm that hurts. My other appendages are quite intact, I assure you," Valentine added under his breath.

"Very well, I shall arrange for you to meet her on the morrow. But first see the royal physician for that arm." Richard knelt to retrieve both swords.

They headed back to Fiddleford Manor and Valentine tried to flex his fingers. Even this simple movement sent arrows of pain through his arm. "The things I do for you..."

Richard's eyes twinkled in amusement. "Oh, cease your worrying. Have I ever let you down?"

Valentine rolled his eyes toward heaven, then quickly back down to earth, just in case Richard's cow came clumping by.

* * *

The great hall of Westminster Palace shimmered in elegance. Candles glowed in multi-tiered chandeliers suspended from the ceiling splashed with signs of the Zodiac. Tiles gleamed under the ladies' satin slippers and the gentlemen's leather shoes, the pointed ends fastened to their knees with sparkling chains. Couples twirled to the minstrels' delightful tunes from the gallery above. Laughter, like the clinking of pewter, echoed throughout the tapestry-hung hall. Fresh rushes strewn about the floor sweetened the warm evening air.

King Edward and Queen Elizabeth huddled at the high table, heads together, jewels and gems threaded through their ermine-trimmed robes, a swaying sleeve spilling a tankard of wine as he playfully slipped a grape into her laughing mouth. Elizabeth's siblings and sons from her first marriage, now titled and landed, jammed the great hall. Her brother Edward commanded the private Woodville fleet that ostensibly guarded the coastline.

Even Richard seemed to be enjoying himself. He stood as far as possible from the power-hungry Woodvilles, off in a corner with his older brother George, in the throes of animated conversation. George was duke of Clarence, a perfidious subversive who caused the king constant torment. His cohort the earl of Warwick aided all his slipshod uprisings and campaigns. Each slapdash revolt ended in humiliating defeat for George, intensifying the rift twixt the brothers. They called a truce after George's most treacherous attempt to seize Edward's throne. Thwarted once again, George basked in the glow of reconciliation, nestled in the family bosom.

George's checkerboard cloak slipped off one shoulder, his crimson shoes with long pointy toes had bells secured to them. *A court jester in the guise of a nobleman*, Valentine thought.

Conversation and laughter rang out, the courtiers exulting in the company of their beloved King Edward. The kingdom was at peace.

But Valentine Starbury was miserable ... and trying desperately to get drunk.

All the laughter and closeness made him feel more or an outsider. Pangs of jealousy gnawed his insides like hunger. He sat alone at the end of the dais, chin cupped in his palm, his other hand thrust into his pocket, turning a coin over and over. Tonight his gold collar choked him, his sleeves bound his arms like shackles.

The scene before him looked familiar yet strange. After three years in France, although happy to be back on English soil, he found it hard to re-assimilate. Even the accents sounded foreign to him. He needed to reacquaint himself with court life, renew old friendships and reflect on what he left behind, from the new perspective of a man.

He tuned out the noise and tried to conjure his mother's voice, but could only recall ragged breaths as she sobbed the tragic news to him: "Father perished in the battle, my child..."

No. Not My Lord Father. The strong, tall soldier who'd handed Valentine his first sword, taking each finger and wrapping it round the cold handle. The battle also took Richard's father, and knowing they went to heaven together comforted the nine-year-old Valentine. But it hadn't consoled his mother. She lay down one night, hugging Father's pillow, and never woke up. Valentine sat clasping her hand all night. As darkness gave way to a dewy dawn, her lips froze into a peaceful smile. He remembered looking up to see Richard's mother, tears spilling from her eyes.

Valentine joined the bustling Plantagenet household that day.

He had a lot of catching up to do with his surrogate family, but now was not the time.

He cringed at his defeat in that duel with Richard. He should have known better than to tax an injured arm. Adding to his dismay was the scowl of distaste he displayed every time a woman walked by. Studying every female in the great hall, he wondered which was the wench he was doomed to woo.

Wishing she would appear so he could be done with it, Valentine searched for the eyes of bile, the hair of straw. But no one of that description flitted, whirled, or even waddled past him. She was probably in her chambers translating Homer.

Aha! The thought hit him like lightning. It was one of Richard's jokes; there was no bovine wench! No one but Richard derived amusement from his bizarre sense of humor. Valentine's last gulp of wine warmed him as he stood.

Forcing a laugh in the spirit of good sportsmanship, he lumbered up to Richard and George. "There's no bovine wench here, Richard. It is typical of you, though, to make me waste my entire evening waiting for the cow."

Richard registered neither surprise nor amusement, which further befuddled Valentine. When would Richard admit his prank? "She'll be here. She revels in dancing."

"This sitting about does nowt but depress me, Richard. I need to be alone for a while, to think. I'm going for a walk." Without giving either of them a chance to join him, he exited the great hall and strode down the corridor to the palace doors. He breathed easier now that he knew the inevitable was delayed. So it wasn't a joke after all, unless George was in on it. But George wasn't a prankster. He was much too busy with wine, wenches and wars.

Valentine strode past the palace gates and inhaled the earthy air to further clear his head. He hadn't realized how stuffy the great hall had been until he escaped court's sweaty body.

London strictly enforced its 8:00 curfew. After the city gates slammed, anyone walking the streets was subject to a stiff fine. But fresh air and solitude were well worth the few shillings if he were stopped.

Whistling a French tune, he strolled towards the riverbank. The full moon's pearly glow lit his way. At the distant curve in the Thames, the Tower's four peaks stabbed the dark sky. Houses leaned into each other along the riverbank, flickering tallows lit in each window, in honor of St. Paul's feast day. Silver-gray sprigs of birch, their green leaves giving the scene a festive air, decorated every door. The bawdy dockside taverns rumbled, their hanging signs swaying in the breeze. Except for the occasional glimmering lantern, the trading ships in port were dark, their masts towering. A few unfurled sails surged and glowed like specters. Wherries, barges and weather-beaten fishing boats bumped lazily against the bank and drifted back out like a row of dazed sleepwalkers. The distant noises drifting from the palace created a discordant hum.

He began to see Richard's reason for needing a private escape. Mayhap this grassy patch under the elm at the edge of the palace grounds could be his.

He stopped whistling.

What a tranquil spot to connected with the earth. He hated his stifling clothes even more now, his loin-choking hose, his moss-stuffed shoes. He craved wetness to soak his head and drench his body.

Reckless from the wine, he stripped his raiment and tossed each item aside in a crumpled trail as he trotted down to the river. The breeze rustled his hair, caressing each exposed limb as he shed each garment: surcoat, shirt, hose. Free, unclothed and unfettered, he laughed at the absurdity of his actions. How appalled Richard would be at flaunting nudity outdoors!

His feet quit dry earth and slipped into the river's liquid warmth. It enveloped him like a cocoon. He plunged under. Water soaked his hair and scalp. Resurfacing, he laughed and tumbled like a child. Breathing deeply, he spread his arms like wings and glided through the water, every muscle stretching and flexing as his arms propelled him forward.

He waded towards the bank, arched his back and floated, gazing up at the sprinkling of stars, diamonds strewn across the heavens.

Soft humming reached his ears from beyond the riverbank—the lilting melody like morning glories twining round a fence, the notes captured him in their sweet cadence. He turned and dropped to his knees.

Peering round the twisted elm, he saw the glowing head of a white horse. It turned to face him.

He still wanted to find the source of the humming, but his clothes lay beyond his plucking, way up the bank!

A woman came into his view next to the horse. Her fingers wound round the reins, pulling the animal towards the bank to drink. As she turned, his eyes lingered on her silhouette. He sank low into the river's murky depths, but he couldn't tear his eyes away. Her skirts gathered to her knees revealed legs so trim, she could run to Cripplegate without stopping.

God's truth! Was she the maiden he'd galloped up to in the outer court after the battle, the one he'd vowed to find again? Aye, it was! This time no crowd would drive them apart. At this moment, no one else in the world existed.

All thoughts of the cow waiting back at the palace forgotten, no one mattered except himself and this lady. With a burst of impulsiveness, he waded towards her.

"I want to hurl you to the ground and make mad passionate love to you!" he itched to proclaim.

Hearing the distant splash, Denys gasped. Someone lurked in the river, watching her. She squinted to make out features. A spark of recognition enlightened her, then gave way to surprise.

"I didn't mean to frighten you." His voice rang out, piercing the silence. "I fancied a dip."

His voice echoed in her mind since that day. "You found me!" she uttered, the only words she could think of. This unclothed and vulnerable figure before her was the same one that made her feel so special, so desirable, towering over her as the pride of the king's triumphant army. But her modesty prevailed: she fumbled about her belt and pulled her skirts down. The hemline fell to cover her ankles.

"Aye, my lady, 'tis I. As badly as I wanted to find you again, I hoped the atmosphere would be more—formal. At least with a bit more than a river to clad me. Do you fancy a dip, too?" he teased.

"Nay, I came out to water Chera and be alone for a while." A hint of breathiness threaded through what she hoped sounded like poised self-possession. For certes he could hear her heart hammering. First things first: find out who he is. "Do you reside in London, my lord?"

"I just arrived at court. My residence is in Surrey. I'm a friend of the royal family."

"Oh, you are acquainted with Unc…er, his highness the King Edward!" That would make things much easier. She wondered why he didn't stand as she scrambled for a way to prolong their exchange. "I never knew knights bathed in the Thames."

"Nay, this is a first. I've never done this before but I didn't feel up to partaking in festivities. I recently returned from France and … memories started coming back and I just needed some freedom. I was invited to the palace for the feast of St. Paul."

"Oh, if St. Paul could see you now," she whispered.

"Pardon?" He moved closer and she inched back up the bank.

"Just thinking aloud." She focused on his features. She couldn't decide if he had more allure in full dress armor or like this, naked and vulnerable. "Do French knights swim nude in the Seine?"

"Nay, not that I know of." He shook his head. "Ancient Romans spent many a leisure hour at the baths, but they were much more sensuous than we stodgy English."

"I must say I have never been in the presence of an unclothed man without the honor of a formal presentation." Her mind raced ahead to a blur of scenes in the future. She quieted her thoughts.

"Oh, if you please. Allow me to present myself. I am Valentine Starbury, earl of Pembroke. As for rising and bowing to kiss your hand, I daren't approach you in this state, I cannot bow lest I dunk my face in the water, and I am as risen as I will ever be."

She tried not to smile.

"And may I ask your name, my lady?"

"I am Denys, and this is Chera." She gestured to her horse. "Her mother died birthing her and she now thinks I am her mother."

"I must sadly inform her, then, that she is mistaken." He looked at Chera. "No palfrey ever had such a beauteous mother. Cannot she discern the lack of resemblance?"

Now she displayed that smile. "And what is your position at court, my lord?" The idea of calling him 'my lord' in his present state of undress amused her. But she had to find out as much as possible about him, to prove him real and not just willed out of her fancy.

"Knight at present, though I trust my proficiency with axe and sword gains favor with King Edward. I inherited my title from my father who was killed in battle when I was nine. The Plantagenets took me in. They are my family in every sense save blood ties. In essence, that's one reason I am here."

"They dared you to swim nude?" she teased further.

"Nay, but were it not for the unreliability of a third party, I would not be here, talking to you. So, I am grateful to that party. Had she arrived as scheduled, I would be in there..." He waved in the direction of the palace, "Forced to make merry and charm my way through the eve with a forced smile."

"You seem jovial enough. What saddens you?" She lowered her eyes. "Sorry. I pry. I just ask out of curiosity. My thirst for enlightenment, of every kind, is one of my most serious flaws, I'm told." She hoped that excused her rudeness.

"'Tis not a flaw at all, but a sign of an active, intelligent mind. I have hidden nowt from you so far! Well, nearly. I daresay there is much more I would know of you. I am obliged to court a lady who needs a suitable *parti*."

Disappointment snatched away her excitement, leaving her voice flat. "Alas, that's one drawback of royalty ... and nobility. This lady...have you seen her portrait?" She didn't want to ask who the lady was. She didn't want to know, her fantasy so cruelly dispelled.

He shook his head. "Nay, I go into this without benefit of a glance at her countenance."

She gasped. "You and she are betrothed?"

"Nay!" Droplets flew as he shook his head. "I would be on the next vessel back to France afore anyone force me to marry anyone sight unseen. 'Tis out of honor that I meet her at all! And 'tis all that I agreed to do, make her acquaintance. If our souls do not resound with compatibility by eve's end, I shall bid her adieu. I shall have fulfilled my part of the bargain."

"Ah." Her sigh of relief could be heard clear across the Thames. *Oh, he's free!* Her spirit soared, along with her heartbeat. "Ah, so 'tis a bargain."

"Nowt more, for certes. To me, the worst way to begin courtship. I'm a staunch believer in love. I will fight the odds and make a love match, not succumb to loveless liaison just to seal a political alliance or save some homely wench from spinsterhood."

"Noble indeed, but presumptuous to brand her homely not having beheld her." She pitied the poor wench.

"I've heard a description, albeit a brief one, from an objective party. I've formed a picture in my mind's eye, and 'tis not pretty." He scowled but quickly replaced it with a smile.

"Well, it is King Edward or George. They can't be objective about any creature in bodice and skirts." She gave him a bashful grin.

"Nay, a more indifferent, detached, and dispassionate soul." He lowered his head.

She nodded. "Of course. The duke of Gloucester."

His head snapped up. "How did you guess?"

"Simple. He is the only person in this kingdom who matches all three of those words."

"That I can't argue." He chuckled.

"But why take his word? The lady may be a ravishing beauty." She flicked a lock of hair off her shoulder and raised a brow before meeting his gaze again. She could enjoy this playful repartee, now that she knew he wasn't betrothed—and no wench of Richard's acquaintance could capture this man's interest. She had a hunch it was one of Richard's sisters and suppressed a giggle.

"Somehow I doubt it. Were she that beauteous, the king would already be wooing her," he stated.

"So what *did* he say about her, my lord?" *What is this bargain?* was what she really wanted to know.

"Oh, nowt especially derogatory." He shrugged. "He never means harm. He tells it straight, exactly as he sees it."

"Aye, Richard is blunter than a dull butter knife." With that she also admitted to herself she didn't want the hapless dowdy anywhere near him.

"And for certes whatever he said to me, he said to her. He isn't one to talk behind others' backs. Nor am I!" he added.

"Is it his cousin with the one gray eye and one green ... oh, what is her name?" She tapped the side of her head. "Gonilda?"

"Nay. She's a relative of the queen." His eyes brightened as he held up a finger. "Now I remember. Her pet name is Dove."

She recoiled as if hit with a bag of rocks. Her fingers numbed round the reins. "Dove, is it?"

He went on, "Aye, and he described her as quite plain, actually." His smile faded. "Her eye color, oh, what was it ... ah, yes, she has eyes the color of ... what was it now ... oh, yes. Bat guano!" His words tripped over laughter.

Turning to quit his suddenly undesirable presence, she slipped. Her feet slid into the muck. His arms wound round her and righted her. Their contact made the stars and all their brilliance sear through her, for this intense surge drained all her vigor. Now they stood waist-deep in water. His intensifying breath fanned her cheek. Before he could vex her any further, she stumbled onto the bank, dragging her skirts behind her.

So she was the hapless wench with the guano eyes! How could Richard treat her so cruelly? The lout! "Bat guano? Is that any way to talk about someone you never met? Do you always judge without first seeing the subject with your own eyes or is your discretion so flawed that you cannot trust it?"

"Those were Richard's words, not mine!" He held his hands up in surrender.

"And in repeating them, you are just as foul." She climbed up the embankment, snatched the reins and stalked away, Chera trotting beside her.

"Do come back! Wait!" His voice grew louder as he caught up to her.

Tears blurred her vision; branches tore at her. She stumbled over exposed roots. She'd been degraded and belittled by the queen before the entire court, but nowt hurt as much as this.

Because it was him. He had the power to hurt her.

And Richard—how could he? He and this naked knight, unfeeling buffoons both.

She led Chera back to the palace, throwing her arms round the animal's neck before parting at the stables. Chera nuzzled her cheek, her warm breath like a soothing lullaby to Denys. "You'll always love me, won't you?" she whispered. Chera answered with a tilt of her head, another nuzzle. Forever loyal, a mere beast, yet so capable of unconditional love.

* * *

Confused at the outraged maiden's reaction to Richard's description, Valentine waded to shore and retraced his steps to reclaim the clothes he'd flung off with such abandon. But they were nowhere in sight. Moonlight illuminated every patch of grass, every clump of dirt, but nothing resembling his tunic, hose or doublet. Then the startling realization hit him harder than the wine had struck the pit of his stomach: the vixen pinched every thread of his attire!

He sprinted down the riverbank like a wounded badger, crouching lest anyone spot him, the breeze caressing his body on parts never exposed to the outdoors before. Despite the absurdity of his situation, he laughed. *It does feel good after all*, he assured himself, with moss beneath his bare feet.

He climbed aboard a slumbering barge, looking for something to wrap around himself, a piece of cloth, a sail, anything, so he could re-enter the palace with a modicum of dignity. He found nothing. He clambered up the bank and snatched a hunk of birch from the door of the first house he reached. Holding it to his loins like Adam's fig leaf, he fled.

Past the formal gardens he pranced, wincing as sharp pebbles stung the undersides of his feet. He reached the gatehouse and sprinted up the path. The heady aromas of roses and honeysuckle failed to calm him. Only a bit farther, past the startled watchmen, whom he greeted with a breezy, "Lovely evening … er … modeling for a statue, holding one pose, tucking in me bum for hours…"

The portcullis was still up. His steps echoed through the tunnel that led to the outer court. Once safely inside, he allowed himself the luxury of a relieved sigh. Nary a soul in sight. Lights glowing from the great hall indicated a few courtiers hadn't yet drunk themselves into oblivion. *Please let the king be retired!* he implored an invisible savior, for even though Edward by no means shared

Richard's prudery, he was king after all, and wouldn't appreciate a titled subject prancing round in such inappropriate attire.

His bare feet slapped the floor as he dashed up the grand staircase and down the corridor to his chambers. Guards were posted at the entrance to the king's chambers, swords glowing in the torchlight. He flung open his chamber doors and scuttled into his privy closet. He relieved himself in the chamber pot, tossed the bough aside, and slid 'neath his sheets. Oh, that vile, wicked nymph, pilfering his clothes. He could wring her little neck! As his thoughts dissolved into disjointed randomness, he dreamed. His lips crushed hers as his hands slid up and down that luscious body.

Chapter Three

Denys sat under the elm tree at the edge of the palace grounds, Chera grazing at her side. After munching on an apple, she began a missive to the Archbishop of Canterbury, telling him of her possible connection to Malmesbury. "Your Excellency, I solicit your help in finding out more..." she wrote as the words flowed easily, her penmanship steady and confident. Oh, to finally take action and trace her origins, after all those years of hushed whispers.

At the sound of thumping hooves, she looked up, expecting a royal page to accompany her back to court. But her breath caught and held as the rider came closer. The streak of white played through his windblown hair, puddling round his shoulders as he halted his mount.

"I am otherwise engaged at the moment, my lord," she stated. Her fist gripped the pen; the quill point pierced the parchment. She didn't want to betray the sparks of excitement he elicited. "Good morrow to you."

"Despite what you wish, I did not deliberately seek your company, nor shall I give you the satisfaction of knowing how I managed to return to the palace yestereve with dignity intact." He stared her down with narrowed eyes, yet a smile played upon his lips.

"Be grateful you escaped with anything intact, my lord." She forced her gaze back to her pen and parchment. "Mayhap you will think before maligning someone you know not."

"If my raiment is out of reach, I certainly shall. I shall think afore disrobing for any reason from now on. Especially in present company." He unhorsed and approached her. She now sat at eye level with his knees and furtively observed the embroidered tunic molded to his torso, his flat abdomen tapering to squared-off hips. Tight hose outlined his masculinity.

The breeze carried his woodsy scent. Moonlight hadn't done him the justice of the bright sun. The cover of night had shadowed the sky-blue eyes she'd marveled at in the outer court. She focused on those eyes once more, still radiant with the innocence of youth, untouched by the hurt of lost love. Her eyes swept over the broadness of his chest now that it wasn't submerged in water or encased in armor.

"Removing yourself at this moment would give me greater pleasure than ever removing your clothes in my company again, my lord." It was no surprise when he took a step closer.

"Come now, don't be so disagreeable. We are even. I vexed you somehow and you inconvenienced me. I admit I started it. I thought I was delirious … when diving into the river for a solitary swim, I never dreamed I'd open my eyes to that same vision I encountered in the outer court. You must admit it would knock the senses from any healthy man. Can we not start afresh?"

If she refused, he would no doubt mount his stallion and call it a day. Something told her not to dismiss him. Aye, he'd talked about her to Richard, but he didn't yet know it. That was forgivable.

"I suppose there is no harm in our being civil, as I am a … a friend of the court, as you are. But I would inform you, I am betrothed," she added, to maintain her distance, in case he intended to narrow it further, as she was unchaperoned.

His smile vanished but he didn't move a muscle. "A nobleman, I presume?"

She nodded. "Aye, of course, a nobleman. Titled and landed."

"And when is the wedding date?" he prodded further.

"Soon." She could not force eagerness into her tone.

"Pray tell, is it to him you write, calling the event off?" He peered at the letter and she clutched it to her breast.

"Have you nowt to do, my lord? Are you not in training?" She dipped her pen in her ink horn.

"I am constantly at practice, with sword or without. I return from the Tower where I attended council. The king prepares for another battle with the Lancastrians." He knelt before her and eased himself down to sit.

She had no reason to hide her alarm. "How I hate these battles! They threaten the well-being of the kingdom and the lives of my loved ones. When?"

He shrugged. "I know not as yet. But if another battle is imminent, I shall join their forces."

" 'Their' as in Yorkists', I trust?" she goaded.

Without missing a beat, he returned, "I know you try to vex me. I told you my father died beside Richard's. These battles won't be over until every last Lancastrian traitor is in his grave. And God forbid it, should King Edward perish in battle, we've George and Richard to continue Yorkist rule."

She began to wonder how well she wanted to know him. "A visit to the confessional is in order for entertaining that thought. Speaking of the king's death is treason."

His smile told her he did not take her a bit seriously. "I've talked with King Edward at length many times. He accepts the reality of death in battle, yet it never stops him from fighting to uphold Yorkist rule. I merely entertain the possibility. King Edward's warfare prowess notwithstanding, he is in real danger of perishing in battle. Should Richard someday inherit the throne if his heirs are unable to rule, I shall be at his side serving any office in which he sees me fit. The kingdom would thrive with a king like Richard."

"You've got it all plotted but the coronation date. Richard king? Not half unlikely, but downright frightening." She shuddered, knowing how Richard shunned advancement beyond his rank of duke. "Besides, he is far down the line of succession."

"You are just peeved about what Richard said about that wench he wants me to woo. 'Tis a good thing she didn't see me last night *au natural.* I would never get her out of my hair then." He plucked a blade of grass from the ground and wove it through his fingers.

"Modesty is not among your brief list of virtues." She gave him a wry grin.

"Nay, I am proud to vaunt my person, dear lady. Years of hard work tilting and jousting and wielding axe and sword gave me my share of knocks and bruises, but have made me quite firm indeed." He ran his hands over the slim hips and muscled thighs straining under his hose. "The art of warfare is not my gift, however. I am far more skilled in the art of statesmanship. Why, King Louis called on me to compose letters to his foreign counterparts, not to mention love letters." He raised a brow. "I assisted him with speeches, and I trust King Edward keeps this in mind when he bestows his next preferment upon one of his knights."

So he aspired to higher office and the title that went with it. For starters.

"On that we are at odds, my lord. You revel in court plots, and I despise them. Are you sure your name isn't Woodville?"

"Farthest from it. Starbury is the name, my lady. And I will earn my higher titles the honorable way, through loyalty plain and simple. Carry on where my father left off."

Not knowing his father, she could make no judgment. The kingdom was so rife with traitors and spies, she didn't know who was whom anymore. He could be Lancastrian at matinmas one day and Yorkist by vespers the next for all she knew.

Aye, physically alluring, but far too immersed in vainglory for her tastes. His ambitions contradicted everything she believed in. Mayhap he would think more sensibly after experiencing the treachery and deceit of court affairs.

She pretended to return to her writing as if never interrupted. He stood, bade her good day and returned to his steed, swung one leg over its back and galloped off. As he rode away, a smile touched her lips. As man and beast descended the grassy slope out of her view, her heartbeat dwindled to an uneasy thump. Her eyes slid shut, his image sharp as if he still stood before her. She let the fantasy linger for a moment longer, then returned to her quest to find her family.

* * *

The letter finished and off to the Archbishop in the hands of the most reliable royal messenger, she strode the palace corridors seeking Richard. If a battle was imminent, he was undoubtedly in prayer, far from the cacophony of voices and minstrels and most of all, Woodvilles. She climbed the great staircase and headed for the chapel.

* * *

Valentine had already found Richard the chapel's front pew, not in his usual pensive pose, but simply sitting there. "Richard," he whispered. "I found her. The one I told you that I saw standing alone in the outer court after the battle." His voice took on a dreamy tone. "I've never seen anyone like her. I met her again today at the edge of the palace grounds and ... oh, I could have ravished her right then and there."

"Were she French, mayhap she would have let you have your wicked way right there in the dirt." Richard motioned him to sit.

Valentine slid into the pew next to him. "She has pledged her troth to another. A nobleman. Oh, if only I'd gotten there first," he continued with renewed exuberance. "But I think 'twould take more than a title to win her."

"Hell's teeth, Val, she may be undowried, or worse—the daughter of a Lancastrian." Richard slid farther down to give Valentine more room.

"I care not. My inheritance is ample I want her even if she doesn't have a farthing to her name." Valentine folded his hands twixt his knees.

"Have you forgotten our bargain? You lost fair and square, my good friend." Richard closed his Book of Hours and placed it in his lap.

"Nay, I have yet to meet your cow." Valentine glanced at an elderly woman lighting a candle near the altar. "I was all ready last night."

"And way in your cups," Richard remarked. "A grand stinking impression."

"Well, what do you expect, the way you describe her? And after meeting this … oh, her name should come to me. Her hair reflected the moonlight, her eyes the green of the forest, her skin so smooth and milky…" He omitted running back to the palace clutching a sprig of birch to his privy parts. "And, might I add, she's feisty to boot."

"Nay, I know no one of milky skin or forestlike eyes." Richard shook his head. "Not in this country. How will you lavish the necessary attention on two ladies?"

"Come, you know me. I can budget my time … and my affections … quite well. I have time for both." He splayed his fingers. "What man doesn't?"

"I don't." Richard lifted his chin with an air of superiority.

"Ah, but that is you, my friend. I refer to us lesser men." Valentine's brow arched as he turned to the sound of the creaky door.

* * *

Denys leaned on the chapel door and grasped the handle as she peeked in. Right she was; there sat Richard in the front pew. Then she heard a voice and realized Richard was not alone. She didn't dare open the creaky door farther.

She stood in stony silence as Richard spoke: "Very well, go chase your nymph all over London if you wish. But only if you meet Denys right now. I shall fetch her and then you must bestow your … procedures upon her."

"So be it. I shall wait right here."

She knew that voice. *By God, 'tis him!*

39

Denys let the door close with a whoosh of musty chapel air. But she stood rooted to the spot. Something held her skirts. She turned back to see what impeded her. Oh, God's foot! The chapel door caught her skirts! It was too late. Even Richard would notice a lady's skirts caught in a door. No sooner did she shove at the door than it swung wide open, and there he stood.

"I ... came to pray, Richard. I am sorry, I did not realize you were here." She kept her tone crisp and detached, trying to maintain poise through her distress.

He handed her the end of her skirts that had torn clear away. "Hello, dear. Do come meet a friend of mine." She glanced toward the altar. He stood there, looking as delighted as if he discovered gold in the holy water, his grin wide. Her heart lurched. She grasped the edge of a pew to steady her trembling hands. *Does he do this to all women?* she wondered.

"I think not, Richard. We have already met." Her gaze dallied on the knight who provoked so unsettling a response in her.

"Oh, you've met Denys?" Richard turned to face Valentine. "You didn't tell me you met her."

"I ... uh..." Valentine's stammer echoed and faded into the upper reaches of the fan vaulting, Richard stood waiting.

Denys's blood began to boil. "I demand an explanation from you, Richard, and will not give you the dignity to explain to me in private. I would have it now. Look into my eyes and tell me they're the color of guano in the face of a hideous cow."

"Hideous?" His brows knitted in puzzlement. "That is not even in my nomenclature, dear. When have you known me to be so vivid?"

"That is what *he* said you said!" She cast a glare in Valentine's direction.

"So you're the 'Dove' he referred to?" Valentine spoke up. "I had no way to know that was you. I only relayed the impression I got from Richard's description—like one of his sisters."

"I would never call my sister a cow, for pity's sake." Richard turned back to Denys, shaking his head. "In light of our sticky situation, I thought it advantageous if the two of you met. We each see you in a completely different light. It was you he babbled and raved about all this while, but I was sure I never met anyone matching his florid description."

"So you're Denys." Valentine's gaze raked over he. She found herself enjoying it, even as she flushed with rage.

"You know you are a sister to me, Denys," Richard spoke up. "But Val insisted that I describe you and I told him how I see you. He is a brother to me, as you are a sister. Now if you'll put your madcap imaginings aside, I trust you will grow fond of him as well."

"We shall see." She excused herself from the tension mounting twixt the three of them.

The door eased shut with a groan and Richard gave Valentine a long, hard look as he walked up the aisle.

Valentine found no reason to restrain his elation. "That's Denys! I am enthralled! Ah, Richard, you're a sly one. Making me believe her a homely slag so I'd be doubly pleased when we finally met. You and your wicked sense of humor. Too bad she found out, but no matter, I shall make it up to her."

"'Twas was no joke. That is the way I see her. Are you so obtuse that you do not understand that?" Richard fixed narrowed eyes on him.

"No dukedoms or manors come close to what you offer me!" He swallowed, his mouth dry as sheared wool. "She told me she pledged her troth to a nobleman. 'Tis to you, I now see. And she harbors as much dread."

"Well, of course. Elizabeth wants to ruin a dear friendship, not to mention my own intentions. But I counted on you to change all that. Now you've made a right culls-up of it all!" Richard turned to leave.

"I can fix it. There's been simmering twixt us since we met. Like lamprey stew, simmering, not boiling, only enough to tease." He gazed out over the fan vaulting and focused on the stained glass windows' jewel tones in the distance.

"Lamprey stew, is it?" Richard chortled. "Mayhap you'd best pull your nose out the pot afore it gets burnt. Forgive my lack of perception, but I don't see her tripping over her skirts to get to you, Sir Galahad."

"Consider yourself forgiven." Valentine bowed his head. "Do you not see the intensity in her eyes? But then, I trust she never looks at you that way."

"Thank heaven." Richard rolled his eyes. "But all you've managed to do is make her cold-shoulder you. Are you sure it was lusty France where you spent the last three years, and not bloody Flanders?"

"So we got off to a bad start. Do not be such a dolt." Valentine glided down the aisle after Richard. " The next time you enter this chapel may well be for Denys's wedding, but rest assured, you won't be the groom!" Valentine knelt and kissed the feet of the Blessed Mother statue before exiting the chapel.

Richard shook his head with the hint of a smile and headed to the graveyard for some peace.

* * *

The familiar too-short knock on her receiving chamber door interrupted her evening meal, but she didn't feel much like eating anyway. Denys opened it herself, having dismissed her maid early.

Richard stood there, trying to look contrite. "I am here to apologize if that is what you want." He closed the door and poured himself to a goblet of wine from the sideboard.

"I don't demand an apology for derogating me in front of that dolt. I've already forgiven you, Richard. Let not the likes of him strain our friendship."

He followed her to the bay window where they sat on the velvet seat. She took a sip of wine before speaking. "I take it you haven't located Anne."

"Nay. But I depart for East Grinstead this eve. There's a chance she is there." He gazed out the window.

"God willing. Meanwhile, I have found a guide to Malmesbury. Hugh Corey, brother-in-law of the duchess of Salisbury's seamstress. A courier from Gloucestershire, he knows the countryside thoroughly. He can take me directly via the quickest route. I was fortunate to find someone who knows the roads. 'Twill make the journey much safer and easier. He is confident we will locate Foxley Manor once we enter Malmesbury. He's available Thursday fortnight, so I depart then, even if you're not in wedded bliss with Anne by then."

"I'm relieved you have a protector and won't wander round unguided, but why so sure that's where your origins lie?" Richard turned to face her. "All we know is that's where Bess rustled up a dowry for you."

"Oh, I'm quite sure." She gave him a confident nod. "When I asked Bess casually about Foxley Manor, she spun one tale after the next. She lies as she breathes."

"How can you tell?" He gave her a sly look.

"She strums her pearls," came her reply. "You know she does that when she tries to talk herself out of a fix."

He nodded in instant recognition. "Oh." He knew it too. "Well, do not put much stock in it. High hopes may lead to heartache."

"I am going to do this, Richard. And not just to get out of our quandary. I need to find my family." She pushed open the diamond paned window. "I need air."

Colored fragments of light illuminated the chamber, mingled with flickering candle flames.

"Speaking of our quandary … and Val…" Richard approached her.

"What about Val?" She feigned indifference. "What's he got to do with our quandary?"

"I fully expected you to take to him. Especially since he's the very one you gushed about—King Arthur and all that. You don't know him at all. I've known him for many years, and he has the most sincere heart in the kingdom. Even you said so, before you knew who he was." Richard leaned on the window jamb. "You wanted to meet someone like him, and what do I do, I go find not merely someone like him, but the very character you blather about. I fling your fabled hero at your feet, and you won't take him!"

She shook her head. "I can't help but falter—I have doubts about him. He aspires to high office. We must be careful these days. What he said may be innocent, but we have enemies and we never know who. He may be in George and Warwick's clutches."

"If anyone is Yorkist through and through it is Valentine. His father died next to mine. He would never harm any of us. Give him a chance. He isn't about to go away, so you may as well get used to him. You may even grow fond of him, as is my wish."

The chamber door burst open and King Edward's Page of Honor stood at attention. " His Highness the king summons your lordship immediately," he addressed Richard.

Richard tapped his foot. "And how did you know I was here?"

"Her Highness the queen told me to look for you—" The page cleared his throat and averted his eyes, "in the company of your betrothed, my lord."

"Why, the nerve of her!" Denys turned away.

"It could be worse, Denys. If you really loved me, she'd try to marry you off to anyone *but* me." Richard straightened his shirt and turned to the page. "Now, what is amiss?"

"The earl of Warwick plots to invade from France, my lord." The page spoke to Richard without making eye contact.

"That fool." Without a backward glance at Denys, Richard strode past the page out of the chamber.

But Richard turned on a heel, rushed back into the chamber and ran up to Denys. "Godspeed on your quest." He kissed her hand and vanished.

"Godspeed to you!" she whispered into the darkness. "Mayhap I'll have a family for you to meet upon my return."

* * *

As the sun peeked over the horizon, a stream of pinkish fingers waved on the new morning. Valentine went through mock battles in the palace's outer court until Mass began. Richard did not attend.

When he didn't appear at breakfast in the great hall, Valentine went to his chambers to fetch him.

A yeoman let him in. Valentine approached the ornately carved bed and pushed the velvet hanging aside. Richard's face looked troubled in sleep, his brow furrowed. He nudged his friend gently. Opening one eye and glimpsing Valentine, he groaned and turned over.

"Come on, rise and shine! 'Tis a belter of a day, and tomorrow's the tourney. You can't win by dreaming of victories, we must get out there and flex our muscles." Valentine wielded an imaginary sword, relieved that his arm was healed. The paste of mandragora leaves the physician wrapped it in worked wonders.

"I do not give a feak if the sun ceases to rise and we plunge into eternal night," Richard mumbled into the pillow.

Valentine bent over to hear him. "Are you ill? Shall I summon the physician?"

"Nay, fetch no one. I heard news last evening that fairly broke my heart." His head no longer buried in the pillow, he pulled the coverlet up over it.

"Oh, I'm sorry you are downtrodden. But do rise and break your fast. You will feel better with a full stomach. I shall practice with sword in the outer court whilst I await you."

Valentine had two mock combats with the young earl of Towton, cornering him both times. Richard arrived, face sullen and drawn, his gait lacking that lively stride.

Valentine greeted him. "Where have you been? The sun is nearly disappeared over the treetops. Have you broken your fast?"

"Nay. Why should I add a broken fast to the broken heart I now possess?" Richard slunk past Valentine, not looking up.

"What's happened?" Valentine followed him to a wooden bench.

The pounding of hooves on hard earth, usually music to Valentine's ears, disturbed him as activity in the outer court intensified. Armored soldiers in shining silver splendor, plumes floating from their helmets, entered the palace gates on horses bearing the Yorkist standard. Banners streamed behind them.

"What goes on?" Valentine turned to Richard. "The tourney is tomorrow, is it not? Or is the next battle about to commence?"

Richard glanced round and stood. "Let us walk and I'll tell you." They passed the gatehouse and strolled along the embankment.

"Aye, it is. Warwick is at it again. He plots to invade from France with Marguerite of Anjou. They are on their way here with a fleet of ships provided by King Louis. My brother George waits in the wings. They will attempt to dethrone Edward again. That is easy enough to handle, for they'll never succeed."

They left the palace grounds and sat on a grassy mound. Valentine looked over his shoulder for the arrival of more knights as Richard drew his knees up to his chin.

"Do we go to battle this afternoon or not?" Valentine persisted, knowing he had to prepare himself mentally for the rigors of battle just as he had to train in warfare.

"Nay, we've to meet with council first." Richard halted and closed his eyes. "You won't believe what they've done with my Anne. Last night I learned they married her to Marguerite of Anjou's son, Edward." Richard's voice cracked with despair.

"Oh, I am sorry." Marguerite of Anjou—wife of the deposed King Henry VI—one of the most tenacious Lancastrians in the realm, was even worse than Warwick. "I see why such a marriage suits Warwick's political agenda. But poor Annie." His heart went out to his dear friend. "I wish there were something I could do. I feel helpless."

"Thank you, but there's nowt to be done." Richard turned and they began to walk back.

"I've begun to realize how devious statesmanship really is—and how I would change things." Valentine's muscles clenched in frustration.

"It's hell-spawned Elizabeth Woodville. Again! She wants me married to her niece, so she'll stop at nowt to thwart my plots. Her and her henchman, Anne's father, Warwick. That weakling Edward is no good for Anne!" Richard kicked a pebble out of his path. "They never even met. Because of that unholy witch and her greed, Anne is lost to me forever."

Valentine's heart plummeted. "I suppose there is no escaping marriage to Denys now." He cupped his chin in his palm and heaved a disheartened sigh.

The only woman to ever fill the aching gap in his life, in a cruel twist of irony, was to marry his best friend.

"Nay, on the contrary. 'Tis entirely up to you now," he encouraged Valentine, his tone brighter and tinged with hope. "Do you want her?"

"Of course I want her! I would marry her now if the king gave his blessing and permission." Just thinking of her put a spring into his step.

"Well, that's not about to happen. My brother never overrules his queen when it comes to Woodville alliances. You must make her your own, or we will all be utterly miserable," he ordered.

Valentine's eyes darted round as his mind spun. Now that Anne was not to marry Richard, he had to capture Denys's heart. He couldn't waste a moment.

* * *

But the call to battle cut Valentine's precious time short. As a squire helped him on with his armor, a messenger delivered a note from him to Denys, asking that her thoughts and prayers be with him.

* * *

Denys did not appear in the great hall at mealtimes, barely ate her favorite dish of saffron-sprinkled oatmeal, or the bowls of figs, almonds and dates left in her outer chamber. She didn't embroider, play her lute, or ride Chera. Her only venture outdoors was her first royal progress, to St. Giles, one of the poorest parts of London, with a bag of coins and a royal guide laden with food. The half-starved rabble gaped at her as she unhorsed and handed out coins. They stood in such awe, they didn't fight, bite, or trample over one another to grab what they could. They simply mumbled thanks and touched the hem of her gown as if she were a saint.

She returned to the palace, dragged herself to her chambers and collapsed on her bed, physically and emotionally spent. But she forced herself out of bed and returned to the chapel, where she spent more time praying than she did sleeping these days. She begged the Lord to lead her to her family. She said another prayer, "Protect those I love in battle—Uncle Edward, Richard, and—Valentine Starbury."

Sitting in the peaceful surroundings, the aroma of incense lingering, she let the perfumed air comfort her. "God, please let my true family be alive and safe."

She opened a page of her prayer book at random and began to read, "…keep me and defend me from all evil and from my evil enemy, and from all danger, present, past, and to come, and deign to console me by Thy descent into hell…" Oh, how apt a prayer it was!

She slipped a small sheet of parchment from twixt the book's pages and unfolded it. The soaring and inflated loops of Valentine's elegant penmanship were nearly as beauteous as the message they conveyed. "Though I willingly challenge the ugliness and cruel hostility of battle, I will hear not the scrape of swords but your sweet voice and see not the ugliness of death but your delicate face before me. I will be honored if you await my arrival in the palace rose garden at the victory parade's end. Until I return, Valentine."

She closed her eyes and inhaled deeply. Mayhap she could fall in love with him. Was it possible to be in love with someone without liking them? She wondered. Strange how her feelings conflicted and collided, weaving and bobbing through her heart like a finely woven tapestry. Did it take the talent of a great artist to manage them, as well?

Back in her chambers, she opened her jewel box and searched out her most cherished possession—not a piece of jewelry; she owned few jewels. It was a wilting white rose, its petals just starting to shrivel round the edges. The rose he gave her, its scent as sweet as if just plucked from the vine. It simply refused to die. It was also the only rose she ever saw without a single thorn.

The other roses on the vine were long gone. But "their" rose lived on.

* * *

Yet another victory parade entered the gates of London. This time, Denys watched from the palace gatehouse as the procession entered the outer court. Now she had a soldier to welcome home. She no longer needed stand alone and watch it happen all around her. Richard rode alongside King Edward. Cheers filled her ears as she glimpsed George, smirking in a new air of confidence, doubtless from a late surge of loyalty. Marguerite of Anjou sat stonily in a chariot, head erect with all the regality she could muster, flicking a handkerchief in the faces of onlookers clamoring for a glimpse of her.

Valentine entered astride his steed, waving to onlookers, bending over to shake hands. Glancing round, she noticed nearly every female eye feasted on the beaming knight.

She sprinted down the winding steps and dashed over to the garden. Just like that very first time, he came prancing up to her on his mount. She'd never experienced the thrill of a soldier coming home to her, even if they didn't embrace and mingle tears like longtime lovers. He unhorsed and held his hands out to her. A bejeweled Yorkist collar of suns and roses glowed upon his chest. They did not embrace, but stood looking into each other's eyes for a long moment. He elicited a warm feeling deep inside her. His eyes spoke of understanding, though she knew nothing of his past, she knew he'd lived through tragedy—and did his best to keep it from destroying him.

"Thank you so much for your note, my lord." She caught her breath. "It meant a great deal to me."

His eyes lit up. "Every soldier needs something to fight for besides the kingdom." She knew much more lurked behind those simple words. "So what happens now? Does the earl of Warwick return home as well?"

"Aye, but alas, he returned in a box. He is slain." A hint of sorrow crept into Valentine's voice upon mentioning the dead earl. Denys detected that he'd admired Warwick. "However, 'twas a victory."

Whose victory? she wondered. The kingdom's? The House of York's? Or his own? As drawn as she was to him, she still had doubts about his loyalties.

He glanced in the direction of the palace, but fixed his gaze right back on her. "The king requested my presence at the council meeting prior to this eve's banquet, so I must bathe, tidy myself up and don ordinary raiment."

"In the Thames again, Sir Starbury?" She smiled, remembering how upset she was that first night, snatching away his clothes. If she had to do it again, she wouldn't change a thing. Except mayhap do it in daylight.

His eyes twinkled in the bright sun. "That romp was strictly on impulse. 'Tis not something one can plot. Or should." He took his mount's reins and they headed for the stables.

"Do you act on impulse as a rule, my lord?"

"Most of my life is one unexpected event after another, so I learned to take life as it comes, not expecting life to go as expected. Life would be terribly boring if it were so, would it not?" They slowed to a stop without even realizing it. The horse began to graze. "Imagine plotting out your entire life, and having every outcome go accordingly. We would die of boredom. Our heartbeats would never quicken, there would be no such thing as a gasp of surprise." He took a step closer.

What happened to the talk of court affairs? she wondered, wanting to experience some of this surprise he spoke of. "I love surprises, my lord. I cannot get enough of them."

"Like this?" And without warning or preamble or as much as a come-hither, he captured her lips in a sweet, yet hungry search. Her lips softened under his patient but demanding kiss. It ended too quickly as he pulled away and they both took a much-needed gulp of air.

"Forgive me, Denys," he whispered, his breath fanning her ear. She shivered as a surge of warmth flowed through her. "I just couldn't wait any longer."

"'Tis quite all right." She released a heavy sigh. "Neither could I. But I certainly see your point now. 'Tis easily understood when shown rather than told."

"I really must prepare for council, and I must be calm, and not—excited." He straightened his tunic. "Shall we be on our way?"

"I'd best go back another way." She glanced round. "The queen's spying eyes may see us together."

He hesitated and she knew he didn't want it to end, either. "Very well, then, good morrow to you, Denys."

"And to you, Valentine," she called him by his name for the first time. It felt so right and natural—like she knew him all her life.

* * *

That eve the courtiers, the soldiers, their lady loves and assorted lesser-ranked subjects feasted on a sumptuous banquet in the great hall. The dancing, eating, and especially drinking continued long after the king and queen took their leave. All throughout the meal and the revelries, Denys wondered where Valentine was. Having looked out for him all evening, she burned with curiosity—*where could he be?*

She swept a liberal helping of leavings into a satchel to give the poor on the morrow. The palace wasted more in one feast than some folk ate in a fortnight.

Richard sat cross-legged at a window seat nibbling on a pheasant leg, a pewter pitcher at his elbow. Denys approached him, and as much as she wanted to ask if he knew Valentine's whereabouts, she restrained herself. "Richard, no one can argue that the Yorkists are the most fearless, most courageous warriors to ever pound a battlefield!"

"Not quite so, Denys. Don't forget Richard the Lionheart and his army in the Crusades." He wiped his mouth with a linen napkin.

"Oh, but the Crusades were over religion, Richard." She gathered her skirts and sat beside him. "You and King Edward's army fight for our land, our kingdom, that's what really matters."

"A spot of mead?" He motioned to a passing steward who filled an empty goblet on the table next to her.

She took a bigger gulp than she should. "Was anyone seriously wounded?"

"The usual casualties on both sides." He sipped his mead. "Oh, and Anne's husband of two days wasn't wounded—he was slain."

She nearly choked. "Dear God! How?"

"Stabbed thrice," he replied in his customary calm manner. "Once for me, once for Anne, and once to spite Bess Woodville."

"Oh, how terrible!" Then she understood. She didn't dare ask the name of the slayer. "Poor Edward."

"Aye, terrible for his mother. But not quite so dolorous for me." He continued nibbling his pheasant leg.

Her eyes slid shut and she relished a fleeting relief, but guilt flooded her. A callow youth—slain in cold blood. "This means Anne is free to marry you."

"Isn't she now." He struggled to keep a straight face. "And how ironic...Anne's father and husband slain in the same battle. So much for Wicked Queen Bess and her ploy to keep me from marrying Anne. It blew right back in her bat-fowling face." He finished the pheasant leg, placed it on the plate before him and wiped his hands. "And lest I forget, I have some truly sad news." His voice now took on an ironic tone.

"What?" She leaned forward.

"The king held a conference this afternoon. He bade me bear a most unpleasant order to the Constable of the Tower." He took another sip of mead.

She held her breath.

"An order of execution for old King Henry the Sixth." He drained his goblet. "He is to die at dawn."

"Oh, Jesu." She lowered her head. "That feeble dotard would live a happy life were it not for his tyrant wife and all her dissidents."

"It was inevitable. Mercifully, his will be a peaceful end." Richard placed his goblet down and wiped his lips with the napkin.

She shivered. "Why is life worth so little?"

"It was much worse in centuries past, my dear. And no more court affairs tonight." He stretched his legs. "I'm positively weary of it. Have you seen Val?" He looked round.

Her heart danced at the sound of his name. "Not since the victory parade ended. He said he had a council meeting to attend. But till this hour? Mayhap a mob of maidens set upon him afterwards."

"In that case we won't see him for a fortnight." Richard smiled. "But that's highly unlikely. He likes his maidens one at a time these days." He tossed her a glance.

"You're sure of that?" Oh, how she hoped so.

"I thought you were to heed my wish and give him a fair chance." He raised his brows in expectation of an answer.

"There is still something about him I . . . can't help but fear." She clasped her hands together, lips tight. "I have my doubts about him, but what I fear most of all is my growing fondness of him."

"Well, your fabled knight is soon to receive a preferment. I asked the king to grant him a higher title and some lands for his courage and loyalty in battle," Richard informed her. "Duke of Norwich in all likelihood, a title held by many of my ancestors. That is, if one of Elizabitch's lot doesn't pinch it first."

She forced herself to stop scanning the great hall for that golden head.

"Have you seen my new nephew Prince Edward?" He gave her a wide smile.

"Aye, I have." She nodded, warming to the image of the strapping baby boy. "Suckling at the wet nurse. He's a sprightly nipper."

"Edward is mighty proud. And I cannot tell you how relieved I am now that he has a male heir. I hope George comes to his senses now that he's farther removed from the throne. . . as am I, I suppose," he added, his tone vague.

"But I fear the House of Lancaster will rise again. With Henry Tudor at the helm," Denys ventured.

"Fie on Tudor," Richard spat. "I expect to hear no more of him. He fled back to France when his mother's funds could no longer feed his army."

"Well, I know the realm is safe as long as you and Uncle Ned and . . . the right soldiers lead the vanguard into battle." She gave him a reassuring nod.

Courtiers began to drift away from the great hall as servers cleaned up and fed the palace dogs the scraps. She bade Richard good eve and glanced round one last time for that blond head and broad chest. Alas, Valentine was not about. Disappointment crushed her as she headed for her chambers alone.

Chapter Four

Candles blazed as the breeze floated through the open windows and rustled the velvet curtains. Queen Elizabeth sat in her post-childbirth chair. Her court ladies surrounded her, toying with their lutes, flutes, viols, and rebecs. Their chirpy prattle drowned out the instruments' twangs and hoots. Denys preferred to play her lute in peaceful solitude, but she attended these ladies' musicales for one reason: to catch up on Woodville antics. The conversation took a serious turn as they gloated over the recent victory over the Lancastrians.

"What a rout! And didn't old Marguerite of Anjou underestimate my Ned's advance," Elizabeth tattled. "The City of Gloucester was barred up tight to her entrance. Then my Ned faced that Lancastrian right wing head on right into the center of the line."

That, Denys knew, was grossly inaccurate. She respected Uncle Ned to eternity and never questioned his battle skills, but she knew it was Valentine who'd led the vanguard, faced the Duke of Somerset and penetrated the center of the line. But it was not for her to correct a queen.

Elizabeth prattled on, "...and my dear brother-in-law Guilford was stabbed to death in the heat of battle." A collective gasp hung halted the string-twanging as she raised her chin with an arrogant smirk. "However, sources informed me twas actually murder, not warfare—and twas no Lancastrian who murdered him."

Murmurs and hushed whispers circled the room. Denys leaned forward.

"The earl of Pembroke murdered him in cold blood." Elizabeth's lips pursed in a line of insistence. "Valentine Starbury," she added for emphasis as her eyes narrowed on Denys.

"I shall hear no more of this." Denys stood and set the lute down. "Pray I must be excused." Dizzy with dread and rage, she gathered her skirts and departed the room, blood pounding. Painful glimpses of her early childhood flashed before her eyes with graphic intensity. Her heart lurched as that long-ago fear reared its ugly head to haunt her ... the scent of melted wax assaulted her at the memory...the candle cast macabre shadows on Elizabeth's jutting jaw...the accusations plagued her more vividly than the beatings... "You stole my brooch, you spoke harshly to Thomas, you pulled Bridget's hair..." Now some untapped chamber of her heart cried out in fierce empathy for Valentine, wrongly and unjustly accused. This time Elizabeth Woodville went too far. She dreaded the news of a trumped-up charge against Valentine. The queen had accused innocent men and condemned them to the block. This could mean the axe for Valentine if Elizabeth instigated false charges. Desperate to speak to her uncle about this, she fled to the royal chambers.

* * *

"Where is His Highness the King?" she demanded of his Page of Honor when she reached his receiving chamber.

"Gone to Sandwich to capture the Bastard of Fauconberg, Mistress Denys," he replied.

Another battle? She hadn't heard about this. Was Valentine with him? She turned and ran down the corridor, her breath in short gasps.

Fleeing the confines of the palace, she raced through the outer court towards the stable. She needed to take Chera for a long ride over the outlying moors, to pray for an end to incessant conflict and for Valentine Starbury's head.

As the groom saddled Chera, Denys heard her name. She turned as Valentine strode towards her, hair streaming behind him, his face pale in the twilight. He glowed in his crimson satin tunic edged in cloth of gold. "Where are you bound in such haste?"

Her surprise at seeing him knocked the wind out of her. "Why are you not on campaign with the king?" Her bemusement gave way to elation, yet she grew uneasy at his nearness. Her heart raced. "I proffered my service, but his highness ordered ... er, asked me to stay and fulfill my duties here. He and Richard will return in a few days."

She hesitated to warn him of the queen's accusation. Mayhap it was best to wait for the king.

He drew her to him and rested his chin on the top of her head. She welcomed his comforting touch. "They will be fine. It is not much of a battle. Fauconberg has no chance. His choices are to surrender immediately or lose his head on the block tomorrow."

Lose his head on the block. The words stunned her. She turned and looked up at him. He looked so clean and touchable.

She couldn't hold back. The thought of him put to death was too much to bear. "There is something you must know. Bess just spewed the most dreadful gossip. It will spread all over the palace and—" Choking on her words, she couldn't go on.

"Calm down." He extended his arms and brought her to him. She sensed that he wanted her to lay her head on his shoulder and seek his comfort. "Now, tell me," he urged, his voice calm and gentle.

"Bess says you murdered Guilford," she delivered the horrible accusation. "Her sister's husband."

He stood silent for a long time. She expected him to lash out and snap off a tree limb, start flailing it about as if brandishing a sword, cursing the witch to eternal damnation.

His laugh numbed her.

She clenched her fists and broke their embrace. "How can you find humor in this?"

His lips curled in amusement. "'Tis absurd, that is how. I did not even witness the killing. I was nowhere near it. Richard and I were foraging with the soldiers. When we returned to our tents, we heard the news."

"But Bess accused you!" She glared at him. "I don't believe how you bray at this."

"She's miffed I wouldn't court her ungainly sister. But 'twas the end of the evening and I was all in. Fret not over false accusations, Denys. They are only words and words mean sod all." His unaffected tone finally calmed her as he gathered her to him once more.

"She's had innocent men arrested on made-up charges and dragged to the block. The earl of Desmond lost his head for telling the king he should've married a foreigner!"

"That was true and Desmond admitted it. I murdered no one and I can prove it. One-hundred-sixty soldiers were with me. If I really killed Guilford, then mayhap I'd have something to worry about." His gaze met hers.

"You don't know the queen, Valentine," she gave him necessary warning. "It matters not when accusations are false. You must inform the king and make sure the royal signet is in its place!"

He laughed again, louder this time. She wanted to protect him and pummel him at the same time.

"I've dreamt about this since that day in the garden." He lowered his mouth to hers. She let him claim her lips, as she'd also dreamt of since that day. His kiss was warm, soft and deliciously slow and leisurely. Her fingers played through his hair. As if both feared what would happen next, they pulled apart at the same time.

Huddled in the warm circle of his arms and resting her cheek on his tunic, she forced herself to breathe calmly. Her heart thumped between them and all their layers of clothes. She took a step back, fighting her excitement at being so close.

"What were we talking about?" he murmured as their hands found each other and their fingers intertwined.

"Uh—foul slander … the queen accusing you of murder. She's done it before, Valentine. I don't want it to happen to you. Just go to the king, please."

"Denys, gossip is something a nobleman is behooven to rise above." His eyes burned into hers. "What sets me apart from other courtiers, royalty excepted, of course, is that I care not what others say about me. As long as I, and those who care about me, know the truth, 'tis all that matters. The king and Richard know I did not stab Guilford, and I pray you know. The queen cannot frame me for it. There are too many witnesses, the king among them. She'll need find another way to punish me for not yielding to the putrid charms of her spinster sister."

He led her through the palace gates and down the narrow path to the river, the site of that unforgettable first meeting. She harbored mixed feelings, delightfully fearful of the responses his nearness stirred in her.

"I heed your warning about the queen, but we must take her accusations with indifference and at times even laugh them off. We of high rank are subject to all kinds of slander and yet we learn to brush it off…" He swept a dusting of soil from the front of his tunic, "like the dirt it is."

A chuckle escaped the depths of her relieved sigh. "We of high rank? You consider us among those ranks, my lord?"

He stepped back and his gaze lingered on her features as no man ever had before. It mortified and flattered her at the same time. "Most certainly. Especially you. You are royalty."

She looked away and nodded, ready to change the subject, but wished she could tell him the truth—she was not royalty, she knew not who she was.

"I know your aunt does not treat you as well as her own brood. But you still have royal blood in your veins, as only a lucky few ever do." He paused and added, "Even if you do not marry Richard."

No, she couldn't tell him the truth. "Ah, yes," she said through a forced sprinkling of laughter, "the best way to ruin my amity with Richard would be to marry. His la-di-da neatness alone sends me widdershins."

He chuckled, adding, "Ah, he is staid, all right. But he seems happy enough with his lot. 'Tis a happy time for all of us, especially for me. If it weren't for that joust I wouldn't be here relishing the delight of your company."

Her eyes widened. "What joust?"

"Richard and I jousted over you," came out so casually, as though he referred to someone else.

"Over me?" She sat there, stunned. "When?"

"I believe it was, uh—" His eyes searched high and low and he shook his head. "I don't remember. But not long ago."

"Richard never mentioned it." Her voice rose. "Why joust over me?" she insisted.

He flipped his hand in an airy wave. "Oh, it was a friendly little spar. But I admit he was the victor. Had I not been suffering an injured arm 'twould have been anyone's game." He held up his arm and flexed his fingers.

"He defeated you? Well, that does not surprise me. He's an experienced and able swordsman." She paused and gave him a serious glare. "But why was it about me, if you don't mind my asking?"

"It was about who would win you. And I won you." He brandished a grin and puffed out his chest as if he'd won the crown and the kingdom.

"You mean to say I was at stake? A sop to bestow upon the loser?" Her fists clenched. "You sparred and whoever lost would be saddled with me? Friendly, indeed! Who was the father of this brain sick jest? I can safely assume it wasn't Richard. He does not possess the imagination, or the gall."

"It was his idea for me to court you to help him escape your arranged marriage. How can you object?" He shrugged, palms up.

She paced in a circle, burning with humiliation. "I will be the laughing stock of court if anyone hears of this."

"No one will hear of it." He stopped her in her tracks. "All I am doing is trying to uphold my end of the bargain."

"Is that what you consider spending time with me?" She faced him. "Upholding your end of the bargain? Then your bargain is done. I hereby relieve you of the chore." Unable to bear the sight of him for another second, she gathered her skirts and fled. Stumbling on a tree root, she toppled over, landing on her side with a painful thump. She struggled to stand and smooth her skirts, attempting to maintain her dignity. Two warm hands gently lifted her as she scrambled back to her feet, brushed her back with sensuous strokes. She turned to face him, to babble some jumble of words, when his fingertips wrapped round a lock of her hair. His hands remained clasped a moment longer than necessary.

"Valentine, remember you're barely a part of the nobility in this kingdom, and are in more hazard than you think. Go to the king and be sure that royal signet is in his hands lest you end up strutting the great hall with your head tucked under your arm!"

"You really are worried about me, aren't you?" His voice took on a reverent tone.

She struggled out of his grasp. "Pray let me go. I need to be alone–to think." Her hem caught on a branch, snagged the satin and tore it to ribbons. He leaned over and unwound the frayed material from the branch, but he didn't hand it to her. He tucked it away under his surcoat. "Just a favor. If I may."

"Valentine, I warn you—avoid Bess Woodville. And for the time being—me as well." With one more glance, she turned and strode up the hill back to the palace. She didn't turn around to look back. As long as he cared not about Elizabeth's accusation, she needn't worry so. He'd managed to calm her a great deal about that.

She slowed her pace to a stroll and sat under a tree beyond the palace gates, trying to sort out her feelings for him. Beneath the lofty airs he harbored a streak of sincerity. He treated her like no man ever had—like a woman, not a little girl. She wanted to flirt but didn't know how. So for now she'd let him lead and simply follow. She was too anxious over the quest for her family to romp through a mummery with Valentine Starbury.

* * *

Richard welcomed Valentine to his receiving chamber the following eve. "Val, you remember my dear cousin, Anne Neville?"

57

"Indeed I do. 'Tis a pleasure to see you once again, Lady Anne. My, you've grown since I saw you last."

Lady Anne gave Valentine a warm smile that touched her brown eyes. "'Tis good to see you again. You have done quite a bit of growing yourself! Hard to believe you used to toss me in the river and flip me upside down!"

"And crack eggs over your brainpan!" He made a fist and tapped her on the head.

"And crush snowballs down my cloak!" She gave his arm a playful pinch.

They laughed as the sweet memories revisited them.

"Oh, come hither, Annie!" The childhood playmates embraced and Valentine held out his arm to bring Richard into the warm circle. The trio wound their arms round one another.

When at last they broke their embrace, Valentine stood back and held Anne's hands. She bore the ravages of adulthood much too soon. The creases around her expressive eyes shared Richard's look of wisdom peeking through that callow innocence. Although distant relations, Anne shared Richard's swarthy coloring. Dark hair peeked out from under the headdress. Her arched brows gave her expression sharp definition.

"You have my gravest respects on the death of your husband Edward," Valentine offered Anne.

"'Twas no true marriage, Valentine." She shook her head. "We did not live as man and wife, not even for a day."

"Nay, indeed not," Richard echoed, his sharp tone piercing the serenity of his chamber. "I called you here to ask a favor, Val, and I trust you will honor my request."

He nodded, knew what that favor would be.

Richard and Anne sat side by side in carved oak chairs and for a moment a picture flashed before Valentine's eyes—Richard and Anne enthroned as king and queen. How regal they looked in their majesty, heads held high with a royal air of subtle superiority, yet how gently their eyes caressed each other when their fingers touched.

Richard looked over at Valentine. "I would like you to stand up for me at our wedding."

Valentine reached out and pumped Richard's hand. "I am happy to. When is the date?"

"On the morrow after vespers. And God willing before the queen can muck it up again." He scowled.

"I offer you both my most heartfelt wishes." They nodded as one.

"Fine." Richard and Anne stood and she tucked her hand into his sleeve.

As Valentine bowed he saw a spark in Richard's eyes he'd never seen before, lighting up in bliss when he gazed upon his bride-to-be. What he wouldn't give to share that same magic with Denys.

After Anne took her leave, Richard closed the door after her and stood by the window. He placed a foot on the window seat and rested an elbow on his knee.

Valentine joined him, looking out over the Thames. The river transport slowed to a halt in the mist of eventide. "Now Anne is again free to marry. And this dissolves your trothplight to Denys."

"Aye, she is relieved, though saddened I will reside in Yorkshire." Richard straightened his doublet. "She expected us to continue on at court."

"The queen knows nowt of your plots, I take it," Valentine said.

"Nay. And Edward will keep it quiet until after we exchange our vows," he added. "But friendship knows no earthly bounds. You needn't hasten to capture Denys's heart. Take your time."

Valentine's smile widened. "I'd rather not. I thank God I lost that joust. Winning her heart is another matter. It may take longer than I thought," he added.

"Well, if anyone can make a woman go from slapping your face to kissing it, you can."

"No doubt, no doubt!"

Richard invited his friend to sit. "Val, I tell you of my wedding in utmost confidence. George mustn't know either."

"Why?" His eyes widened. "Would George interfere with your marriage?"

Richard snorted. "The Grey Mare won't give up her quest to hitch me to Denys. After the council meeting, Edward told me Elizabeth had the gall to send George to him to ask he deny us permission to wed."

He blinked. "Hell's teeth, what did Edward say?"

"Exercising elder-brotherly authority, Edward told him to pizzle off." Richard sneered.

Valentine whistled in disbelief. "Getting George to do her dirty work now? Why, she'll stop at nowt."

"This time George has a stake. You know he married Anne's older sister. As such, Isabel stands to inherit all her mother's estates. Elizabeth has convinced

George that Anne must stay an old maid in order for him to keep Isabel's inheritance. Over his customary flagon of malmsey last eve, George let slip that he intends to keep all of Isabel's inheritance. Now I really must marry Anne immediately. I must protect Anne's inheritance, and keep it out of George's greedy clutches."

"Well, if you can overcome all these obstacles, you and Anne truly are meant to be together!" Valentine tilted his head with a smile.

"Aye, I believe we are. And I wish to sire heirs just like any man," he said after a pause, still looking out over the river.

"But you truly love her, do you not?" Valentine asked.

He turned to Valentine. "I always have. Now I finally get to marry her. Isn't that a rare occurrence!"

* * *

On what was supposed to be Richard's wedding day, he entered Pluckley House, George's townhome, pushed his way through the crowd of jugglers, fools, and random hangers-on, laughing and singing drunkenly off-key to the minstrels' sloppy playing.

In the great hall George sat at the center of it all, a full-breasted wench on his lap, holding a goblet to his lips as his left hand 'slipped' down her front, his fingers fumbling with the crimson lace of her bodice.

Richard approached his brother just as a vulgar joke sent raucous laughter through the room. He held out his arm and shook George, causing a stream of wine to spew down the wench's front. She squealed, throwing her head back in delight. Then her eyes met Richard's and she nudged George. His eyes widened at the sight of his brother.

"Richard! Ye decided to partake in the subtle pleasures of life and it's about bloody time! Grab a tankard and a wench and join the festivities! But shed some of that blasted raiment first. Such foppery is not needed here."

"All right, George, where is she? I demand to know." Richard's voice never rose above normal level, and this was no exception, yet its sinister tone dared anyone to defy him.

"Ay? I didn't hear you." George held up a hand. "Quiet! His Grace The Duke of Gloucester is present." The noise died down to a curious buzz.

Richard paid no heed. "Where is she?"

George wiped wine from his chin and tossed the wench from his lap. She tumbled to the floor, giggling.

"Where is who? And do not look so glum, Richard." He chucked his baby brother on the chin.

"What have you done with Anne?" Richard spoke through clenched teeth.

"Anne who?" George's eyes crossed in confusion.

"Your sister-in-law, Anne Neville, you puttock, you know who! Where is she?" Richard clutched George's arm and shook it.

George blanched, for his adoring brother never spoke to him this way. Fury blazed in the young brown eyes. "Calm down, Richard," he chided in a hushed tone.

"I will be calm when you tell me where she is." He spoke through clenched teeth.

"By order of His Highness the king, I no longer am warden of Lady Anne. I neither know nor care where she is." George waved Richard off and turned back to his revels.

Richard vowed, "I will find her, George, and when I do, God help you."

The Duke of Gloucester's slight figure glided through the great hall and he slammed the double doors behind him. With eyes aglare at the lot gaping at him, he snapped, "Go back to your frolicks and quaff 'till you drown." He strode out of Pluckley House, his velvet cloak flowing like liquid.

The revelers looked at each other, shaking their heads, the age-old question in each of their minds: Did the king's starchy brother ever have any fun?

* * *

Denys went to visit Richard one more time before his wedding. She strode past the guards through to his retiring chamber and knocked. He didn't answer, so she went on in, as she was accustomed to doing.

He scurried about the room, wearing one shoe, bareheaded and in a plain linen shirt and hose, his lips twisted into a tight grimace. "Richard! Why aren't you in your wedding raiment? Where is your Esquire of the Body? The wedding is but an hour away!"

"No it isn't." He peered under a chair.

She shook her head in disbelief. "What—"

"Not now, Denys, I have somewhere to go." Pulling his other shoe out from under the table, he slid into it. He jammed a ring on his thumb and slammed his jewel box shut.

"Richard..." She grasped his sleeve but he flitted away like a feather in the wind and headed for the antechamber.

"What is amiss?" She wedged herself twixt him and the door. His eyes bored through her as he jerked his thumb, but she did not heed his signal of dismissal. "You look like you're about to kill someone."

"I will. But it'll have to wait. And if you don't want me in your marriage bed on Twelfth Night, you'd best let me go find Anne." He headed for the door.

"Oh, no!" She followed on his heels. "She's missing again? On your wedding day? What happened this time?"

"This time, Her Pestilence convinced George that Anne must stay an old maid so he keeps all his wife's inherited bounty. So he's the one who spirited her away to hell knows where!" He opened the door.

"You will find her!" she called after his retreating figure, quit his chambers and wandered aimlessly through the corridors, passing courtiers singing, plucking their lutes, or hurrying to their duties. Shuffling her feet through the rushes spread on the floor, she ran her hand over the elaborate frames of the portraits lining the walls, looking into the eyes of long-dead monarchs, their ancestors and descendants. Knowing she wasn't part of this long and enduring line tore at her heart. Oh, if only she knew who she was, she could escape Woodville clutches! Forcing herself to push the horror of her aloneness out of her mind, she wondered where Valentine was. Lonely as she was, she wanted to hear his pealing laughter and watch the breeze ruffle his hair. Looking into the outer court, she didn't glimpse him among the knights milling about, or the servants rushing back and forth carrying sacks, pails, and firewood. With squeaking wheels, wagons laden with supplies entered the gates. A stray hen waddled by and a kitchen wench dashed after it. But Valentine was nowhere to be found. As she decided to take Chera down to the river for a walk, the royal messenger she'd sent to the Archbishop galloped up to her on his graceful mount. Staying astride the horse, he touched his hand to his hat.

Her heart stopped.

"Mistress Denys, I've a reply from the Archbishop of Canterbury."

Her breath caught in her throat. Hand trembling, she took the parchment he handed to her, folded over and embossed with an elaborate wax seal. Her answer, at last! God willing, the long-buried secrets of her origin, now in her hand!

* * *

"So where did you find Anne?" Valentine put the finishing touches on his dress for the evening, selecting rings and chains from his jewel box.

"In Shoreditch, in the kitchens of a friend of George's, dressed as a cook-maid." Richard scowled out the window.

Valentine looked up. "You jest."

"'Tis the truth. George spirited her off to the place, the jackanapes … sometimes I do not know how he got into this family! The grief he has wrought upon us turns my blood green! That's why he hates Elizabeth; they're too damn much alike!"

"How did you find her?" Valentine slipped a gold Yorkist collar over his head and smoothed it over his chest.

"I went to George's friends first. She was not with either, so I went to his enemies. Fortunately, I only had to question twenty of them before I found her. Imagine if I had to go to the entire five thousand!" Richard slid out of his black tabard. "Ah, the funeral's over. I should change into something less dismal."

"What funeral?" Valentine took a white sarcenet tabard and dark green doublet from his wardrobe and laid them out on his bed.

"The Earl of Hereford." Richard's voice dragged with fatigue. "Executed yestermorn for treason."

Valentine stumbled backward in surprise. "God's truth! Another one? I didn't see him side with the Lancastrians during the battle."

"He didn't. He was always on our side. He just happens to be the latest suitor to turn down Elizabeth's sister's hand in marriage. Elizabeth conjured up a list of charges the length of your arm, he went to trial, of course the judges were all her brothers and nephews, and they found the poor fellow guilty of dallying with Marguerite of Anjou and thusly guilty of treason. Imagine, Marguerite of bloody Anjou! I doubt her husband ever even romped with her. But that was Elizabeth's charge, which grew and grew—next thing you know, the sorry sod's in the Tower and they're building a scaffold—" He drew a finger across his throat in a cutting motion. "Were I not the king's brother, she'd find cause to lop off *my* head for not marrying her blooming niece."

A clearer picture of Elizabeth Woodville formed in Valentine's mind and he suppressed a shudder, remembering Denys's warning. Mayhap he'd laughed it off too easily. But King Edward assured him he was in no danger. This mollified Valentine, yet he wondered… "I've learnt when in the presence of Her Highness to keep my gob shut."

"Unless it's to vomit out how lovely she looks or smells." Richard scowled as if sick to his stomach just talking about her.

Valentine straightened the sleeves of his doublet. "I've endured much worse, my friend. Remember, I spent time in France."

"Ooh, la pew!" Richard held his nose.

"May I help you choose a tabard for the evening, Richard?" Valentine stood before his full-length looking glass and turned this way and that.

"My Esquire of the Body can do that, Val, you needn't bother."

"No bother at all." Valentine turned to face Richard. "You did me a great service by defeating me in a joust that I was haughty enough to call. That resulted in my having to court the fairest maiden in the land, whose heart I intend to capture, and I daresay she will surrender it as easily as the Lancastrians give themselves up to you."

"Is that so? It may not be so easy. The Lancastrians are men. The fairest maiden in the kingdom is not exactly eating out of your palm, is she, Sir Golden Rod?" Richard cast Valentine a sly grin.

"Nay, but after tonight she may be nibbling. I have written some enthralling poetry and picked the sweetest flowers from the garden. I will stand under her window and recite my verse in the moonlight with my silver-tongued French." He released a shaky sigh, still not feeling as confident as he sounded.

"Your silver tongue would do something else French had you not let slip about our sparring and driven her away," Richard remarked.

Valentine slipped into new pointed-toe shoes and fastened the ends to his knees with ropes of pearls. "Oh, I expect by the morrow she'll forget all about that. All it takes is our exchange of logic and we will be in accord."

"Mayhap you're right, Val." Richard nodded. "If anyone can make a lass forget what she did yesterday, you can."

"So when is the wedding?" Valentine wiggled his toes inside his shoes.

"On the morrow. Before dawn. And no one knows about it this time. Just Edward, you, Denys, and the priest. And God willing, this time—Anne." Richard headed for the door.

"I shall be there." Valentine held out his arms and did a few slow dance steps, imagining Denys before him, and felt not a stirring in his loins, but a warmth in his heart. With a deep breath, he let the essence of her perfume fill his head, he hummed a song of romance, as if they shared their very first dance…

"What on earth are you doing?" Richard's voice brought it all crashing down around him.

"Why, dancing." Valentine blinked, his reverie fast fading.

"Well, since you're having such a gay time, I'll leave you and your invisible partner to carry on." Richard quit the chamber with a thin smile.

* * *

The Archbishop's letter was blunt and to the point. Having no record of her birth, he was unable to help her ascertain her true parentage. She dropped the parchment into the fire, her heart crushed, her face streaked with anguished tears.

She thumbed through the journal she kept all those years ago, when she and her noble "cousins" learned to read and write. She remembered a palfrey Uncle Ned had brought her, the way Thomas Woodville shoved her aside so he could ride it first, how she'd run away to write in her unsteady scrawl about his cruelty. Now she read that troubled child's story, a tale of the events leading up to the startling revelation that she was not a Woodville after all.

She finally found the entry she sought.

"They said Denys bla-bla-bla-bla Malmesbury," the entry read.

Now she would find out what the bla-bla-bla-bla was. And with God's blessing, that would lead to who *she* was.

Later that eve a messenger came to her chamber with a folded and sealed sheet of parchment. Her pulse surged. Another note from the Archbishop? Had he found something? But hope plummeted as she broke the seal and saw Richard's writing. He requested the honor of her presence at his wedding in the dead of night.

* * *

Richard and Anne exchanged vows in a hushed ceremony at Westminster Palace's secluded St. Stephen's Chapel. Denys focused her attention not on the bride, but on Valentine Starbury. His cape was of the richest red velvet, furred with ermine. Gold studs glittered on the rolled brim of his hat. He stood beside

Richard and handed him the gold wedding ring. Richard's eyes looked pleasantly calm as he and his bride marched back down the aisle, Anne's white veil flowing behind her. Denys felt Valentine's hand on her arm and she grasped it a bit too possessively. As he walked her out, she imagined she and Valentine were the bride and groom, leaving the chapel amongst the well-wishers, their gazes meeting for the first time as man and wife. What kind of husband would he be; would he be faithful? Or would he flaunt his mistresses before the court like Uncle Ned? Would her wedding night be as delightful as she always dreamed? Then she stopped to ask herself why she entertained such thoughts. Wedding Valentine Starbury? Letting him take her virginity? She shivered, out of shame as much as delight, and forced herself back to the moment. Richard was married; another symbol that her childhood was over. She approached the bride, kissed each of Anne's cheeks and Anne smiled warmly. She approached Richard. "I wish you happiness in your marriage." He thanked her and whispered into her ear, "Just as I wish you happiness in yours."

* * *

As she and Valentine parted at the chapel door, she didn't let her gaze linger. "Did you speak to the king about Elizabeth's accusation?"

He nodded. "Aye, I did, and he assures me I'll enjoy the company of my head for many a year to come."

She relished a rush of affection for her goodhearted uncle. Oh, how could he have married that woman? "I'm truly relieved, Valentine."

"I can tell." He gave her a playful grin.

"I would invite you to the solar for a game of chess, if time permits," she challenged.

His eyes widened. "You play chess?"

"A bit. 'Tis a pastime." She tried to sound casual. "The sky looks threatening. I hope you are up to the challenge."

"Count me in! I must break my fast with the council, but have a few minutes." He gave her a cocky grin. "Set up your chessboard forthwith."

She nodded, bobbed a curtsy, and took her leave.

Smiling to herself, she wished she'd seen that joust, and the look of crashing defeat on his face when he yielded. But to see his surprise at her utterance of "checkmate" with a few quick moves would more than make up for that!

* * *

"Now, chess is my game!" Valentine inspected the pewter king and queen as Denys took the sunniest window seat in the solar. "Shall we make it more interesting by wagering checkmate within twenty-five moves?"

Denys omitted to mention that she had played chess since Elizabeth's son Anthony, the more human of the two, taught her at age three. "Or are you unsure of yourself, my lord?"

"I go easy on you, dear lady. Call your forfeit and let us proceed."

She rotated the board so that he would had the white pieces, a great advantage, as he would make the opening move. "I'll make it easy for you. You can have white. Prepare for an even more humiliating defeat than at the blunted end of Richard's sword."

He blanched, covering it up with a seething smile. "Are the stars in your favor today or do you just feel lucky?"

That you will find out. However, it surprises me that you do not wish to play for a wager." She adjusted each piece in its square.

"I never gamble with a woman." He studied the board.

"You gambled *for* a woman," she shot back. "And you say you won her."

He continued to study the board without yet making his opening move. "Although my pride yet eludes me, it is well within my grasp, is it not?" He moved a pawn forward two squares.

"Physically, yes, but figuratively, your prize may as well be out in the heavens for all its proximity to you." She brought out her knight.

He brought out his same knight. "Infinitely greater prizes have slipped through my hands, dear lady."

Trying not to let his pointed remark distract her from the board, she returned, "Then your hands have even less skill than your sword." She brought forth her king's pawn and assessed her position.

"My sword skills leave nowt to be desired. As for my hands, they can perform magic beyond thrall." His eyes left the board and burned into her.

"Then why did you not challenge Richard in thumb-wrestling? You may have won."

His gaze dropped back down to the game. "Mere child's play."

"Shall we play for a forfeit then?" she goaded.

He looked up at her. "Of what nature? I am sufficiently landed; I need no girlish gauds."

"Not chattels," she countered. "An accord similar to the one over which you so haughtily sparred Richard."

"What is it?" Ignoring the game, he fixed his gaze on her.

"If you win, uphold your pact with Richard and pursue me to your wits' end. If I win..." Her smile caused him to slump back against the wall, his eyes taking on a dreamy look, rememorating melting ice. "Then that pact is void and you end your pursuit of me."

"But I cannot! My wager with Richard was fair and square and I am honor bound."

"This new accord subjugates it. Do we have a deal or do you blunder at this game such that you cannot chance it?" She knew he wouldn't dare back down.

"Very well, we have a wager." Their eyes stayed locked over the chessboard and held in the silence.

"'Tis your move, my lord," she informed him.

Finally shifting a pawn to protect the one under attack, he heaved a sigh. "Losing confidence?" She captured his pawn, baiting her checkmate in next move if he recaptured her pawn with his.

He emitted a confident "Hrrmph!" and took her pawn, falling into her trap.

She advanced her rook, but did not release it. "Now that is checkmate, but I had you at unfair advantage. I shan't hold you to the bargain." She moved her rook back.

He looked up at her. "What unfair advantage?"

"I've played chess since the age of three. Very few in this court, the king included, ever defeat me. It would be unfair to have humiliate you further." She forced herself to keep a straight face.

He backed away from the board, resting against the alcove. "That is honorable of you. Or didn't you want to win because you realize your folly and welcome my pursuit?"

That brought an amused grin to her lips. She returned the pieces to their starting positions and began a solitary game. "You shall never know, my lord. However, do know that honor is my greatest virtue." She spoke whilst moving the pieces of both sides as he watched in reverence. "I would never cheat nor take advantage of your lack of skill in an area in which I excel."

"Such a contrast from the rest of your family, I must say. So un-Woodville-like."

"All the more evident I'm not one of th—" She stopped herself too late. Clenching a fist around a black pawn, she clapped her other hand over her mouth, springing up, whirling away from him and the storm of questions that was bound to follow.

He stood and approached her. "Not one of them?"

She waved her hands in the air. "Forget I said it."

He turned her to face him, gathered a few stray strands of her hair and touched them to his cheek. "You are not the queen's niece?"

"I did not mean to say it." But she felt oddly comfortable telling him. Unlike Richard, he wasn't busy rounding up a council for his new life in the north. He had the time and inclination to listen. And how badly she needed someone to lean on!

"There is nowt amiss with being taken in by a noble—"

"I care not a whit to be noble. I never belonged to them and I do not belong now. I am no Woodville, I abhor the thought that I must live under their roof!"

"You are nowt like them. It matters not who raised you." His soft tone comforted her. "You are still you."

"Oh, but I will find out. If it takes till my last breath, I will find out who I am. I never believed the Woodvilles to be my true family. It goes beyond our many differences in nature, temperament, and values. I just do not fit in. My suspicions are deep, and have been for some years now. When I was young, I overheard Bess and Uncle Ned speak of Malmesbury in regards to me, and of an orphan. Ever since I heard those whispered fragments, I would ask Bess again and again, 'Tell me about my mother and sire, Aunt Bess, please!' But she would slap me away or command a server to remove me from the chamber."

"Why not tell you the truth?" Eyes downcast, he shook his head.

"I think she has a dark secret under her pointed hat. But I cannot go on not knowing. I do not remember much, but I wrote down what I could. It is well that nobles have their children taught to learn to read and write, or I could not have recorded it. It began to haunt me after Uncle Ned took the throne and I saw the Woodvilles for the powermongers they are. That heightened my suspicions. I share none of their qualities, even if only a niece. I resemble them in no way, especially not her. I saved that childhood journal all these years. I wrote their mention of Malmesbury. Richard says Bess offered him a dowry, Foxley Manor, in Malmesbury. When I mentioned Foxley Manor to her, she gave me a cuckoo story, and I caught her in the lie. I wrote to the Archbishop, but he was no help. There is no record of my birth."

"What will you do now?" he asked.

"I depart for Malmesbury on the morrow to find Foxley Manor. If it is a red herring I will try another way. I shall not stop until I find my true beginnings." She gave him a resolved nod.

He clasped her hand. "Denys, let me go with you. I shall guide you every step of the way and be there when you need counsel, should it not prove fruitful."

She shook her head. "Your concern is touching, but you need not hold my hand. I've hired an able guide. Just..." She faltered before the words spilled from her lips.

"Just what?" He gripped her fingers. "I shall do whatever you ask."

"Just be here for me when I get back." She drew herself to him.

"Of course I will. I've nowhere else I'd rather be." He lowered his face to hers, his eyes closed and their lips met, quenching a hunger he'd not known before her. A soft moan escaped from deep within his throat as he stroked her cheek with feathery touches.

She pulled away, rubbing her lips as if to wipe away any trace of his kiss. "Do not take advantage of me, I have had enough of that."

"How is a kiss taking advantage? You enjoyed it as much as I." His voice softened. "Did you not?"

"Nay, you addle my wits ... just let go." She broke their embrace and left the chamber.

"I will be here," he called after her. "Waiting..." he whispered under his breath, "...to know you better. No matter who you are."

* * *

Mounted atop Chera, with by her guide Hugh Corey, her maid, a pair of royal guardsmen and one of King Edward's grooms leading a pack horse carrying clothes and provisions, the queen unknowing, Denys passed through the palace gates. Handing out coins and sweets to gaping city folk, she led her retinue along the ancient city wall.

They clip-clopped through London's busy streets, through the stinking refuse. Crows cawed, sweeping down into the streets, tearing at rotten carcasses with their beaks. Merchants and costerd-mongers shouted out: "Come, eat, come! Hot pies, pies of goose, beef, mutton, hot pies, hot!" Black oak against white plaster framed the dwellings, colorful shields representing their trades. A wealthy merchant's house, adorned with colorful stained glass windows, stood among the craftsmen's dwellings. Robes of bright reds, blues, and greens draped the folks, their pointed shoes just as colorful. Barefoot children darted in and out of the crowd. Carts rumbled and church bells clanged in the distance.

They crossed the bridge over the city ditch, its mire of ordure giving off a foul odor. On the rutted road over the open moor, farm buildings, barns and almshouses surrounded them. The church bells faded and the barking of dogs grew loud as they rode by a kennel beside a stream. Houses, on piles driven into the earth, stood in clusters over the marsh. The party followed well-worn tracks as the clouds thickened. Once free of the city's confines, Denys welcomed the cold sprinkle of raindrops on her face and hands.

"Malmesbury in five days, then I shall know who I am, God willing," and Mother Nature answered with a new burst of rain to refresh her. She threw off her headdress and let her hair tumble down her back.

* * *

As Denys journeyed to Malmesbury to find her beginnings, Valentine thought he could help by staying at the palace.

Richard traveled north with his bride to Pomfret Castle, his new official residence. Some servers remained, washing linens, covering the floor with fresh rushes, and scrubbing the privies.

Valentine would catch up with Richard later. He had something to do first.

The rope-thick vines covering the palace's north wall made it as easy to climb as the grand staircase. An open window let fresh air into Queen Elizabeth's dressing room. He scaled the vine, scrambled through the window and landed on his feet.

A row of chests stood against one wall. Headdresses hung from hooks, each pair of shoes in its own wooden box. Satin undergarments were folded one atop the other, on a shelf along the opposite wall. A frilly cloth draped a dressing table. A pile of ivory combs lay beside a row of horns filled with lotions.

In the queen's privy closet he found stacks of padlocked trunks, knowing their contents must be cataloged here. He had to find what he sought, even if it meant sleeping here on a pile of Elizabeth's chemises.

No one could challenge the organizational skills of Elizabeth Woodville. Her compunction for method unsettled him: each meal needed be served her orderly way, each plate removed and each goblet rinsed before the next course. Every server had to check in and out upon entering and departing the palace, every horse had its name etched on its stall, every bale of hay and slop bucket was accounted for, every expense recorded by the fastidious queen herself. She drove the poor Lord Steward round the bend with her constant inventorying of the bakehouse, buttery, and saucery. She sat with the controllers every Wednesday to balance the accounts. No one spent a farthing without her approval, and heaven help the auditor who added up a column wrong.

Torches blazed in the queen's chamber windows into the wee hours, the account books under her scrutiny. Surely she'd filed away documents pertaining to her beauteous silver-haired charge.

He looked through a leather-bound ledger on her writing table, neatly penned in straight columns. He thumbed through another ledger, and another. Finally he found a book that did not list finances. It listed her siblings, their spouses and children, birth dates and places. Each name had a number next to it. Surely a code of some sort, an index to her stacks of files. His finger ran down the list of names, turned the page and skimmed another list. The Plantagenets: Edward, the departed Edmund, George, Richard, and their other siblings, with their dates and places of birth. Some had numbers next to them, some did not. He turned another page. The Woodvilles were a huge clan. The listing went back to the early 1300's, before Edward III. She certainly knew where she came from. Then on his way back, retracing all the names, he saw it. It had no birthplace or date next to it, just the number 5. The name he'd sought.

Denys Woodville.

But what was the number 5? He checked the other names with 5's next to them—Elizabeth's aunts, uncles and cousins. As it grew dark, he snatched a torch from the bedchamber and retraced his steps into the private close-room, settling among the trunks. Flickers of torchlight caught Romans numeral on the front of each trunk. The trunk embossed with "I" sat at the very bottom, "V" at the top.

Using a night-stool for a step, he swung the trunk out over his head and let it drop. Dust billowed as it hit the floor. He climbed down, twisted the rusty lock till it broke and eased the lid open. It was crammed with letters, their musty odors mingling with the scent of the wax that had once sealed them. They all had one thing in common: they were written by people with a '5' by their names in the book. Now, which pertained to Denys Woodville?

The torch down to an orange glow, he reached the last few letters. Straining his eyes to see, he stood and stretched his legs.

Then he found it…

A short letter with flowery script covering one side of the page, signed Margaret Holland, Countess of Somerset. Who the devil was she? Its significance lay in the body of the letter, where 'the babe' was referred to several times. It was dated "Monday next after Martinmas, 1457," in the tradition of using saints' days to date letters. Martinmas.

Running through the saints' names and dates, he remembered it was on 11 November, the feast of the plowman, when the great slaughter of the animals took place.

He'd done all he could for one night; it was pitch dark and the torch had dwindled to nowt. Shoving the trunk back into place, he groped his way out of Elizabeth's closet into the antechamber. Torches glowed in the distant corridor. Tomorrow morn he would look more thoroughly through trunk 'V.'

As he passed through the outer chamber, footsteps echoed behind him. Flattening himself against the wall, he glimpsed a white apron as a server lumbered down the hall. She was corpulent, her dress was filthy, and she reeked of a stench he could detect ten feet away. It was Kat, the only female cook in the court's kitchens, by virtue of her bulk and strength, she was how he pictured Denys as per Richard's blunt description.

He hoped she would waddle by without seeing him. The footsteps stopped. *Oh, no.* He held his breath. She'd caught him.

He had to think—fast. "Good eve, lass, what brings you to the queen's chambers at this late hour?" He crept back along the wall.

"What brings *ye* 'ere?" Her sharp accusing tone betrayed a dockside accent. She entered the antechamber and slammed the door shut. Now they stood confined in this too-close space.

"A secret royal mission. 'Tis frightfully dark in this maze of a palace." He shoved the letter down the back of his hose and wiped his forehead.

He feared he was in more trouble than the time he arranged separate dalliances with King Louis's two daughters, and they both arrived in the garden at the same time!

Just as he had then, he now broke out in beads of cold sweat.

"Well, tell me what you're doin', white knight, or I report ye to the queen." She placed meaty fists on her hips.

"Kat, I am simply…" He tried to appeal to her by using her name. "I'm not trying to hurt anyone, you know how I respect the king and queen."

"Tell me what you're doin' then," she repeated.

"A mission for the king. Seems our good queen mislaid the privy seal and the king needs it. But she will be mighty vexed she learns the king sent me here, so do promise you won't tell her?"

"Privy seal my arse." She sneered.

"But 'tis true!" he insisted.

"I bet you're sneakin' round for The White Hog of Gloucester. I seen the two o' you diddlin' together so much, methinks you're after each other or some-such." He'd heard those of low birth refer to Richard as "The White Hog" from his emblem, the White Boar. No one of nobility would dare refer to him this way, except maybe the Woodvilles.

"P'r'aps if you take me mind elsewhere, I'll forget I ever seen ye and won't tell 'er 'ighness ye were 'ere." She edged up to him and ran a finger down his cheek.

"Take your mind off it? Very well then. How about a game of chess?" He backed away with an agreeable smile.

"Nah!" She licked her lips, baring rotted teeth. "'ow 'bout ye acquaint me body with yours?"

"How about ye acquaint your body with a fresh cake of soap?" he rejoined.

"What I have in mind has nowt to do with clean." She reached out to snatch his privy parts.

He slid out of the way. She tried to flutter her lashes, but this pitiful attempt at femininity failed him.

"Alas there is nowt I can do to pleasure you. A physical defect robs me of my manhood, as it were. I am not a man in the true sense." That was easy enough to say at the thought of touching her.

"Ye speak the truth, me lord?" Her tone softened…an attempt at sympathy, he hoped.

"Aye, I speak the very truth. I was wounded in the Battle of Tewkesbury, both me and my horse. We rode into battle man and destrier, out a pair of geldings." He reached behind him to smooth the letter, bunched up twixt his buttocks "The beast soon perished, poor thing. But I … nearly lost it, had it fairly stitched back on. It ceased to serve in the carnal sense."

"And it don't work no how?" She inched closer. He retreated, his back against the wall. "Your story warms me heart," she uttered. "But I wanna see for meself." She made a lunge for him.

He sidestepped out of her reach and pointed an accusing finger. "Mayhap I should tell Queen Elizabeth about you trying to bed me in the royal chamber." He turned the tables on her. "Just what are *you* doing here?"

"Scrubbin' the bloody privies in punishment for servin' Her Highness burnt toast. Lookit me hands!" She held out raw and calloused palms. "Look how they be from scourin'!"

"Cease!" he commanded and she froze.

"What's that on your left hand? Be that a witch's mark?" He forced himself to approach her. "Mayhap you are witching a king's errand."

"Nay! 'Tis but a wart, me lord!" She snatched her hand away. "I ain't no witch, please..."

As she sobbed he knew dread would snuff out any tattle about this incident.

"Then be gone lest I demand you remove your chemise and prove you've not an extra teat!" he demanded.

She backed out, flung the door open and fled in a cloud of body stench and kitchen grease.

Heaving a sigh of relief, he looked both ways before removing to his own chambers, where he ordered a bath and scrubbed every inch of his body. He lit a small fire and burned the letter. He didn't dare keep it or return to Elizabeth's chambers to put it back.

"Oh, Denys, the things I do for love!" Longing for her made his heart ache, but he knew this would bring him one step closer to winning her.

* * *

Valentine entered the ancient and elegant Pomfret Castle's gatehouse, un-horsed and handed the reins to a stable lad. A page led him to a chamber where Richard conferred with his council.

After announcing the next meeting's day and time, Richard dismissed them. "Val, what took you so long? I thought you changed your mind and joined court on progress."

"Nay, progress is too like battle but with none of the glory. I needed attend to a task." He sat in the window seat and looked over the busy river.

"I have meetings in London and will depart on the morrow. Lodge within if you wish," Richard offered.

"Thank you anyway." Valentine waved the offer off. "I'll return to London."

"I thought you might," Richard displayed his half-grin.

They quit the chamber and Richard led him to the outer court. A gentle breeze played with Valentine's hair. Breathing deeply of the fresh country air, he closed his eyes and enjoyed the twitter of birdsong in this moment of peace.

"A monumental task if it took near a week." Richard stretched his arms over his head.

"'Twas indeed." Valentine recalled the journey's duration as the fresh air goaded his appetite. "Is there anything to eat?"

* * *

After a hearty repast of roast quail breast, wings of swan, mussels, whelks and cockles along with slabs of buttered bread, a bowl of strawberries and a handful of almonds washed down with ale, they headed back outdoors. "Do say we're not heading for a graveyard."

Richard removed his hat, stroking its feather. "Nay, we'll stop here on the mound."

"I'm helping Denys find her real family, Richard, but she doesn't know yet. 'Twill be a thrill and a reward to know I help in her quest. It may even help capture her heart, but that's not my only motive." He sat on the ground and chewed on a sprig of mint.

"I know you are in her thrall." Richard sat cross-legged. "But do not get too spellbound. Denys can be enchanting and most vexing at the same time, the way she builds fictional realms round herself. She can be a flibbertigibbet at times. If her plight isn't to her liking, why, she just fixes it in her brainpan. And it is difficult, nigh on impossible, to tell her otherwise. Even if she rememorates truly what she heard when seven years old, it was likely Bess's joyful cruelty in toying with Denys's feelings, playing up to her pensive nature. Should this not bear fruit, even you may be unable to console her."

"Ah, but I'll make up for it. Besides, I made a promise to you and I will keep it."

Richard snorted. "I knew you would fancy her once you met."

"There's plenty to fancy." He closed his eyes and pictured her. "Mayhap too much." He chortled. "If I help find her family, then all the sooner she will marry me. A double ceremony would have been grand."

"You are more of a dreamer than she!" Richard cast him a sly grin. "Nay, Anne and I needed to be wed in the utmost haste under a cloak of secrecy. I couldn't afford the luxury to woo at leisure."

"Leisure? Indeed!" Valentine laughed. "Pursuing her takes so much of my vigor, I'll barely be awake on my wedding night!"

* * *

Valentine rode alongside Richard over the broken stones of the straight Roman road leading back to London. Their horses' hooves thundered across ancient wooden footbridges over babbling streams. Diverting southwest, they traveled narrow paths through deep woods, surrounded by trees of ash and chestnut that cleared into an extensive marshland. Mist shrouded the hills beyond. Gorse and bracken scented the air.

They reached Leicestershire before sunset on the third day. After lodging at the local inn, he and Valentine went on a twilight ride, the cool air on their faces. They unhorsed at the top of a hill and Valentine pulled a half-eaten quail, a shriveled plum and two squashed fruit tarts from his satchel. "Care to partake, Richard?"

Richard shook his head and stood looking out over the tilled fields. Patches of light and dark green spread over the earth under the hazy sky streaked with wispy violet fingers. He sat on the ground, drew his knees up and hugged them to his chest. "What is this place?"

"Market Bosworth, according to the marker we passed." Valentine bit into his juicy plum.

They sat in silence as the sun bowed lower in the sky. Valentine pulled off his surcoat and tunic and sprawled out bare-chested in the grass. "Ah, sweet earth! You should lie down, let your bare skin breathe of the fresh soil." He attributed Richard's silence to the sudden changes in his life.

Before Valentine finished his plum, Richard stood and headed for his mount. "I must be gone."

Valentine took his last bite and tossed the plum aside. "Why so soon? Stay and watch the stars come out as we always did. We shall name the constellations if you can remember them."

"I cannot stand it here." Richard shuddered and ran his hands up and down his arms. "I am chilled. Something about this place…" Richard mounted and tugged on the reins.

Valentine jumped on his mount and caught up with Richard at the bottom of the hill. "Richard, are you ill?" His eyes were glazed, unseeing behind a medley of dark tormenting thoughts.

Richard said nowt, but turned and galloped back toward Leicester, leaving Valentine confounded. How could someone who lolls in graveyards for hours be so ill at ease in a peaceful place like Market Bosworth?

* * *

Malmesbury—an ancient town of narrow winding streets, wattle-and-daub cottages, and busy shops. Cleaner than London, it did reek of waste and rotted trash. Denys and her party entered through the East Gate and rode down the High Street. A large banner in the main square read "Cross Hayes." On this market day, dwellers scuttled round dressed in their custom of rough woolen clothing, bags of goods slung over their shoulders or over the backs of mules. As she passed stalls displaying sweets, biscuits and other treats, her mouth watered at the spicy aroma of gingerbread.

The market teemed with squawking chickens, grunting pigs, and mongers hawking their wares. Wooden awnings creaked on rusted chains above the stalls. Burlap bags and pots clanged against the beasts' sweaty rumps. Expert hands prodded and squeezed piles of fruit. Customers argued over prices with fishmongers.

She purchased a dozen cakes and enjoyed her freedom to walk among the villagers, trying to catch a word or two as they chattered in the unfamiliar Wiltshire dialect.

Her eye caught an array of colorful cloths and ribbons hanging in one shop, but her eagerness to complete her task pushed her ahead. Her appetite gave way to a wave of unease as she walked a bit farther and glimpsed the Abbey beyond the Market Cross.

"I am going to the Abbey," she told her guides. "Follow me." With steady strides, she led the short walk to the Abbey.

She leaned on the heavy door and entered the cavernous Abbey. As she pulled the door closed, she shut out the swirling dust and hot sun. A friar stood at an ancient tomb to the left of the altar with his back to her. He turned just as the slice of sunlight closed on him.

They met halfway down the aisle. "Good morrow to you, Father. I am Denys Woodville. Who is the Abbott here? I need to see him."

"Ah, that be John Aylee. I shall fetch him for thee." As he vanished into the shadows she sat in a pew, fell to her knees and prayed that her journey ended here.

Moments later, the Abbott approached her. His soft plumpness comforted her as the sun's rays slanting through the stained glass landed in a glowing rainbow on his bald pate. "May I 'elp thee, my child?"

She slipped out of the pew and greeted him. "Your grace, I am Denys Woodville and would be grateful for your assistance."

He nodded. "'Ow may I be of thy assistance, Mistress Woodville?"

"I seek my family. I was given to Elizabeth Woodville as an infant ward of King Henry the Sixth. I am told there is no birth record, but I believe my family hail from these parts."

He gasped as if taken by surprise. "Dost th'a know thy family name?"

"Nay, I know not who they are, but I wish to check the records and see who was born that year."

As he shook his head, her thrill of expectation dissolved. "Yer a furrener?"

Since anyone from even a few miles away was a 'foreigner' she nodded, but made haste to explain: "I reside at court now, but my true family hails from here."

"They books of birth records date only to 1350," the Abbot informed her. "They murre recent books were destroyed by fire, oh, nigh on twenty year 'go. I shall fetch the surviving one fer thee."

As he took his leave, she knelt and prayed some more. For all she knew, the mother she sought could have knelt in this very same pew, hands clasped, head bowed, praying for her daughter's well-being.

He returned, handed her the book, and she tried not to rip the pages in her haste. She turned to 1457. "I believe this was the year of my birth," she told him. The town recorded three births that year, all boys. She checked two years before and after; three females born in those years were now dead and the others still lived, married to yeomen. "Your grace, do you recall a baby girl born to folk who died soon thereafter?"

He shook his head. "Nay, lass, but if King Harry's men or any furrener come to Malmesbury to take away a babe nigh on twenty year 'go, I shall 'ave r'memb'r'd it."

"May I ask—do you know of Foxley Manor?" She held her breath awaiting his answer.

79

He pursed his lips. "Nay, nowt of Foxley Manor. Might have changed hands, been renamed. The community started wi' the invasion of the Saxons, when it be part of Wessex. The name Foxley dost sound most strange to me."

"How about deeds?" she pleaded. "I must find Foxley Manor."

"Tha all gone in fire, Mistress Woodville, right along wi' the birth records. A shame, it twere." He shook his head.

She couldn't help but wonder if he was lying. She thanked him and, eyes stinging with tears of defeat, went back out into the brilliant sunshine which now glared harsh and cruel.

Hugh waited at the entrance and together they asked townsfolk if they'd heard of Foxley Manor, but to no avail. They either gaped at her and the royal colors draped over Chera, or shook their heads as if she spoke another language. In a way she did.

Still no luck.

An elderly man crossed Silver Street, leading a mule with one hand, a bag of dry goods slung over his shoulder. "Oh, please let him know!" she begged as she and Hugh approached him.

The man's face lit up in recognition when she spoke the name, as if trying to recall a hazy memory. "Aye. 'Twas once called Foxley Manor, nigh on twenty, thirty year 'go, but changed dwellers several times. I know not who the lord was, but divers tenantry dwelt there, and now—oh, I haven't bin tha' way since afore this old mule was born."

"Do you know where it is?" She spoke so fast she had to repeat herself.

He pointed. "Aye. At the edge of town, due west, on the Bristol road, the far bank of the Avon. Foller the Gaerstons Road to Goose Bridge."

She knew many streets had the Saxon suffix "Gaerstons" meaning the green field.

Hugh nodded. "The river's right over yonder." Turning back to the old man, he asked, "Do you know the names of anyone who ever lived there, or who lives there now?"

The man shook his head. "I know not who lives there or lived there. Last time I 'eerd 'f t'were many year 'go. I don't ge' out round these parts much more, don't hear any local piffle."

"Any Woodvilles live near these parts?" Denys prodded.

"Nay, no Woodvilles." He shook his head. "Can't say I ev'r 'eerd that name. Me name be Blanchard, but nev'r 'ard of a Woodville round Malmesbury."

She almost envied him, never having known a Woodville. "Thank you." She reached into her bag and handed the man a few shillings.

Turning to her retinue, she pointed with a shaking hand. "Onto the Avon!"

Over the stone Goose Bridge they rode, her heart thumping, mouth dry as salt cod. Then she saw it up ahead, surrounded by trees at the foot of a sheep-dotted hill—a two-storey house of red sandstone fronted with oriel windows and an arched front door. She left Chera with her maid, unhorsed and motioned for Hugh to follow as she ran up to the door. She knocked and rattled the latch but got no response. She peered into one of the windows. "Dark as a tomb," she commented to Hugh. They went round back but could not open the door nor see through the windows. Fierce determination lit a fire in her belly. "I need to gain entry to this house and will find a way."

He waved his hands to and fro. "You cannot force your way in, milady, 'tis a crime, you can be hanged for that, or the pillory if you're lucky!"

She placed a finger to her lips. "Shhh. No one will know if we're quiet about it."

"We?" His eyes bugged out.

"Pay heed, Hugh. This is likely my ancestral home. I need to gain entry and find clews to my family. Follow me and keep an eye out."

The back door looked a simple affair, but not so when she rammed her shoulder against it. "Owww!" She rubbed her shoulder as Hugh looked round, shuffling from one foot to the other. "Hugh, fetch a good sized bough." He dragged a large fallen branch to the door and grabbed hold of it.

"I am going to ram the branch against the handle and it should shatter the latch on the other side." She drew back. "One-two-three!" The branch rattled the door but did not budge it.

"Oh, Jesu, help this wench." He clasped his hands together.

"I am not giving up that easily." Once again she drew back and smashed the branch against the door handle like a battering ram. The door rattled but did not open. "One more time." She battered the handle with a series of rapid thrusts. The door swung open, groaning on rusty hinges. She stumbled inside, dropped the branch and regained her footing.

She turned to Hugh. "I'm in! Follow me!" She peered around, her eyes adjusting to the darkness. The house was bare; not a table, chair or wall hanging remained. She tried to remember ever having lived here, even as a babe. But not the slightest trace of memory came to her.

"Hugh, stand guard here." She began to walk through the airless rooms.

The residence would be elegant if furnished and inhabited. But now, hollow and devoid of warmth, it felt forsaken, abandoned. She wished it were hers so she could pretty it with cheerful tapestries, elegant tables and chairs, fragrant flowers, sweet rushes on the floors.

And this was her dowry!

She climbed a staircase to a central corridor and entered a cold empty bed-chamber. She unlatched a window and swung it open. Inhaling the clean air on a breeze that chilled her skin, she wondered who'd lived here, loved here, died here. And what it all had to do with her.

Wandering from chamber to empty chamber, she halted in a door-way—rosary beads attached to a locket hung from the far wall. Heart hammering, she moved closer to get a better look. It hung by a nail; she retrieved it and turned the locket around. It framed a tiny oval portrait of a young woman. Oh, God, who was she? Denys focused on the eyes, trying associate that face with a long-forgotten memory. The woman looked bereft, as if in mourning, her dour lips turned downward in a frown. Her eyes, dark and troubled, echoed her black raiment, the only adornment a string of pearls circling her throat.

She enclosed the rosary in her fist and went back outside.

"I found this hanging on the wall, Hugh." She held it up to him. "She looks not like me, does she?" Her voice defeated, she'd so wished for some resemblance; that would give her a glimmer of hope.

He studied it, but shook his head. "Not much, lass. Except a bit in the eyes."

She took another close look. "So what? I've seen green eyes on many a girl." She slid the rosary and locket down the front of her chemise. "Let us depart, there is nowt for me here." Heading for Chera, she couldn't wait to be gone from this forsaken place.

"But this could well be it," she said over a sigh as she mounted Chera. *Foxley Manor. My dowry. My family home.* But unless someone could identify the young woman in that portrait, she would never know.

Now more than ever, Denys felt lost; utterly lost, with no place to call home, no family to call her own. But she tried to regain hope by looking far into the future. She would find her family and be break free of Elizabeth's control, free to search out a loving, caring mate. This was but the first step on a long, tedious journey. If she did not find them today, she would find them on the morrow or the next day. She refused to depart this earth without knowing where she came from.

Head high, shoulders no longer slumped, she whipped off her headdress and crammed it into her satchel. As Chera's strong legs galloped over the green earth, her hair streamed behind her in the wind.

Spent, she led her party back down the High Street to the White Lion Inn. Next morn she headed back to Westminster Palace—but God willing, not for long—to plot her next step.

* * *

Denys returned to the palace as cleaners cleaned the privy closets, swept the floors and opened windows to let in fresh air. She peeked into the great hall. In preparation for the evening's banquet, scullery maids polished the tiles on hands and knees. Servitors spread linen cloths on the tables and set them with plates and goblets. The crystal salt cellar separating nobles from commoners stood at the high table's center. Adjusting her headdress, Denys headed towards the chapel for vespers as Valentine rushed up to her. She embraced a pang of excitement.

His dress was in the fashion of a noble of his rank. His blue velvet doublet furred with red fox, sleeves lined with blue satin. A gold girdle cinched his waist, gleaming with rubies and sapphires. A long feather trailed from behind his bejeweled cap.

"Meet me at the twisted elm, we must speak to," he whispered out the side of his mouth.

"Why not tell me here and now?" She desperately needed to release her frustrations and defeat on his strong shoulders. But he looked too troubled.

"I'm sorry, Denys, here and now is neither the place nor time. But we must talk. It regards your…" He brought his lips to her ear. "Your search."

"You found something? What?" She clutched his sleeve as her heart surged.

"Just meet me there as fast as your legs can take you." He turned and skirted the worshipers gathering at the chapel door.

She hastened down to the elm tree at the river's edge. Valentine stood there, watering his mount.

She approached him. "What did you find?"

His eyes shone bright. "I discovered that Margaret Holland, countess of Somerset is somehow connected with your—"

The pounding of hooves distracted him. He looked up with a wave of greeting and an obliging smile. "Cheers, Alan. What brings you here?"

She turned to see a squire atop a sleek brown mount.

"His highness the king summons you forthwith, my lord." He removed his hat. "We depart for Smithfield and tomorrow's tourney."

"I shall be there." Valentine waved his dismissal.

But Alan did not depart. "I have orders to bring you back to the palace, my lord."

Valentine glanced at Denys, rolled his eyes, headed for his mount and galloped away ahead of Alan.

"I know you try to gain my favor, Valentine Starbury," she said to the departed knight. "I shall pursue this. But if it shatters my dreams once more, I shall hold you accountable."

* * *

After court retired for the evening, the queen summoned Denys to her chambers. "Why were you dallying with that low-born soldier during vespers?" Elizabeth's eyes narrowed to hateful slits.

"Valentine Starbury is now Lord Valentine, duke of Norwich," she reminded the queen.

A frown tugged at her lips. "I do not give a whit for his title. Why were with him?"

"How dare you spy on me." Denys twisted the fabric of her skirt in clenched fists.

"Cease your smart mouth and answer me!" Elizabeth took three strides to within slapping distance.

"He is Richard's best friend. He is very kind to me." The words came out before she realized she'd defended Valentine Starbury.

"And you've been whoring with him since The Hog wormed his way out of marrying you," she accused.

"Certainly not!"

"I know you slithered off to the riverbank like a strumpet after that lecher. Your manner is that of the lowest order—a common tart. You disgrace our family and I shall not let you give the Woodvilles a bad name." She scowled.

Give the Woodvilles a bad name? That was akin to saying Attila the Hun was unruly at times.

"Valentine is far more courtly than your wasplike lot. He treats me with the chivalry of the most noble gentleman. He's not even hinted at a tryst." In defending him, she defended her own honor.

Either Elizabeth had something against Valentine, or he was her latest cohort and this was all an act to cover it up.

She began to wonder if the ambitious Valentine Starbury wove some pernicious plot in exchange for a Woodville favor or two. After all, the king bestowed only the highest titles upon Woodvilles. Giving the dukedom of Norwich to a non-Woodville carried a vestige of suspicion.

The queen dismissed her with a casual swat of her hand and a characteristic last word: "I have an arrangement in mind for you and it does not include someone of his ilk."

Denys swatted her own hand back at the queen but only after she turned to quit the chamber.

* * *

That eve as the queen's maids undressed her, she noticed something amiss: a trunk sat askew atop the others, its lock broken. She ordered a maid to fetch it down, flung it open and sifted through the contents. All appeared in order, but she checked the old ledger just to be sure. She'd listed every letter in that trunk and from whom it came, but didn't find Margaret Holland's letter. She checked again and for certes, it was gone. She thumbed through the other letters again. None were missing. Just this one.

In her inquisition the queen railed at her bevy of maids, attendants, ushers, pages, barbers, and higher ranking staff: King Edward's gentlemen of the chamber, Lord Chamberlain and Lord Treasurer. She interrogated each on their whereabouts of the last fortnight and what they knew about the missing letter. Kat the cook looked as innocent and perplexed as any of them. The queen discharged the unfortunates who faltered. Elizabeth knew she'd dismissed these servants unjustly, because she had a good idea who really stole that letter.

* * *

With court at the tourney in Smithfield and Richard up north, Denys set out on her way to meet the countess of Somerset, or if she was no longer alive, her descendants. But first she stopped to call on the duke of Clarence at Pluckley House.

After an apology for interrupting his banquet, she asked him, "George, do you know of Margaret Holland, countess of Somerset?"

"Stay, my dear lady, stay!" He shoved a brimming wine goblet into her hand and led her to the end of his high table, away from the laughing, milling guests and lively music from the gallery above. "A young Genoese expeditioner by the name of Colombo is about to arrive from Bristol. He has seen the far reaches of Iceland and the desert shores of Africa. Whilst he be brags of his travels, I will see if he handles tankards of malmsey the way he can navigate his vessel." He winked. "I hear Genoese are weaned on wine. 'Twill be interesting indeed."

"Oh, George, I'd love to stay and watch you drink him under the dais, but I hasten to embark on a quest of my own, just like this ... what was his name?" she shouted over the noise.

George led her to a seat. "Cristoforo Colombo, quite a mouthful, is it not? Now what about Holland?"

She stayed on her feet, too excited to sit.

"Margaret Holland, countess of Somerset. Do you know aught about her?" She repeated her request.

George swirled his wine in the goblet. "If I remember rightly, Margaret died nigh on ten years ago and her title reverted to the crown. King Henry then bestowed it upon Edmund Mortimer's sister Cecily, descendants of Edward the Third's son Lionel. But they are of no blood relation."

Crestfallen, she lowered her head, shoulders slumped. "Oh, she's dead?" But she lifted her head and held it high. "I will find her descendants, then. Naught is going to stop me, whether it be disappointment, inclement weather or slamming into stone walls at every turn." She kissed him on the cheek. "Thank you, George. You are a well of knowledge."

"All the more reason to rue a wasted talent." He grinned. "I trust you'll find your family. And if I know you, you won't give up till you do. And how goes life with you? Has Sir Starbury yielded to your charms, or shall I say, how hard has he fallen? I see how he looks at you. 'Tis not the lusty eye of a lecher, dear one, 'tis the gaze of stars sweeping over the heavens. His eyes are laden with stars and you're his heaven!"

George always chose such eloquent passages—so mystical, yet portraying such a distinct picture. He was a master poet in the guise of jester. Not even Uncle Ned, for all his striking good looks and battlefield brilliance, could match George's gift of golden-tongue.

"Wait, lass, more comes back to me now…" He tapped the side of his head, eyes closed. "Margaret Holland's son Ian—oh, where does he live—" His eyes flew open and lit up. "Ah, Witherham! A village near Leicester. You should be able to find him there. You can travel one end to the other in the blink of an eye. He's a blacksmith, I believe, or a silversmith…some sort of smith."

"Thank you so much, I shall go there!" She was thankful George's memory served him best when in his cups.

She let him return to his banquet. It was to honor his wife's birthday, but she saw no sign of Isabel in the great hall. No surprise there; George hosted many a merry revel after forgetting to invite the guest of honor.

Mayhap her own birth records did not exist, but the countess of Somerset's certainly did.

As she departed, three well-dressed hooded men followed, far enough behind her to keep suspicion at bay.

* * *

George had been correct: Witherham was so small a hamlet, they passed through thrice without stopping. As usual, her retinue of maid and grooms caught the villagers' attention—they rushed from their wattle-and-daub cottages to stare rapt at the young woman on the graceful palfrey draped in royal colors. Apparently no one of note ever passed through, except prisoners being dragged to their execution.

Two narrow lanes lined with small cottages, an ancient stone church and graveyard made up the village of Witherham. Nestled in a valley below lush hills dotted with bushes and sheep, green strips of farmland surrounded it. Clouds dipped low to meet the hilltops over a feathery horizon.

Ian Holland welcomed her to his cottage, his hands covered with candle wax. His eyes danced in amusement when he smiled.

When Denys explained who she was, he bowed and swept his hat off, bowed to her maid, bowed to her grooms, bowed to the mounts. He told her he was a wool merchant. He was also the village candlemaker, blacksmith—George had been correct in that—and chapeler, maker of caps. Caps lay everywhere, of every size, shape and color, caps with rolled brims in the latest fashion, caps of cloth and leather and the roughest burlap.

"I am here because I believe you and I may be kin," she stated.

His listened, dipping wicks in melted wax as he did. "My mother was countess of Somerset," he verified. "But I spent my childhood at Kenilworth Castle under the duke of Bedfordshire's ward."

"Have you brothers and sisters? Aunts, uncles, or cousins on your mother's side?" Her voice quavered as she tried to calm herself with even breaths.

But he shattered her hopes once more when he told her no.

She showed him the woman's portrait in the rosary. He shook his head, showing no sign of recognition.

As nightfall approached, Ian promised her, "First thing on the morrow we shall appeal to the Lord Mayor of Leicester and check the churches' birth and death records. I shall help ye at my best, young maiden." He stood and began to stuff a small box with caps. "These are for the duke of Gloucester, the duke of Clarence, and whoever else is lucky enough to pinch what he can. I shall be much obliged to grace every head at court."

"'Tis grand of you, Master Ian." She nodded her thanks. "Do you know of any inns for myself and my party?"

"The nearest inn is a mile out of Leicester, much more adequate for your ladyship. Alas we have none hereabouts fit for a royal retinue." He shook his head.

"We are not royal, Master Holland. I come as your peer," she corrected him.

After a supper of meat pies and ale, they all rode to Leicester, Ian leading the way on a wiry old palfrey. Intending to rise at dawn to see the priest, whom she hoped would be more help than the abbott in Malmesbury, she climbed a narrow stairway to her sparse third-floor room of the White Boar Inn and sank into the well-worn bed. The low ceiling beams nearly touched her head, and the floor was uneven, but the leaded glass windows let a sparkling array of colored moonbeams spill into the room.

She dreamed of a faceless family she couldn't see nor hear, but whom she knew and loved.

The hooded followers took a room at the Rose and Crown up the road. But they did not tarry. In the dead of night, they stole out the back door and headed for the White Boar.

* * *

In her sleep, Denys smelled smoke, but burrowed deeper into the goosedown pillow. Moments later she almost choked. She opened her eyes and let out a blood-curdling scream. Orange tongues of flame reached for her, leaping out of the darkness. She jumped out of bed and groped for something to cover her naked body, snatching up the coverlet as thick smoke stung her eyes. Tears blurred her vision. She backed up against the far wall, screaming for help. Ian broke down her door and rushed up to her.

The fire spread the entire length of the wall and reached the bed. With a *swoosh* the bed caught fire. She gagged for breath as Ian wrapped her in the coverlet and pushed her towards the window. "Jump, lass, jump!" She looked down at the ground, three floors below. Before she could register another thought, she felt a firm shove between her shoulders. As she plunged to the ground, she screamed as if her lungs would burst.

Her last memory was the metallic taste of blood.

* * *

When she woke, her body throbbed with pain, her right side felt badly bruised and swollen. A serving wench propped her up and forced a goblet twixt her lips as a physician approached her bed. "How do you fare, lass?"

"Where am I?" She glanced around. She was no longer in the White Boar.

"We are in the home of the lord mayor of Leicester, Mistress Woodville," she explained. "The White Boar caught fire. It burnt nearly to the ground."

Fragments of memory came back—the flames, the heat, her choking and falling, but not hitting the ground. "Where were the rest of you?"

"On the ground floor, we escaped." Her maid Mary reached over and smoothed her hair. "But the governor of the inn and Master Ian both perished."

"Sweet Jesus." She turned her head away and wept, sick with remorse.

When she regained her full senses, she requested that her servitors fetch the vicar of the church—and the birth and death records, which hadn't perished.

Propped up in bed, she combed through the old documents.

Margaret Holland, countess of Somerset, had no living relative. Her brother died with no issue. No girl babies were born to either of them in 1457 or in the years preceding or following.

Another red herring, this one ending in tragedy.

Now she wondered—did Valentine Starbury deliberately mislead her?

Her bruises not yet healed, she hired a litter to carry her back to court. They stopped several times each day to rest and took only well-traveled roads.

* * *

A fortnight later, the full moon saw Queen Elizabeth in her foulest of moods. With her infant son at the breast of a wet nurse, she had time for her usual persecution of servers and high born.

After her summons to the royal chambers, Denys stood in the doorway waiting for the queen. Elizabeth swept down the corridor, her crimson veil billowing out behind her, looking as if she rose from the flames of hell. The servitors scurried away. Alone, she and Denys faced each other.

"I shall come back later, Aunt Bess." Denys turned to leave.

"Stay right here!" the queen thundered. So Denys obeyed. It was better to be abased here then before the entire court.

"Thief!" she shrieked, her face blotched with rage, her eyes spitting sparks of fury. "You broke into my trunk and went through my letters!"

"I know not of what you speak!" Denys shot back, this accusation flooring her. She stumbled backward. "I never broke into anything."

"You broke into my private trunks, searched through my letters, damaging them," she shrieked. "Who but you, trying to find your parents. Well, they are dead, and did not want you anyway. Now get ye gone, before I cut off your arms and beat you with the bloody ends."

Denys drew herself up to her full height and the queen took a step back.

"Whatever knave broke into your trunks, it was not I. I was not even here," she stated, her voice even.

"You are a liar," Elizabeth countered in a faltering voice.

Denys turned her back on the queen and quit the royal chambers.

Her suspicions repeated over and over in her mind. Only one person would break into that trunk.

If he actually had.

She strongly suspected Valentine Starbury setting the trap she fell into, nearly losing her life in the process. Who was Elizabeth trying to fool?

Valentine and the queen were in this together. The thought struck a bolt of fear through her, as if hit by lightning.

* * *

She finally regained her strength. Nowt remained but the emotional scars, so she prayed several times daily for the souls lost in the fire.

Then she heard unsettling news. Richard bestowed the governorship of Yorkshire upon Valentine Starbury. He departed court and traveled to take up residence in Yorkshire.

Relief came with a feeling she couldn't define.

That eve, Denys committed her thoughts to paper for the first time since the fire. Sitting at her writing table, she poured her heart out into a new journal. "*Although burdened by despair of not knowing my family, I have faith I will find them.*"

Then, deciding on lighter fare, she wrote a heartfelt letter to Richard, for he counted on her for court news.

She kept her letter light; she refrained from outpouring her loneliness over missing their long talks, their intense chess games, their hard rides over the moors. She omitted the tragedy and her narrow escape. Her pen raced across the parchment as she reported anecdotes about court, especially the most recent turn of events. Last eve an inebriated George met a comely redheaded tart at a riverfront tavern and sweet-talked her back to Pluckley House, spiriting her past his wife's chambers to his own. When he snuggled up for a final frolic, he glimpsed a curly red wig coiled twixt their bodies. By the rood, his mistress of the night—another man! George brayed louder than shattering glass as the varlet leapt through the window to his escape.

Someone knocked at her chamber door. Expecting the messenger she'd summoned to deliver the letter to Richard, she gave it to her maid who answered a knock at the door.

Valentine stood in the doorway, hair windblown, eyes searching the chamber. His gaze met hers, imploring her to give him one last moment. She inhaled his scent of leather and fresh air.

The maid unknowingly handed the letter to Valentine and he took it, looking down on it, then back over at her.

She nudged the maid aside and snatched the letter from his hand. "Do not touch this letter."

Here he stood, the man who'd plotted with Elizabeth, caused the death of several innocent people, and nearly caused hers. How can she have been so attracted to that regal bearing, those lips that made hers tingle with delight?

He was nowt more than a two-faced deceiver, treasonous to his final act.

"What is this you dispatch to Richard?" He gestured at the letter.

"None of your business. Now get ye gone. I shall never trust you again." She swung the door shut. He caught it and pushed it wide open.

"We may never see each other again, so you will listen to me. I was sick with worry for you. Every night I spent hours in chapel praying for your recovery," he pleaded his case. She turned away, unable to look at him, yet something forced her to imbrue his image into her memory, the blond locks, the expressive eyes...

You gave me false leads. And I believe it was deliberate and goaded by the queen. I almost died and a few good folk did die. I shall never believe another word you say." She went to the window and stood looking out, her back to him.

He approached her and placed his hands on her shoulders. "Nay, I was not false. Please hear me out."

She shook him off her. "Guards! Remove this knave from my chambers."

Her summons sent a pair of guards charging into the room. They seized Valentine and dragged him away, his protests and pleadings echoing through the corridor.

A shadowy figure sped past Denys's doorway, flitted down the corridor and headed for the queen's chambers.

* * *

The following eve Denys supped in the great hall for the first time since the fire. The music was just as bright, the courtiers as ravenous for fare. King Edward's fool stood beside him, displaying his usual knack for sending the king into fits of laughter.

Queen Elizabeth rose from her seat at the high table. A hush descended over the great hall. "His highness the king and I bid you good evening." Her commanding voice carried through to the far reaches of the hall. King Edward, sitting at her side, smiled warmly, turning an apple by its stem.

"I announce the upcoming nuptials of an outstanding knight," the queen went on, looking out over the hushed crowd.

Denys sat in confused silence; no one had mentioned a word about a knight's wedding.

"By order of Queen Elizabeth...Valentine Starbury, duke of Norwich, is to be married in a fortnight," she announced.

That surprised Denys. She pitied the poor lass who would suffer his hypocrisy, his incorrigible ambition, his—

"To my niece, Denys!" the queen proclaimed, looking right through her.

"No!" She shook her head at all the polite smiles and nods. Then the great hall burst into applause.

Elizabeth raised her tankard. Everyone stood, the minstrels, the courtiers, the king himself rose to his feet, smiling through the look of apology in his eyes.

Denys maintained her dignity and somehow survived the toastings, the platitudes, the insipid murmurs of approbation.

Her groom-to-be was unaware of any of this, on his merry way to Yorkshire!

* * *

Denys entered the queen's chambers without an appointment. She intended to declare her refusal to marry Sir Starbury and leave court forever. Still mired in a confused fog, she managed to find the words. "I will not obey your order to marry," she stated.

"Either you marry him here or I shall have you wed in the Tower. I am wedding you to him as a reward—to him, that is. As of now your chambers will be guarded round the clock." Elizabeth snapped her fingers and two men-at-arms emerged from the shadows, clasped Denys's arms and steered her out of the queen's chambers.

As her feet scattered rushes in her haste to keep up, Denys shook at the thought that her body was to be given to Valentine Starbury in reward for the evils he did at the queen's bidding.

Chapter Five

The queen's guards surrounded Denys twenty-four hours a day. They flanked her chamber doors, held vigil at the foot of her bed, observed her every bite at mealtimes, oversaw her privy visits, at her embroidery, at her music, and followed her back to bed. How could marriage to Valentine Starbury be any worse?

Escape was impossible. She had no ally; she wasn't even allowed to write letters.

She sat in her chambers plucking her lute strings, deep in thought. She pondered the revulsion that shuddered through her when her aunt commanded she wed Richard; she tried to rekindle that same contempt now, at the thought of marrying Valentine. But it was like trying to hate flowers and romance; she couldn't force herself to despise him. She couldn't stop her heart fluttering as she pictured him in her mind's eye. She couldn't control the heat spreading through her body at the memory of his first kiss.

She even began to believe he'd told the truth when he pled his innocence. Could he commit such unspeakable acts as to plot her death with Elizabeth?

Nay, she refused to believe him party to such villainy.

She took the white rose from her bedside table, scooped up the fallen petals and started to toss it all into the fire. But she couldn't. She held it to her cheek, breathed in its lingering scent, and returned it to the drawer.

Do you really want to escape? she asked herself.

Her answer came faster than she expected.

* * *

As Denys slept she felt a gentle brush upon her cheek. She smiled dreamily, knowing it was real; that familiar touch, strong fingers roughly calloused, yet so tender. With a yawn, she opened her eyes to a kind face smiling down at her, eyes as blue as the morning sky. "Uncle Ned!"

"'Aye, 'tis I, dear one." The king perched on the edge of her bed. "Good morn. Afore setting sail for France, I had to bid you Godspeed. My little Denys will be a married lady soon."

She sat up and wrapt her fingers round his. "Protect me always."

"I wish I could attend your wedding, my dear." His voice lowered, thick with regret.

"Uncle Ned, I will miss you so much. I knew this would happen someday, but now that 'tis upon me, I—" She faltered. "I don't need to explain. You know how I feel."

He nodded. "I know, dear. Don't think a man doesn't feel just that way when facing marriage. I would live my days in joyful bachelorhood, but forces stronger than we dictate our fate and we must obey."

"I had to become a woman sometime." They shared a laugh, for they knew since she returned to court, prate often centered on the queen's spinster niece.

"Valentine will make a fit husband, I promise," he assured her with a wink.

"He's not proposed to me himself. Mayhap he's as happy in bachelorhood as—" Her voice lowered. "—as you were, sire."

"I feel he'd have proposed had he the chance. Richard summoned him to Yorkshire so hastily, he barely had time to don his boots. But from what I see, though he never shared this with me, I know he wishes to win your heart. Many a marriage takes place without heart, sadly, far too many…" He sighed, yet without losing his dimpled smile.

She knew he'd referred to his own marriage. "I always wanted someone to love me, Uncle Ned. Oh, I know you love me. But I mean—that way." She turned away, her cheeks hot.

"In the way of romance." He could always put into words what she couldn't. "Roses and moonlight. Kisses and nestling. Two souls joined as one."

Oh, how he knew!

"You shall have your wish. And I shall see you again on my next northern progress."

"Oh, please do." She wound her arms round those shoulders that looked massive even under his plain linen shirt.

He planted a kiss atop her head and cupped her face in his warm hands, wiping tears away with his thumbs. "Don't cry, Denys. I'm always here for you, but you'll soon have a husband to discover earthly delights with, and trust me, there are many."

She knew Uncle Ned to be well acquainted with earthly delights.

He stood and slipped on a heavy robe in royal purple. Uncle Ned became King Edward once more.

* * *

Valentine had been notified of their upcoming wedding and, though there'd been no time for a reply, Denys was sure he was the most mightily pleased man in the kingdom.

On the eve of her departure for Yorkshire, she answered a knock at her chamber door. The queen's dressmaker unfolded a satin wedding gown, its neck revealingly low, sleeves slashed and flowing, the bodice trimmed with rubies. Trying it on with the assistance of her ladies-in-waiting, she marveled at the high-waisted skirts that began under her breasts and the smoothness of the embroidered satin underskirt. It was close fitted to flaunt her curves, to enhance the lines of her neck and shoulders—exquisitely crafted, a work of art.

Only it wasn't white. It was the brightest crimson, the color of fresh blood gushing from a new wound.

"Why a red wedding dress?" she asked Elizabeth afore her departure. "For you to wear white would be farce, a mockery of the church and a blot to this family. The entire court knows of your lewd behavior with this knave," came her scathing reply.

Denys gathered the dress, bunched it up and flung it into her hearth. Orange flames blazed to engulf it. "Unlike you, I won't be delivered of a child in six months' time!"

Elizabeth's hand drew back and struck Denys's cheek. But the sting hurt no longer. Soon she would be free of Woodville bonds forever. She counted the minutes until that final passage through the palace gates, to her future.

"You have only your own children to abuse from this day on, Aunt Bess, for I am no longer your charge. And as such, I no longer obey your commands." She turned her back on Elizabeth Woodville for the last time.

* * *

Denys closed her last trunk lid. As grooms removed it from the chamber, she took one final glance round the stark room and left Elizabeth, her smoldering wedding dress and her bitter memories behind.

* * *

Middleham Castle loomed in the distance as Denys and her retinue crossed the stone bridge over the River Ure. She had never seen it before, but if shown a hundred castles, she would know this was Richard's favorite. The Norman keep stood at the center and towered above the outer walls. She crossed the drawbridge and entered the busy outer court. A groom took her mount and a page led her inside.

Walking through the private quarters, she recognized items King Edward gave to Richard: a velvet chair, paintings of Edward III and his sons, elegant sets of golden candlesticks atop heavy carved tables.

They reached a private bedchamber and she began to remove her gloves.

"Tell the duke of Gloucester that Denys Woodville has arrived and wishes audience," she ordered the page as she surveyed the chamber—comfortable, but lacking style. It was Anne who oversaw adornment of the private chambers.

Her maid fitted her with a peach satin gown trimmed with damask, pulled her hair back and crowned her with a tall steeple headdress, looping the muslin train. It caused her great discomfort. She swept it off and replaced it with a velvet circlet.

The page returned. "The duke of Gloucester awaits you in the rose garden, Mistress Woodville."

Joy put a skip in her step for the first time in weeks. Oh, to see her dearest friend again! She followed the page down the exterior staircase and out into the gardens. Richard sat on a stone bench twirling his hat twixt his fingers.

"Richard!" She broke into a run. He smiled, placing his hat on the bench. She rushed up and embraced him.

"I am pleased to see you, Denys, and wish you most heartfelt happiness in your upcoming marriage."

She sat beside him and smoothed her skirts. "Let us dispense with falsities, Richard. Bess trothplighted me to him in punishment."

"Marriage to Valentine punishment? The storied character plucked from King Arthur's table round?" Richard gave her that sly half-smile she missed so much.

97

"He is." She nodded.

"He's the one you fancied, Denys." Richard crossed one leg over the other and grasped his ankle.

"He was." She nodded again.

"You described him right down to the toenails." Richard glanced down at his well-groomed nails.

"You are correct." She nodded once more.

"I thought you'd arrive today in wedding raiment counting the minutes till he says 'I do.' What can possibly cause perturbation?" Richard's eyes bored into her.

"We don't love each other," she stated.

He looked surprised that could be required for marriage. Well, for her it was. "Valentine is smitten with you, how can you not love someone so ardent and taken with you?"

"Ardent, taken, smitten? That's not love, Richard. Nay, that is not my lot. I fear that the love of a husband and my true family are lost to me forever. Which reminds me—" She groped under her bodice. Richard looked away as she slipped the rosary out and held the tiny picture up to him.

"Do you know this woman?" She held it out to him.

He studied the picture and shook his head. "I have no clew."

"I found it at Foxley Manor." She slid it back down her bodice.

"When were you there?" he asked.

"After you left court. It was deserted, empty of all chattels except this, above a doorway. If Foxley is connected to my family and yet Bess now owns it, she overlooked this." She patted the item concealed under her bodice.

He glanced at her hiding place and looked away. "Have you asked round?"

"I've asked all worth asking. But none know her." She released a heavy sigh. "To come this close…"

"Well, now, you have marriage to look forward to, a new life. I'm sure you'll be as happy as Anne and I. We both enjoy visiting our tenants and subjects, we have endowed for two universities, we instituted the Middleham Fair, life is much more smooth than it ever was at court. Starting a new life is the best way to purge the old."

"I am pleased for you indeed." She gave him a heartfelt smile. "I commend you on your wise choice of mate."

Richard polished his sapphire ring on his doublet. "I am blest. As you will be, too, when you and Valentine become man and wife. He's noble and greatly regarded in these parts. I do not merely speak of the subjects' fealty to their lord. He has turned more than one noble female head since his arrival, and I daresay they will continue to turn should you not claim him."

"So he is a varlet here, as he was at court?"

"Nay, impossible." He shook his head. "I keep him too busy for dalliances. Besides, since he learnt of your trothplight, he has decorated and prepared his manse for his bride. He has near gutted Lilleshal and re-built her from the floor up!"

"Has he now?" Her heart softened at the thought of Valentine going to such lengths for her arrival. "It sounds to me like sheer gaudery." Try as she might, she couldn't force favor into her tone—or her heart.

"You certainly don't know Valentine as I do." Richard's gaze intensified. "Do you not trust my judgment?"

"Of course I do. You may know Valentine, but did you ever marry him?" She knew he enjoyed such rhetorical questions; they gave him a chance to return a jest.

"Just think of us as one big family once more. Minus the Woodvilles. What is wrong with that?" He splayed his fingers.

A smile escaped her glumness.

"There will be shared evenings, there will be children…"

She rolled her eyes. "Oh, now you really get ahead of yourself!"

"Not really." His lips spread in a warm smile. "Not as much as you think."

"Richard, do you mean—"

"Aye." He squared his shoulders. "I am going to be a father."

"With—with Anne?" she stammered, the idea incomprehensible to her. Anne was so young.

His eyes fired a tumult-filled glare. "Well, who else?"

"But it seems so sudden, that is all," came her quick rejoinder.

"Life is sudden, my dear. And every so often, we must catch it up so it does not pass us by. Your husband-to-be is to arrive shortly and I expect you wish to prepare. I bid you good day for now and will see you this eve in the great hall." He stood and gave a little bow.

She remained in the garden till the sun vanished over the distant dales. She needed to be alone, to think, to do just what Richard had said; to catch up with the changing events that passed her by with dizzying speed. But she would not let chance happenings master her destiny. Events had no beating heart, no blood, no life, no mind. And damned if such would master her fate.

In the end, she would triumph. This was merely the road to that end. Twould be fraught with barriers, rugged paths, and streams swollen with muck.

Aye, anyone could guess she conjured her storied knight from legend. But part of that fancy was to fall in love with him, and it wasn't so. She would always be second in his life, behind his council, his duties, his aspirations for greatness.

* * *

"'Tis bad luck to see the groom before the wedding, so I shan't." She sat up in bed and pulled the coverlet up to her neck. Weak sunlight cast wan shadows throughout the chamber. A gentle rain streaked the windows, the weather outside as gloomy as she felt inside.

"But the wedding is ten days off," Mary, her maid, insisted.

"No difference, I shall see more of him than I ever want to once we are wed. I see no reason to face him now." She dismissed Mary and got out of bed for the first time since she arrived. Her limbs ached, her eyelids heavy from disturbed sleep. How she wished she could simply sleep the next decade away and awaken to find her loving family. As for now, she needed go through the motions.

* * *

"'Tis bad luck for the bride to see the groom before the wedding!" was all she would say to anyone who asked why she didn't join the duke and duchess of Gloucester in the great hall or watch the mummers or play chess, cards, or dice.

By day, as Valentine tended to business as governor of Yorkshire or attended council meetings, she escaped the castle and rode Chera through the lush countryside. But by nightfall she spent her time reading, plucking her lute…

…and thinking about this stage of her life ending and the next about to begin.

* * *

She answered a rap at the door, expecting Anne's tailor Henry Ive.

Valentine stood there, his presence so overpowering, her breathing halted.

She didn't remember him so tall, dressed as a nobleman in a velvet doublet of mulberry, a House of York color. The satin sleeves flowed in folds, nearly reaching the floor. Rings of colored gemstones sparkled on his fingers. A feather peeked from the rolled brim of his velvet cap, studded with jewels. Before drinking in another inch of him, she moved to shut the door. "I've nowt to say."

Her efforts were hopeless; she was no match for his strength. He pushed the door open, entered the chamber and closed the door, shutting out the world.

He removed his cap. "I care not for daft superstitions. I must explain what I could not when those brutes dragged me off."

"I doubt I'll believe you," she spoke her true feelings.

"Listen to me, and you will know, 'tis the truth." His eyes pierced her like daggers. She would not let her heart become airy as a cloud again. But here he stood, so close, so commanding, allowing no means of escape.

"Very well. You have three minutes."

He straightened his tabard. "I entered Elizabeth's chambers when court was away. A scullery maid caught me and, oh, never mind what happened hence. Suffice to say it was harrowing."

"More harrowing than nearly burning to death and plunging from a third-storey window?" Her voice stayed calm, yet her heart thumped like Chera's hooves in full gallop.

"Nay, my darling, I shall never forget how I worried over you. But I solved Elizabeth's mysterious filing code and found a letter. Written by the countess of Somerset the Monday after Martinmas, 1457, it mentioned 'the babe' several times. Martinmas is in November. I told you of the countess that day we were interrupted."

"It reeks of conspiracy with Bess. Unless you can convince me otherwise." She crossed her arms over her chest.

"Because I want you to know who you are. And now that I am to be your husband, I can help all the more." His pleading eyes nearly melted her. Instinct told her he spoke the truth. "I believe in your quest, Denys."

"I shall find my true parentage on my own, without your help. If I must marry you, so be it. More marriages are arranged than not. But that is where my duty to you ends. As for now, I am in no one's charge and wish to see neither back nor front of you until our wedding. Good morrow." She forced herself to look away from those eyes that begged for something she neither understood nor could give.

"Is there nowt else you care to say so near the day we join forever?" He took a step closer.

She shook her head. "My marriage to you is a punishment."

"Are you the only person you can think about? Do all you see exist for your own convenience?" he goaded. "They must. I know no one who particularly enjoys your company."

"Then why are you here?" she asked.

"To tell you the information I gave you was not contrived to send you to your death. To let you know I helped in your quest and truly regret it did not lead to your family. To tell you that I only desire your happiness and wish to share it as your husband. Although my first efforts led to tragedy, I have all the more reason to earn your trust. And to ask, if I may be so bold, that you enter our marriage in hope that we find a happy life full of meaning." He paused and smiled. "Hell's bells, Denys, as thrilled as I am to marry you, I am just as astounded as you. Marriage was the last thing on my mind." He touched her lips in a fleeting kiss.

She moved closer and with one sweeping motion, he whisked her into his arms and lowered his lips to hers in a warm kiss that made her body grow stiff and weak at the same time.

His mouth consumed hers in demanding but patient passion. Her feeble attempt to push him away faded into the darkness that engulfed them as the last of the glowing rushes drowned in their holders. As her arms started to wind their way round his neck, he eased her away and studied her in the faint light reaching through the window.

"That meant more to me than title, new lands, and the life I am given here in Yorkshire. I shall see you next at the altar on our wedding day." He placed his cap back on his head, touched its brim, turned and vanished into the darkness.

"Goodbye, Valentine." Her voice trembled, but retained the sternness she meant to convey. Safe behind closed doors, out of his sight, she let a smile curl her lips.

Her heart told her he was sincere. Just as her heart told her that she had a family awaiting her.

* * *

Early next morn, a timid tap on the door assured her it wasn't the beaming bridegroom on the other side.

It was Anne Neville, her slight figure dwarfed by the ornate silver tray she held, heaping with savories, a goblet and a white linen serviette.

"Good morrow, Denys. The servitors believe you ill, so I bear sweetmeats to cheer you." She entered the chamber and placed the tray on the bed, turned and grasped Denys's hands.

"Thank you so much, Anne. How very thoughtful." She picked up a sweetmeat and sank her teeth into it, savoring the confection.

"I am pleased by your trothplight to Valentine. He is a knight exemplar, a most trusted advisor of Richard's and mine. The north country is far better off with him here." She took a confection for herself but only nibbled on it.

Denys wiped her hands on the serviette and focused upon Anne's middle, flat as the day they'd first met. But she saw in Anne's eyes a mirror into her own future.

"Are ye with child, Anne?"

"Aye, I suspect I am three months along already." She beamed. "Richard longs for a son so badly."

She gave Anne a nod and replied in a warm tone, "I offer you my very best."

Anne lifted Denys's chin with her forefinger, forcing her to look into those young brown eyes, round with concern. "Are you sure you feel right? I can summon the physician. Is it a digestive problem? Ague? Surfeit?" Her voice was so caring, Denys began to wish she had a sister like Anne. Dear God, mayhap she did!

"I am fine, Anne." Her voice steadied and she found herself desperate to share her feelings. "I once believed Valentine Starbury was everything I ever wished, but he is so ambitious, so brash, so sure he can conquer any enemy single-handed. Now I must marry him. Oh, he provokes such diverse humors in me! I long for him one minute and take fright the next. None of these feelings are love. So Bess has the last laugh. That rankles most of all."

Anne sat on the bed, pale as the day outside, her skin glowing with that alabaster transparence of childhood. "Hardly. There are far worse punishments to inflict upon you. She could have dredged up some wizened old letch with a paunch. I think she does you a great favor. He is devoted to the kingdom and our subjects. He will make just as devout a husband. As for his ambitions, his father having perished in battle makes him all the more determined to carry on his work."

"But he won't stop till he achieves the highest office in the kingdom. Devout? To me it seems he thirsts for power." She hated to harbor these doubts, but could not help it. "It is so hard to trust him."

Anne shook her head. "Richard trusts him with his life. Surely you don't doubt Richard's judgment of character."

Denys honestly couldn't admit Richard's choice of wife was bad judgment, but men didn't judge each other the same way. "But I fear him, Anne. I also fear *for* him. He thrives on guile and strategems. He will surely get himself killed. 'Tis as if he seeks it."

"Ah, he is a man. Give him a chance." Anne's voice hovered on the edge of pleading. "He thinks the world of you." She went on, "He has spared nothing preparing Lilleshal, with the most exquisite marble and tapestries and chattels—"

"He likes his luxuries." Denys shrugged.

"Oh, but that is not all," Anne continued. "'Tis not only the house. 'Tis how he speaks of you in the house, and his eyes light up. 'Tis you he speaks of incessantly. Even before trothplight he spoke no end of you."

Denys's mind unclouded for the first time since arriving, sharpened with curiosity. "What of me does he speak?"

Anne laughed lay her hand over her middle. "Oh, he is smitten as any man I ever saw. He speaks so highly of your determination to find your parents, for one."

"So he told you I was taken in by ... her." The mention of the Woodville name repulsed her like a leech on her skin.

"Nay, Richard told me first, but only because he considers you family. Do you object?" Anne asked her. "I'll never tell a soul."

"Nay, what harm in your knowing? Of course, I shall try to see the good in him, since he will be my ... my husband." Her voice broke as she nearly choked on the word. "But even you must have discerned that zeal in him, the way he talks of Richard bestowing high positions upon him, his lofty path already mapped out—it scares me so to hear him talk that way. The next step is treason—read your history, Anne. He sets no precedent."

"Valentine is deep in his doings here. Neither he nor Richard desire a return to court, and King Edward has many years to rule before he yields the throne to his son."

"For that I am grateful, because court is the last place I ever want to return. Oh, to be out of there, 'tis like release from the Tower dungeons. I cannot tell you how it feels to be free, just for this pitifully short time."

"Then why are you sequestered in these dark chambers, when you should be out there?" Anne waved towards the window at a slice of sunlight peeking from behind a bluish-white cloud. "The sun may be hiding, but it is warm, and the grass dewy. This morn I saw Valentine run through the rose garden barefoot like a colt. He certainly makes the best of what life gives." Anne stood and her gown's coppery sheen echoed the joy in her eyes. "Please eat and join me for a ride over the moors."

Anne smiled so genuinely it lifted Denys's heart. "Very well." The sweet-meats' fresh baked aroma drew growls of hunger from her empty belly. "I shall be down shortly."

"Chera will be bridled and saddled by then. Tra-la!" She quit the chamber in a flutter of satins and rosewater.

Denys enjoyed a luxurious stretch, then took bites from all five confections, basking in the solitude that had formerly imprisoned her.

* * *

She turned Anne's dressmaker away. She did not want a new wedding dress. She regretted she had nothing dowdy and somber, for she did not feel joy a bride should.

The eve afore the wedding, Anne came to her chambers with a luscious white satin gown lined with pearls, the skirts inlaid with colored gemstones in diamond patterns, the sleeves embroidered with gold roses. The veil, just as splendid, frothed with yards of lace and a circlet of heart-shaped pearls.

"Anne, this gown is exquisite! Wherever did you get it?"

"It was my mother's wedding gown. Both she and my sister were married in it. Since my own wedding—as you know, was so rushed, I had not time to fetch it from home. I want you to wear it. As Valentine and Richard are like brothers, you will be my sister."

Tears welled up in Denys's eyes as Anne spread gown and veil on the bed. "Thank you so much, Anne. I know not what to say."

"Say nowt." She smoothed the material down. "Just give Valentine a chance. Let our children grow old together."

Denys wrapped her arms round Anne and held her close. She felt the slight swell of Anne's middle twixt them and at that moment knew what carrying a child would feel like.

* * *

Through the mist of her veil, she saw the man who within minutes would be her husband, a vision of grandeur in his crimson doublet. She glided down the aisle as if an invisible force drew her to him. The chapel glowed from candles lining the altar. The sun streamed through the stained glass, throwing patterns of soft pinks and greens on the stone slabs beneath her feet.

She joined him at the altar and he spoke his vows as if in prayer, his heartfelt gaze riveted to hers, his voice somber and deep with meaning. She forced herself to avert his gaze, so piercing, so earnest, it burned through to her soul. Although she still harbored grave doubts about this man, she regarded the way he spoke to her with his impassioned eyes. He lifted her veil and she felt the quiver of his lips as he kissed her. When their eyes met for the first time as man and wife, she saw him struggle to hold back a grin.

"So kind of you to come to my wedding," he murmured out of the side of his mouth.

* * *

The marshall ushered the bride and groom into Middleham's great hall to the flourish of trumpets and clarions adorned with Valentine's coat of arms. They sat at Richard and Anne's side on the dais. The hall filled with worthies from surrounding shires, Lord Mayors, Aldermen, judges, bishops, and their respective retinues.

She kept her mind on the lavish wedding feast and the array of jugglers, mimes, fools and minstrels, for she knew her life would not be the same after the great hall was swept clean.

After grace, a procession of servers entered the hall bearing trays of food, and butlers served wines and ales. Then came another course: roasted swans and peacocks in full feather, boar's heads, suckling pigs, cranes, larks, roasted rabbits, venison, all spiced and seasoned with pepper, cloves, mace and other rare spices.

After the celebration, Richard and Anne bade them Godspeed on their journey to Valentine's manor home of Lilleshal, two miles down the road.

"Remember what I said," Anne whispered into her ear.

She nodded, turning to Richard. He embraced her and bade her farewell. "He will take the best care of you. On my orders." The hint of a smile creased his cheek.

How she wished they were young and free again, galloping over the moors astride their mounts, hair blowing free in the wind. How suddenly it all changed.

Nodding to him and Anne, she crossed the drawbridge with her new husband—a charming knight, but ambitious plotter. A wealthy noble, but hardworking statesman. He loved life's pleasures, but also beheld tragedy in his own past. Knights of legend had no fears, no problems, suffered no grief.

Valentine became the third most powerful man in the realm without trying to usurp the throne or spy on his peers. She had to respect him for that.

But where did love fit in?

Chapter Six

The estate of Lilleshal nestled in a valley beside a stream afloat with swans. Farmland and cottages surrounded the manor house. A mesh gravel paths led to its three front entrances. Lush gardens blanketed the outer court.

Denys marveled at its grandeur. It fully reflected Valentine's stately pomp and his love for splendor. Gleaming in red sandstone, a round tower at each corner rose in gallant protection against enemies. Diamond-shaped windowpanes gleamed from the torchlight within. The gatehouse was a fortress in itself; the closed portcullis enhanced the unbroken line of fortification.

A retinue of servers bowed and curtsied in greeting as bride and groom crossed the drawbridge and into the gatehouse. A watchman emerged from the guard chamber, raised the portcullis and let them through. A maid hurried through the inner ward carrying pails slopping over with milk; a stable boy walked a palfrey. Two grooms rushed up to help Denys unhorse. An usher led them and their servers up an external stairway to the first storey. Tapestries and bronze sconces graced the sumptuous corridors. The floors gleamed, strewn with rushes; the stained glass of each arched window housed gods and goddesses of legend.

Exquisite as it was, she suppressed a shiver at this small version of court. Just what she'd longed to escape.

I'll never feel at home here, she thought, with nowt to look forward to, her heart heavy.

"You are now mistress of the manor, Lady Starbury." Valentine held out his arm. "Let me show you to your chambers."

She linked her arm through his and they ascended the stairs. At the end of the corridor, he opened a door to her new chambers. She peeked in. Prettier than anything she ever had in Elizabeth Woodville's charge, it was clear he'd ordered it decorated to a woman's liking: the bed hangings and curtains dripped with lace in pink and lilac. Pink lace adorned the cushions. The sweet scent of violets floated up from the rushes on the floor. Very feminine, but not what she would have chosen.

Her quarters and raiment were never luxurious by royal standards. But now, wed to the closest advisor of the Lord of the North, she vowed to enjoy it.

"I realize we are now husband and wife, Valentine. By the laws that bind me to you, you have a right to my bed, but not my heart."

His eyes threw out blue sparks when he looked at her. She expected him to strut up to her, throw her on the bed and demand married man's rights.

But he neither made a move toward her nor did he reveal any hint of desire.

"Were you hoping to quarrel? Well, I hate to disappoint, but I do not intend to pillage the honor you so valiantly guard. I have never forced myself upon a woman nor will I ever. You are free as you like to search out your parentage, join me on official progress or stay here and grow lilies. 'Tis up to you. So, if all is to your satisfaction, dear wife, I withdraw to my chambers."

He spun on his heel and walked away.

"Valentine!" She called without thinking, more out of surprise than anything else.

He turned to face her, eyes twinkling in the torchlight.

"I ..." just want to bid you good eve. 'Twas a lovely day, was it not?"

"Indeed so. The weather was splendid and the cooks were in top form. Now good eve to you." Kicking his leg up, he swung the door closed with his foot.

She knew not whether to laugh with relief or cry with anger. So many disturbing feelings converged upon her, no one stood out. She still feared his governorship of Yorkshire would feed a dangerous hunger for more power.

But his sudden and blunt exit from her chambers perturbed her. *He'll be back*, she assured herself.

She was now a married lady, with station, esteem, this exquisite estate. But she wished Uncle Ned were here to assure her that the benefits were real.

She began to plot: two visits to the poor a week, two women to sew coats for the poor, increase the yield of vegetables in the garden to help feed them, a troupe of musicians to entertain them. The future looming before her didn't look so dismal after all.

She unpacked her trunk and found her most favored nightwear—a pale blue linen gown, threadbare at the elbows, but the last trace of her Castle Howard years, the only time in her life she felt wanted.

Shedding her wedding raiment, leaving it in the middle of the chamber for a maid to pick up, she slid the nightie over her head and inhaled deeply of its familiar scent.

She climbed into the big empty bed. The featherbed enveloped her, and she found it the most comfortable bed ever. She pulled the cover over her head and tried to leave her past behind, her new life to begin at dawn.

* * *

Valentine's duties as governor took him all over the shire, to council meetings with Richard at Pomfret Castle, to towns and villages to visit tenants, assess their efforts and settle disputes. As a result he left her alone for weeks on end.

Her first priority was helping the poorest villagers. It brought her out, made her feel wanted, and she smiled through tears at the looks on their faces when she and her guide rode into an impoverished hamlet, handing out boons of food and soft linen squares, a prized luxury in itself, but when wrapped around coins, a gift from heaven. The dialect sounded strange, but she could still make out the heartfelt thanks they shouted up to her, their angel on horseback.

She also kept busy overseeing the household, directing the marshal as he aired the hall, freshened the rushes, cleaned and beat the hangings. She aided the steward in ordering and inventory supplies; she sat with the controller and balanced the ledger. She even helped prepare meals, startling the scullery, from the steward down to the cooks' helpers. She enjoyed trying variations on recipes and mixing different types of herbs, substituting mint for garlic or cinnamon for parsley. Her 'lampreys in galytyne,' a roast seafood dish made with ginger powder, raisins and bread, became her specialty. They grew peas, beans, cabbages, apples and pears on the estate, and her expanding kitchen garden added several new spices and herbs.

She hired resident musicians, formed fours, and arranged her favorite tunes for singers of all ranges to harmonize. She had an organ delivered and played it several hours a day. Music eased her aloneness.

She spent hours poring over genealogy messengered from governors of surrounding shires and mayors of Wiltshire towns, not really knowing what she sought. She had no names or places to start with. She began to anticipate Valentine's homecomings.

Restlessly awaiting his return from York one afternoon, she mounted Chera and rode a few miles in that direction. The freezing air filled her lungs with bracing crispness as she burrowed deep into her ermine cloak. The remnants of last eve's snow dusted the earth with a sparkling blanket of blue-white. The cold turned her breath to ice crystals in the slanting sun. Thin streams of smoke curled skyward from village cottages. All was quiet, except for the echo of Chera's beating hooves on the ground. She halted the palfrey and, from atop the hill, swept her eyes over Lilleshal and her manor. The sandstone glowed and the stream twinkled in the sun's weakening rays. Lights flickered in the windows as surrounding shadows grew long, casting a gleam on the earth. As she tugged Chera's reins and galloped back, a rush of warmth welled within her. She could not wait to nestle before a fire in the winter parlour, her fingers wound round a chalice of mead. The thought of sharing the eve with Valentine gave her a rush of uneasy foretaste.

She supped with the staff in the great hall, glancing out the window every few minutes for some sign of him. When at last he arrived after midnight, she was abed, but she leapt up and ran to greet him. A cold draught scented with outdoor freshness rushed at her when he passed by. She treated herself to a gaze at the muscles under his doublet.

"Valentine! Welcome home!" Her voice echoed down the corridor.

He turned, a question in his eyes, as if surprised to find that she lived here; they'd seen so little of each other since the wedding. At first it was a relief; she'd planned on self-sufficiency as mistress of his manor. But she now knew how empty a houseful of dutiful servitors could be.

"What awakens you at this hour?" He made no move towards her. "I thought I was light on my feet, or are you a poor sleeper? I can remove myself to the stables if you require complete solitude." The torchlight behind him cast a halo about his head.

"Do not jest. It is awful to be alone." She approached him and halted at arm's length.

"I thought you would be thoroughly engrossed in discovering every last nook of the place, tiptoeing through the secret underground passageway, exploring the cellars—general prowling about."

"Prowling may be your style, but it is not mine." She crossed her arms over her chest.

"Do not be so sure, my lady. You and I are more alike than you care to see. When we want something, and I do not mean chattels, I mean what we cannot touch, such as truth, we stop at nowt to achieve it. You should prowl all around here. And, if you tire of the house, visit the old churches, the Roman ruins, the Druid megaliths. York is rife with Viking remnants. The burial ground of St. Alkelda at the foot of Middleham Castle is rich with old gravestones and the church is just as interesting. With your imagination you can see past worlds and transport yourself back to days of pagan rituals..." He moved closer and she took another step forward. Now they stood within kissing distance. "...when they sacrificed virgins to their gods. If you lived in those days, you'd not live long."

"Oh, fie!" She held up her hands. " You are mordant. No comfort at all."

He slid out of his cloak and draped it over his arm. "You left a warm feath-erbed to venture into a cold corridor for comfort? What comfort awaits you here?"

"The comfort of human company. But it seems I am mistaken. There is none to be found." Her better judgment told her to turn and stalk off to her chambers, but she couldn't tear her gaze from his tousled hair, his face reddened by ex-ertion. Though cold from the ride through the frozen night, he gave off waves of warmth. She longed to feel his arms around her, to hold him close, to press her cheek to his chest and spark desire in him.

"As I remember, dear wife, you bade me farewell long ago at your chamber door, and called the palace guard to drag me off. You've been so intent on find-ing your family, you shun my help. Are you intent on me now, because you still haven't found your kin?"

"'Tis nowt to do with my quest. I am companionless, that is all. I am not yet used to these surroundings. And poring through genealogy that leads nowhere just adds to my desolation. I feel more unwanted than ever." Her voice broke in a forlorn sob. Stinging tears sprang from her eyes. But he did not take another step towards her. "I simply wanted to welcome you home."

He slipped out of his shoes and fixed his eyes upon her. "Aye, I allow it was a heartfelt greeting and I am grateful, but I am weary and ravenous. So return to your warm next of slumber whilst I enjoy a repast, a warm bath and my bed."

"Oh, let me!" She wound her fingers round his and the cold of his hand seeped into her. "Let me prepare your bath."

He broke away. "My groom attends my needs. No lady performs such menial work."

"But you are my husband and … we'd both enjoy it." She didn't need to force conviction into her tone.

"By the king's orders I am your husband. Certainly not by the will of your heart. I have seen enough of love to know when it is true. This is certainly not. I shall not force the issue, nor will I loll about waiting for your heart to open to me. I know now your only thought was to escape Elizabeth Woodville and find your family, not to love me. Therefore, I shall not compromise nor dishonor you. Contrary to your belief, I am a gentleman, and shall ever be so. Now I retire to my chambers … alone. I bid you goodnight." He bowed, turned on a heel, and vanished into the darkness, leaving his shoes behind for a servant to tend. The closing of his chamber door was not loud, but a gesture indeed.

She stood a long time in the chill shadows, seething with fury, bursting with sorrow, and learning how cold a bedfellow honor could be.

* * *

Denys sat in the solar doing needlework as servers brought supper: roast suckling pig, crane and lark.

Valentine returned from settling a dispute twixt his tenants on the Scots border. "Sad tidings. Anne birthed a dead child."

"When?" She abandoned her embroidery as he gazed into the fire with sad eyes, lips drawn into a frown.

"Tuesday last. Such a delicate lass is Annie. I doubt she will ever bear him children. She is too frail." His gaze stayed fixed to the fire.

She compared Anne's slight figure with her own sturdy build, and thanked nature for granting her a stout constitution. She could carry a child with ease. Her hips would well allow passage in labor and her heart beat strong enough for two.

She suffered a pang of hurt for Richard and Anne, mourning the innocent babe who never took a breath.

"I hope for children of my own someday," she thought aloud.

"So do I," he echoed, and across the great length of the solar their eyes met. They sat and supped in silence.

* * *

Next morn, Denys mounted Chera and rode the few miles down the road to Middleham.

Though she was bedridden and barely able to hold her head up, Anne's eyes lit up when Denys entered the bedchamber. Her hair fell in a tangle around her slumped shoulders.

Denys gently arranged the pillows about her. "You appear fare well, Anne, considering your misfortune. I am so sorry, as is Valentine. I stopped in the chapel and said a prayer for the dear babe's soul."

"Thank you, Denys." Her voice strained. "I shall try again. I am eager to give Richard a son. Even a lass, he said, will suffice, as long as we are both healthy."

"That is kind of him." She looked away, bursting to spew a stern rebuke, to forbid she try for any more children, for it would surely kill her.

"What of you, Denys?" Anne tilted her head. "Are you breeding as of yet?"

"Nay, not a chance." She did not care to discuss her unconsummated marriage. "But I pray it happens soon."

Anne asked Denys about her family search, and Denys vented her frustration, thankful to have someone to listen.

When, at the end of the visit, Anne bade Denys Godspeed, she gave her a roll of parchment on which was limned her own genealogy. "Mayhap something is there, a name may spark a memory. Such things do happen. Names and places from the past come out of nowhere, from dark corners of our minds. What a delight should we be related, you and I!"

Denys nodded with feigned eagerness. "Thank you for your generosity. This is such a precious document." But she doubted any connection to the Nevilles.

Richard still hadn't returned, but she did not wait. She had come to see Anne, after all, and Valentine's duties brought him into Richard's company so often, she felt connected with him always.

* * *

Denys arrived back at Lilleshal and her lady-in-waiting removed her cloak.

"So how fares Anne?" Valentine asked.

"She looks painfully gaunt, but her spirits are high." They headed for the solar, she rushed up to the blazing hearth, lifted her skirts and let the warmth thaw out her frozen legs. "She gave me her genealogy to trace, told me to dig deep in my memory and mayhap some name or place will surface."

"That was more than kind, with all she has on her mind." He stood beside her.

"Aye, it was." She slipped out of her shoes and sat on the tapestry rug, stretching her legs straight out to let the fire warm her feet.

"Did you see Richard?" he asked.

"He was not in residence." She rubbed her hands before the flames.

"Where was the kingdom's greatest warrior? Jousting with Mars, mayhap?" His comment took her by surprise. She turned to look at him, but he turned his back to her.

He crossed the solar and stared out the window, leaning on the frame, drumming his fingers restlessly. "Valentine, is something amiss twixt you and Richard?"

"Nay, nowt at all. I practice my swordsmanship until I can barely move my arm, and my hand is frozen into position round the hilt of an imaginary sword." He turned and approached her, standing twixt her and the fire. "I will challenge him again, and this time I will win." His tone carried such a vehement tone, her heart took a leap.

"No need, Valentine. He only won so easily because you were already injured."

"But he still bested me." Raw vengeance crept out from behind those words.

"What of it?" She attempted lightness. "He could never win serfs' hearts here the way you do. That is your strength, and warfare is his. You have nowt to prove to him or yourself."

"I need prove nowt to him. I must prove it to you!" He faced her and their eyes met. "Then mayhap I'll chisel a nick into that stone you call a heart."

"You need prove nowt to me either." Sufficiently warmed, she backed away from the fire.

"It takes more than a honeyed tongue to be a man," he argued. "It takes courage to hazard one's life for one's beliefs."

"You are fully a man. I never doubted that." She approached him.

"'Tis not the fact that I lost a joust that rails me. 'Tis that I lost over you. So I will take him on again and I will win. I will take on the entire French army if I must. Whatever it takes to prove myself to you, then you will beg me to love you!" His hands clamped down on her shoulders. Their lips nearly touched.

"Conquests will not make me love you." She made no attempt to escape his grasp.

"Then what? Am I never to know?" His eyes spat chips of blue ice and his brows knitted into a rigid line.

"Love is never forced. You cannot even force your own flesh and blood to love you. No one was able to make my mother love me enough to keep me. It comes naturally, not as a medal for valor. Conquering a heart isn't like conquering an army. 'Tis much harder." Her arms wound round his waist. Her pulse quickened.

"When the queen ordered me to marry you," he spoke as if telling a story, "I danced and tumbled with joy, I thought, 'A-ha! I've won her now!' for that was the one thing I would have that no one else could. The king has his court, Richard has his north country, but I was to have Denys Woodville, the only woman I ever wanted. And now you are my wife and I still do not have you." He paused, relinquished his grip.

A strange urge to comfort him came over her. "I am not a banner or standard to parade round. Winning me isn't like winning a battle."

"'Tis because of battle I lose everything." He talked as if to himself as he moved away and sank into the chair by the fire.

Her heart went out to him in painful compassion; behind his confidence, he was as lost as she. Now she understood what Richard meant that day. Valentine hid behind a curtain of his own anguish.

"Don't think in terms of battle. I am here now, and you won't lose me that way," she assured him.

"I can't lose what I haven't won." He stooped over and stared into the flames.

"You are a titled and landed nobleman. You have that. I do not even know who I am. Think about that." She raised her voice. "You married a bastard, raised by the most hated family in the realm, married to a man who will not touch me." She glanced round the room for hovering servers.

He stood and glared. Suppressed tears glistened in his eyes. "You know who you are. 'Tis no matter who your parents were. You are the duchess of Norwich, my wife. I want you to be proud of me, to look up to me, to respect me. I want a wife who loves me for me, not an unwilling victim of a mad queen."

"I will grow to love you. I am nearly there already. Just be patient." She sensed the strain binding their souls like cord, defying either of them to sever it. She turned and in a rustle of velvet and satin underskirts, left the room.

He stared after her, forcing himself still. Oh, that cadence in her walk, the delicate swing of her hips, the spring in each step now in such harmony with his own bodily rhythms. Yet each passing day brought increasing vexation, it now approached physical pain.

He breathed deeply of her scent until it faded into the folds of the curtains. He knew what kept her from loving him with her entire soul. Not until she found out who she was could she love anyone entirely. He had to somehow prove to her that he'd not abandon her as her parents did.

"God Jesu," he wailed, his cries dying beyond the beamed ceiling. "Give me the chance to save her life, give me the chance to *find* her life, then at last she'll love me!"

* * *

Secluded in her bedchamber, Denys unrolled Anne's genealogy parchment. She was descended from John of Gaunt, a son of Edward III. Both Anne and Richard, as most nobles born in the kingdom, were descendants of Edward III. Denys savored a ripple of excitement. *Could I possibly find my parentage somewhere in this document?* she wondered. *Does my name truly belong on this parchment? Am I a descendant of Gaunt from one of his three mistresses?* she wondered.

She rolled the parchment back up, repeating the names of long-dead noblemen: "Beaufort, Beauchamp, Neville, Stafford." She knew these names since childhood.

Combing through her diary, she pondered every mention of a visitor or lad being knighted. She re-read her entries about feeble-minded King Henry VI, of his ill-fated battles, his triumphs and failures, and his controlling wife, Marguerite of Anjou.

If she was in King Henry's charge as an infant, his living relatives might remember her.

Mayhap King Henry sired her himself and, slipping in and out of mental incontinence, failed to recognize her! She could be a princess in her own right, an unsung princess of a dead king, but still of royal heritage!

She began to conceive fancies of life had King Henry acknowledged her, how different her upbringing would have been. She would have suffered no public disparagement, no angry outbursts—no Elizabeth Woodville.

But then she would be a Lancastrian, a deadly enemy of Richard and his family.

Did she want to find out? Aye, more than ever! Even were she Lancastrian by birth, it mattered not now.

Too excited to sleep, she dug out the original document she obtained at court and traced the branch to which King Henry VI belonged.

He had two Welsh half-brothers, Edmund and Jasper Tudor. Alas, Edmund died over twenty years ago. Jasper could mayhap lead her to success, but for one caveat—he was married to Catherine Woodville.

Elizabeth's cousin.

She trusted Elizabeth's relatives no more than she trusted the Grey Mare herself. But this was a risk she must take.

Now how to locate Catherine Woodville and a Welsh guide?

Only one person could help her, and she'd trust him with her life.

King Edward—Uncle Ned.

She penned a letter to him and ended it with her name smudged in tears. These days, she couldn't think of Uncle Ned without weeping. How she longed for his warm embrace, his winks of assurance. She knew he would accompany her to Wales himself had he the time. She re-read the letter out loud, as if he sat across from her. "Oh, Uncle Ned," she sighed, closing her eyes, his hearty laugh echoing in her mind.

His reply came so quickly, she knew he must have employed a string of couriers to reach her, as he did in war time, to convey urgent messages. Not only did he provide Catherine Woodville and Jasper Tudor's whereabouts, a manor home called Talyllyn, he proffered a Welsh guide, to arrive afore week's end! He ended his note, "You're forever my little Denys, love always, Unc Ned."

She laughed and cried at the same time, folded the letter lovingly and kissed his royal seal.

Her heart racing with excitement, she wrote to Catherine and Jasper Tudor that she would travel to Wales and wished to call on them. She didn't mention the real reason; she would take no chances.

* * *

Valentine was out inspecting tenant cottages the day her guide arrived. Owen Gwynne rode at the head of the trio Uncle Ned had sent to guide and guard her. Denys took an immediate liking to Owen. With hair whiter than the snow that dusted the ground, and cheeks a ruddy brick-red, he was the most talkative man she ever met. Even as Denys assisted her kitchen servers in packing provisions for the journey, Owen filled her ears with tales of bygone days, the civil strife under King Henry VI, resulting from Marguerite of Anjou's doings. Too eager to embark upon her journey to await Valentine's return, she left a brief note to tell him she left for Wales under the king's guide.

The other men in the retinue were young; Bruce was as quiet and broody as Owen was chatty. Something in Bruce's manner and carriage reminded her of Uncle Ned, with the bearing of a true knight, straight and tall atop his mount, arms that could wield the heaviest sword. Peter, a freckled Irishman and frustrated seaman, wished to traverse lands south of the continent, a captivating idea to Denys. Although only a barren desert was known to lie in the southern hemisphere, she admired his curiosity, a trait she proudly shared. With the usual boasting of Irish seamen who considered their talents at sea superior to the English, he recounted his beliefs: "Land lies to our west as well. The Vikings and Norsemen barely scraped the shores of Iceland, Greenland, Vinland, and Eric the Red's expedition across the Danish Channel. Oh, to have shipped with Eric the Red!"

On this bright cloudless day, she mounted Chera and headed west with her three guides. The crisp air pinched her face, the landscape sharp and clear. Snow-capped trees framed the majesty of church towers that soared into the powdery sky. The midday sun spilled a white glint upon virgin snow, untouched by even the smallest sparrow tracks. In the distance, patches of velvet green gave way to brown, peeking through white crystals sparkling over the hilltops like fallen stars.

They reached the outskirts of Yorkshire over icy roads. By nightfall, newly fallen snow rendered the road nearly impassable. She considered turning back, but trusted the weather to improve. Snowdrifts would not stand twixt her and her destiny.

They spent the first night with one of Valentine's tenant farmers and gorged themselves at daybreak with eggs, salt bacon and milk. Because the weather would not allow an open-air meal along the way, their next repast wouldn't be until that eve.

Shortly after the sun rose, they traversed open fields, a copse of trees a mile or so in the distance. The virgin white ground glimmered in the sun. Patches of white flecked the distant hills. Falling snow buried the heather and bracken. Her belly growled with hunger. Much as she enjoyed Owen's talk and demeanor, she wished Chera had wings to soar over hills and treetops to Wales. But as they trudged along, the white flakes dissolved into icy blobs on her face. She longed for a fire and a warm tankard. But as they hoofed on they chatted, making the stinging whipping wind bearable.

The flakes gave way to a strong wind. Blasts of blinding whiteness stung her flesh, numbing her with cold. She tried to move her stiff fingers without dropping Chera's reins. Within minutes she lost sight of Owen's mount at her side.

"Owen!" She extended her arm, but grasped air.

"Right here, snow maiden." He came up alongside her and the tips of his fingers brushed hers.

"Stay by me, I'm getting blinded!" Snow coated Chera's mane and the horse sneezed several times in swift succession. Denys lost Owen again, but knew he and the others rode a few paces away. He'd proven himself an expert wayfinder. He wouldn't get them lost.

Bruce and Peter sang a drinking tune, but she paid no heed as blasts of icy wind tormented her. With her gnawing hunger and desperate need for a warm bed, she'd even welcome a simple straw pallet.

As they reached the forrowed path winding through the woods, the snow shrouded them. Somehow Chera picked her way down the snow-swathed path. The horse's feet plunged into its depths with every footfall. Darkness began to fall. Instinct warned her they couldn't possibly come forth from these woods before dawn. The bare trees provided scant cover, without a house in sight. Blinding snow pelted her eyes. She heard the men, but could not see them.

In the darkness, Owen trudged up to her, a flickering and hissing lantern before him. She halted Chera. The horses formed a loose circle, their puffs of breath providing the only remnant of warmth.

"We must pause," Owen said. "We can go no farther, not until daybreak. I am losing my bearings. All paths look alike in the snow and dark."

"But where shall we sleep?" she pleaded.

"Sleep?" Owen brayed. "We mustn't sleep. To sleep out here is to never wake."

"Can you not spread blankets on the ground so we can rest?" she proposed.

"Dear child, the snow is knee deep. A blanket will freeze to a sheet of ice. The snow is too deep to lie in. And there be packs of hungry wolves about. Nay, we must move about to keep our humors coursing. We have wine and other sustenance. We shan't starve. We will sing and tell stories. Worry not, my dear, the night will pass soon enough."

She yearned to unsaddle and stamp her feet on the frozen earth. But the snow would swallow her up.

"Can we not make a shelter from tree branches?" Desperate for ideas, she would take any wretched comfort and refuge from this misery of the elements.

The men laughed. "None of us has an axe," Peter said. "'Twould be difficult, unless, Mistress Denys, you can gnaw wood like a beaver and dam us all up from the deluge when all this melts."

"Enough idle chatter," Owen declared. "We must keep these beasts moving. Let us go in circles, singing "Day of the Hunt" as we do. By then nigh on fifteen minutes will have passed. We shall rest at fifteen minute intervals until daybreak, then resume our journey.

"This will be the longest night of my life," Denys moaned in the general direction of the lantern, for he and his mount were invisible once more.

"It will be the last if we do not," came his grim reply, as the song's opening lines battered her ears in loud discord.

"How pleasant it is, when the sun is shining brightly,
To ride out early in the morning
With keen huntsmen and hounds as my companions
Chasing the deer among the forest leaves..."

The snow eased. Owen and the others whipped out flasks and began to imbibe. They shared their victuals; Peter gave her a delicious rough brown bread and after one slice, her stomach growled for more. They munched apples and pears, feasted on chicken and consumed enough to keep hunger at bay, if not the cold.

After another round of songs and ribald jokes, begging her pardon, she began to enjoy the moment, and looked to her journey's end. Then she would—God willing—find her place in life.

The blackness lightened to pale gray as dawn broke behind them.

All quiet, all talked and sung out, they pushed on. How she longed for sleep. Never mind a pallet, a stone dungeon floor would be a comfort. She patted Chera's neck and murmured encouraging words of affection to the weary animal.

The windblown snow gathered strength again as the first sign of daylight peeked through the straggling snow-laden branches.

Owen rounded them up to organize the next leg of their journey.

"We shall carry on till we see somewhere safe to stop, anywhere, anything that offers shelter." She could tell he forced a cheerful tone. "In my judgment, we are ten miles or so from Macclesfield, a town of goodly proportions. When we reach it, we should seriously consider staying until this tempest blows out."

Denys heartily agreed, her body so frozen, she almost forced her imagination to feel it. A few moments of intense attention enabled her to bask in the warmth of a roaring fire, to breathe the smoky aroma of crackling logs.

The singing began once more, halfheartedly this time. She hummed along, not knowing the words, but this was her last refuge from dread, for they'd traveled all day and once again the sun began to angle late afternoon shadows on them. She shut out their weary voices and began to sing hymns.

* * *

"Owen, where are we? There hasn't been a house in sight. Are you sure we didn't turn north into the far reaches of Scotland?" she begged, her lips frozen into numbness, hardly able to form words. She raised her hand to her nose and lips but it did nowt to warm them. Her numb fingers could barely hold the reins. Utterly spent, she blanked for seconds at a time and bounced awake with the horse's unsteady stride. Slipping in and out of awareness made her addleheaded. She cried out, her eyes wildly attentive yet seeing nothing.

Owen inched up, reached over and clutched her shoulder. "Are you well, lass?" His voice was familiar and comforting, but she had no strength to turn and face him.

"Aye, I think so," she muttered.

"Good. Because we approach a rise here, and I hope your horse has strength left to climb it. If she don't stiffen up solid, she'll come out of this with the strongest hind legs in the kingdom."

"Where are we?" Her voice croaked with weariness.

"If I have my bearings, this be Todburn Forest," Owen called over his shoulder. "On the other side of this is Macclesfield. We will stop there."

"How long?" She drowned in despair.

"The rest of today and part of tomorrow, I reckon." He handed her a flask and she groped for it, trying to clasp her stiffened fingers round it, but it slipped to the ground, swallowed up in the deep sea of snow.

"I've got another, but if you can't take it, I can try to reach over and hold it to your lips, lass."

"Never mind," she whispered, lips cracked and dry. Her teeth chattered so that she doubted she could sip from a flask.

The weary party trudged through a waste of trees. Dead branches scraped her cheeks as they picked their way through, the path now buried. She had no strength to lean over to avoid them.

Something in the chaos of her random thoughts told her to pray. By now she'd lost all feeling, her utter numbness foreboding the deep sleep she knew she was about to enter. But she was no longer afraid. She welcomed death as a warm passage into a world of comfort and light. Through her stiffened lips she mouthed a prayer learned as a child: "Keep me and defend me from all evil and from my evil enemy and from all danger, present, past and to come." She begged mercy for her soul, bursting with sadness at the thought of never seeing Valentine again. She pictured his face, racked with worry, and regretted not telling where she was going. Oh, if only she weren't so stubborn, refusing his help, blaming him for the tragedy in Witherham and suspecting him of plotting with Elizabeth. "Please, Valentine," she begged, wishing she could clasp her hands in prayer, but they felt frozen round Chera's reins, "Please forgive me. If only I had another chance, I'd be the best wife a man could have." She wept, not for her oncoming death, but for him, how she'd left him so rudely. "I'd make it all up to you." She tried to stop the tears before they froze her eyes shut.

In her addled daze, anger sparked and gave her weary body an edge of vigor. No! She refused to die without seeing him again; he needed her! Early death was not in her plans; she could not, would not die until she fulfilled her destiny here on earth.

She forced her feeble fingers to move, the skin so taut she feared it would crack, but she started slowly. In a few minutes, they were partially mobile. She called out to Owen for the flask. After some groping in his saddle bag, he pulled one out and leaned over to give it to her.

She reached for it, pulled off her glove, grasped it with her bare hand and held it to her lips. The soothing liquid trickled down her throat and breathed life back into her. She licked her lips. They warmed, tingling as self-awareness returned. "I can feel my lips, I can talk! My feeling came back!"

Owen nodded. "They be good tidings, for I see shelter of some sort up yon."

Shelter. The word gave her the same comfort as the words 'feather bed' under normal circumstances. Her heart leapt and a surge of excitement rent her ragged weariness.

"Where?" She squinted into the falling snow.

Owen shifted course to the right and she followed. The snow was not so deep here in the thick of the forest, and Chera easily walked in the footsteps of Owen's horse. Through the tangle of bark and branches she could make out a mass of fallen trees a few feet high, arching across the ground like a wooden cave. It was shallow, it was low, but it was cover, and would provide scant but very real shelter from the harshness that tormented her spirit, sapped her strength, drained her life.

"Oh, sweet Jesu!" Tears welled in her eyes, her lashes still weighed down with bits of ice.

Owen and the others unsaddled. Bruce helped her down from Chera, her legs so stiff, her feet so numb, she couldn't feel the ground when he set her down. It took all her strength to clutch the front of his cloak to keep from sliding to the ground.

"She's spent," a distant voice said. "Lay blankets in there and let her rest."

A pair of hands slid under her back and behind her knees. Her head lolled to one side as someone carried her to the shelter, wrapped her in blankets and lay her on the ground under the woven branches.

The warmth she'd so desperately craved felt like the embrace of the sun. Be this death? If so, she welcomed it, because she was at peace.

* * *

Shouting woke her from a deep sleep. As she opened her eyes, patches of brightness shone through the weave of branches over her head.

Awareness returned in fragmented patterns and gave way to sheer terror. Dark figures tore at each other, cursing, grunting, spitting! Filthy and ragged, they rained merciless blows upon her men. Two more leapt from the woods, armed with longbows. She gasped in horror as a black hail of arrows whirred by. Owen clutched his chest as an arrow pierced him. He cried out in agony and crumpled to the ground in blood-soaked snow.

One savage thrust at her, tore her cloak and crushed her with his bulk. His stench made her gag. She screamed and beat him with her fists, but he clearly enjoyed the struggle. He wrenched her skirts to her thighs. Raw cold stung her skin. He grunted like an animal, his breath smothering her face with foul blasts. She forced her eyes shut and gritted her teeth. *Oh, God, please God, let this nightmare end.*

As she gasped for air, his body stiffened and fell on her. She struggled to escape the burden of his weight. A pair of powerful arms lifted him off her and Peter rolled the lifeless body onto the ground. He pulled a dagger, dripping with blood, from the assailer's back and gathered her to him. "'Tis all right, love, I killed him." Her tears of fright stung her raw flesh. She trembled like the brittle branches around them.

Seeing their fellow vagabond in a lifeless heap on the ground, the band of robbers rounded up all the horses. Chera reared in protest as one of them tugged harshly on her reins and pulled her away. Too stunned to move, she sat until complete silence reigned.

Bruce approached and rubbed her hands twixt his. "We're safe, they've gone," he assured her. "They got what they wanted."

"Owen!" She crawled from the shelter. Peter followed as she approached Owen lying in the snow, his breath coming in torturous gasps. She knelt by his side, bloody snow soaking her clothes and stinging her skin. She carefully worked the arrow from Owen's chest as more blood poured from the wound. A dark red puddle spread over his cloak.

"Owen…" she whispered. His eyes opened, rolling, his breathing rasping and hollow.

Bruce and Peter carried Owen into the shelter and she crawled back in after them.

"Put his head in my lap." Branches painfully dug into her scalp. They placed his head in her lap and she cradled it.

"We must try and get help," Peter said as they backed out of the shelter on their knees.

"How?" She looked up at him. "They've taken our horses … everything!"

"It stopped snowing and the day is bright and clear. We can make our way on foot."

"We shall separate." Bruce squinted at the sun to get his bearings. "If I head northwest and Peter southwest, one of us should reach help. Peter and I shall meet hence."

"You are leaving us here?" she shrilled in dismay.

"You must stay with Owen. Worry not. We'll be back to fetch you. If Peter and I both go, 'twill double our chances of finding help. Have you a better idea?"

"Nay." She shook her head, unable to grasp their sorry plight, much less dream up a better way.

"Fine. God willing, one of us will return soon. Let us go, Peter."

They separated after a few paces and she gently rocked Owen's head. "They will be back soon with help. We shall get out of this, all will be well…"

He began to stir as his eyes leveled on her face. A hint of a smile broke through the wanness. He took several labored breaths. "I am dying, lass, I breathe my last."

"Nay, you are not!" She refused to believe it. "They have gone for help."

"Listen. Do not speak, just listen." He took another wheezing breath and spat out. "I can tell you now, for in a few moments I will be gone, so 'twill matter not. I know of your quest to find your family. I know because the queen found out about us guides, and ordered me to mislead you on the journey to Wales and be sure you learnt nowt. I feared for my life if I did not obey her, but now my life ends, so it matters not."

Her breath halted. Her heart seemed to stop. "How could she…"

"Listen!" He attempted to raise his voice. "After having been in King Henry the Sixth's service, I returned to him many years hence to aid in matters of the treasury. It was during that stay, at Mass, I saw a man hand an infant to him—oh, she couldn'a been more than six, seven months old. 'Take good care of her,' the man said. 'She may be of value someday.' That is all I remember him saying. King Henry took the babe and looked down at her. His face blank, he knew not what to do with her. Then he straightaway handed the babe to the nurse who hurried off." He paused for breath, turned and coughed blood onto the ground.

"Oh, Jesu!" she gasped. "When was this? Do you know what year?"

"What year..." A series of sighs followed a shake of his head. "I was forty, or was I ... I must have been forty, it had to be then..." His voice grew weak. She leaned over to hear him. "I was born in fourteen-seventeen so it had to be fourteen ... oh, fifty-seven?"

"The year I was born!" Her heart leapt. "Owen ... who was this man who gave the babe to King Henry?"

"His name was..." He succumbed to a fit of coughing and shook his head from side to side. Blood seeped through his clenched teeth. She pulled one of her skirts up to his mouth to wipe it away. "John," he rasped, his breathing shallower. For a moment he stilled. Then his breath rattled again and his chest rose as he struggled for air.

"John?" She begged him with her eyes, locking into the gaze that left her and now stared up at the sky, "John who?"

"John..." came out in a whisper. He coughed, choked, and took his final breath. His eyes opened wide, then the lids slipped over them for the last time. His features relaxed and settled into eternal stillness. His chest no longer rose and fell. No more air or blood escaped his lips.

But amidst this tragedy, she took heart from the fact that Elizabeth knew she was on the right track. If nothing was there, there would be nothing to mislead her about.

Whatever Elizabeth had to hide, it hid in Wales.

She bowed her head over Owen's lifeless form and prayed for his soul.

* * *

Daylight faded. The sky darkened. She said a prayer for Owen's soul and crouched beside his body, slipping out of awareness and into blackness once again.

John ... John ... John who?

Chapter Seven

The sweet taste of wine warmed her as an embrace comforted her. She leaned forward into folds of velvet. It was Valentine, she knew it. Her heart burst with gratitude. Enclosed in his warmth, she felt wanted for the first time in her life.

She moved her hands and feet, lifted one knee, then another, with caution, in fear of broken bones. "Oh, dear God, I can move!" She wiggled her toes, enjoying the movement, the ability to control her body. "'Tis heavenly!"

Through the curtain of her lashes, blue velvet swam into view, the glitter of topaz that echoed soft candlelight. Sturdy shoulders supported a head of dark blond hair reflecting each candle's glimmer as it gave off a glow of its own.

But it was not Valentine. "Richard! What ... where am I?"

"You are at the home of the earl of Nottingham. The earl brought you here in a litter. He lives near the shelter where they found you. You are but a few miles from Kettlewell, where I was in residence when he summoned me."

"What happened to Bruce and Peter?" She searched his eyes, silently begging for good news.

"Bruce summoned help and led us back to you." He handed her the goblet and she took another sip. "They are both all right."

"Oh, thank God..." She released a sigh of relief. With her next breath, the horror rushed back, haunting her with their chilling particulars—the vagabond's assault, clinging to Owen, cradling his head, the name "John" on his lips as he breathed his last, the surname passing into the beyond with him. "Owen..."

"Owen died of his wound," Richard told her. "You half froze to death. You would have perished had they not found you."

"He died in my arms. Oh, poor Owen." Her eyes spilled over with tears. "Did you summon Valentine?"

He took the goblet and rearranged the pillows behind her head. "He is on his way."

As she drank more wine, he gave her a slice of buttered bread. "Oh, Richard, I was so very cold. I couldn't move, I was sure I would die."

"Do not dwell on it, my dear. You are warm, you are safe, and you shan't set off again until the spring thaw." His voice seemed to come from a distance.

Each bite of bread gained her more strength. She now conceived more worldly thoughts. "I wonder if Valentine worried about me."

"Don't be daft, of course he worried," Richard chided. "He couldn't sleep nor eat."

"He never cared before." She shook her head. "You have no idea what our marriage is like. He is so distant, so cold."

"Likely he is unused to married life and yet to find his way as a husband. 'Tis not his nature to be cold. I know he feels a lot more than he lets on," he assured her.

She would have laughed if had she the strength. "Nay, he shuns me. At first it was a relief, for I mistrusted him. Then his manner waned to a chill apartness."

"Have you talked to him about it?"

"Aye, and he will not touch me until he is sure that I love him and go to him willingly as a wife. I care about him a great deal. But he refuses to possess my body without possessing my heart. But how can I love a man who won't take me in his arms and treat me as his wife? We go in circles like this, I fear we'll forever circle each other instead of . . . coming together." She hoped she spoke daintily enough not to discomfort him.

"Denys, men have drives that women, in their stable family circles and well-defined duties, cannot comprehend. We war, brother against brother, to claim what we feel rightfully ours, whether it be or not. Valentine wants to be loved. Your body means nowt to him without your heart. He can dally any tart that strikes his fancy, most men can. But to win a maiden's heart, that is a different matter altogether. That prize all men covet. He wants your heart, Denys. Then and only then will he give you everything he has."

"Sometimes I don't know if I can. I wish I felt otherwise. I lie awake in my bed as he lies in his and wish so strongly he would come to me. I try going to him but always back off." She took a sip of wine.

"Hearts are vessels to be filled," Richard said. "They have immense capacity. True love cannot be rushed. It does not flood you after one tryst in the bed-chamber. It must come gradually. I talk not of lust, which can consume you like a shower of hot embers. You both must allow it the time it needs. But when it happens, you will know. And it is worth the wait. He will see you quite differently now, for he almost lost you."

"Oh, how I prayed, when I believed we would all perish, I begged for a second chance!" She shut her eyes.

"Now you have it. And so does Val." Their eyes met and though she could still see a spark, it held a remnant of lost youth. *Do I look that way too?* she wondered. "How did you learn all this wisdom, Richard?"

"Simply by living, my dear. Valentine has seen tragedy and so have you. Both lost your parents, both believe yourself abandoned. You both hold back, but for different reasons. You will learn how much he cares, but you must show him *you* care. And it takes time, not words." He took her hand, warming it twixt his palms. "He should be here any time now." Richard glanced across the chamber. "When he arrives, I will depart."

She gave him a warm smile. "Richard, I think I am closer now to finding my true beginnings than ever!"

His eyes lit up. "Pray tell."

She wet her lips. "After the robbers fled, I held Owen Gwynne's head in my lap as he spoke his last words. In 1457, he saw a man he knew hand a babe to King Henry the Sixth. The man's name was John. And the babe was a girl."

"John who?" Richard asked. "Did he know the surname?"

She shook her head. "John was the last word he spoke. He took his dying breath, his eyes rolled back and he shut them forever."

"Hell's bells, Denys, do you know how many men in this realm are named John?" Richard folded his hands, his rings clinking together. "You could visit every man named John and not find the right one in five lifetimes. He is likely long dead."

"But surely you can find out, you can access all the court records," she be-seeched.

"I've known many a John? Do you want me to summon every one of them?" Doubt clouded his eyes.

"Nay, only those old enough to have given an infant girl to King Henry," she stated.

"I shall ponder it." He tapped his fingers on his chin. "Things have odd ways of creeping up sometimes, even in dreams."

The chamber door opened and Valentine entered. A shadow of stubble peppered his chin, roughening his smooth lines. He appeared to be tortured by some unrelenting demon. She knew it was because of her. A stab of guilt pierced her heart.

"Valentine!" She reached out and he paused to take her hand, as if afraid to touch her. "I am so sorry for all I caused you! But I am well, I can almost stand."

"Do not. I am happy to carry you." He spoke as if to a wounded soldier in battle. He looked at Richard. "She gave us quite a scare here." She could tell he struggled to keep a tremor from his voice.

Richard stood and straightened his surcoat. "I shall depart as promised. Denys, I shall aid you in your search as best as I can. But you survived fire and robbers in one lifetime. Miracles do not happen in more than threes. Do not become greedy."

"Oh, Richard, I know you will unearth something!" she cried out to him.

"John," he muttered under his breath, shaking his head as he strode out. "Whoever solves this mystery deserves knighthood."

Valentine sat at the edge of the bed and brushed her hair back off her forehead. Lines of worry creased his features. "How do you feel?" His tone gave her a spark of hope.

"I feel fine, a bit weak. Mayhap I'll tell you all about it later. If you would hear it."

His hand trembled. She looked into his eyes and he averted his gaze for an uncomfortable moment. "Tell only what you will. It was a dreadful ordeal. I prayed every second and thank God you are all right."

"Richard said you worried about me." She paused. "Did you, Valentine?"

His gaze swept her face, then leveled squarely on her eyes. "What do you think? When that storm hit I routed out with every servitor in the house, saddled every horse in the stable, and those without horses went on foot. Then I summoned Richard and he saddled his mounts. They were still straggling back when I left to come here."

She tried to sit upright. "Is everyone all right?"

"Everyone returned relatively unharmed except Kevin, the stable lad." He spoke slowly, his tone full of remorse. "We know not what became of him. A search party is still out for him."

"Oh, dear, the poor lad." She shuddered in shame. "Oh all the misery my reckless expedition caused…"

"We made a five-mile circle round the grounds, and Nottingham's messenger intercepted me. I sped straight here." His eyes brimmed with tears. "Oh, why couldn't it be I that saved you?"

She took him in her arms to comfort him.

"You stubborn, stubborn woman! To go to such lengths, to tempt the grasping fingers of death twice already just to seek the truth. I am proud of you and could shake you at the same time!" He leaned into her embrace and held her with a care and tenderness she thought he would never show.

"'Tis not bravery, Valentine. 'Tis blind faith. I know in the end, I shall find them. I have to believe that."

"See, I told you we are more alike than you care to admit." He drew back and clasped her hands.

She smiled as Richard's words echoed in her mind. Much as she misliked Valentine's ambition and unyielding perseverance, they shared these traits.

She would wait until they arrived home, and exchange vows once again—not just spoken, but with hearts and bodies, truly joining as husband and wife.

"I shan't go anywhere again without you or without telling you first … in person," she promised. "But that matters not, for I near the end of my search!"

"How?" His eyes twinkled.

"When my guide, Owen, lay dying, he spoke the name 'John' with his last breath. Owen was in King Henry's service when I was an infant."

"John? How does that possibly help?" He gave her that same addled look Richard had.

"I will not stop until I unearth that very John that served King Henry," she declared.

"There are hundreds of Johns from that time." He splayed his fingers. "Half of them are likely dead."

"Someone must know. I am close. I can feel it in my bones. Have you ever had such a feeling?" She leveled her gaze on him.

"Aye, many a time." He nodded. "But I've been wrong often enough, too."

"All I have to do is find the right John and I am on the way to my family. My real family!" She pumped her fists and raised her head to heaven.

Valentine asked, "Did you and Richard have a nice visit?"

She nodded. "Aye, it was very short, but pleasant."

"Did he tell you Anne is breeding again?" He gave her an expectant smile.

"Nay. Why did he not tell me?" She rolled her eyes. "Oh, that addlehead."

"You are just rescued from being frozen to death. Mayhap he felt it a poor time to share his own news. His concern was you."

"But Anne is so frail. How could he?" A tinge of annoyance tightened her lips.

"I am sure she had her say in the matter." His smile widened.

"But why not tell me? How could he omit such a thing? I would warn him of the dangers." She said a silent prayer for Anne. She did not want the dear girl to die. "How badly did Richard need a son to imperil his wife so?" She could never see Valentine forcing her to breed were she that feeble.

* * *

At home the following eve, he refused to leave her side. He had supper sent to her chamber and they dined together. He hadn't paid her this much attention since he was wayward and fancy free.

She let him see the locket and likeness of the girl she'd found at Foxley Manor, but he showed no recognition.

"We'll find them." He handed it back to her. "May I show this to the other lords round Yorkshire? You never know."

She clasped her fingers round her cherished possession. "I do not want to let it out of my sight. 'Tis the only link to my heritage…" But she handed it back to him. "Yes, take it, Valentine. I trust you. Besides, I've shown it to everyone I could possibly think of."

He took it from her, raised it to his lips and kissed it. "I promise I will guard it with my life."

* * *

Richard's call to battle came next morn. With King Edward about to invade France, Richard needed 120 men-at-arms and 1,000 archers. As indentures raised the army, Valentine summoned all his tenants and their weapons. Richard's chief officer of arms arrived at Lilleshal with a stack of banners and badges displaying Richard's emblem, the white boar, for each soldier to wear.

"Must you go so soon?" Denys pleaded as he rounded up his contingent on the grounds amidst a cluster of shiny plate armor, streaming plumes, and colorful banners. She had so much left unsaid…

"Aye, I must. King Edward is by now in Calais and we must cross the Channel. Charles the Rash counts on us." As a grin spread over his face, she knew she could hold her knight back no longer. He would move mountains to rush to the king's colors.

As he pulled her to him and kissed her farewell, pounding hooves, clanging armor and shouts of eager soldiers surrounded them. "Keep well for me, and if you start another quest for your heritage, do so by messenger!"

"Please come back safely," she begged.

"God willing." He looked to the heavens. "Some things aren't up to us. They're up to Him."

His squire handed him his helmet. He slid it over his head, closed the visor, and raising a gauntlet in farewell, departed.

She fell to her knees. "I love you," she whispered, as he vanished round the curved path, leading his men to the far shores of France. "Why do you want France?" she asked after him, alone but for chirping birds nestled in trees lining the path. "Is France so beauteous she is worth dying for?

* * *

She received but one letter from him that month, about to depart France for Peronne with the king and his army. The cold clutch of fear seized her heart. Oh, why must he fight every battle of every war? She read on: "*The French will not put up much of a fight; the memory of their rout at Agincourt is still fresh in their minds.*" At the end, he wrote, "*Please keep well for me. I need you.*" He signed it, "*Your loving husband*"

She pressed the letter to her heart and prayed for his swift and safe return.

Both her quests had ended in tragedy, Elizabeth intent on thwarting her. But, dear God, why? She must have a reason other than cruelty. The queen always had reasons. The name "John" that Owen exhaled with his last gasp held the final clew. "But what, oh, what is it?" She pounded a fist on her writing table in despair.

* * *

She rehearsed her declaration of love for Valentine, thrilling at the thought of union with him after such a long frustrating time. She missed him terribly and wondered if he missed her as much.

Pounding hooves under her window flooded her with relief. She flew down the stairs to greet her husband on his return from France.

He stood at the entrance to the stables, handing his mount's reins to a groom, his back to her. Holding her breath, she waited for him to face her.

His triumphant smile warmed her more than the sun as they embraced. She nearly melted at his touch, though layers of clothes and furs separated them.

She stroked those powerful arms that wielded battle axes and swords, felled the soldiers of enemy armies. "You are so cold, dear husband. Come inside and warm up by the fire. I have made you lampreys in galytyne. I shall tell the marshal to lay our table with the best plate. The cooks baked beauteous apples into luscious pies. Then I want to hear all about your triumph."

"Delectable," he uttered, turned and trudged toward the house. "But before aught, I must bathe."

She gave orders to the marshal, butler and pantlers about the evening meal. Allowing him time to bathe, she went up to his bedchamber. She'd not set foot in this sumptuous room before. Red silk adorned the walls. Gold leaf rimmed the red ceiling. The bed hangings matched the red velvet curtains shot with gold threads. The red coverlet shimmered in gold embroidered swirls, the carpet delicately woven in exquisite design. He sat fireside in a black satin robe, rubbing his temples.

"Oh, please let me. I am good with headaches." She knelt before him, moved his hands away and caressed his head with a circling motion.

"I think I died and went to heaven." His weary voice barely reached her ears. "Are those your fingers or the wings of an angel?"

A joyful grin spread her lips as he opened his eyes. "I see the face of an angel before me."

She studied his strong features, the determined ridge of his brow, the expressive lips. And those eyes—although it bothered her to admit it, his eyes were the most beauteous when he was troubled.

She walked him to the bed, lay him down and slid beside him. "Valentine, facing death makes you see things very differently."

"No need to tell me, my dear." He yawned and shut his eyes.

She placed a hand over his heart. "When I was dying, I prayed, not for a second chance at life, but one chance to tell you..." She faltered and swept a lock of hair back from his face.

"Tell me what?" His heart slowed to a steady beat. His muscles relaxed.

"I was as worried about you in battle as you about me freezing in the forest. I know you didn't doubt my ability to take care of myself."

"The most rugged of men scarce survive your ordeal. I go to battle thoroughly prepared. So what do you want to tell me?" he asked.

"That I did not regret my own life's end, but did regret leaving you behind. Without having told you..." she whispered as he planted feathery kisses on her neck. She shivered with delight at her husband's touch for the first time.

"Tell me what? That you learn to suffer my rude presence?" he asked.

"Mayhap."

"You can endure my crude inclinations?" He nibbled her ear.

"Do I not?"

"You begin to enjoy my company?" His grin gleamed in the moon's pearly light as she matched it with hers. "I am known to on occasion."

"Mayhap you are falling in love with me?" His mouth descended upon hers. He traced a finger down her neck and over each breast through her satin chemise in slow circular motions.

She sighed under his touch. Dancing flames smoldered deep within her.

"Tell me what is in your heart, Denys."

She slid her hand inside the robe and stroked his chest, her breath matching his with increasing fervency.

He slipped her chemise over her head and slid her skirts up to her waist. She wriggled out of her nether garments.

"Tell me what you are afraid to, and God knows you've said it in your head often enough ... oh, tell me!" he commanded betwixt kisses as his body covered hers. Her legs parted and wrapped his waist. "I know what you want to say, so tell me! Tell me you are in love with me!"

Her hips began a primitive circular motion as of their own free will. He moved to enter her and she thrust forward to meet him, to take him into the depths of her soul.

"I'm in love with you, Valentine, oh, I'm so in love with you!" After a stabbing pain, a galaxy of stars exploded throughout her body. They cried out in unison, their bodies sliding in their mingled sweat, glistening in the pale moon.

* * *

At noon they rose and dressed. Breakfast, left at the door by his groom, remained untouched. As Valentine slid rings on his fingers, he told her of the battle. "We were at Agincourt, on the very field that history occurred, when Edward made King Louis an offer of peace," he explained. "Everyone was for it, and Louis accepted. He not only agreed, but will pay Edward fifty thousand crowns a year. He also paid a fortune in ransom for Marguerite of Anjou. She will return to her birthplace and spend the rest of her days there. However, there was one person against this treaty with France. He refused to sign."

"Who?" she asked.

"That born enemy of the French." He smiled. "Our duke of Gloucester."

Her eyes widened. "Richard opposed the king's treaty? How did Edward take it?"

"With his usual good nature, as he presented Richard another grant of estates." He shrugged into his doublet.

"I am astounded." She blinked, shaking her head. "Richard never disagreed with Edward on anything."

"Richard is coming into his own, and does not see everything Edward's way. Remember, he all but rules the north. Edward renders him a king here." He ran a comb through his hair.

"I wonder if that inclines him to become king…" She dared not finish the thought. It was tantamount to treason.

* * *

On land granted by the king in Wetherby near York, Valentine began to build a sumptuous new manor, Denysbury, meaning "Denys's Castle." She didn't reckon its magnificence until she sat with the steward and auditors to tally the exchequer. Thousands of pounds to have three hundred thousand bricks carted to Wetherby, a legion of Flemish masons to lay them, a team of builders to lay out the main house and outbuildings, in the tradition of Westminster Palace, with marble from Florence, stained glass from Venice, and tapestries of Arras. Stables, gardens, and a chapel to surround the manse. Just like Valentine, it would be a regal exemplar of nobility.

"We do not need this!" she admonished as they supped in the solar. She lifted her goblet for a sip of wine and a sparkling ruby necklace slid to her lips. He stood behind her to clasp it round her neck.

"This is not necessary, I do not need gems dripping from my neck." She stroked the teardrop-shaped ruby nestled twixt her breasts. "I do love it, but it is not necessary." She gave him a big smile.

"Nay, it is not necessary. That is the beauty of it."

Chapter Eight

"He is a little angel." Valentine and Denys leaned over the cradle to gaze upon Richard and Anne's new son Edward.

A pang of longing darkened Valentine's eyes, but nowhere did it match the emptiness in Denys's heart. Oh, how she wanted her own child. She took a moment to pray for that miracle.

Anne, suffering a slow recovery from the birth, remained bedridden. Denys visited her chambers, found her asleep, and backed out.

That left Richard, Valentine and Denys at leisure for the first time since Valentine learned who Richard's 'hideous cow' was.

"Let us fetch wine and cheese and sit out under the stars," Valentine proposed as he linked arms with the both of them. "We can jabber away the evening."

But Richard looked preoccupied—his stooped carriage of old betokened much more on his mind than jabbering. "A grave matter has just come to my attention and I am not good company tonight."

They walked down the corridor and entered Richard's private solar. He sat in a chair at the window and they sat on either side of him. "What is amiss, Richard?" Denys asked. "You can tell us."

He looked at each of them. "George."

Valentine and Denys exchanged troubled glances, knowing that name meant crisis.

"What has he done now?" Valentine folded his hands in his lap.

"For one thing, his wife is dying of consumption. But Anne must not know, she is delicate enough already. If she knew her sister soon breathes her last, she would perish." He continued to stare out the window.

"Oh, I am sorry, Richard." Denys knew Isabel's life was fraught with misery, from her marriage to George at her father's pushing to the birth of her son Edward, branded "addleheaded."

"The Duke of Burgundy has died, leaving behind his daughter Mary. As Burgundy is our biggest ally, Edward summoned a Great Council from which I returned yesterday. George was present." Richard scowled at the mention of his brother's name. "George figures in his crafty mind that ere Isabel lies cold in her grave, he will wed Mary of Burgundy to keep Burgundy in English orbit. He makes no pretense to hide his intention to use this marriage to usurp Edward's throne again."

"What of Mary of Burgundy?" Denys asked.

"Mary wants no part of it. She needs a prince, not a greedy duke. George was vexed enough by that. Now, to top it all, Bess Woodville, of course, demands Mary marry her brother Anthony. Another opportunity to advance the Woodvilles." He whistled through his teeth. "George is irascible. He ran through the palace, screaming and yelling, refusing food or drink, accusing Bess of trying to poison him. He made a right goat of himself. Edward is at the end of his rope with the lot of them." He shook his head. "I could see in his eyes his longing to escape it all, start anew and be someone else. Since his coronation I think Edward wishes he were been born common without the perils of kingship."

"So George is back in his place," Denys concluded. "Until next time."

"I doubt there will be a next time." A rare expression of fear darkened Richard's eyes. "He has done worse, much worse. He rounded up a rabble, spread word that Edward practices supernatural arts and poisons his subjects, and babbled that Edward is a bastard. If that weren't enough, he accused Isabel's former servant of poisoning his son. The servant was brought before a judge and hanged."

She clutched her chest, nearly choking.

"George wove all these feigned charges to suggest she was a Woodville accomplice," he went on. "For revenge, Bess started to drive Edward to distraction with tales of George, what an evil villain he is, recounting the many times he tried to usurp the throne. My final eve there, at the high table, Bess declared that her sons by Edward will never ascend the throne unless George is gone."

"How did they leave it?" Denys asked. "Surely Edward would not let harm come to his brother, not for the Woodvilles' sake."

Valentine sat through all this, not saying a word. He fiddled with his rings, eyes fixed to the floor.

"Bess insisted George be arrested and held in the Tower. If she gets her way, his days are numbered." Richard's voice trailed off as he lowered his head.

Denys gasped and Valentine's eyes widened as he leaned forward.

"I pleaded with Edward to give this serious thought." Richard bit his lip. "But as much as it pains him to say so, he sides with his wife. Oh, that witch!" He pounded his thighs with clenched fists.

"Now Bess's sons are one step closer to the throne." Valentine's voice droned, devoid of feeling.

Richard sat up and shot Valentine a meaningful glance. "As am I."

* * *

The minute they arrived home and stepped inside, Denys clutched Valentine's arm. "This is all most frightful." Her voice wavered.

He flicked off his cloak and removed his pourpoint and shoes as they headed for the stairs.

"Fret not, Richard knows what's best for the kingdom. Bess drives them all mad. You should know better than anyone, being raised by that witch. Richard detests the Woodvilles almost as much as you do, and with reason. They make his family's life living hell."

"Something tells me Edward isn't the only one to want George out of the way." She held her skirts and followed him upstairs.

"I do admit, he is as popular as a bubo in the armpit." He led the way to their sleeping chambers.

"Valentine, did you notice how calmly Richard takes it all?" She caught up to him and they walked side by side.

"When do you see him look anything but calm?" He glanced down at her.

"You know George's end would bring Richard's succession a step closer."

"At least Bess wouldn't be queen anymore." He gave her a half-smile.

"Do not jest, Valentine. The kingdom craws with pretenders." She shuddered, knowing too well how treacherous court could be.

"The biggest pretender of all is Henry Tudor, and he's in exile in France. He rears *his* ugly head when his mother bribes spies, but do not worry your pretty head over it. Margaret Beaufort lives at Hawarden on the Welsh border and knows her latest spying venture had best be her last, or it's the Tower for her, too. The crown is safe on Edward's steadfast head." They reached his chamber door.

"And I hope it stays that way." She faced him and rested her head on his chest. "I do not want to talk any more court affairs. Do you know what tonight is?" She looked up at him and traced her fingertips over his jawline.

"Tonight?" He shook his head. "Aside from the night our servers are off duty?"

She led him into the bedchamber. "Tonight is our six-month anniversary, and I want court affairs out of our bed, for I have other plans."

* * *

She took a leisurely bath in the cushioned tub, the warm water scented with lavender oil. As the sweet scent soothed her, her thoughts remained on Valentine and what she planned this eve. She pictured him abed, muscles relaxed, breathing calm, face peaceful and relaxed. She thrilled at the idea of sliding under the covers, teasing him into wakefulness, his warm lips parting beneath hers ... oh, she wanted to share his laughter and his troubles, to assure him that he had nowt to prove to her, were he king or commoner. She wanted him at her side when she found her family, to share his joy, his pain, his life. She savored this warm yet frightful sensation. Her heart fluttered with a discordant cadence. She'd dug far beneath his aspect and found the gentle, loving man who flooded her with warmth at every thought of him.

Her own knight of legend. Her own Galahad.

She rose from the tub and wrapped herself in the towel. "I am deeply in love with you, Valentine!" she sang softly. It didn't matter whether he heard because in a few moments, she would show him.

All was quiet when she entered her chamber. She unwound the towel and slipped on a satin nightdress, brushed her hair until it shone, dabbed lavender oil on her neck, on the insides of her knees, elbows and thighs, and stole away to his chambers. She opened the door to his inner chamber and tiptoed in. The chamber glowed in the firelight from the hearth. She stood for a moment, watching his chest rise and fall as he slept.

She crept into bed next to him and began to gentle the mat of curls on his chest, slid her hand lower and lightly scratched his inner thighs with the tips of her nails. He was naked under the coverlet. He stirred with a sleepy groan, rousing a pulsing ardor throughout her, sending an urgent fan of flames through her loins. She tore the nightdress off and whipped it across the room. He smiled sleepily and turned to face her. With a soft moan, he held out his arms and drew her into his warmth.

In the gleeds of soothing release, he clasped her hands and they caught their breaths. They lay in silence, the dying fire an orange bed of embers. The torch in the hallway cast shadowy light, mingling with morn dawning through the curtains. They talked of his family, how he wished his father could see his beauteous wife, and their hopes to find her own family.

"You may journey to the ends of the earth to find them, as long as you come home to me." I love you," he whispered.

"Oh, Valentine, it means so much for me to hear that!" She rested her head on his chest.

"Cold?" He slipped his arm around her neck, nuzzling her hair. His warm breath brought gooseflesh to the surface of her skin.

"Not anymore," she answered, her voice barely a whisper, for he lit a fire in her whenever he touched her like this.

* * *

A week later, a messenger arrived bearing Richard's standard and a note from him. George had been sentenced and executed. "My only consolation is George went as he would want to go," Richard wrote. "Drowned in a cask of Malmsey wine."

"He went with a smile, Denys," Valentine assured her, his voice dry and heavy with defeat.

They went to their chapel pray for George's soul. She closed her eyes and pictured his wily grin.

George, who'd wanted the throne so badly, he committed subversion to seize it.

George, who betrayed his own brothers.

George, whose ambition sent him to his grave.

This put Richard a step closer to the throne—with Valentine poised to reach the pinnacle of his power.

She shuddered. "Who is next?"

He drew her close. "Oh, come now, Denys. Why think someone else is doomed just because the king put an end to George's mischief?"

It was no comfort. A strange harbinger caused her to tremble. This kingdom was destined for tragedy.

George's execution was just the beginning.

Chapter Nine

Hands clasped, Valentine and Denys strolled Middleham Castle's grounds on this sunny second Tuesday after Easter. Bright daffodils and bluebells promised spring, the air sweet with primroses, May blossoms, apple, cherry, and pear blossoms from the orchards. An endless azure sky streamed with ribbons of clouds. The kingdom reveled in a two-day Hocktide festival. Valentine and Richard's tenants visited Middleham laden with eggs, and their lords catered them a feast. They enjoyed tournaments, jousting, archery, puppet shows, and minstrels played merry tunes. Striped tents topped with fluttering flags surrounded them.

A collective gasp knifed through the music and laughter. A messenger astride a horse bearing the royal standard galloped away. The surroundings silenced. Heads bowed. Ladies wept.

Denys ran to Richard and Valentine standing on the drawbridge. Valentine, his face white with surprise, embraced a weeping Richard.

"What is happened?" She wrapped an arm round Richard's shoulders. "What is it?"

Richard pulled out of their grasp and covered his eyes as if to ward off a pounding headache.

"The king is dead." Valentine's voice trembled with grief. Richard turned away and knelt at the edge of the bridge.

No. Not Uncle Ned! Her protector, her ally, the closest she had to a father. The news stunned her stock still. "Oh, Richard, I am so sorry. We all loved him so very much." *The kingdom without Uncle Ned. Oh, God save us all.*

Richard stood, excused himself and crossed the drawbridge to the inner courtyard.

Valentine knelt to the ground and retrieved a message that had slipped from Richard's hands. "This is from Lord Hastings, lifelong enemy of the Woodvilles. 'The king has left all to your protection, goods, heir, realm,'" he read to her. "'Secure the person of our sovereign Lord Edward the Fifth and get you to London.'"

"But Edward is just a boy!" She recoiled in disbelief.

"I'm sure Richard has something in mind." He spoke while re-reading the note.

"But he won't be thinking straight!" She peered down into the moat. Sunlight glinted off the water, slapping the castle wall.

"One of us will." He left her to catch up with Richard.

Still stunned, she prayed. Fear tormented her through her grief. "Oh, God," she begged, "please watch over these men."

Scenes of Uncle Ned came to her without pattern or design—her cheeks cupped in his warm hands—in gleaming armor astride his war horse, blowing her a kiss. Oh, what she'd lost, what the kingdom had lost! Dear, beloved uncle. The king they called Golden Boy.

"God help us."

The sun slid across the sky, stretching the shadows. A gentle wind played through the leaves. Time and nature marched on. The kingdom carried on as well.

Now he belonged to heaven, and to him she prayed. "Uncle, please guide them, let them not fall into enemy hands." As she lifted her face to the sun, Uncle Ned warmed her from above.

* * *

"I still don't want to accept that he's gone, Valentine." After the castle settled down for the evening. Denys shut their solar door and turned to face her husband. "What happens to the kingdom now?"

"I read you the message." He tapped his feet, words rushed, tone impatient. "They need Richard in London immediately. Parliament made him Lord Protector. Until he gets there, we have no king. This is extremely dangerous. Prince Edward is the son of Elizabeth Woodville, you know what will happen when Woodvilles wield influence over the boy."

She sat beside him. "Surely Prince Edward has councilors. They wouldn't let her anywhere near the council chambers, would they?"

"It depends who outnumbers whom." He gathered her into his arms. "Richard wants me in London with him. I must depart tomorrow morn."

She pulled away. "Whatever for?"

"As his chief advisor. He knows his faults and asked me to help." Valentine gave her an uneasy smile. "Worry not, darling. My talents complement his. Pack some raiment and follow me in a few days."

She shuddered. "I am afraid, Valentine," she admitted.

"Have faith in me. Oh, my father would be so proud. I'll finally oversee something far bigger than Yorkshire." His voice held a slight quiver.

She said no more about it and left him alone with the memory of his father.

* * *

Valentine departed with a retinue of his and Richard's retainers and followers to join Prince Edward at Stony Stratford on the way to London. Denys pulled chemises, blouses, skirts and undergarments from her wardrobe chests and packed them into trunks. But she halted every few moments as if hearing the dreadful news for the first time. Uncle Ned gone, England kingless. She stopped to stare at the wall and tears flowed. The bursts of action—Valentine's departure, Richard gathering a council—made it all dreamlike—a heart-stopping nightmare.

She said one more prayer to Uncle Ned.

* * *

She arrived in London as servants readied Burleigh House, their Chelsea townhome. Planning to visit the children in St. Giles, she stopped at the market to purchase an array of sweets and pasties, she went to Totten Orphanage by herself for the first time.

"Our angel is back! Tell us a story!" The children flocked to her, brimming with excitement. She smiled into their brightened eyes.

She sat on a wooden crate and handed out sweetmeats and pasties. They devoured the treats and awaited her tale. "I told you of King Arthur, Queen Guenevere and Merlin. They lived long ago. Now, one more special king belongs to our history. I shan't tell you a legend this time. Today my story is true, from my own fond memories. It is about a brave and fearless warrior, my late uncle, King Edward the Fourth." Never having set eyes on him while he lived, they sat rapt as if she told of fabled King Arthur.

But to Denys, he would always be Uncle Ned.

* * *

The following eve, Denys raced down the corridor of the Tower of London's White Tower towards the council chambers. A meeting had ended; council members and bishops gathered round Richard outside the chamber. Elizabeth Woodville's brother Lionel, as a council member and Bishop of Salisbury, clamored for Richard's attention. Edward Woodville, commander of the Woodville fleet, elbowed his way up to Richard. An array of guards, liveried nobles and hangers-on stood nearby.

She approached Richard and when he finished his discussion with the group around him, she tapped his shoulder. "I must see you right now."

He turned to face her, eyes sullen and troubled, his brow creased, as if warding off the remains of a nightmare. His black mourning attire darkened his eyes, dulled his complexion and cast a somber mood over his entire being. He did not want to be here; she knew it.

A guard closed the inner council chamber door, leaving them alone. Books, papers and ink horns lay scattered on the table, mappae pinned to the walls. One object in glittering contrast to the chamber's starkness caught her eye. She could not halt the gasp that escaped her lips. Atop a pillow in regal splendor on a sideboard sat the crown of England.

"Richard, what is this?" She gestured round the chamber. "Where is Bess? Where is Prince Edward?"

"My nephew the prince is safely secluded in the Garden Tower and Bess Woodville is even safer … or should we say the kingdom is safer. She is in sanctuary in the Abbot's lodgings at Westminster with her other children. But not before naming herself Queen Regent." His voice turned bitter as if her name left a sour taste in his mouth.

Her jaw dropped. "Bess named herself Queen Regent?"

"Aye, but she could call herself Queen of the Nile for all it matters." He sank into the polished wooden chair Uncle Ned had used as king. It seemed to swallow Richard up.

She took the chair beside him. "Richard, I am fearful for you and my husband. All these advisors clamoring about you and Valentine, some pressing you to take the throne, others backing the Woodvilles. Loyalty means nowt to these men. They will turn on you before your very eyes." Her voice broke with a sob.

"Look at history. The last King Richard, a boy king, had his uncle murdered when he came of age. Boy King Henry the Sixth's Lord Protector was murdered. Worst of all, both were dukes of Gloucester! Don't let it happen thrice. Put Prince Edward on his throne and come back to Yorkshire."

He cut his hand through the air. "Cease the superstitious babble, you sound like that bloody soothsayer Bess had mixing love potions for her ugly sisters. We do not live history. We are here and now. Lest you forget Prince Edward is half Woodville?" Richard's voice lowered, tinged with resignation. "I dare not return to Yorkshire leaving Bess Woodville sway over that boy. Our lives and lands are in peril."

As she remembered Valentine saying those exact words, her insides churned in fear. "Court crawled with Woodvilles during Uncle Ned's entire reign, they had their pox-ridden fleet in place, Bess was as contriving as ever, and he handled it all. You can certainly keep them at bay."

He shook his head. "'Tis not so simple. There is no telling how they will bend and sway a boy of twelve. Do you see that Woodvilles make up a great part of the council? Not to mention the bishops. The clergy has been pro-Woodville since Henry the Sixth."

"And how much control do they really have at this moment?" She feared the answer.

"For starters, their little navy, formed, they claim, to protect us from French pirates, is growing. Edward Woodville gathers more ships as we speak." He let out a mocking laugh. "Oh, and you should hear him defend his arse in council. What a load of tripe. 'We must protect our realm from invaders, protect the coast towns and merchant shipping!'" he aped Edward Woodville's thready voice. "Does he play me for an idiot? I know bloody well he fills those ships with his own men. What a jest, they think they're seamen now."

"What does Anne say about all this?" she wondered out loud.

"'Tis not her place to say aught," Richard stated, his tone stern.

"Have you no thought for her concern over your fate? How she must want you home?" Her voice gained volume as vexation tightened her chest.

"She is on her way here as we speak. 'Tis a blessing she is quiet on the matter. To have her prate in addition to all you lot would addle me no end."

"I beg you, Richard," she pleaded. "Oversee Woodville treachery and the Woodville fleet from the north."

He made a fist and pounded the chair arm, his ring rapping on the wood. "I am here because my brother wanted me here. I respect his wish. I served him in life and I serve him still in death. He made me Lord Protector of his Realm, on paper embossed with the royal seal, but in our moments of private conversation, he spoke from the heart. He told me what he wants."

"He had no idea he would die so suddenly," she argued. "No one did."

"He did not want the kingdom to slip into Woodville hands. He had serious reservations about his sons being able to rule justly while Bess and her family still lived." He glanced at the crown across the chamber. His eyes lingered on it longer than she thought they should.

"When Prince Edward is crowned, your protectorship ends," she told him what she was sure he already knew.

"We shall see," he said in a curious manner. "And though Woodville allies be few and far between, they are formidable. Do you know what Margaret Beaufort did?"

She shook her head.

"She paid someone to pinch the Great Seal and take it to Bess, with just about everything else they could pilfer from the palace, including half the royal treasure." He stared her down with a countenance of wild-eyed lust for power. "Margaret Beaufort holds a distant claim to the throne. She may attempt to make it hers or for her son Henry Tudor. She covets the throne as badly as Bess, mayhap more."

"You mean she may finance yet another army for Henry Tudor to try and usurp the throne yet again? With all this going on?" The mere thought struck her as folly.

"I know not if it'll be Henry Tudor or just another ugly Lancastrian lot. But all hell can break loose and all the faster if I trot off to Yorkshire." He dropped his head into his hands and rubbed his temples.

She saw his solemn predicament, the painful decisions he must make, how quickly time ran out. No longer lord of his northern marches, Richard now carried the burden of the entire realm on his shoulders. And it showed.

She turned away to gaze out the window, at the river streaming with barges and trading vessels, farther afield at the stretch of marsh to Battersea and the blue-green Surrey hills beyond. Threatening clouds hovered over them. She felt trapped twixt elements unknown, at the mercy of whichever way this storm blew.

"Take one step at a time. Do not talk of thrones and pretenders yet," Richard added. "'Tis too early to know. I am here, that is the important thing, and I will not leave."

"And it all will go to your reckoning?" She turned to face him. "You don't have the command over life that you think."

"It may not fall into place the way I wish, hard though I will try." His look of feared defeat confirmed that. "Our parts are cast from the day we are born. 'Tis in the stars, since the dawn of time man has known that. 'Tis the way we fit into divine order. Whatever's meant for us happens whether we want it or not. I am summoned here for a reason. 'Tis my supernal fate to be here now, and I shall not defy that fate."

"I don't believe in stars or astrology," she countered. "I believe in free will and I use it. I make the decisions, I am not ruled by fates or Babylonian phantasy. You're in no hands but your own." She knew full well Richard could easily control his own life.

"Enough has gone amiss in my life, things happen beyond all control." He turned to gaze out the window.

"With all respect, they only go amiss when you let them," she relayed the cold truth as she saw it.

"Oh, really? Then you willed Bess upon yourself? And were you not most willfully against Valentine Starbury? And I let my father die?" He turned to face her. "Nay, thank the bloody Lancastrians for that!"

"We all die, Richard. It's part of the cycle. We go to heaven in the end, no matter which path takes us there. Some of us lose parents, some outlive our brothers and children."

He gave a solemn nod as his hands shook. Oh, how she wished they could escape this terrible predicament!

"Am I not trying to do what is right for this kingdom?" he beseeched. "I understand your fears, I know you are deathly afraid. But I cannot afford that. I cannot run away. I cannot be fearful. I must crush the Woodvilles and thwart all rebels, be it Margaret Beaufort or her pock-faced son." He stood and smoothed his doublet. "I must go, I have work to do."

She stood and turned to leave. "Very well, but please tread carefully. Watch them all."

"They are busy enough watching one another." Her childhood friend, now the most powerful man in the kingdom, quit the chamber.

* * *

Sir Valentine, dressed like royalty, knocked on Burleigh House's front door. The usher let him in as Denys rushed up to him and fell into his arms. "Oh, I am so happy to see you, my darling!" They shared a loving kiss and headed to the solar.

As they sat down to dinner the steward served wine and her favorite blueberry mead. "What happened in Council? How is Richard?" She took a sip of mead and savored its sweetness.

"Parliament proclaimed him Lord Protector of the Realm, as per Edward's will." He sipped his wine.

"And you?" She unfolded her serviette and placed it on her lap.

"He made me his chief advisor for the time being." He sipped his wine.

"For the time being? The only rank above that is king." A server brought brown bread and swirls of butter.

He dismissed the hovering server and buttered his bread. "This all happens fast enough. Don't rush things, please." He took a bite of bread.

"But you enjoy all the intrigue, don't you?" she goaded, though she knew the enormous responsibility thrust upon him showed and replaced his callowness of unfettered youth.

He scraped his chair back and went to the open window. He blocked out all light except the glow around his figure.

She turned to face him. "This is what I dread, ever since Richard got the news of Uncle Ned's death and rushed you to court with him. We'll never see our beloved home again." Tears of longing sprang to her eyes as she pictured her lovely garden, those purple moors. London had none of it. London only brought back bitter memories of court mischief, back-stabbing and powermongers. Now they too were trapped in it.

"Cease all dread, Denys." He approached her and placed his hands on her shoulders. "Ponder the good. With Richard as Lord Protector, we are royal courtiers and may have any castle, any manor, any lands we wish. We have a retinue second only to the royals themselves. Court banquets and feasts are ours to attend. You and myself at the high table instead of Woodvilles. It will be me who rides through town to the blasts of clarions and trumpets." He shut his eyes and displayed a dreamy smile. "Silks, ermine and sable, cloth of gold and silver, sparkling jewels on your fingers and around your beauteous neck."

He approached her but she pushed him away and hid her face behind her goblet. "I want none of that. I want to go back to Yorkshire, to our home, the only realm I love. I do not want Westminster Palace and all its gilt and flash. I care not for jewels and banquets and royal trappings. Or dare I say 'traps'?"

"Well, it is what I want." He thrust his thumb at his chest. "Since age nine when I lost my father, I longed to live the life he never lived, to attain what he fought for but never lived to see. Now is my chance to make him proud of me—" He paused, then said in a somber tone, "and to make you proud of me."

Servers brought their first course, bowls of lampreys in galytyne. Valentine took his seat across from her.

"I am already proud of you!" she affirmed. "I am proud that you govern Yorkshire."

"This I must do, Denys. Just as you must find your family. I'll never be king, so this is my chance for greatness. This is my quest."

"It scares me so." She could barely speak, her mouth dry with fear. "We already have the Lancastrians as enemies. Henry Tudor strives for the crown and his mother spies on the court. The Woodvilles are power hungry as ever. Now Richard moves in on the throne with you at his side. Why couldn't he leave us in Yorkshire?"

"He needs me," came his simple answer, with no trace of conceit.

"I know it too well." She dipped her spoon into her bowl but had little appetite.

"My father's last words to me were 'Give back to the kingdom, something noble.'" He spoke as if to God, in a tone she'd never heard before. His voice rumbled, sending a chill up her spine. "Now is my chance." He took up his spoon and swirled it round his bowl.

"Valentine, I know you want to pay him homage. But you already do that so beauteously. I'm sure he didn't mean you to a martyr—or a saint."

"Nay, although sainthood is all well and good. Saints make most beloved leaders. We mortals have worshiped them throughout history. Yet they make paltry husbands. And tedious, stale, lifeless lovers." The last wedge of light faded as a groom entered to kindle a fire in the hearth. "They are humble..." Valentine's spoon clinked against the bowl. "...and monkish..."

She put her serviette down, stood, went round the table and sat upon his lap.

"It will all work out, I promise." His hands began to unlace her bodice. "You have nowt to fear, I shall always look after you."

And oh, how she wanted to believe that no harm would befall any of them. Yet the slightest disagreement twixt Valentine and Richard could destroy them all. They had so many enemies. How she hoped the delicate balance would be upheld. The entire kingdom depended on it.

Servers brought dinner on silver trays, eyes averting the embracing couple oblivious of their meal. "Leave it," Valentine instructed and turned back to her. "My love, I will give you a life fit for a queen." They stood and he led her to the cushioned window-seat overlooking the garden. The sun's fading rays limned the petals, darkened the green leaves and silver birch, and cast burnt orange tones on the walls.

"No more talk of court affairs tonight. Talk to me of love." She searched his lips with hers. Her hands ranged over his arms.

His eyes pinned her as never before, searing her soul. "You're the woman I love. Please never leave me. I could not survive alone. My animal instincts would best me. For that is what men are. Animals. Fighting, gorging, spitting beasts. I need you to keep me tame."

"Making love keeps you tame? You become a wilder man than I can picture in battle." She stroked his cheek.

"I simply perform my marriage duties," he stated with a straight face.

"I was never instructed in those duties, my lord. Not even by Bess Woodville." She rolled on top of him.

"You have a wondrous natural talent for it."

* * *

Next morn, a squire handed Valentine a note from the cloistered Elizabeth Woodville to celebrate her daughter's sixteenth birthday. The note stated the child's wish to see Denys also. He grinned as an idea popped into his head. He woke Denys and told her about the message.

"I will not go." She nestled under the coverlet. "I have nowt to say to Bess Woodville. We spoke our last when she sent me away."

"Do you mind if I go?" He spread her hair over the pillow.

"What do you care about her daughter?" She opened one eye and looked at him. "And why see Bess? Have you not seen enough of her cruelty and deception? She wants something, Valentine, she would not ask us to go simply because she enjoys our company."

"Young Elizabeth is but a child, a helpless cub caught in a bear trap. 'Twould do her the world of good to have company. But, yes, you share my sentiments exactly. She is not the only one who can want something. I want something from the queen, and I intend to get it." He kissed Denys on the cheek and turned to leave.

"Wait!" She reached out from under the coverlet and snatched at his tunic. "What are you going to do?"

"I will beat that old hag at her own game." With a sly grin he strode out of the chamber.

Denys could not go back to sleep. She tossed and turned, stomach churning with fear that he asked for trouble, involving himself so closely in this struggle for the crown. She rang for her lady-in-waiting to bring breakfast and fill a bath. She would prevail on him to return to Yorkshire with her, but this time move him by the needs of his own subjects rather than the tumults of this sundered court.

* * *

"Your highness, we are honored to be asked here. But Denys is not well." Valentine bowed before the deposed queen by dower, brooding on a nest of cushions like an overaged hen. "It has been a long time. I hope we can forgive past quarrels."

"Taking my niece off my hands more than makes up for any quarrel we had, Valentine." She raked her eyes over him. "Much has happened since then." Wisps of gray hair escaped her headdress and floated around her head like strands in a spider web.

Young Elizabeth appeared and Valentine bowed to her. "Lady Elizabeth, you look ravishing. My, you grow more beauteous each birthday, and I daresay after another sixteen you will be twice as beauteous as you are now."

Young Elizabeth's figure was slender, no bumps, few curves. She was quite boyish but for the wavy blonde hair tumbling down her back, her peevish pout the only feature Valentine found appealing.

With a mirthful laugh she sat on a wooden stool and spread her skirts around her.

Elizabeth Woodville's other children attended along with her remaining hangers-on. They regarded Valentine with suspicion, knowing him to be Richard's closest friend.

During the modest meal of venison stew, Valentine noticed young Elizabeth made eyes at him and pouted when he glanced her way. After a lone server cleared the table, Elizabeth Woodville led him to an outer chamber.

"Valentine," she employed a tone last heard to beguile her husband into raiding the treasury for another trunkload of sable pelts, "The duke of Gloucester pledged allegiance to my son Edward and as you know, set his coronation date for the twenty-third of May."

"He has, your highness." Valentine proceeded with caution, for he refused to divulge particulars discussed with Richard in the council chamber.

"Our own council has ordered my son's coronation date be the fourth of May," she declared, pinning him with her eyes.

"Your council?" Valentine blinked, astonished. There was no true council until Richard gathered one in the name of Edward V. Her council was not only unlawful, twas a product of her imagination.

"My son will be an extraordinary king, as was my Golden Boy, will he not?" She gave him a malicious grin.

"Oh, he has inherited King Edward's benevolence, his courtly charm and his ability to beguile people, I have seen Prince Edward with his many admirers." He nodded.

"Traits which Gloucester sorely lacks." Her lips tightened, exposing deep creases. She refused to refer to Richard as Lord Protector or even duke, brazenly slighting his titles.

"He is Lord Protector," Valentine said it for her.

"Not for long. As soon as my son is crowned, he is naught but another soldier."

"The duke of Gloucester's talents lie more in the direction of his army on the field, your highness," he corrected her.

She cleared her throat. "With Lancastrians snapping at our heels, we need every soldier we can muster."

"And all our generals," he added.

Unheeding that, she continued, "As Edward's mother, I wield enormous power when my son is king. I stand beside him to ensure every decision is in the realm's best interest."

In greedy Woodville interests, you mean, he itched to say, but kept quiet and let her prate. He burned with curiosity—*what does she want from me?*

"I shall bestow titles on loyal subjects as I choose, with the king's consent, of course. Edward looks up to you as a most chivalrous knight. He always thrilled at your jousting and your practe at the quintain, as did all my little ones, but Edward was always the most impressed," she flattered.

"Why, that is high praise indeed, your highness," he replied in all sincerity.

"You enjoy your position as governor of Yorkshire, do you not?" she pressed.

"Aye, your highness, very much. I have captured the hearts of many of our subjects," he boasted, knowing Elizabeth used flattery as bait to ensnare.

"But that is scant reward for a great knight. Think of the glory a relative of the king is booned."

"Relative?" he echoed, confused.

"Denys is my niece. You are a member of the Royal Family upon my son's coronation. Think of the riches we can bestow. After all, only half the treasure is currently in our possession. We have yet to procure the other half."

Her intentions were now clear—to drive a wedge betwixt him and Richard. "We includes me, your highness?"

"A simple question, Valentine. What do you prefer, to be treasurer of the royal chamber or governor of Yorkshire?" Eyes of steel bored into him and he returned the intense stare with his own. He smiled to acknowledge her offer, but inside he seethed. The nerve of her, to think he could be bought, that he would betray his lifelong friend to set her twelve-year-old child on the throne!

She clearly had no idea how folk in the north respected him and Richard. She'd never ventured north of Warwick.

Same old Elizabeth Woodville, thinking to buy anyone she pleased, if not with money, with favors. But this time it would come back to bite her bony arse—and a large bite at that.

"So, your highness, you ask me to procure for you the other half of the royal treasure, and in return you will make me treasurer of the royal chamber among other boons?"

"For now." She gave a one-shoulder shrug. "You can strike your handsome countenance on a coin. Just think—your own likeness jingling inside pockets and purses all over England."

"Why, I am astounded, your highness. To be chosen for such a worthy position ... right next to the king." He forced a flattered tone as he inwardly cringed with loathing.

"Edward's coronation marks a new passage in our history, a new beginning. As such, I shall start my life anew with my family about me in my old age, I want to bury painful memories and make amends to any I wronged. That includes my dear niece Denys. All I ask is that you aid me attain that amity."

He'd heard enough. His heart pounded as he saw the perfect opening for his own ploy. But it must be couched in terms she understood. Greed and self-interest. Pleas from the heart would fall on deaf ears. He must put on a great pretense. Without skipping a beat, he put down his own marker. "Your highness, I am honored at the chance to serve Edward as king and be a member of the royal family in such an exalted capacity. But I see a fly in the ointment. I must ask a favor of my own."

"And what is that?" She raised a plucked brow.

"I must know Denys's line of descent. As her husband, I am entitled to know who you chained me to. If she is the bastard daughter of some mischance rut, I can never be royal. I must be satisfied who she really is before I can serve Edward." Oh, how those necessary lies pained his heart.

"I know not of her family." As Elizabeth spoke, he noticed her sagging chin, her fading beauty.

"Then tell me who gave her to you. Only then can I be sure of my part in your proposition." He kept his voice calm.

"So this is contingent upon you knowing her family?" She bobbed her head like a bird of prey.

"Only with true information from your highness. 'Tis only fair," he bargained on. "How else can I weigh the value of this enforced marriage to me?"

"You won't consider it otherwise? Even though I hand you the highest position at court?" She placed a fist on her hip.

He almost laughed. She had no court to speak of. And if his and Richard's efforts came to fruition, she would never set foot in court again. She did not yet know him to be Richard's closest advisor. It all happened so suddenly.

"Nay, your highness." He sliced the air with his hands. "I cannot consider your proposition until you reveal who you took her from. I must be sure of her royal stead."

She clucked and clacked and sucked at her remaining teeth. "I cannot tell you because I do not know myself," she finally replied, her tone defeated.

Valentine stared her in the eye. She looked away and twisted her pearls.

"Your highness, you have information and I know you do. There is no need for deceit and foot-dragging. It is in our common interest that I be sure of her family. Only then can I do all in my power to secure Edward's throne."

"You serve yourself well," Elizabeth admitted with grudging admiration. "Mayhap I married my niece better than I thought."

"Your highness, we are too old for secrecy and lies."

"Tell that to your friend Gloucester," she shot back.

"We discuss Denys, your highness." He got back to the point.

"Ah, yes, Denys. The only person in the realm with problems. Denys, who whirls the world by the culls, yet is so sad she knows no kin. Poor little thing. Why not pillage my trunks again and see what else you can find?" A wicked gleam shone in her eyes.

"May I? Oh, thank you! Do tell where they are, I shall start with trunk Number One." Valentine bent forward in a mock-sweeping bow.

She raised her arm, palm open, as if to slap him. "I know it was you, you popinjay." She actually smiled. "But there was no royal offer on the table then, so how did my niece get you to do it?" The smile still on her lips did not reach her cold hard eyes.

The claustrophobic panic of a trap halted Valentine's breath. Hoping she didn't notice his momentary falter, he gathered his wits and resumed their verbal joust. "Twas my own doing. I needed to know if Denys was worth my woo and what lands and estates might become mine."

She hesitated as she weighed his answer and finally nodded.

He hid his satisfied grin behind his hand. Ah yes, self-interest and greed she saw as no fault.

"Oh, very well." She waved her hand through the air. "I approve of your determination, so like my own." Her voice sweetened, but still grated on his nerves. "Is it not enough your children will know *they* are royal, accepted by me, the queen?"

"I have a right to know who Denys is, and be sure of our bargain," he stated bluntly.

A spark lit her stormy gray eyes. "Go to Bishop Stillington. He has all kinds of information. That is all I can tell you. And for that you should be grateful," she chirped, eminently pleased with herself. "He lives at the foot of London Bridge on Thames Street. You may use my barge. But you must wait until the morrow. They are making repairs to it."

"Thank you, your highness. I shall seek him straightaway. But I can't use the royal barge. It wouldn't feel right, not yet being proven royalty. However, I thank you for your offer. And long live King Edward the Fifth!" He lowered his gaze and bowed out of the room, turning quickly so she would not see his spreading grin. "I've got the old witch now," he mumbled, skipping down the hallway.

Like an adder, Elizabeth's instinct for self-preservation lay coiled and ready to strike. He had impressed her with his words but something was amiss. The honeyed lilt when he spoke Denys's name belied his play. "That ingrate bastard will never find out who she is," she proclaimed. "She is about to become a widow. That is the last anyone will ever see of Gloucester's right hand, Valentine Starbury. He thinks himself so clever. But no one betrays Queen Elizabeth of England." She retrieved several gold pieces from the hole dug into the wall for the filched royal treasure. She summoned her lady-in-waiting. "Hold out your hand. Take these." She dropped the coins into the astounded maid's palm with delicate clinks. "Run to my boatman, give him these." She handed the maid five more coins. "Point out Valentine Starbury to him, and tell him to scuttle whichever barge he takes to cross the Thames ... render a small enough hole so it will not sink till halfway downriver to London Bridge."

Elizabeth rubbed her hands in glee. The disarrayed old Bishop Stillington could barely hear, much less remember who birthed whom. But it mattered not. Valentine would never reach the dotard's house. He would pay for his false bargain with a Woodville—with his life.

* * *

Valentine stood on the riverbank with the crowd awaiting barges to take them down or crossriver. The massive London Bridge spanned the Thames, London's main waterway. It also served as a street, clogged with shops and crowded houses. From where he stood he couldn't see the traitors' parboiled heads spiked atop the bridge, but he knew Richard would abolish that grim tradition when he became king.

He approached the nearest barge and tipped his hat to the boatman. "Why such a throng here?"

"Ebb tide, my lord. Currents are too strong to cross. Come back in a bit 'n I'll take ye over." The smaller boats bobbed about as the current swirled round the bridge's piers.

Valentine thanked him and took respite at a riverfront tavern until ebb tide abated.

An hour hence, he quit the tavern, glutted with savory meat pie and ale.

He returned to the waiting boatman who helped him aboard. "To the home of Bishop Stillington at the foot of London Bridge." The boatman's bulging muscles strained as he plunged the bargepole into the water and launched the barge. Valentine settled back to enjoy the ride.

After a few minutes it seemed the river had swelled; he attributed that to high tide. But he then remembered the tide had just ebbed. It couldn't rise this fast. Feeling dampness in the bottom of his shoes, he found them soaked. The drenched moss inside thickened round his feet like mud. "Hey!" he signaled the boatman. Valentine stood as water surged on the port side, behind the boatman's seat.

The hole at the bottom of the barge broke open. Gushing water deluged the barge. He lost all sight of the boatman. Swirling water tugged his body under. The barge swayed and rocked like a storm-tossed buoy. Valentine clung to the side. Waves pounded his face like vicious fists of anger. He watched helplessly as the boatman washed overboard, screaming as he plunged beneath the swirling tumult.

The barge drifted wildly, caught in the current that tried to tug him into the watery depths. The barge whirled and smashed into the bridge's pilings. The force of the collision threw him face down on the barge's floor. Gasping for air, he groped blindly for something to hold onto. Another foamy rush of water surged through the barge's gaping hull. It began to overturn, sliding bow first into the river. He sprang to his feet, the bridge's stone parapet a few feet away. If only he could reach it...

The barge surged and tossed, shattering on the pilings with violent thrusts. Through misty eyes he saw someone atop the stone parapet reach out to him.

He dove over the side of the sinking barge and swam for his life, his muscles straining to fight the forceful current. His feet flailed like the tailfins of a minnow escaping the teeth of a pike. With the last trace of wind left in him, he reached the parapet and the misty figure trying to reach him.

He leapt into open arms, chest smacked chest, but the force of the current dragged him back, out of his rescuer's grasp.

Gulping precious air, he hung from the parapet, gripping the rough stone, fingers about to break. He felt a tug on his arms as hands reached down for one more desperate pull to safety. Tumbling against his rescuer, Valentine choked, coughing up water. Two men dropped a rope from the drawbridge and it fell between them. They looped the rope round Valentine's waist as floating barge fragments whirled beneath his hanging legs. They heaved Valentine to safety atop the drawbridge and laid him down. Someone threw a blanket over him. Utterly spent, he blacked out the world.

* * *

He opened his eyes to a tangle of white hair and wizened eyes fraught with concern. "Wha … what happened?" His voice drowning in liquid, he spat up water. The old man before him held out a cloth.

"You nearly drowned, lad. My physicians looked you over, declared you past recovery. I'll save last rites for some poor soul who's not so lucky."

"Who … who are you?" he rasped.

"Why, I be Bishop Stillington. Your barge foundered apart right behind me house."

"Your excellency," he burbled words and water together.

"That's right, let it up." He patted Valentine on the back. "Next time, spit onto these cloths on the floor. Now stay in bed and say not another word until your voice dries out."

"Tell Denys…" A wave of weariness swept over him and he slid back into unconsciousness.

Able to sit up next day, he entreated the bishop to send a message to his wife. "Tell her I survived a sunken barge, worry not, but please come the second you finish reading this!"

* * *

The messenger arrived after Denys left that morn to bring food to the poor of Whitechapel and re-tell the story of King Edward. She supposed Valentine had sat up all night with Richard making plans…

* * *

After four slices of gammon, three boiled eggs, two slabs of buttered bread and a pint of ale, Valentine gained renewed strength in his battered body. Now to find His Excellency and discuss what he'd come for. He peered out the bedchamber window at Bishop Stillington in his walled garden, twisting a pear off a branch.

He gnawed at it, spat, and pitched the uneaten part to the ground. A terrier dashed after it.

Valentine pushed the window open. "Your Excellency, may I have a word?" he called down to the bishop. Stillington looked round as if he couldn't fathom where the voice came from. He scratched his head, shrugged, and plucked another pear.

"Up here!"

Stillington looked up, saw Valentine and headed inside. When he entered the chamber and approached the bed, Valentine saw him clearly for the first time. Trusting blue eyes looked at him from behind the film of cataracts. He looked like a shy billygoat about to mate for the first time. "I want to thank you for taking care of me. I am the duke of Norwich, our Lord Protector's close advisor."

Stillington nodded, but Valentine wasn't sure he'd heard or even knew who the Lord Protector was.

"The duke of Gloucester is lord protector," Valentine clarified.

"Hell's teeth, I know, do you think I live at the edge of the world here, my lad?" He chuckled, his voice laced with mirth. "Ye had a close call out there, ye be lucky ye take water so well. The other poor sod perished."

"I am deeply grateful, Your Excellency, and shall do anything in my power to thank you." He clasped the bishop's hands.

"Teach me to swim like you, lad." He gave Valentine a toothless grin.

Valentine laughed. "Your Excellency, I sought you out and was coming here. My wife Denys is seeking her family and I hope you may hold a clew as to who sired her. She was given to the Woodvilles in infancy. Queen Elizabeth raised her as a niece."

"Woodvilles? Elizabeth?" He snorted. "That catzo, I be glad to see her put in her place."

Valentine blinked, unsure he heard correctly. "Is she aware of your contempt, Your Excellency? 'Tis she who sent me here."

"She is oblivious to all contempt, thinks everyone, top to bottom, should kiss her corybungo. I know naught of your wife's parentage." He shook his head. "I had some birth records and such. I used a few for kindling to keep me bones warm. I have a trunk full of patent rolls and such. Ye are welcome to search it, when ye are mended."

"Can you bring them to me?" Valentine's heart raced. "I need something to do whilst I regain my rigor."

* * *

Denys rushed to the bishop's house. "Is he all right, Your Excellency?" She peered over his shoulder for her husband. "Why is he here?"

"Seeking your kin." Bishop Stillington polished a pear.

She gasped.

"He survived a mishap. His barge foundered and near sucked the whole Thames up into it." The bishop made a waving motion with his hands.

"Oh, Jesu!" Her heart surged. "Where is he?"

"Sleeping like a babe." He held a finger to his lips. "Shhh. Let him be."

"Let me look in on him, please!" She leapt the stairs two at a time and peered into the darkened chamber in which he slept. She approached the bed.

"My darling," she whispered. "You get well soon now. I shall visit every day until you recover and be waiting when you come home."

He stirred and opened his eyes. They lit up when he saw her.

"Darling, how do you feel?" She leaned over and embraced him.

"A bit addleheaded, as if I imbibed too much cheer." His words came slow and unsteady. "I don't remember knocking my head but there's a knot the size of my fist on my brainpan."

"Did a physician see you?" She smoothed hair from his forehead.

"Aye, the bishop summoned his. He said I need a few days' rest." He glanced round. "Are a few days up yet?"

"Nay, it was only yesterday. How did you get here? The bishop said you sought my kin."

"Bess told me to come here," he said. "It was during the river crossing that the barge foundered. It had a hole in the hull."

She recoiled as if stung. "Why talk to her about me?"

"I went to make her relent and tell me who gave you to her. 'Twas to be a surprise for you." A coughing fit interrupted his words.

"Valentine, have I not told you time and again she tries most damnably to keep it from me! I would be not a bit surprised if she deliberately rent the hull of that barge. Please, Valentine, she is ruthless, stay clear of her."

"I know that. And she knows I know. I did not go to her as a callow youngling surmising she would happily reveal your parentage. As I thought, she offered bribes, treasurer of the royal chamber, a vast sum, and my likeness struck on a coin if I procured the rest of the royal treasure for her and join the Woodville faction. I refused until she provided something for me first. I told her I would join Edward, secure him on the throne, remain loyal to him as king, and deliver the royal treasure only if she would give me the knowledge she keeps from you. She led me to the bishop, but alas he burned his birth records. She well may have scuttled the barge, but she could not scuttle me. I am an excellent a swimmer, unlike the poor boatman who swirled under to his death. It took all I had to save myself."

"Another death! Has she no heart at all, not even of stone?" Denys clenched her fists and stamped her foot. "Stay away from her, Valentine, please."

"Now you see why Richard wants no son of hers to be king?" he asked.

"As long as she lives, I do." She nodded.

She cradled his head in her arms until he fell asleep, then slipped out of the Bishop's house with a promise to return after vespers.

* * *

Bishop Stillington entered Valentine's bedchamber that eve carrying a small wooden casket. Valentine eased the worn lid open to reveal sheaves of torn and yellowed papers. His spirits plunged. What could be of import in here? But with nowt else to do, and no strength for the journey home, he began to sort them.

He scanned each document without interest. Finally his weary eyes lighted on the names Edward Plantagenet and Lady Eleanor Butler. He could not believe what he was reading. His heart began to pound. He read it again under close scrutiny, out loud, to verify 'twas no dream.

Old Bess had diverted him here to keep her secret, unknowing of an even bigger one to be found in this place.

He pounded on the floor, summoning a server to fetch the bishop.

The bishop, panting and wheezing, entered the chamber.

"Your Excellency, you must see this!" He waved the document through the air.

Stillington plucked it from Valentine's hand, held it at arm's length and bobbed his head like a rooster looking it up and down. "Ah, the patent rolls from when King Edward was but a lad. This changes things for certes. I forgot I had it."

Stillington read a passage aloud and Valentine sat up in bed, breathless as when his rescuers dragged him out of the Thames.

"This is a troth-plight from Edward Plantagenet to Lady Eleanor Butler, before he married Elizabeth Woodville. They did exchange vows right under my nose, they did indeed. Lady Butler was a widow, quite young, in fact, at the time." He looked at Valentine over the top of the parchment. "Aye, lad, good King Edward was not legally married to that old Woodville scold at all, not at all. He already had a wife. That putative prince of hers is no more fit to be king than my terrier doing his four-legged prance out there in the garden."

"But this is amazing." Valentine stared at the document in wonder. "Why did this never—"

"Oh, his grace did pay me for my silence in his lifetime. And so I forgot it through his lifetime. Old age took most of my memory and now I just be an old man who burns all I can glean to keep warm. It be a miracle this paper survives. 'Tis twenty year old and a bit, I should say."

"You say you promised King Edward you'd not speak of this in his lifetime," Valentine said. "But now that life has left him—"

"If this be made public, it changes the course of history, lad. We steer the crown of England with our own hands." He held out his hands, bony and slightly atremble. "Well, mayhap not my hands..."

"But do you not see what the Woodvilles have wrought on this kingdom? We're at the brink of war!" Valentine shook his fist.

"Ho, ye need not tell me." His tongue played with a loose bottom tooth. "I would see that Woodville scold and her bastard issue sail through Traitors' Gate afore anyone in this kingdom."

Valentine broke in, "Then you agree the Lord Protector must know of this."

"Aye, he'll know what to do. Heh, heh. This be good as the crown upon his head. Aye, I shall accompany you to the Lord Protector but not afore you recover."

"I am recovered!" Valentine struggled to sit up.

Stillington lowered Valentine back down onto the pillows. "Recovered? Tallywags! Stay abed yet. You get up and start playing silly buggers, you'll be right here flat on yer back like a plaguer."

Heedless, Valentine leapt out of bed. "Nay, we must go now!" A wave of dizziness dazed him and he crumpled to the floor.

Two servers lifted him and laid him on the bed, pressed a cool cloth to his head and covered him with blankets, for he'd begun to shiver.

He awoke next morn with a renewed surge of strength after breaking fast with more bacon, eggs, fresh brown bread and ale. Valentine secured the precious document in the satchel Stillington had given him. Fully dressed in the ill-fitting but elegant tabard, cloak and hose the bishop provided, he found His Excellency in the solar breaking his fast.

"What are you doing up and about..." He stood and tried to wave him out. "Get ye back to bed, lad!"

"I am fit, Your Excellency, we must take this document to the Lord Protector forthwith! Except we will not go by barge if you do not mind." They left the house and mounted two of Stillington's palfreys.

Valentine tugged on the reins. "To the Tower of London!" The sheet of parchment rose and fell under his cloak with every beat of his hammering heart.

Chapter Ten

Denys entered the Great North Door of the magnificent Westminster Abbey.

Since her first visit at age four, the resplendent shrine enchanted her. The Great North Door's gaping arches soared high, flanked by stone pillars, beaten by age into a rustic beauty. Subdued light spilled through rows of arched windows on either side of The Nave, caressing each corner and fold of every carved tomb. The hollow recesses of intricate design allowed radiant fragments to peek from the shadows in immortal splendor.

She gazed up at the arched ceiling's fan vaulting. Her feet whispered over smooth stone slabs carved with names and lifespans of the long dead whose bones reposed in the vaults below—kings, queens, and royal infants carried away with their first breaths. The ancient carvings danced in time with the pulsing heartbeat of hovering spirits. Chapels branched from The Nave, graced with the same haunting beauty. The glow of flickering candles hurled ghostly movements on the shadowy carvings. Twixt the towering pillars, the walls bore carved images of the immortals, eyes staring blankly into eternity. Marble figures rested on their backs with hands clasped toward heaven atop splendid tombs, prayers in Latin chiseled into their marble coffins. The stained glass windows glowed in tones of ruby, sapphire, and emerald.

She felt so small within these ancient walls that enshrined her beginnings and those of her countrymen. Yet she savored the joy of living enclosed within centuries of death. She inhaled the musty stillness of age. The air reposed peacefully, surrounding her with age-old godliness. Drawing breath, she tasted its invisible yet mighty strength and heavy closeness. She wandered these elaborate tombs, to read about lives left behind. Her fingertips glided over cold marble.

Wanting to be alone and undisturbed at her worship, she went to the Abbey's most secluded chapel, St. Paul. Tucked away in a corner, it contained an altar and a confessional. Golden light glowed from a single candle within. Ascending its two worn stone steps, she peered through the spikes topping the arched door. She knelt at the altar, bowed her head, and clasped her hands.

She did her most private devotions in the overpowering silence of this chapel. As she prayed, a soft sweeping over the paving slabs disturbed her—the scratch of mice or human footsteps? Hushed, conspiratorial voices filled the air and grew louder as several robed figures entered the chapel.

She turned and faced the doorway. There stood John Alcock, Bishop of Worcester and president of the Council. She couldn't pray as he stood there. Another man came into view—Edward Woodville, an arrogant upstart even more hated than his sister.

They entered the chapel and gathered at the altar. They didn't see her, but turned and waited as others came in. She could not slip out now. Woodville was cooking up a plot. They were not here to swap ale-quaffing tales.

She tiptoed into the confessional and closed the door. The air in the close space choked her. The voices approached and grew clear. She held her breath. Feet scraped over the stone floor as rich fabric rustled. Her eyes adjusted to the dark. She squinted through the screen at the figures surrounding Edward Woodville. They wore the alb and cope, the ecclesiastical vestments of bishops. He bowed to each—his brother Lionel, Bishop of Salisbury; John Morton, Bishop of Ely; Thomas Rotherham, Archbishop of York; John Russell, Bishop of Lincoln and Keeper of the Privy Seal; and Edward Story, Bishop of Chichester—every bishop on the council.

As Woodville began to speak, she could not believe what she heard.

* * *

"Where is the Lord Protector?" Valentine demanded of a guard as he and Bishop Stillington reached the White Tower.

"In private chambers, my lord." A page led them to the top floor. They reached Richard's audience chamber and Valentine rapped on the door. "Your highness, 'tis I, Valentine, with a visitor of good esteem."

Richard appeared shoeless, his shirt wrinkled, fingers and neck devoid of jewels, hair disheveled.

Valentine cringed, assuming he'd interrupted something intimate. "Oh, I'm sorry, Richard. Did I get you out of bed?"

Richard's eyes grew wide. "No, not at all. Are you all right? Denys told me of your dreadful mishap. I went to His Excellency's house to see you when I heard, but you were fast asleep. Do come in."

Deeply touched by Richard's concern, Valentine gave him a quick embrace. "I am fine, I feel as strong as an ox. But we must speak to you. 'Tis of great import."

"Very well. Come in and make yourself at home." Richard glanced at Stillington and they exchanged polite nods. Richard ran a hand over his eyes and swung the door open. They followed him into the king's retiring room, still eerily strewn with Edward's chattels—a shaving blade here, a silver basin there, as if he would return any minute. One item outshone all else—on a purple silk cushion, awaiting its next wearer, sat the crown of England. The sight of it stunned Valentine, for he now knew who that wearer would be.

"Richard, we have news that changes everything!" Valentine slid the document from beneath his cloak and made a formal introduction: "Your Excellency, I present Richard Plantagenet, duke of Gloucester and our Lord Protector."

Valentine noted the pleased grin Richard gave him. The bishop bowed as Richard unfolded the parchment.

His eyes swept back and forth, growing wider with each pass. When he reached the end, he looked at Valentine, vigilant as ever, shaking his head. His tongue darted out to wet his lips. Valentine filled a tankard on the table beside him with ale and thrust it into Richard's hand.

Richard took a sip. "Is this lawful? Edward was precontracted to another woman when he married Elizabeth Woodville?" he directed the question at Stillington, plucking grapes from a gold bowl.

"Before God and man ... fie, these grapes have big seeds!" Stillington spat them out the window.

"Edward Plantagenet ... to Lady Eleanor Butler, daughter of the earl of Shrewsbury..." As Richard re-read the document, his head moved side to side in time with his eyes.

"Edward wed Elizabeth Woodville in haste, did he not?" Valentine asked.

"It was a secret! He told no one for two years." Richard leaned forward and clasped Valentine's shoulders, as if to wake him from a dream, prove to them both that this was indeed real. "Val, do you know what this means? My path to the throne is cleared. Prince Edward is illegitimate!"

"That is so, my friend and king." Valentine beamed for his dear friend and for Denys. He knew in his heart that his father lauded them from heaven.

Richard closed his eyes, nodding, as if all this were ordained. "God has chosen me to be king."

"So how does it feel, King Richard?" Valentine reeled, giddy in the knowledge that they had just begun a bounteous new life.

"It feels like … it feels like…" Richard folded the document and pressed it twixt his palms.

Valentine pulled Richard to his feet, hugged him, rocked him back and forth. "It should feel like a rapt tumult of the wildest ecstasy of lovemaking you ever imagined, even in your most wicked, wanton fantasies!"

The bishop, standing off to the side, nodded wholly in agreement. Richard eased from the embrace and patted Valentine on the arm. Trying to hide a smile, he turned to the window and gazed out over his realm.

* * *

They finally left him alone. Bishop Stillington took a full minute to bow his way out of the chamber.

Valentine saw the Tower as if for the first time, from gleaming floors to carved ceilings trimmed in gold leaf. They passed through the private chambers, walls lined with paintings of kings gone by, a parade of constant succession over the centuries. As they passed through the doors out to Tower Green, the air carried the scent of honeysuckle. Valentine turned and gazed up at the four spires atop the massive White Tower, approached the gates and looked out over the river at the misty Surrey hilltops beyond. All the realm's exquisite palaces, castles, abbeys and the ancient memories they held, and every inch of lush green land beneath their feet—was now a large part of his life.

"I did it, Father, I did it all for you! Now are you proud of me?" he beseeched the heavens, not to gain reply, for in his heart he knew…his father was smiling.

An uneasy twinge tugged at his heart and he forced it away. Denys would learn to value it all as he did. He knew their love would surmount her fears. He knew the obstacles—formidable enemies lurked in the shadows, the same foes that killed his father. But all Denys need do was settle in. If God answered her prayers and she found her family, the entire kingdom would lay at their feet.

As he left the Tower's main gatehouse, a heavy weight lifted from his soul. Already one with his beloved wife, he was now one with his kingdom.

He parted company with Stillington and popped in on London's finest jeweler to bestow yet another sumptuous creation on her.

* * *

"I wanted a private meeting, Your Excellencies," Edward Woodville's voice rang out, no longer hushed. "Gloucester's council contains many hesitant to join our cause. We must stay Gloucester's protectorship and bring young Edward under our sway. Too many hesitate to place a boy of twelve on the throne. Why, I know not. Look at his advisors! Woodvilles handle power with poise, if I say so myself. Our council needs administer the upbringing of our lord King Edward the Fifth, and protect him from opposing elements within the government, namely, The White Hog and his lickspittle henchmen."

"The clergy will always support you," Rotherham spoke, "especially since old King Henry was overthrown and mercilessly murdered by Plantagenet hands. My lord, it confounds the bishops in the council why Woodvilles have the bad name when 'tis Plantagenets who usurped the throne and seek to do so yet again." A round of clucks echoed and died out.

"Precisely. To that end, we must move swiftly, slaughter The Hog, and crown my nephew Sunday next." No one objected. Woodville cleared his throat and carried on: "Both my brother Anthony and I are devout sons of our Holy Church, because of the misfortunes suffered by our family, not least at the hand of folly-fallen Clarence, a Plantagenet fittingly in a deserving grave at the hands of his own. I dedicate myself to the cause of God—I wear a hair shirt as I speak—I humbly beseech your excellencies support England's new king, our lord Edward the Fifth."

"Long live the king!" one of the bishops thundered.

"Do we have the loyalty of the clergy?" Woodville asked.

"Aye, we will support King Edward in any way we can," Story spoke, "but execute Gloucester? Take him alive. You may need a pawn later on, surely. I never could see the sense in killing—"

"On that," Woodville broke in, "I will discuss it with the Queen Regent and my brother Anthony. But take him we must. 'Tis absolute at this point. Killing him—" He paused. "Now that I ponder it, 'tis sinking to his level."

"In any event, my lord, I speak for the entire church in that we much prefer a regency of Woodvilles over Gloucester and his Godless cohorts." Alcock spoke again. "Have you heard the blasphemies laymen commit since Golden Boy Edward the Fourth usurped the throne? Divers clergy accused of false crimes, turfed into prisons and their chattels pillages whilst they languish in filthy cells. Golden Boy lifted not a finger, turned his pretty face 'tother way. Now his brother yearns for power, and only Lucifer knows his intentions. It is safe to assume the same accursed Plantagenet blood runs through his veins. Young Edward must be crowned forthwith."

"We proceed with a plan, Your Excellency," Woodville replied eagerly. "And in great haste, for the longer The Hog holds authority, the more peril to our supporters. I would share our plan to seize the regency, devised yestermorn by myself, the Queen Regent, her son the marquess, my brother Anthony, and Lionel—" Silence followed as he bowed to the Bishop of Salisbury. "We're about to besiege all England."

Silence. Surmise. Denys could almost see their pupils dilate.

"I have fortified the Woodville fleet with several more vessels, using the portion of the royal treasure we retrieved. We've leased two Genoese ships, Spanish carracks, currently the largest in the fleet—carracks are the largest sailing ships in Europe. They are now anchored in the Downs, twixt Goodwin Sands and the east coast of Kent. I am proud to say, as commander, our fleet is on course to a grand success!"

"Good news indeed, my lord. You make a fitting admiral, If anyone's sails are full of wind, yours are," came Alcock's reply to that. The other bishops nodded and murmured in concord.

Woodville replied with a half-amused 'hrrumph' and carried on, "The two chartered Genoese are neutral and wish to offend no one, but I suspect their motives. One of the captains is a mariner named Colombo. I believe he will ask a boon from the royal coffers to finance future expeditions."

"What culls, to ask the crown," Alcock addressed the others and they nodded agreement.

"The other vessels are safely in Woodville orbit," he informed them. "We quietly launched a few caravels to Calais to safeguard the port. We will send more up the Thames to stop the trade there and send The Hog up the river. Some will head north up Scarborough way, and others to Wales. We may even ferry Henry Tudor over if we need Lancastrian blood to show The Hog we mean business. But I greatly hasten."

"You, Edward?" Salisbury piped up in an overstated tone.

"Our end is to crush The Hog and his henchmen. Once we control trade, we have him. A fleet of Spanish carracks cannot stop us," Woodville declared.

"Have you sufficient finances?" Alcock asked. "Shall we clergy back up our faith with gold?"

"Er, I was coming to that, Your Excellency. We have half the royal treasure on one of those ships out there, with the other half soon to follow. I shall call on the church only if The Hog isn't as easily put down as we foresee. All we need for now is your loyalty—and your silence."

"You have both," came his reverent reply.

Denys's heart raced as this conversation knocked the breath out of her.

When they departed, she dashed out of the chapel, up the west aisle in the shadows of tombs and fled the Abbey through the Great West Door. She mounted her palfrey and galloped to the Tower as fast as its legs could take her.

* * *

As Valentine quit The Crown and Cushion after a pie and ale, Denys charged up the road towards the Tower, her hair streaming behind her. Spotting him, she slowed the palfrey to a trot and halted. He darted into the road to meet her.

"Valentine!" She reached over to embrace him and nearly slid off. "I came to see you this morn and watched you sleep for hours, oh, my darling…"

He grasped her hand. "I am fine, Denys, truly. We shall talk of that later. But why such haste? I don't like the look of you—your face flushed and eyes troubled so." A headdress poked out of a bag hung from her saddle.

"I must find Richard anon. Follow me!" Her hand slipped from his as she spurred the palfrey on.

He knew she wasn't after Richard for a game of chess. He obeyed and followed.

* * *

He caught up to her at the entrance to the White Tower. He unhorsed and tossed the reins to a groom.

"Denys!" He clutched her elbow as she ran down the corridor past the guards, who exchanged amused glances.

"Valentine, 'tis is a matter of life and death for us all!" She panted as he followed on her heels.

They reached the door to Richard's audience chamber. She waved the guards away, entered his private chambers and burst in without knocking. He stood at the window, one foot propped up on the seat, studying a document. He'd donned a doublet, gold Yorkist collar, rings and shoes.

And something else. The crown.

"Richard!" At the sound of his name, he swept the crown off and placed it on a cushion. He turned as Denys rushed up to him. "Edward Woodville intends to capture and execute you and use their fleet to close off the ports and take Calais!" Breathless, she gulped air. "He has the support of every bishop on the council! Oh, Richard..." She struggled to keep her composure.

"Execute Richard?" Valentine shook his head in disbelief. "They could not have found out this quickly!"

"Found out what?" Denys turned to him.

"That King Edward and Elizabeth's Woodville's marriage is void. Prince Edward is a bastard and Richard is our king, in name and by right," Valentine gushed.

Numb with surprise, she gasped.

"Why so hasty, Val? I am not king yet. We've not even set a coronation date." Richard folded the document and turned to Denys, fixing his eyes on her. "How exactly do they intend to take me?"

"Can we escape to Yorkshire tonight or is it too late?" she asked. "Has he launched ships yet? Have you declared yourself king publicly?"

"Blast it, Denys, stop asking questions and answer me!" Richard thundered. Eyes aglare, he took a step forward and the chamber fell into stony silence.

Denys bowed her head in obedience. "I overheard it in confession."

Richard's face registered confusion but he motioned her to carry on.

"They've made anchorage in the Downs, twixt Goodwin Sands and the east coast of Kent. And they have two neutral Genoese galleons. They intend to take Calais, hasten up the Thames, seize control of every port from here to Scarborough—and execute you!" This time she couldn't hold back the tears.

Ever-composed Richard picked up a tankard and flung it to the floor. "This is the last bloody straw!" He heaved a deep breath. "I'll have every one of those ill-breeding maggots for this! Woodville corpses will line the bottom of the Channel when I'm through!"

"Richard, wait." Valentine clutched Richard's sleeve.

Richard plucked his hand off like a piece of lint. "Oh, ballokes! I've waited too long already." He began to circle the chamber and Valentine followed. Watching them made her dizzy.

"Listen a moment, Richard." Valentine blocked his path. "Hanging the entire Woodville clan and their sailors, sinking their ships will not make you the benevolent lord these Londoners want. Instead, offer all soldiers and sailors who desert their fleet a royal pardon. At this time, forgiveness is more effective than lopping heads or sinking boats. Such a virtuous act will be praised by all and gain many loyal and devoted subjects. Nobody wants to fight the best general in the land. Think how noble and righteous it is, and the admiration that will follow. You'll be adored here much as you are now in the north."

Richard stopped circling and sat on the window seat. "Admiration, you say?" He turned his ruby ring round his pointer finger. "How be it, I denounce Edward Woodville as an enemy of the state right now and shall put a price on his befouled head."

"Fair enough, but what of my suggestion?" Valentine sat beside him.

"Very well, but how do we tell them they are pardoned? Send the message out in the beaks of gulls?" His lips angled into a grin of derision.

Valentine tapped his finger on his chin. "There is a way. We must get close enough to Woodville's vessels to spread word of our pardon offer."

"We?" Richard raised his brows.

"Summon the bravest souls you can muster, furnish them with boats to row out to the fleet and cry out their pardon if they lay down arms and disperse. Simple, Richard. Ever so simple." Valentine stood and smoothed his hose.

"Aye, I can use more supporters. 'Twill be a great humiliation to the Woodvilles, too. Simpler than rounding them all up for the axe man. Too messy, that, I daresay." Richard scowled in malignity.

"For this delicate and daring venture, you need loud men with brass—" Valentine cupped his manhood in his hand and gestured, then remembering his wife was present, pretended merely to scratch himself. "—er—with pluck."

Richard let a smile play upon his lips. "Don't let me interrupt your plucking, Your Delicacy."

Valentine gave a mighty shrug and laughed.

Denys could hold her tongue no longer. "Valentine, this is dangerous. It is not a battle in truth, 'tis a peacemaking, but remember who you deal with."

"Fret not, my darling," he assured her. "We have the formidable backing of some worthy salts. That adventurer from Portugal, Richard, what's his name?"

"Edward Brampton?"

"Aye." He nodded. "A most fitting second in command. I shall make the first approach to the Genoese ships. You did say they were neutral, darling?" He turned to Denys.

"Aye, Edward Woodville said so. They're also the two biggest ships of the fleet by far."

"Grand!" He rubbed his hands together. "I shall start there. A few goblets of Tuscan wine and they'll serve Woodvilles to us on a silver platter."

"God's truth, Val, do you never stop thinking about food and drink?" Richard returned and the two of them strode from the chamber.

"Wait!" Denys called after them. "What about this void marr—"

"Not now!" Richard called over his shoulder. "We will talk after vespers. Until then, not a word."

Too shaken to think, she slowly rode back to Westminster Abbey, away from the tumult, the jostling courtiers and their sweaty bodies.

This time she paused at Edward the Confessor's ancient chapel. Grayish yellow carved pillars met in arches all around her, gracing the tombs of past kings and their queens. In the center rested Edward the Confessor, who ruled until his death in 1066. She knelt beside his tomb, its low archways cut into an ornate carved block of stone, its chiseled Latin worn with age. She prayed for the man about to be king—and for his closest friend and councilor.

* * *

After vespers, Valentine set out for Kent. Denys waited until the worshipers filed out of the chapel, then went to join Richard.

"He will be fine," was the first thing he said.

She slid into his pew. "Oh, I pray so. He's never gone to battle without you."

"'Tis far from battle, Denys. 'Tis an olive branch he bears, not a sword. A transaction. What he's best at and I'm worst at. Aside from those old salts I chose to accompany him, no one is more fitting to bargain with Genoese." He slid his Book of Hours into its velvet pouch.

"Still, with all going on—"

He cut in, "Someday we may battle again, and even fight in separate fields … but on the same side, of course." The timbre of his voice told her he trusted

Valentine completely. "So, how fares marriage? Have you gleaned Valentine's gentle qualities? We all know he has them. Valentine is a kind and loving man yearning to please."

"Aye, he is much attentive of late." She smiled secretly at the memory of his touch.

"Of course. I knew he would be." Richard nodded as if he saw exactly what she referred to.

"But you were right. A need to prove himself consumes him at times." A rush of tenderness and affection for her husband warmed her heart. "But that *is* his more delicate side, Richard. It renders him easily wounded."

"I trust it will not destroy him. As his wife you must help him. We men cannot always be strong. You must ensure his weaknesses do not undermine him or your marriage."

"How can I when he never admits these weaknesses?" She crossed her ankles.

"By loving him, my dear. Simply by loving him, as I said before, do not merely tell him, *show* him." He gave her a resolved nod. "Do you share special moments? On dark cold nights when draughts whistle through the house, does he keep you warm? Does he comfort you when you feel ill, or lend compassion, or esteem the way you run the household? Is he attentive to you? Then do the same for him. He beams brighter than the sun when he looks at you. He ventured all to help find your parentage. He is forever thankful he was fortunate enough to win you."

Her gaze shifted inward to her soul as she pondered his words. "He looks at me as no man ever before—his eyes light up like beacons."

"I know how much you love him, and it didn't take long at all," he spoke the truth.

Denys would have hidden her smile from anyone else, but not from Richard. "Oh, how right you are, you made me see my true feelings. I love him with all my heart. But we went from Yorkshire gentry to this..." She waved a hand in the direction of the palace, "...with you practically on the throne and Valentine running the kingdom at your side."

"There's nowt to fear." Richard's fingers tapped on his Book of Hours.

"This all happened so fast, as if lightning struck and hurled us all here, and now we sit in the palace, you soon to be in Uncle Ned's place on the throne." Gooseflesh prickled her arms. She chased it away with her hands.

"You feel struck by lightning, I feel I got here in the blink of an eye, it happened so fast." He shook his head.

"But this void marriage of Uncle Ned and Bess. That is most stunning. I physically faltered and fell when I heard," she admitted. "How on earth did this come out?"

He explained Valentine's unearthing of the document and Bishop Stillington's revelations, the stark wonder with which he'd read it in the Patent Rolls.

It was all too much for her after everything that happened in the last few weeks. Heart racing, mouth dry, she searched his eyes, dark and pensive. "I dread to ask but I need the truth. Do you want to be king?"

His gaze did not leave hers. She detected the trace of a smile. "God wills it so, it seems."

She recoiled as if struck. "I need take one day—nay, one hour at a time. All I hope for is Valentine's safe return and an account of his triumph. But he'll come back to this … all this tumult. The anguish hits me the harder because it happens before my eyes. The council chamber can be more dangerous than a field of battle. Even as they are divided twixt clergy and anti-Woodvilles."

"That's why we labor day and night to bring a semblance of order, get Parliament running again and oust the Woodvilles once and for all. After my coronation, we'll settle into regular and peaceful life under my reign."

"But that's months away." She hugged her arms to ward off a sudden chill.

He glanced away. "Sixth of July, actually."

That stunned her. She gasped. "So soon?"

"The sooner the better," he stated, a tinge of annoyance in his tone, that she dared question him. Yet the smile still played upon his lips. "Oh, you are laying it on with a trowel!" He gave her a dramatic eye-roll. "I know exactly what I am doing. I have but one request of you as my most loyal subject—my most loyal lady subject, that is." He sat back and crossed his legs.

"What is it? I would do anything if I can serve you better."

"Be a dutiful wife and serve your husband. Leave matters of state to us. You think I have problems, just wait 'till Bess Woodville finds out she's got a nest full of illegitimate offspring." He tried to stifle a laugh and failed.

She tittered, softly at first, then joining in sudden hearty laugh as both their voices echoed through the shadowy chapel.

Oh, how good it felt to release all that pent-up tension. "When was the last time you really laughed like this?" She wiped her eyes with the end of her sleeve.

"The last time I saw Bess, when she missed the bottom step and plopped down on her prat."

"Serves her right!" They shared another laugh, but she quickly placed a finger to her lips. "Shhh! We mustn't laugh here. The chapel is not a place to make merry."

His expression became serious again, his lips tight. "Fret not. When all the dust settles and we are safely in our ordained places, laughter will flow freely."

"I pray so." She clasped her hands together.

"Just hold your thoughts of Valentine. A prayer or two for him will not hurt," he suggested.

"Oh, he believes he needs no prayers. He cheated the arms of death the other day, and walked away from its embrace like it was nowt." Her voice shook at the memory.

"Now, is that not a worthy trait?" he goaded.

"But you sent him off afore he could savor it. Just wait 'till he returns," she warned. "He will never cease to sound his triumph over the Genoese and the Woodvilles."

"Valentine believes his greatest victory was to win your heart." His words and his tone rang true. "'Tis quiet without him about," he admitted. "I do hope the Genoese mariners esteem what I sent them."

A peerish thought arose and she decided once and for all to get it off her chest. "Richard, are there wenches on any of those ships?"

"I think not. If any were, I'm sure they'd be rather salty by now."

* * *

She counted the days till Valentine's return. In the dead of the ninth night, she heard the familiar cadence of his footsteps on the stairs and darted out of bed to meet him.

"Valentine, my love, thank God you are home! Are you all right?" She ran her hands over his body, searching for dressing or wound.

"Nay, all went well." This sounded so stoical, it was almost Richard-like.

"Let us embrace. I waited so long ..." Their arms wound round each other and they shared a deep kiss.

He led her towards the stairs, shed his doublet and tossed it over the railing.

"Now do tell how it went!" She clasped his arm as they climbed the stairs.

"Two of Richard's old salts, John Wellis and Thomas Grey, took command of the fortifications at Portsmouth. They supplied our little navy. Richard sent Lord Cobham with a small sea force to Denysr and Sandwich to hold the ports, in case of a Woodville attack. Edward Brampton and I went to the Downs, where their fleet sat. Brampton and I sailed right up to the great Genoese hulk straightaway and hailed them that we came in peace—and were famishing. They asked us aboard, methinks eager to share a hearty feast. We planned it so we approached at the hour most people finish their supper, so their bellies were full, and their wits dulled. The captain's name is Colombo. He's a Genoese expeditioner. We had quite a winsome commune."

"Colombo—the name sounds familiar," she recalled as they reached the top of the stairs. "I've heard it before. Aye, of course! He came to London. George held a banquet in his honor … that is, what George passed off as a banquet. Consumption was of the liquid kind. The party didn't interest me enough to stay and meet him. I was in a rush to go and find the Countess of Somerset that day and in no state to linger at one of George's drunken revels."

"Aye, Colombo mentioned that," Valentine said. "French hostilities cut short his first voyage to England, so he went to Portugal. He later visited Bristol and London on his way to Hibernia and Iceland but could not get an audience with King Edward. He has very provocative beliefs about the world. He was most cordial over an eve of wine and congress, speaking freely about Woodville ploys over the years, Edward Woodville's motives for the fleet, their intent to seize Richard…" He paused to yawn. "I explained how, if they wrest England's crown, God only knows how trade would be affected. He agreed and broke the back of the fleet. The rest followed him into London and yielded to us on the embankment at Westminster. Edward Woodville, coward that he is, fled to France to cool his heels with Henry Tudor. We won't see either of their hides again." They reached his bedchamber and he stood aside for her to enter.

"Valentine, your deed will be retold over and over in years to come!"

He slid out of his shoes. "Living it is far more thrilling than the telling."

"Have you notified the council of your success?" she asked as they nestled on the bed together.

"Nay, I came straight here, not even stopping at the Tower. I left that to Brampton and Cobham. Somehow I think they'll waste no time informing the king of their great success."

"King?"

"Why, Richard, of course." He waved that away.

"Valentine, I was in a torment of worry every minute. There has been more than I can bear! A rash of arrests and executions, two of Bess's brothers beheaded for treason, and Uncle Ned and Bess's children proclaimed bastards because of his plight-troth to Eleanor Butler."

He sighed and wrapped an arm round her shoulders. "These are times of great tumult. I never promised an easy, smooth transfer of power. Let us just serve the kingdom as best we may."

"I try. You have no idea." She began to unlace his shirt. "I know this was your first battle without Richard," she said as he trailed kisses down her neck. He gathered her hair in bunches. "I worried myself frantic that you might not cope without him, but prayed you would, and you did. I am so proud of you."

Their mouths locked as their arms wound round each other. She eased away. "You once said that a noble's wife never performs such menial chores as bathing him. Well, you are not just any noble. You are a valiant soldier, our kingdom's bravest. Is it a menial chore if we bathe each other?"

"That sounds even more fun than crushing Woodvilles." He let her remove his undertunic and hose.

"We'll use my tub." She pulled him to his feet. "'Tis bigger than yours."

The fire blazed in her retiring room hearth as a maid prepared a bath at her behest, filling her tub with pails of hot water which she scented with lavender oil. She closed the door and removed her chemise, kirtle, and petticoats. Valentine shed his nether garments, sank into the fragrant water and stretched. He rested his head on the tub's edge.

She eased in beside him and smoothed hair from his brow. The warm water embraced them. How good it felt to be so close to him.

"Love me, love me right here, Valentine!" She wrapped her legs round his waist as passion consumed them, their souls in cadence with the universe of ecstasy that bound them together.

Afterwards, they lay in bed, arms and legs twined about as she drifted off into slumber.

Chapter Eleven

Richard's coronation was the most magnificent in the history of the kingdom. Denys, thrilled to be part of it, beamed with pride at Valentine's achievements, but doubt tormented her when he readily accepted his position as Chancellor of England.

King and peerage rode through the streets of London to the coronation in unequaled magnificence among magnates, prelates, knights and household attendants. The crowds cheered along the entire route from the Tower to Westminster. Richard, finally out of mourning for his brother, looked truly regal draped in a purple velvet ermine-trimmed robe over a cloth-of-gold doublet. Pages surrounded him, draped in white robes. Anne, weak and frail, rode in a richly decorated litter, attended by crimson and blue satin-clad ladies on horseback.

The procession made its way to Westminster Abbey over rolled-out red cloth. Denys walked in state alone behind Richard's sister, while Valentine, as first officer of the coronation, followed the king, with the honor of bearing his train. To Denys, he was the most resplendent of all, his blue velvet robe blazing with gold threads that glittered in the sunlight.

A priest carried a great cross leading the procession of abbots and bishops. The principal magnates followed, bearing swords and maces. The duke of Westminster bore the scepter. The duke of Windsor carried the jeweled crown on a cushion of royal purple. Bishops flanked Richard on each side, a cloth of estate borne over his head. A company of earls and barons preceded the lords carrying the queen's ceremonials. Denys followed, leading another line of noble ladies, knights and squires.

The procession crossed The Nave to a burst of song. The king and queen approached the altar. As the haunting refrains of the pipe organ echoed through the Abbey, Cardinal Bourchier anointed them with the sacred chrism and set the crowns upon their heads. After High Mass, the procession filed out over the red cloth amidst the blasts of trumpets and clarions.

At the coronation banquet in Westminster Hall, Richard sat at the center of the high table, Anne to his left. "Long live King Richard!" resounded throughout the hall.

At dusk, attendants entered with flaming torches. Leading the procession of subjects, Denys approached the royal dais. She dipped in a bow, clasped Richard's hand, and kissed the coronation ring. Only then did it strike her with full force—the ring was no longer Uncle Ned's. It belonged to King Richard.

"God bless you, your highness." She looked into his eyes. They did not glisten quite as brightly as the jewels in his crown, but he gave his first smile as king.

* * *

Languishing in sanctuary, her sons sequestered in the Tower, Elizabeth Woodville knew she'd lost everything in two short months. Their fleet had also failed. "Damn Valentine Starbury!" she spat. How had he survived that scuttled barge? She could flog herself for sending him to Stillington! "Oh, what a mistake to set him on that path to my downfall," she wailed, gazing forlornly at a painting of her two sons, Edward and Richard, knowing she'd never see them again. "Useless to me now!" she railed, unapologetic for her self-centered character.

* * *

Along with Valentine's appointment as Chancellor came an annuity of eleven hundred pounds, plus castles at Stokesay and Rockingham.

As the moon dusted their bed with pale beams streaming through the open window of their chamber, she took deep breaths to relax—but couldn't. "Oh, Valentine, I shall never get used to all this."

"The throne is safe, and Elizabeth Woodville is sequestered. Henry Tudor is more of a threat than she'll ever be." Scorn gave his tone a bitter edge.

"He hides in France," she countered. "And hasn't set foot on English soil in ages."

"We must still guard against his spies and followers." He sensed her unease and rubbed her neck muscles. "His mother was seen to hand Bishop Rotherham a large parcel, and we doubt it's a donation to the church."

"Will you seize Tudor and hold him in prison? Or battle him again?" Old fears crept up on her, steadfast as a lingering ague.

"Nay, Richard is not like Edward. He likes to leave well enough alone. 'Tis not his manner to strike first."

Denys couldn't help but think that her husband's was. "Please do not provoke anything, Valentine. I could not bear to lose you in battle."

"Are you so in love with me that you cannot bear to be torn from my presence?" he teased as his hand slid down to rub her shoulders.

"You know I am. I also hate battles and wish everyone peace." She began to relax under his welcome touch.

His fingers traced the curvature of her body. "We are men. We can't help fighting. Just as we can't help loving." He slid off the bed, placed another log onto the expiring flame and returned to her. "Now, what were we talking about?" His face glowed in the flickering firelight.

Her unease dissolved as that ardent, nighttime feeling came over her. She nestled close to him. "Fighting, loving … something like that."

He propped himself up on an elbow and lifted a strand of hair from her cheek. "Love and war…how alike those two passions are."

* * *

At Valentine's ancestral estate of Fiddleford Manor, Denys spent hours in the gardens planting roses, lilies, violets, all the flowers she loved. Their delicious scents floated through the house with the cuttings she brought in each day. It was almost as peaceful as their Yorkshire sanctuary, but the buzz of London filled her with life and zeal. Adjusting to the city, she began to enjoy its narrow winding streets, the mongers shouting the virtues of their wares, the throngs rushing about to perform the tasks life demanded, the swarm of trade along the Thames. Now and then she walked the dusty streets alone, as a common subject, blending into the crowd of brightly colored cloaks and the rosy cheeks of children. She and her guides visited poor areas and gave out bread, meats, and fruit from her garden. It rewarded and saddened her at the same time.

Would she be one of these had Elizabeth not taken her in? Could the ragamuffin girl who devoured the strawberry tart and licked her dirty fingers be her own sister?

She never stopped wondering.

* * *

Now that Richard was king, she needed to make an appointment for an audience. How she missed the freedom to prance past the guards at each of his outer chambers, then through to his retiring chamber.

He'd become unreachable. But today, she would see him alone, without a hovering retinue.

Two guards conducted her to the White Tower's audience chamber where he sat signing documents. The crown rested on a cushion within his reach. He looked up and began to smile, but didn't finish. As he stood to greet her, she bowed. But she spoke as an old friend. "Oh, Richard, you look so regal, but so very tired. Is it all catching up with you?"

"It has caught me, surpassed me, and left me in the dust." With his weary reply, he eased back into the chair and rested his head in his hands. "Such an immense burden of obligation, simply overwhelming. At times I find it hard to believe I am here. I expect Edward to walk through the door any minute and shoo me away." He resumed his erect carriage.

"I fully understand, Richard. Part of me refuses to believe Uncle Ned gone. I still see him when I close my eyes, I still feel his hands around mine, I hear his laughter." Would she never stop grieving for Uncle Ned or stop missing him? "But you handle it notably well. I trust you will soon fall into comfortable ways and adjust to being king as in any other position."

"Kingly ways?" He puffed. "It will be years before I am comfortable. There is so much to do."

"Valentine loves every minute, just as I feared he would," she murmured.

His eyes sharpened, restoring a glimmer of confidence. "My Chancellor is more popular than I," he said without a trace of indignation.

"I noticed." She nodded. "I wish I could slow him down at times."

"'Tis your wifely duty to drain his vigor when he has too much pluck." Richard tilted his head and tapped his fingers on the table. His rings sparkled in the sunshine pouring into the chamber.

"That just envigors him more," she returned with a smirk.

"Find Bess Woodville's potion crone. I'm sure she can brew a batch to stir or pacify him as you will. That witch's potions helped kill both my brothers." His tone dripped bitterness.

"Richard, please. Leave Bess in the past. Put her out of mind. She can harm us no more. It must gall her to rancor that you are king. Just think of her fury holed up in her spartan chamber, the Woodvilles smitten from the palace as if taken by plague. Her attempts to kill us all failed. The kingdom is yours. You must bear its burden, but you must also enjoy it. 'Tis grand to see the royal tournaments, feasts and banquets Bess forbade me."

He lifted the last document he'd signed and studied the royal seal. "Grand, is it not?"

She took a deep breath and squared her shoulders. "Richard, I am here not only for an audience, but to seek a favor."

He placed the document back on the pile. "What do you need, an increase in Val's salary, a castle by the sea, mayhap?"

"Nay, you are ever more liberal to us. I need only one small favor of you. Help me find the man who took me from King Henry as a baby."

He nodded. "Ah, yes, the mysterious John. I wish to help, but cannot look into it forthwith."

"I understand you cannot go off and scour the kingdom for him. If you can but find me a list of King Henry's courtiers, I can continue the search myself."

He held up a hand. "You will not go on another winter search. No travel twixt November and May. That is a command, spoken to you by your king."

"I heed and obey thee, my liege." Addressing her childhood friend this way gave her a strange dread. "But with summer upon us, there is no difficulty in travel. Bess is powerless. I trust there will be no more mishaps."

"I shall assist as I can, now I really must resume affairs of the realm. Give Val my blessings and tell him I shall see him when Parliament convenes." He turned to another stack of documents.

She stood to leave. "How fares the queen? I've not seen Anne since the coronation."

"She is not in good health." His eyes clouded as always at mention of Anne's increasing absences from court gatherings.

"I am so sorry, Richard." Her heart ached for them both. "Please, if there is anything I can do—"

"Just continue to be kind to her as you always have. She needs all the love and care we can bestow." His gaze dropped, his voice lowered.

"That is the very least I can do." She bowed and they parted.

* * *

Court glittered in greater splendor than the late King Edward's. Mummers, jugglers, tumblers and fools performed every eve, minstrels played lively music in the gallery, courtiers took to dancing, dice and checkers.

Valentine and Denys sparkled with all the splendor due their new status. They dressed in more extravagant raiment than ever, his doublets and surcoats of the richest velvet, his undertunics of satin or fine Holland cloth, his head always topped with a velvet cap gleaming with gold fleurs-de-lis or shot through with gems. Her attendants draped her in gowns of velvet lined with satin or cloth-of-gold, furred with ermine or sable, blazing with patterns and swirls of gold, studded with jewels. Her satin sleeves flowed to the floor in layers, every finger beringed.

Queen Anne, ailing and bedridden, could not make many appearances. Denys wished she could cheer Richard up as he sat beside her empty place at the high table, but a spark always brightened his eyes when his darling son Edward skipped into his arms.

On progress in Cambridge, Denys and Valentine heard news of tragedy. The little boy had slipped away in his sleep. The king and queen, overwhelmed by grief, rushed to Middleham for Edward's funeral.

The inevitable buzz spread through court: who would Richard name as heir to the throne?

"Be thankful we do not have these tribulations, Valentine," Denys said as they rested in bed.

"A king's biggest burden is to choose a fitting heir, absent legitimate children." Valentine tucked the cover around her shoulders as the flames in the hearth died down to glowing orange embers.

"Who should his heir be?" She warmed her hands in the crook of his elbow.

"The Bill of Attainder bars George's son from the succession," Valentine replied. "Mayhap his sister Elizabeth's son Jack de la Pole. He is the eldest untainted nephew, and God willing, will be of age when his time comes."

Denys smiled, though lingering grief over George's execution still weighed on her heart. "How happy George would be to see his son ascend the throne. And Richard loved George so."

"He will make his choice soon." Valentine's tone carried a note of foreboding. "There is no shortage of more distant would-be kings. Margaret Beaufort will surely put in a claim if succession isn't secure."

"That would be quite a feat, there being no precedent for a female monarch. And Henry Tudor's mother, of all people. Is she a threat?" Denys asked.

"Not so much her. She's subtle and stays out of the way, quietly financing her son's invasions. She seeks no glory herself, only for him." Valentine bunched the pillow under his head.

Denys nestled close to him. "I've never even seen Margaret Beaufort."

"She keeps a safe haven in Wales. Well out of the way," he assured her.

"Valentine, will England ever have a queen born to the throne?" She'd wondered about this since childhood.

He nodded. "Aye, some lucky lady will be born to rule. Alas, not in our lifetime."

"Mayhap in our children's," she mused.

He turned to face her. "Speaking of children..."

He took her in his arms once more.

Chapter Twelve

"We received an interesting missive today." Valentine sat across from Denys in the solar as his Esquire of the Body slid satin slippers onto his master's feet.

Taking his serious tone the worst way, Denys clutched her hands to her girdle before they could tremble. She knew how Valentine made light of the most threatening danger—he thrived on adversity, all the more to vaunt his valor in besting it. "Oh, no, what now?"

His smile eased her. "Nay, 'tis good tidings, that Genoese captain from the Woodville fleet. Cristoforo Colombo."

"Aye." She nodded. "The one you caused to disburse the fleet."

"Aye. He repeated his ideas about the world we don't know, and Richard took that for what it is worth." A steward brought a tray laden with cheese and grapes, and another server placed glasses of mead on the table.

"How so?" She took the closer glass.

"A teaser if you will, to obtain an audience. He claims he can reach the Orient by sailing west. And he wants to explain to the court how he will do so." He picked up his glass and took a mouthful.

"Why, I have heard that before. Irish mariners believe land lies to the west. Peter the seaman lad talked of it on our ill-starred journey to Wales. He retold legends of such voyages." She plucked a few grapes from the tray.

"Richard has granted an audience to Colombo, not just out of curiosity for what lies west, but out of regal graciousness, and gratitude for his part in dispersing the Woodville fleet." He ran his finger round the rim of the goblet. "And if our presumptions are correct, Colombo will arrive upon our shores forthwith. But Richard is no fool. Of course we discern his base motive for this visit."

"Of course!" She plucked up a cube of cheese and nibbled on it. "He wants to discover the unknown bounds of the immense and stormy Ocean Sea, to claim distant new lands full of curiosities beyond our wildest imaginings."

"We figure a more mundane reason." He looked over at her. "Riches. And to achieve riches, he needs a patron." He grabbed a handful of cheese cubes. "One with vast funds at his disposal."

"You must esteem the man's knowledge of the sea, not to mention his pluck, his strong belief in what others would dare not dream. Would you not want your legacy to live throughout the ages?" she challenged.

Valentine gave her a proud stare. "I am Chancellor of England, I will be remembered for all time."

"You may be a prince among men to your tenants and a god to the serfs who depend on you for their sustenance, but in the eyes of fate, we are but specks of dust on a minute island. Ponder what lies ahead. Your service to the kingdom will pale against Colombo should he succeed. His name would be lauded by the whole world, not just England." She snatched up some grapes, leaned over and popped one into his mouth.

"Oh, you and your chimeras!" He frowned as he chewed. "We suffer strife enough keeping this land from invasion and ruin without fretting what lies over the Ocean Sea. If new lands lay there, do you not think some fearless expeditioner would have found them? Besides, Marco Polo already found the Orient. We well know where it is and how to get there."

"Not by sea, dear husband." She shook her head. "A possible sea route provokes much thought. Listen carefully to the man when he says his piece. I certainly will. We may be about to embark upon a turning point. And I would very much like to hear about it firsthand. This time I shall meet the Genoese who would touch the farthest corners of our world. I never thought him such a worthy mariner with such advanced ideas. George described him a seaman keen to glut himself with wine until he fell on his prat, tottering off to his next banquet."

Valentine stood and brought her to her feet. He sat back down in his chair and sat her upon his lap. "Wherever do you get this insatiable yearning for gossamer spheres we cannot see, hear, nor touch?"

"I know not. Mayhap my mother. If that be so, I may never know." She settled on his lap and rested her head on his shoulder.

"I venture you and Colombo will chat for hours about an infinity of almosts, what-could-have-beens and mayhaps." He handed her his goblet. "Here, take a sip."

She sipped and gave it back to him. "Valentine, remove your fetters, look beyond the coast of Cornwall and imagine what lies across the Ocean Sea. No one knew of Greenland until the Norse went to see what was there. Mayhap the Genoese mariner is more perceiving than you think. This did not all come to him in a fleeting fancy. You know how steadfast the seafaring Genoese are. They are ocean-bound wayfinders and astronomers. I shall receive him here, in this very house, should the court not find him of uttermost interest."

"Chase your mystical remote lands, my darling." He drained his goblet. "As for the king and myself, we have a kingdom to run—of diminutive proportions when you ponder what may lie far beyond our shores, but for us, the entire world weighs upon our shoulders."

* * *

Councilors, nobles and curious hangers-on packed the royal outer chamber, clamoring to glimpse this mariner whose stirring conjecture kindled every fancy. But Valentine was not among them. The new president of the Council of the North was busy putting the finishing touches on its creation.

Denys arrived an hour early. She already felt empathy in her heart for this fellow seeker, whose lifelong quest mirrored her own. He too sought something unknown, mayhap even unreachable, yet no one dared discourage him. She would not miss meeting him this time. She hoped to sit him down in the privacy of the inner chamber, away from the pressing crowd, plumb the depths of his soul and learn what forces drove him beyond the terrors of lesser men.

She wished to offer blessings and encourage him never to quit in the ugly face of adversity.

Her eyes swept across the chamber. Tired councilors stood in groups, their faces drawn and strained. Pages scuttled about carrying trays laden with goblets and tankards. Voices clashed like a band of untuned viols. Then through a parting in the crowd she discerned a head of dark auburn hair and pair of sharp blue eyes. His hands sliced the air in a display of expressive gestures as he spoke. He stood in vigorous contrast to the wan Englishmen around him. An olive-skinned man beside him translated his words into English.

He looked away but her eyes stayed locked on his. He looked again and this time riveted his attention in her direction. They exchanged smiles. She elbowed her way through the crowd and during a lull in conversation, introduced herself. "Cristoforo Colombo, it is a pleasure to meet you. I am Denys, Duchess of Norwich." Colombo took her hand and kissed it. She bowed as his interpreter translated.

He relayed Colombo's admission that he was still learning English. Richard had already asked him if he spoke French, but his French, too, was halting. So he had to speak through the interpreter, "Silvio Lentus," he presented himself with a sweeping bow. "Lentus means slowly," he explained. "And what better name for an interpreter?" Colombo gave a magnified shrug, throwing his hands up with a flourish that she found pleasingly charming. His hands, so dexterous at accompanying the nuances of his phrasing, needed no rings in order to sparkle.

He stood erect, ruddy features glowing with the roughness of the seas he traversed. His beaklike nose hosted a light scattering of freckles. His sharp eyes reflected her own passion for truth. As the melodious language flowed from his lips, she stared in awe. This man visited places she only dreamed of, and had the desire to go even farther. When Richard led him and Silvio into the receiving chamber, she followed on their heels. "I am not letting him out of my sight, Richard. He is as obsessed as I am with finding the nearly impossible," she told the king in a half-whisper. Richard returned her sparkling gaze with a mildly amused half-smile.

"Tell me of your travels, Signor Colombo, tell me about distant shores on which you stood, and where you intend to go next," she gushed after servitors brought goblets of wine with plates of cheese and fruit.

Through Silvio, he told her of voyages to Ireland and Iceland. He described his first long voyage, to the island of Scio in the Aegean, "Homer's place of birth," he said. "The island is the gate to the Orient, the most enchanted land in all the world we know." He gestured with his hands as he spoke. "Their costumes full of color, overflow with silks, pearls, gems to make your mouth water. Scio is a wondrous island. Her main commodity is mastic."

Denys winked at Richard, knowing this was but one of an abundance of unknown delights from the world's far reaches.

Colombo signaled Silvio and the interpreter proceeded to place several gift boxes before the king. Thanking him, Richard opened the boxes and lifted out delicate bottles in glittering jewel tones of red, purple and green, decorated in gold leaf. Their stoppers diffused the sunlight streaming through the window and cast rainbow bands onto the table.

Silvio translated Colombo's words: "The glass vessels are Venetian, by Mastropietro, our most famous glass craftsman. They are very delicate and my gift to you. They contain mastic, from the mastic tree. It is used to make perfume, sweets, and..." He motioned at four covered drinking vessels full of the cloudy liquid, "...this is to be sipped, rolled around the tongue and savored, like finest wine. It is grown throughout the Mediterranean, but southern Scio's mastic bark is readily discernable from any other, for it yields the most aromatic and redolent scents and tastes. The Ottoman Caliphs consume copious quantities for their..." Silvio faltered as he searched for the right word. "...many wives."

Denys pulled the glass stopper from a bottle and breathed in the foreign elixir. Heady indeed, it stung her eyes with its caustic aroma. Its mystical essence exceeded English rose and lavender oils, downright stale by comparison.

"Of all the sensual beauties on Scio, the scents spurred my imagination," Colombo said through Silvio. "My sense of smell is my strongest. At sea, I use it to detect winds and currents, but Scio inspired me to press on beyond. It is a land of enchantment, an awakening of the spirit." As he spoke, Richard ventured a sip of the mystical mastic a repugnant scowl. Trying hard to hide a smile, Denys turned, re-fixed her gaze on Colombo and continued to bombard him with questions.

They learned a lot in those first few hours of their acquaintance with the expeditioner, of the most import that the king of Portugal refused to finance his voyage across the Ocean Sea. She sensed Valentine was right and Colombo would solicit the English crown's support. No offer of monies tumbled out of Richard, though. Denys wanted to hear much more about the voyages, the lands and peoples, without broaching money. All too soon he departed for an audience with Richard's newly created Admiralty Office.

Denys leaned forward to address Richard. "He is the most amazing person I ever met. He is so like me in wanting to find what he knows is out there, and willing to overcome all obstacles to do so. Oh, what a dauntless spirit!" She threw her head back and sighed with wonder.

Richard rapped his fingers on the table. "Not dauntless enough. Or was it politeness that kept him from pleading me to raid the treasury?" He raised a brow as laugh lines creased his cheek.

"'Twas your first meeting, Richard. He observed custom. Mayhap he awaits your offer. Will you consider the crown endow monies for his expedition?" *Please say yes*, she silently begged.

"Denys, if I were simply a wealthy noble with time on my hands, without the vexation of my immense burden of expenses, I'd venture monies on the chances of his odyssey increasing my capital. But my burdens here in my own realm border on unbearable. I have neither time nor inclination to offer him assistance or support." Adjusting his cloak, Richard started to stand. She reached across the table and sat him back down.

"Oh, Richard, linger with me a few moments more and experience something not of this land!" She held one of the delicate bottles out to him and he looked away, fanning his hand through the air. "Sniff this ambrosia. 'Tis something out of a dream!"

"Out of Houndsditch, more like." He wrinkled up his nose. "It pongs." He pressed his palms on the table, stood and headed for the door.

She tugged on a lock of her hair and flicked it over her shoulder. "You and your patronage partiality. Signor Colombo bursts with confidence and the knowledge to back it up! Mayhap the king of Portugal missed the opportunity of a lifetime. Consider being part of this dream."

"I cannot chase dreams right now." He approached the door and a page followed. "Were I lounging upon a pile of silken pillows like an Ottoman caliph, my most pressing decision being which concubine to tumble next, mayhap I could. But if what lies beyond the Ocean Sea is anything like that potion … ugh!" He pointed to the bottles of mastic. "'Tis worse than anything Bess Woodville's alchemy ever brewed up … I shall stick to my simple hippocras, thank you."

"So he is turned away by another monarch?" She hung her head in despair.

"He has my heartfelt prayers, but I cannot back them with gold. I cannot begin to fit him with ships. I have England's fleet to build." The page opened the door for him.

"Oh, I do wish we could help him. Those lands beyond the Ocean Sea need claiming." She stood and rushed over to him, determined not to give up.

"And the land beyond this chamber needs governing. So to work I return." He strode out the door, cloak trailing behind him.

She sat back down and pondered a while, sipping the wondrous ambrosia brought to her lips from so far away.

* * *

During Colombo's stay at court, Richard graciously seated him on the dais at his side, arranged grand tours of the palace and Westminster Abbey, and took him falconing in the forest. Others were less kind, notably the doubters who branded him a moonish wanderer too outlandish for their practical sensibilities. Valentine renewed his acquaintanceship with Colombo cordially enough, but he and his fellow councilors couldn't resist a jest or two. "Don't imbibe that Scio plonk, Richard," Valentine warned the king one eve as mummers and jugglers entertained court. "The English for mastic is shaft-softener." Richard hid his grin behind his goblet and cast a sideways glance at Colombo clapping his hands to the music.

* * *

"I asked Cristoforo to visit," Denys told Valentine toward the end of the Genoese's stay. "We will look at the mappa mundi together and I plan to sing for him."

"That will send him back over the ocean faster than the Woodville fleet dispersed," Valentine jested, not looking up from his pile of papers.

"I am in no mood for feeble wit, Valentine." She placed her fists on her hips. "I am serious."

"Too serious." He laid his pen down, approached and gathered her in his arms. "Trying to find your family is a lofty enough enterprise. Now you want to help claim unknown lands across the Ocean Sea!"

"Sweet Jesu, Valentine, I don't intend to go with him. I enjoy listening to his ideas and beliefs. They confound me, and yet inspire me, too." She lowered her voice. "His marine shrewdness almost matches the ingenious governance of the Chancellor of England." She traced his jawline with her fingers. As his lips descended upon hers, she shut out all but the intoxicating aura of the man she loved.

Their usher entered and announced himself by clearing his throat. Denys and Valentine jumped apart. "Signori Cristoforo Colombo and Silvio Lentus wait without, my lord and lady."

Colombo presented them each with a gold pendant from the city of Elmina, where he voyaged a year before. He promised to show her Elmina on the mappa mundi as she fingered his delicate gift in the shape of a cross with rounded edges. A spark of inquisitiveness brightened Valentine's eyes as Colombo implied that more gold could be gotten there, but she cast her husband a warning glare, for she had no intention of exploiting Colombo's talents and bravery to acquire even more riches.

After a meal of roast boar, roast swan in full feather and her own creation, lampreys in galytyne, Denys and Valentine led their guests into the solar. Colombo brought his mappos and unrolled it flat on her writing table. They anchored the corners with tankards.

"I thought you said the world was round," Valentine jested, but she paid no heed, too taken with the jagged seacoasts. Colombo showed them England and where Cipango and Cathay lay in the Orient. The Ocean Sea's immensity entranced her. There had to be more to the world than they knew!

"I intend to find out what lies to the west." He nodded as Silvio spoke, conviction brightening the mariner's sharp blue eyes.

"I believe you that the world is round, so surely there is another side of the Ocean Sea," Silvio relayed to him in his own tongue.

"And who inhabits it, if anyone?" he asked, but she couldn't venture a guess.

He explained how he used stars to find his way. This interested Valentine and led to an astronomy discussion. They shared stories of the mappa mundi they'd seen with a flat earth bordered by dragons, of mariners swallowed up by what Colombo referred to as 'the abyss,' widely believed to be at the edge of the earth. But he assured them he shared the convictions of learned scholars in Florence that Asia is what lies across the Ocean Sea.

Denys took Colombo and Silvio for a walk in her orchard. She plucked an apple from one of the trees she lovingly nurtured and presented it to him.

"These are deliciosus, domina, fit to grow on Scio!" He munched away in delight. "Are all England's apples so juicy and sweet?"

"There are divers kinds. Some are sour." She plucked another and took a bite. "But these grow under my tender loving care. I sing to my trees." Smiling at his amazed expression when Silvio relayed her words, she explained. "I believe plants thrive on nurture as do humans. They, too, crave attention and company. As do people, they need praise. So every day I sing to them, dance among them, stroke their leaves and tell them how lovely they are. In summer I tell them, 'You will bring forth bounteous sweet fruits,' and at harvest time, I praise their abundance. This orchard and my gardens are my pride and joy." She gestured at the trees and plants. "I grow many herbs and vegetables. My garden at home in the north is just as extensive, but alas, we are there so seldom, as Valentine needs be by the king's side. But this orchard is my little patch of Yorkshire right here in London." They ambled twixt the rows of apple, pear and plum trees through the walled orchard that sloped down to the river.

She filled two baskets with fruit for them to take home.

"These will be eaten so fast, I will return with empty baskets!" Silvio translated for Colombo.

"Come back anytime, Cristoforo," she offered as they gazed out over the river. "Even after you've claimed lands on the far side of the world full of wondrous new delicacies, you can always help yourself to my home-grown apples."

Before leaving he took Denys's hand and gave it a gentlemanly kiss. "Bonum nocte, domina." He cupped her cheek.

"When will you return to England?" she asked. Valentine had already bade his farewells and returned to work.

"I know not, but I pray soon," he said through Silvio. "King Richard and his council do not much believe in my expedition."

"Oh, 'tis not so, Cristoforo," she assured him. "We are all very supportive. But we are also in jeopardy, we face the menace of invasion and restive rebels. King Richard's mind and treasury are overwhelmed. But I believe in you. I do not have a royal treasury to disburse, but you have our prayers and belief, especially mine. For I, too, quest through heartache and frustration."

"Your goodwill is deeply gratifying, Lady Denys, but I need monies. That is why I appealed to the crown of Portugal, and now here. But I shall not falter. Even if the journey to find patronage is longer than the journey for which I seek it."

"I know you'll never falter. I see it in your eyes," she spoke from her heart. "I can see through to your soul, a restless inquiring soul that hungers for what you cannot readily see. It is called faith, and one must be bold and brave beyond human endurance to possess it."

"And how can you know all this, from our few brief meetings?" He spread his hands, clearly curious.

"Because I am on a quest of my own, Cristoforo. I too seek a world. It is not of the magnitude of the world you seek. 'Tis my own personal world of family." She pressed her palms to her chest.

Silvio translated her words and Colombo, with his vigorous hand gestures, eagerly prompted her for more. "You see, I know not who I am. I was adopted as a baby and I want to find my true family. I do not intend to give up until I find them. Like you, I believe they are out there waiting for me, as are your lands beyond the Ocean Sea. Our quests are alike in that regard."

As he looked into her eyes, she sensed how well they understood each other despite lack of common language. "I wish I could find them for you, dear lady," he said.

"As I wish I could help you. But for now, all we can exchange are prayers. There are other crowned heads," she encouraged. "Richard is not the only one. And though I have a quest of my own, I am also in thrall of your past accomplishments and what you plan to accomplish in future. I will not forget you and your dream. If you have to, seek patronage from every crown in Christendom to launch your voyage west. Never, ever give up."

"Thank you. We part in French ship," Silvio said as Colombo kissed her hand. She glared at the interpreter.

"French? How long have the French been involved?" Her voice wavered in suspicion. After all they'd done for him, he was courting the French?

"No, no, not French people! French ship, French ship…" Silvio corrected, shaking his head, hands flailing.

"Oh, *friendship!*" She laughed as the men nodded and then shook her head in wonder. "How badly can we interpret one another? So where do you go now?" They re-entered the solar and Silvio gathered their mappae.

"Back to Portugal and my young son."

"Have you no wife?" she asked, out of curiosity she hoped he didn't take as more.

"I did, but Felipa, she is dead." Silvio's voice carried a note of sadness as he translated.

"I am so sorry." She cringed at the awkwardness of conveying her regrets through an interpreter.

"But she left me a most precious gift, my Diego. He is but five years of age, but when older, he will voyage with me."

"Oh, how marvelous! Father and son, discovering new worlds together! Oh, you will make history, Cristoforo. Please keep in touch," she requested.

That brought a smile to his face. "I shall, domina," he replied in halting English.

After they parted, she leaned on the door and gazed into the torchlight on the wall, flooded with wonder.

She leapt back with a start, for Valentine stood in the doorway. His dress now more magnificent than as governor: purple pourpoint trimmed in sable; gold pendant suspended from a gleaming chain; the white boar adorning his chest. A jeweled girdle bound his waist.

She approached him. "How long did you stand there? You're so quiet, such stealth."

"I learned that necessity at the French court. But, alas, I'm still no match for King Louis's regal and exclusive demeanor. Neither am I Genoese discoverer with fantastic goals that may change the course of history … world history, at that." His words carried a tone of lightness, so far from his torment in the past when he'd not yet won her heart. But she detected something buried deep within his words that the twinkling in his eyes couldn't hide.

She wrapped her arms around her husband and held him tight. His hair brushed her cheek. She planted kisses on his neck. "Colombo doesn't come close. For all his flair and sense of adventure, he is just another man compared to you. You need never worry that my heart will belong to anyone but you."

"What did you two—er, three—talk about?" They eased apart and walked to their hearthside chairs.

"I found my thought and feeling kindred to his." They sat side by side. "He wants to launch a quest, but runs into endless frustrations, as I do in seeking my family. That is why I champion his cause. We both seek what we know is out there, but we've yet to find our way. For him it's stars, currents and winds. For me it's more veiled. I steer my ship on misty memories and long-dead names. I wish you were more supportive of him."

"Denys, no one is more supportive than I of your quest." He took her hand. "You know what I have done already and I will continue to do so. But the king-dom is a great weight to carry. Unknown lands to the west, or wherever else he wants to voyage, we cannot endow right now. I hope you understand that."

"Of course I do. But we are equally steadfast in our quests. Having my own, I know how vital his is to him."

"Do not be allured by flowery language, overdone hand gestures or excessive vigor. He wears me out just listening to him!" He stifled a yawn.

"We are kindred discoverers trying to shape our destinies, nowt more," she corrected.

"I can be somewhat of a discoverer myself, domina." He stood and brought her to her feet. His lips descended upon hers and swept her up into an ocean of ecstasy so immense that even Cristoforo Colombo could never cross.

* * *

When she entered the solar next morn, she glanced at the oaken chest that contained her genealogy and other documents of import. She hadn't opened it since before the tragedy in the woods, but behind the glass door her papers lay scattered as if rifled through. She opened the door and examined the papers. Then she saw what was amiss: the genealogy she procured at court, Anne Neville's tables, the tables from surrounding shires—were all gone.

* * *

Before court went on progress, Richard sent her a roll of Johns named in King Henry's court records.

John Grantham, King Henry's chief steward, now served a noble family in Windsor. John Lyghtefote of Maidstone was King Henry VI's barber. She went to him and left John Grantham to Valentine.

On the back of her palfrey and with a retinue of servants, she traveled to Maidstone. The sun bathed the golden wheat and rye swaying in the fields. Despite the warm comfort of the rays, the burglary and theft of her genealogy rolls gnawed at her like a festering sore: who had stolen them? Not Elizabeth, sequestered from the outside world. Did Elizabeth send the thief to hinder her search? That thought prompted Denys to peer over her shoulder every few minutes, although her guides surrounded her, hands on their daggers' hilts.

Upon entering Maidstone, she asked a merchant where to find John Lyghtefote. He directed her to a shop on the edge of the market square next to a butcher's stall.

As always, the crowd parted when her retinue rode down the narrow streets. Hawkers stopped shouting their wares, squeaky wheels ground to a halt, and voices hushed at the sight of Valentine's splendid colors draped over their mounts.

She introduced herself to the old and feeble John Lyghtefote, explained herself and showed him the woman's small likeness in the pendant.

As he shook his head, her shoulders drooped in dejection. "Sorry, milady, 'twas not I who delivered an infant to the king. The Prince of Wales was born there, but we all knew that, for they heard Queen Margaret's labor screams in the far reaches of Scotland."

"Please, my lord!" she goaded him. "Do you remember any other Johns you served with?"

His eyes wandered as he stroked his chin. "Oh, there was John Grantham and a few others, long gone."

She asked their names anyway.

He thought a moment longer and held up a pointer finger. "One more John comes to mind, surname of Butts. He lives near Smithfield, was King Henry's Exchequer. Never forgot the name, for he always had a butt of malmsey on hand.

"Butts. I shall remember that, too. Thank you so much, my lord." Blinded by tears of frustration, she headed home to await Valentine.

* * *

He returned home next eve and gathered her in his arms. From the look in his eyes, she knew his visit to John Grantham bore no more fruit than her expedition.

The dam burst and she released all the heartache she'd kept inside these last few months. "Oh, Valentine, I will never know who I am, it becomes more unbearable every day."

"We will find them, Denys, dead or alive, we shall find them. We have other names here. All is not lost." He tightened their embrace.

"How can Bess be so cruel as to keep this from me?" She swept tears away with her fist.

"I honestly do not believe she knows." He shook his head.

Denys took a deep cleansing breath and felt a weight lifted from her shoulders. "I cannot help but agree at this point. No one could be that heartless, even her. I must give her the benefit of the doubt, if only for my own peace of mind. I cannot imagine my fate had she not taken me in—I could have been a homeless urchin begging for alms in St. Giles. What irony—now she is virtually homeless."

* * *

Valentine rearranged his schedule, and two days later they traveled to Smithfield to find John Butts. "Exchequer is a high position," Valentine assured her as they exited the city gates and trotted down the rutted road. "He should know, he must know…"

Smithfield's parish priest directed them to John Butts's timber framed cottage perched on the edge of his farm. Valentine and Denys arrived as darkness fell. No candlelight flickered in any of the windows.

Valentine helped her unhorse and they hitched their horses to posts by the front door. "Look. The door is ajar." He knocked to no reply.

"We can't just barge in." Denys clutched his sleeve as he swung the door open and called out.

"Anyone home?" Still no reply. Denys cringed at this invasion of a stranger's home as they crossed the threshold and entered the dark cottage. Their feet slid on the worn rushes on the floor. Valentine groped his way along the wall, found a torch and lit it. The torch blazed into life.

"Hallo?" Valentine headed for the staircase and peered upwards. But stillness surrounded them. The torch cast a glow over the chattels: a plain table, chairs and cupboards. She followed him across the hallway into a solar.

"There's no one home, Valentine, let us depart and…" As she turned to exit the solar, her head snapped back as if struck. She let out a piercing scream of terror.

Valentine rushed to her side. She clung to him, trembling. A corpse sprawled on the floor heaped with burnt rushes, features blackened beyond all recognition.

Valentine approached the lifeless form. "This was no accident."

"Oh, the poor man!" She backed away, unable to breathe. "We must fetch the bailiff!"

They rushed to the nearest cottage to raise the hue and cry. Sleepy villagers led Valentine and Denys to the bailiff's home. Who would murder an ender villager? And why?

* * *

When they got home, Valentine summoned their servers for inquisition about the violated oaken chest. All denied seeing a stranger enter the house.

"Someone thwarts my every effort and I don't think it is Bess," Denys concluded after they dismissed the staff. "This is heartless murder, a good honest life taken for no reason but to keep me at bay."

"Don't be fearful." He held her and stroked her hair. "I shall never let anyone harm you. I will post two more guards at the door day and night. Do not travel without two more armed guards. Not even to market. You are not to be alone."

She wrapped her arms more tightly around him. "But who could possibly want so badly to keep me from my family?"

"Why, it could be…" He halted and shook his head. "I cannot think why. But the secret of your birth is vital and deadly to whomever it is."

* * *

The coroner determined that John Butts was killed at least two days before Valentine and Denys found him.

"That would be the day I saw John Lyghtefote, the man who told me about Butts." Denys clutched his sleeve as a surge of terror shook her. "Valentine, someone is tracking me. Whoever it is knows our every move!"

Once again he held her and tried to soothe her. But by now he was far from calm himself.

* * *

She intended to solicit more of Richard's help after joining him on progress. They set off for Windsor to meet the court. Armored knights bestride staunch mounts milled around filled Windsor Castle's outer court, plumes and banners streaming behind them.

One of the knights approached Valentine and Denys with discomforting news: "Lord and Lady, Henry Tudor had invaded from France."

She clenched her fists. "Why will he not give up?"

"He is no match for us." Valentine scowled as she clutched his arm, plated in gleaming silver. "We shall return anon, do not fret."

King Richard led his army of 9,000 to fight their deadliest enemy.

* * *

Whilst the men were away, Denys penned on parchment the Johns yet unseen. John Smith, John Drury, John Freke and John Knolles were the last. But where to find them?

An idea dawned. Why not ask Marguerite of Anjou? Married to King Henry all those years, surely she knew!

The widow queen had nothing to lose. Exiled to France, she would surely help spite Bess Woodville.

Denys wrote in French to Marguerite, possibly her last hope.

She dispatched the letter by messenger and prayed Marguerite would help her—another lost soul.

She dashed a note to Valentine but doubted he would get it. The only person besides Richard who'd shared her triumphs and shattering defeats was Anne Neville.

Granted an audience with Anne, she and her queen wandered the castle grounds with their ladies and the royal guard. The sun's golden rays glinted off the Thames like floating gems. They stood on the bridge spanning the calm currents as swans glided by.

"Anne, I have a new lead. I should have thought of her a long time ago." Her voice shook. "Marguerite of Anjou!" Anne's eyes lit up. "Why, how marvelous. She may have seen you given to King Henry. She was his wife, after all."

"And if she does not remember, she can still tell me of those men named John!" With a spring in her step, Denys could hardly contain her excitement.

"That is a joy to hear. I truly hope your search ends soon. How fares life with Valentine? I remember your apprehension about your wedding." Anne lowered her eyes and her voice.

"Valentine never leaves my thoughts." Her stomach churned as always at the thought of him in battle. She didn't share this with Anne, who she knew harbored the same fear for her own husband in that same battle.

She wanted to proclaim her declaration of love for Valentine, but Anne was still in mourning for her son and Denys would not further vex her by gushing over her bliss. But, she thought again: *This is Anne, the would-be sister who honored me with her own wedding gown.*

"Oh, Anne." She smiled. "I have grown to love him so very deeply."

"You are such a beauteous couple. So suited to each other." Anne tossed a pebble into the water.

"To think Bess married us as a punishment." Denys laughed in irony. "Another cruel barb that missed its mark."

"Ah, yes, he is a rare gem. Were I you, I'd clad myself in armor and guard him with raised lance."

Those words alarmed her. She halted and clutched Anne's arm. "Is he so bad a soldier?"

Anne turned to her. "Oh, nay, Richard has nowt but praise for Valentine's skill in the field. I refer to his charm, his handsomeness. I would guard him jealously. Look at the ladies at court. They sigh and nearly swoon when he walks by."

She knew he'd had his pick of the court upon his return from France. Wenches of every shape, age and size clustered about him like bees to honey, but no one dared make eyes at him in her presence—they knew he was hers and hers alone.

Anne went on, "Richard tells me that on the march they overnight at the nearest lord's castle, Valentine is always the center of attention … the ladies' attention, that is. 'Tis harmless trifling, Denys. Do not take it to heart." She paused. "There is one lass to be wary of…but not in any serious way," she added in haste. "She is but a child with dreams of Galahad in her young heart."

"Who?" Denys's heart quickened.

"Bess Woodville's daughter Elizabeth. She is sixteen or seventeen. She fancies Valentine something fierce." Anne brushed it off with a toss of her head. "But do not fret. As I say, 'tis a young girl's fancy."

Denys's chest tightened. She looked down at her hands, clenched into fists. She unclenched them and spread her fingers. "Young Elizabeth is no longer so young. Often I wonder why Bess hasn't married her off." Denys pictured the lass's shining hair and eyes like the midnight sky, possessing all Bess's faded beauty. "She's likely the most beauteous of the younger women at court." She turned to face Anne. "Why did you not tell me before?" Her voice hardened.

Anne placed an assuring hand on her arm. "I did not think it of import. It still is of no import. She is a falcon set free from a cage. Bess only recently released her to Richard. Think how you would feel if just released from sanctuary. Besides, she is at Middleham for the most part. Valentine hardly sees her. Not only that, he hardly notices her."

She knew Valentine hated to reject anyone, for any reason. Callow Elizabeth could take his kindness the wrong way. "It likely means nowt," she forced herself to say, yet wondered if her husband's worshiper carried her fancies too far…

"Something else, Anne. Burglary. A thief broke open my oak chest at Burleigh House and purloined all the genealogy."

Anne gasped. "Was anyone harmed?"

"Nay, not at all." She shook her head. "Nowt else was disturbed. It was as if the thief knew where to find them."

"Has young Elizabeth been in Burleigh House?" Anne asked.

Denys nodded. "You're a step ahead. Aye, a few times on feast days and such. But why would she want any of those documents?" She shook her head in bafflement.

"Mayhap she works at her mother's behest," Anne ventured.

"I wouldn't put it past her." Denys tried to keep bitterness from her voice. "I wouldn't put it past any Woodville. There is something in those documents Bess doesn't want me to know. Something of my family."

Anne moved close. "You're a fighter. I know you will find your true lineage despite the obstacles Bess throws in your path. The Woodvilles will get what they deserve—every last one of them."

"Spoken like a true queen." Denys's heart swelled with pride for Anne. "And thank you for that. It is everything to me to know how much you believe in me."

"Your story will have a happy ending." Anne smiled, but it faded as she spoke again: "The consumptive ills that weaken me will bring me to my grave sooner than later."

"Do not talk of that, Anne." They crossed the bridge together arm in arm. "Live for the moment. The moment is all we have right now."

* * *

Valentine and his retainers marched through the palace gates in triumph, banners streaming. Valentine unhorsed, his squire removed his helmet and gauntlets, and he snared his wife in a loving embrace. Coupled with the relief that he survived battle, she thrilled to welcome her knight once more—as she always dreamed.

With Henry Tudor routed to Brittany and his mother in the Tower for treason, peace once more reigned over the land.

* * *

Court convened at Sandal Castle in West Yorkshire. As always, mummers, jugglers and fools entertained the courtiers, who feasted to gluttony. Upon the army's return, Richard made another grant of lands to Valentine and other valorous warriors. He also gave Valentine Reggie the fool. The expert juggler, singer and dancer joined the retinue to keep their spirits high—Richard constantly forecast yet another Tudor invasion.

"His mother is imprisoned. Is she not his only source of revenue?" Denys asked Valentine one eve as they wandered the castle gardens.

"Lady Margaret runs her son's life well enough from the Tower," he informed her. "She's married to Thomas Stanley. He wavers tween sides like a turtle on a fence post. Whichever side looks strongest is the side he joins. Besides, Henry gathers a faction of his own. Mostly Welsh. Richard feigns indifference, but deep down I can tell he is deeply troubled."

"But with stalwart followers like you, the duke of Buckingham and others, Richard has nowt to worry about." She tucked her hand into the crook of his elbow.

"Oh, but people turn, Denys. Lord Stanley might not be alone."

"Who else?" she asked.

"I am not worried about anyone else right now, but it happens. No one is completely steadfast." His voice carried a hint of caution.

"Not even you?"

He stopped and turned those piercing eyes on her. "You think I could turn against Richard and join Henry Tudor?" His voice rose in anger.

"Of course not." She shook her head. "It is nowt to do with matters of state. I know you would never betray Richard; you've proven that time and again."

"So what is it, then?" he demanded.

"The problem is not an it." A hare dashed across their path. "It is Bess's daughter Elizabeth."

His gaze wandered, as if trying to find young Elizabeth. "Oh, her. What of her?" They resumed walking.

"She is enamored of you. Do you not notice?" she goaded.

A grin curved his lips and he laughed. "What if she is? She knows I am married to you and am spoken for." He tried to wrap his arm around her but she pulled back.

"Don't embolden her any more than you already have, Valentine."

"Embolden her? How have I done that? By letting her know she is worthy, by treating her to a dance or two on occasion? Come now, Denys, she is too callow for me." He smiled as if recalling a fond memory. "She reminds me of you when we first met, trying to escape Bess's clutches. Now Bess is sequestered, Elizabeth is out of her scrutiny and samples life for the first time."

"Be that as it may, I believe she may well have stolen my genealogy," she voiced her suspicion.

He slowed his step. "Why on earth would she do that?"

"For Bess, of course. But I would not be surprised if it also had to do with her fancy for you which would lead her to loathe me."

"No...she is no thief. She knows not where her loyalty should lie, with her uncle whom she feels usurped the throne from her brother, or with the hated Woodvilles, who have all but crawled back under their rocks, yet they are her family. But thief? Nay. She is tormented and torn. You were able to divorce yourself from the Woodvilles and ascertain that you are not one."

"What good is it? I still do not know who I am." This haunting thought made her suspicion of Elizabeth pale in comparison. "What good is not being a Woodville if I do not know who I am?"

"We will find them, Denys," he declared, and this time she did not pull away when he held her. "If it is my last earthly act, I shall make sure you find them."

"Just do not foster young Elizabeth," she warned. "Even to be polite. She'll take it the wrong way. I wish Richard would marry her off."

"God help the poor sod who gets stuck with Bess Woodville as mother-in-law." Their matched grins turned to peals of laughter as he began to tickle her. She shrilled with delight and lifted her skirts as she fled from him, enjoying the chase as much as the inevitable capture. Round the maze they scuttled, darted round corners and brushed against vines. She reached an impassable end and he gathered her in his arms.

As he planted kisses over her face and neck, she wrapt his arms around his waist, as much a part of him as his soul.

Their lips met, and his mouth devoured hers. A rush of desire coursed through her as her she stroked the smooth satin of his hose. Their embrace tightened.

"Not here, Valentine! Richard walks through here all the time. Let us withdraw to our bedchamber." She tried to sound stern, but his nearness entranced her. She tingled from the hot trails his fingertips traced on her face and neck.

"Richard would make a swift and silent reversal, his face hot and flushed, at the sounds of lovemaking within a mile of his earshot. I'm sure he tries not to hear himself at it." As they laughed together, she gazed at the stars twinkling above, breathed in the perfume of primroses and sweet blossoms.

They withdrew to their bedchamber—with no sign of Richard strolling by.

Chapter Thirteen

As Denys read a letter from Cristoforo Colombo, Valentine entered the solar.

"Look, Valentine!" She held it up as she took a sip of mead with grapes plucked from a bunch at her side table. "Cristoforo is returned from the Canaries, off Africa. Oh, the people there are such curiosities. He says they still live quite primitively. They paint their bodies, have no shipwrights, and are completely backward in every way."

"What else did he find there?" Valentine plucked a few grapes and popped them into his mouth.

She detected an eager tone never displayed before in talk of the stalwart mariner. But she knew this tone—as demonstrative as when he gushed about battle or matters of state.

"Nowt to interest you." She leant forward and placed a grape twixt his lips. "Plants and flowers never before seen in our lands, and warm winds that bring the most balmy weather."

"Anything of value? Gold, for instance?" He sat beside her and drew his chair closer.

She put the letter down and looked her husband in the eye. "I am not interested in gold. Why are you?"

He shrugged. "Only curious. I trust he does not venture into the vast blackness and hazard his life for warm winds and bushels of mastic." He sat back and stretched his legs.

"His quest is not mundane," she scoffed. "He wants to find new worlds, not new riches."

"Nay, but capital is ventured only to reap dividends and returns. His quest will cost many thousands of pounds, Denys. No one wants to lose everything they endow simply to voyage into the unknown."

"He hasn't asked us to endow him." She sipped her mead. "He appealed to the crown, but Richard gave only his Godspeed."

"He will succeed. Men ... and women ... of that mold do not give up. No one knows that better than I." He beamed at her.

She returned his smile. "Now then, if I can move you to see the value of a voyage across the Ocean Sea to mankind, I can certainly move you to take the rest of the evening off."

He sighed. "Oh, I would love to, truly I would, but the council is holding a special session."

"The council can wait. Your wife cannot. Now ... can the council do this?" She slid onto his lap and planted kisses on his neck.

"Now *this* session holds my interest!" He lowered her to the tapestry mat before the fire and they made love before the crackling embers.

* * *

Though worried over more invasions, Richard cordially welcomed Cristoforo back. The Genoese brought a flair and spark that roused Richard's elegant but solemn court. Cristoforo brought spices from his travels to Guinea, wines from Portugal, exquisite Venetian glass and more mastic from Scio that Denys so loved. In return, Valentine took his gleaming gold collar from around his neck and slipped it over Cristoforo's head. The mariner thanked him in English, and even Richard began to look like mastic agreed with him.

* * *

Valentine and Denys held a banquet at Burleigh House, inviting Admiralty Officers and notable English mariners. They swapped legends with Colombo about great Norse seamen, and what lay beyond the Ocean Sea. Spreading his mappa mundi out on their table once again, he showed them his proposed voyage, to launch from the Canaries. As the guests gathered around, he traced the route with his finger and spoke whilst Silvio translated: "Here there are trade winds that blow northeast to southwest. They blow counter in the southern hemisphere." He described the calm regions around the equator, impressing everyone with his knowledge of winds, currents, and stars. "I admit I seek gold and spices, all the treasures and delicacies of the east, but the prospect of finding new lands most drives me."

* * *

The next morn as Denys studied the household accounts and Valentine tended his duties at court, her usher announced a visitor.

His russet-colored doublet and hose augmented his auburn hair. The collar Valentine gave him gleamed on his chest.

"Cristoforo!" She greeted him with a smile and clasped his hands.

He bowed, returning her warm smile.

She looked over his shoulder. "Are you alone? Where is Silvio?"

"I come alone," he said in halting English. "Perhaps we can speak French?"

"*Oui!*" She led him to two chairs in the solar and they sat side by side. "I thought you didn't know much French."

"Very little," he admitted in French, signing with thumb and forefinger a small amount, "but it is so like Genoese, twixt the four languages, I trust we will understand each other."

"Four languages?" She sat forward, wide-eyed.

"Genoese, English, French, and..." He counted on his fingers. "Hand language!" He splayed his hands, then asked her to take him for another walk through her orchard.

The language barrier did not pose a problem since she understood his halting English and he understood French. But they had no need to talk much. They walked under the cool autumn sun giving way to a bright new day in the comfortable silence betwixt them. She gave him a basket to fill with fruit from her trees. The sweet aromas of fruits surrounded them.

As they approached the house, he turned to her, set the basket on the ground and stepped closer. His eyes echoed the deep blue-green of the sea, telling her what he couldn't convey in words, no matter how mellifluous the language.

"You are most beauteous, Denys." His voice rumbled in his lilting but hesitant English. "Would that I could take you with me to the Orient. I wish that you could be with me always."

"I understand and am flattered," she replied in French. "But I am happy here. I have a husband I love very much." She sighed. "I would go nowhere until I found my family, even were I free."

He nodded, giving her hands an affectionate press. "You get it up for me." He spoke this faster than any other words he'd said in English.

She pulled away and tugged at her bodice. "I … I beg your pardon?"

"Get up, go up…" He spread his fingers, palms up. "How you say … give me a shove … make me rise."

"Oh, I make your *spirits* rise!" She released a relieved breath as he nodded. "Our languages get crossed and tangled. When you say one thing it can very well mean something so very different!"

He shrugged. "What I say?"

"Never mind." She patted his arm.

"I know words have different meanings. But you say in English … what canna you do?" He smiled and brushed her cheek with his fingertips.

He retrieved the basket of fruit and she linked her arm in his as they left the orchard together.

Back inside, she opened her writing desk, took out a velvet pouch tied with string and placed it in his hand. "This will aid you in your quest. 'Tis no fortune, but Valentine and I want you to live your dream and know that we helped make it come true."

Thanking her, he slipped it under his cloak. He lowered his head and kissed her on one cheek, then the other. "You will find your family. I only wish it were I. God bless you, darling Denys." He touched the brim of his hat.

"Godspeed, Cristoforo." She blew him a kiss as he rode away to find his world, and she returned to hers.

* * *

Marguerite of Anjou's message arrived the next day.

Denys offered the messenger a night's stay, a hearty meal and a handful of gold coins. She broke the seal and tore at the message with trembling hands as Valentine stood at her side.

"She must know who gave me to King Henry. She was there, she must know!" She unfolded the parchment.

Marguerite's stark handwriting stood in contrast to her flowery French. Denys read it out loud: "Several men named John served King Henry, but the oldest and most true, John Pasteler, served him from the very start. His surname meant sweetmeat cook, his occupation at the time of his service to the king. I remember him carrying a babe and giving it to King Henry, who handed it to a lady attendant." Denys was sure her heart stopped. "Dear God, the answer I've been looking for! But there is more." She read on, "John Smith..." She looked up at Valentine. He motioned her to read on.

"He, too, cradled a baby in his arms not long after—or was it before? I am not. Memory fades in old age." Denys took a ragged breath. "There were births at court in those years. A girl was born to a scullerymaid and one of the king's pages, John Norris. The child's mother went off, leaving the child as a ward of the king, but I know not what became of her. An usher named John and his wife had a baby I remember the king holding. Both John and his wife died of fever. I am not aware of the child's fate."

The message slid from her hand onto the table. "There are so many, I could be any of them." Marguerite's failing memory left Denys confused and discouraged. "This is worse than not knowing, now I shall never know."

Once again she became that abandoned child.

He embraced her. "Until end of my days, I will try to remember every John I ever heard of, from my earliest memories to my years with the Plantagenets after my mother died. We'll find him, my darling, I know we will."

She relaxed and breathed easily in his arms. "How can I ever lose hope when I have you?"

* * *

On Christmas Eve in Westminster Palace, the great hall glowed with Yule fire. Holly, ivy, and bay adorned the palace halls and scented the air. London was bathed in candlelight and blanketed in fresh snow. Green boughs decorated doors and parish churches. Carolers' voices blent in harmony. Mummers played in the streets. The great hall flowed with mummers, jugglers, fools, ale and wine. Richard's court was not as lusty as Edward's, yet Denys stumbled upon amorous pairs coupling in palace corners and nooks during this joyous season.

As courtiers exchanged gifts, Richard gave his councilors, retainers and staff wine, spices, and coin. He presented Denys with several dozen ermine bellies she'd praised when his tailor visited, the less-luxurious miniver being out of fashion. He gifted Valentine with Carrera marble blocks for Dovebury's hearths. Their gift to Richard was a jeweled tankard he christened Perkin. She thought it silly that men "named" their tankards, but since her shock at learning they also named their privy members, naming a tankard didn't seem so strange. She and Valentine spent many a night whooping with laughter guessing what the male courtiers named their own. They agreed Richard likely considered the lewd practice pure lasciviousness.

"But on second thought," Valentine said, "Richard's of such regal stock, he must call it Ethelbald."

At dinner in the great hall, he and Richard clinked tankards. The king and his trusted chancellor toasted each other's health, arms draped over each other's shoulders.

Valentine and Denys had just finished dancing, wine flowed, and she returned to the dais with him, aglow from malmsey she'd imbibed. Slipping her hand under the table, she whispered, "How is Canute the Great tonight?"

* * *

Richard's spies learnt that by summer, Henry Tudor would strive once more for England. Denys could not vex him by asking more help finding mysterious "John", the only known link to her family. She hardly saw Richard except for a rare appearance in the great hall. With Anne ill and preparation for yet another battle with Henry Tudor, Richard's time was not his own. When she did see him at Mass, he sat alone, head bowed, with no time for greetings before rushing to council or Anne's sickbed.

As chancellor, Valentine plotted late into the night…how many soldiers to call? How to fortify the coast? How to keep from losing the kingdom in battle?

He wrote speeches to deliver to Henry Tudor, drew up treaties and pacts, made alliances by trothplight, plotted ways to drive Tudor back to France. He drew up battle formations, using chess pieces for opposing armies. It seemed a game to him, directing all these lives and testing Henry Tudor's patience trying to outplan and checkmate him.

"This isn't work to you at all, is it?" Denys asked one eve as they sat in their winter parlour. "This is a game you're playing."

His head wasn't bowed, his brow wasn't furrowed from deep disturbing thoughts, no dark shadows around his eyes. In contrast to Richard, who bore the burden of the world on his shoulders, Valentine thrived on it all. But he still found time to go riding, dancing or sit before the fire with her…and make exquisite love to her.

"What do you mean … a game?" He did not look at her, his eyes fixed on the rolls of peerage supporting the crown.

"All this…" She gestured at the rolls. "Alliances, support, plots to exchange lands and territory, preparing for battle."

"We must maintain a strong defense, for Tudor has a most crafty spy—his mother," he shot back.

She blinked. "Margaret Beaufort is imprisoned."

"Aye, but she's married to Lord Stanley and I don't trust him. He made his peace with Richard by agreeing to support him, and Richard made him Constable of England, even though I advised against it. He's turned before. He joins whichever side looks best to him at the time. Richard is just too trusting."

"I'd hoped we heard the last of Henry Tudor." She ground her teeth in frustration. "Once and for all I wish you could crush him with one swift stroke."

Valentine shook his head, smiling. "It takes more than an army to bring down an enemy, my dear. It takes courtliness. Richard hasn't the eloquence of his brother Edward, but he has the army and the mind to execute a stratagem. Purging Tudor from our world solves our present problem, but not forever. It would be like laying a patch over a festering stab wound. After Tudor is defeated, someone else will rise in his stead. We need pacts for peace as well as war, in order to keep the peace and stay the hand of usurpers."

* * *

On Twelfth Night, the great hall glittered, decorated in shimmering greens, reds and golds. Logs blazed in the hearth, wine flowed and servers brought course after course on gold and silver platters. But once again, the seat beside King Richard on the dais was vacant, as were his eyes when Denys observed him up close. Impending invasion was the least of his worries, as Queen Anne was not foreseen to live much longer.

Denys approached Richard as servers began clearing the plates. She glanced at the mountains of food on his plates that his taster still happily consumed instead. "How is Anne?"

"Unwell. All the festivities finally did her in." He took a sip of wine.

"They all love her so. After the contempt Bess wrought, Anne is a beloved queen indeed." Her heart ached for the poor girl—so young, far too young to be facing the end. "Richard, please talk to me if you need a shoulder…anything at all."

His sad eyes scanned the great hall as courtiers danced, laughed, and reveled. "The doctors advise me to shun her bed."

"Pardon?" She leaned forward to hear it again; she couldn't have heard correctly.

"I am ordered to shun her bed. I shall never have my heir." He drew a deep breath and expelled it as he swept his hand over his eyes.

She clasped his hand. "Do not say that. You have heirs—your nephews."

"I know that and I love my nephews with all my heart. But they are Edwards's sons, not *my* sons—blood of mine and Anne's." His lips tightened into a thin line.

She knew what he meant and her heart burst with sorrow for him. Maybe if things had gone differently, if they had followed Elizabeth's order and married, he would have his heirs today. But she and Richard could never love each other in the true sense. It never could have been. And she never would have married Valentine...

"May I go to the queen? I shall sing for her and play upon my lute." She pushed her chair back and stood.

"Of course. She loves you like a sister." His eyes expressed all the gratitude he had no strength to speak.

* * *

The flames in Anne's hearth cast eerie flickering shadows over her sick bed. Denys gagged on the stale air. A chambermaid stood over Anne, holding out a linen cloth as she coughed.

As Denys approached Anne, memories flooded her mind: the glorious wedding gown Anne gave her, the kindness she showed when everyone, including Richard, had elbowed her aside. She prayed for this brave soul, the queen so beloved by her subjects, reduced to this pitiful figure coughing her life's blood away.

She dismissed the server and took her place at Anne's side.

Anne opened her eyes, glazed with exhaustion. "How kind to visit me when you could be enjoying the festivities." Her voice barely a whisper, it seemed each word took a major effort. Denys did not want to tell Anne that the mood in the great hall was far from festive. "How fares Richard?"

"He holds his head high, as always, Anne. He very much looks forward to your joining him again, as does the entire kingdom." She smoothed strands of hair from Anne's forehead.

She turned away. "I shall never return, I lie waiting for God to take me."

Denys grasped one hand and warmed it betwixt her palms. "Do not talk so. You will be fine, you have been ill before, we all have! You will recover. You must. You know how much Richard needs you."

"Apparently God needs me more. Richard has his kingdom. I am but one weak and trifling being." Her eyes slid shut.

She stroked Anne's cheek. "No one knows better than I how much he loves you."

"He has never shown it, Denys. I see you and Valentine together, laughing. He holds you in his arms, he lifts you up and whirls you about…" She took a labored breath. "Richard has never told me. He has never left my side except to go to battle or meetings, but he has never made me the center of his life, as he has been mine."

"But he has always kept to himself. Do not think for a minute that he does not love you," she tried desperately to lighten Anne's spirits.

Anne took to another coughing fit and Denys held a clean cloth to her lips. She sank back onto the pillows with a raspy sigh. "Tell me about you and Valentine."

"Why, everything is just fine."

She looked up at Denys and gave a weak smile. "You're sure of his intentions toward you now?"

Denys's heart grew warm. "Oh, yes, it was difficult getting him to open up, but he did. He wants to prove himself to me, but he really needn't."

"I know the torment Valentine has suffered for a long time now. I think Richard's need for Valentine at his side helped him work through all that." Her voice gained volume, the smile still on her lips.

"Torment? You mean his need to prove himself?"

"That's part of it." She looked into Denys's eyes. "You know Valentine's father perished in battle. When he was only nine, Valentine saw the unspeakable, his father's severed head atop Micklegate Bar. He vowed vengeance, and when old enough, became a spy for King Edward's first general. Enemy soldiers seized him and held him at Ludlow Castle, and within moments of his execution, Richard arrived with a column of soldiers and forced his release. He's always felt indebted to Richard for saving his life."

"Dear God. That's why he wants to be at Richard's side through all this?" Denys fingered the teardrop pearl resting on her chest.

"Nay." Anne shook her head. "Richard knows without Valentine, he'd make a calamity of it all. Matters of states aren't Richard's strength, battles and wars are."

"And Valentine does not feel a complete man until he pays Richard back," Denys concluded.

"If I know Val, he'll never feel he repaid Richard. You and he are very much alike. You're both on quests you need to fulfill. But you must see that having each other is enough, even if you never achieve your goals."

Denys released a relieved sigh. "Thank you for telling me this. Valentine never would."

"Nay, he makes no show of being honorable." Anne's smile died on her lips with another coughing fit. This time she spat drops of blood.

"Would you like me to sing for you, Anne?" The queen nodded and Denys picked up her lute from the foot of the bed. She began to play it softly and sing their favorite song, "When a Knight."

"When a knight won his spurs in the stories of old,
He was gentle and brave, he was gallant and bold;
With a shield on his arm and lance in his hand
For God and for valour he rode through the land.
No charger have I, and no sword by my side,
Yet still to adventure and battle I ride,
Though back into storyland giants have fled,
And the knights are no more and the dragons are dead.
Let faith be my shield and let joy be my steed
Gainst the dragons of anger, the gorgons of greed;
And let me set free, with the sword of my youth,
From the castle of darkness the power of truth."

Before she finished, Anne lay asleep. Denys slipped off the bed and tiptoed from her chambers.

That was the last time she saw Anne alive. The queen passed away in early spring, her frail body no longer able to fight the consumption that took her away.

* * *

As Denys approached the chapel of Edward the Confessor, Richard stood over Anne's grave. He stroked her name carved into the stone and left the chapel. Denys stayed graveside and prayed for the queen's soul, for her king, and for the kingdom.

* * *

On Midsummer's Eve, Valentine, Denys and Richard walked through the royal forest near Sandal Castle after a day of stag hunting.

The bloodhounds', brachets' and greyhounds' barking faded into the distance as the hunting company led the dogs back to their kennels.

Caught up in the mood, Denys playfully blew her ivory hunting horn. Its soft bellow echoed through the trees and died in the depths of the forest.

The trio separated from the retinue and approached a cluster of tree stumps. Valentine sat upon a stump and she stretched her legs out on the grass. Richard remained standing.

"I wish you would sit, Richard." Valentine offered them slabs of bread from his pouch. Denys gladly accepted but Richard declined.

"It's these blasted rumours, all the rumours." Richard paced in wide circles. "Rumours I poisoned my wife, rumours I had George executed, rumours I had Edward killed ... sweet Jesu!" Shoulders slumped, he clenched and unclenched his fists.

"Do not let rumours vex you." Valentine opened his wine flask. "Some folk live such empty lives, they have nowt to live for but to wag their cruel tongues. We know none of it is true."

"'Tis Bess Woodville, I know it," he spoke as if he hadn't heard Valentine. "She started it all, she kindled the flames of hatred against me that spread like a bout of plague, but she is the source. Even as king I cannot escape her foul sorcery. And they now gossip that I want to marry her daughter!" A bitter laugh escaped his throat. "I would dive into boiling oil before I would marry any daughter of hers. Even the thought of that witch as a mother-in-law sickens me." He spat on the ground.

"Bess cannot harm any of us. There are real threats, like Henry Tudor," Valentine warned.

"Henry Tudor is but a pustule on my arse." Richard scowled.

"I know. But he is steadfast. He has spies and finance. His mother sold Maxey Castle to some Irish popinjay to finance that last invasion of his. Nonetheless,

I believe his next invasion will be his last." Valentine's voice boomed with confidence. "And do keep a close eye on Thomas Stanley, even though he's with our side on the face of it."

Richard gave a half-smile. "Val, my friend, only you would surely never turn on me. I trust you as no other. I could not even trust George." He turned to Denys. "And you..." He bowed his head. "I slighted you. I promised to help you but it fell by the wayside."

She approached him. "No, you've had so much to bear..."

"I shall keep my promise. I shall dig and dig until I unearth the answer you seek."

"I wrote to Marguerite of Anjou but her reply left me more confused than ever." She closed her eyes and pictured Marguerite's sea of words. "So many men named John, all leading me nowhere."

"Did she say anything helpful?"

"There was a John with a babe in King Henry's charge, all right. And another, and yet another. Any of them could be me." She gazed at the patches of sky peeking through the treetops.

"I shall see what I can do." Richard took Valentine's flask, placed the opening to his lips and took a swill.

"She gave me names that amount to nowt." Denys slid her foot back and forth in the dirt.

"Show me her message." He handed the flask back to Valentine. "I shall see if it contains any modicum of sense."

One of Richard's pages galloped up on a slick mount. He swept off his hat and bowed his head. "My liege, the evening meal is served. Your faithful court awaits you." He bowed his head again and trotted off.

"Duty calls once more." Richard led as they headed to the castle. Courtiers swarmed round the feast. "See how difficult it is to be king? I must fight off invaders, rule a discontented rabble, and eat when I am not the least bit hungry. Why in hell would I kill anyone for this?"

* * *

"Every other man in Christendom is named John Smith." Denys inspected the month's household accounts, but her mind was not on the entries. "Commonest name in the kingdom."

John Smith was the name Valentine remembered from his visit with John Grantham. "With only John to go by, we have done quite well." Valentine took a swig of ale from Percival.

"We have not done enough." She rubbed her tired eyes. "Until we have found him."

"It may be years," he warned. "We may divert. John isn't the only road to Rome, you know."

She looked up at him and tucked a stray lock of hair back under her head-dress. "What do you suggest? Oh, Valentine, you have no idea what it is to be adult and still feel yourself an abandoned orphan."

His tankard on its way to his mouth, he halted and pounded it on the table as their eyes met. "How wrong you are. You forget I lost my parents at a tender age." His voice wavered. "What I would give to have them back." He approached and rubbed her neck. "I do want to help, and I know in my heart that we will find your family."

"But you have fits when I go off by myself," she countered.

"In blinding snowstorms without telling me, yes." He gave a wholehearted nod.

"The storm did not begin until after I left," she stated.

"You should have turned back. 'Twas madness to trudge on in those conditions." He dug his fingers into her neck muscles.

"What do you propose?" She relaxed under his touch. "If you believe it might lead to my family, mayhap you can beg Richard a leave to go with me. How will we proceed?"

"Priests." His hands slid down to her shoulders.

"Priests?" Her muscles stiffened. "That sounds unlikely."

"King Henry the Sixth's favorite companions were priests. Old Henry was like a virtuous monk, he spent more time praying than ruling, which Queen Marguerite did well enough. Let us find the priests who kept his company. 'Tis possible one of them baptized you. If so, it may be recorded somewhere who your parents are."

"Very well, where to start searching out priests?" She sighed in contentment as his fingers worked their magic.

"Westminster. Some of King Henry's priests are still there, and if their memories fail them, they can tell where we can find others. If that does not bear fruit, then we try the churches within the City walls. There is Saint Andrew

Undershaft, Saint Peter in Cheap, and Saint Paul's on Ludgate Hill. Then we can venture farther out, St. Martin-in-the-Fields—"

"Very well." She reached back and grasped his hands. "I shall start with the priests at Westminster. And when we find the priest who baptized me, I want to be baptized again." She turned to face him. "Because I am starting my life over."

He knelt and planted kisses on her neck. "I can see how finding your family will make you feel that way, but I love you no matter who you are."

* * *

Next morn, Denys accompanied Valentine to Richard's council chambers.

Valentine bowed, she dipped her head. All this formal rigor among old friends made Richard scowl and scoff, but Denys wanted to honor Uncle Ned's memory above all.

"Now that we've dispensed with pompous customs, sit, both of you." Richard gestured to two chairs across from his writing desk. They sat as he straightened a stack of documents. "What brings you here, my faithful friends?"

"Denys is going to test a few more memories for her quest." Valentine sat and folded his hands betwixt his knees.

"Whose memories?" Richard pulled a ring off and slid it back on.

"The priests who befriended King Henry during his reign," Valentine replied.

"I believe one of them must have baptized me," Denys added. "Is that not a distinct possibility?"

Richard nodded, stroking his chin. "I suppose."

Valentine cleared his throat. "If possible, I may ask your leave to accompany Denys to the more far-reaching abbeys of the realm."

"Aye, as you wish," Richard agreed without hesitation.

"You find no problem with that, Richard?" A touch of hurt clouded Valentine's eyes.

"'Tis all right! Go!" Richard waved his hand in assent. "I have enough problems with would-be usurpers and their spying mothers without gaining the reputation of a tyrant. So you have my best wishes. Good luck and Godspeed. Denys, I hope they can help. If not, do not despair, for we shall seek out another road."

Denys stood. "I am off to Westminster to see the priests. Valentine, take care of our king." She dipped her head and exited the chamber. He blew her a kiss.

Valentine turned to Richard. "Before we get to business, I must get a meal down you."

"I do fancy a game pie with a tankard of strong ale, now that you mention it," Richard mused.

"Then let us savor the first repast we've had together in months." He stood and stared at the door Denys just exited. "I've never met anyone as resolved as that woman I married! She won't give up till death stops her, even if that's what it takes, a final personal audience with God to tell her who she is."

"That is where we are alike, Val, the three of us." Richard placed his documents in a drawer and locked it with a key from his belt. "Never afraid to die for a worthy cause. Would that I die for a worthy cause rather than waste away, as Bess Woodville is now fated to do."

"Do you still believe her a witch?" Valentine followed Richard to the door.

"If she is, her powers wane," he replied over his shoulder.

"As yours grow, my liege." Valentine gave Richard a slight bow, not as low as custom demanded. "May I lead my king to my favorite dockside tavern, in discreet disguise, for a hearty repast?"

"Mint peas with that pie and ale?" Richard gave Valentine a pat on the bum.

"Your subjects mustn't see you in a dockside tavern. Some flour to gray your hair, some tattered raiment and we're off!" They exited the chamber, two hungry and thirsty old friends.

* * *

As Valentine traveled to King Henry VI's resting place of Chertsey Abbey to meet the priests, Denys appealed to those at Westminster Abbey who'd known King Henry. Several priests shared fond memories of the ill-fated king but none remembered baptizing a baby girl during or close to 1457. Nor did they remember a John present at that time or know the woman in her small picture.

"King Henry was pious, indeed," recalled white-haired Father Carney as they wandered the ancient cloisters. "He bellowed 'Fie! For shame!' at any wench displaying bosom. When they brought Marguerite of Anjou over to be his bride, twas *he* who blushed, all the way to his marriage bed!" His eyes fastened on long-ago memories. "His highness was addled, but kind. Folk pillaged his lands and treasure till the crown sank hopelessly mired in debt. His own household officers stole from under his nose. Fond memories of dull-witted King Henry aside, Father Carney did not remember baptizing a baby girl that year.

But Father Welde, despite advanced age, sported coal black hair and a fit body, and remembered more than all the rest combined: "A man gave an infant to King Henry at Mass in his chambers when the king was too ill to attend chapel."

"Do you remember who else was there, Father?" Her heart raced as she wiped her damp palms on her skirts.

"'Twas Christmas service, if I remember..." He shut his eyes, deep in thought. "I ministered. Now let me see..." He tapped his fingers on his front teeth. "Oh, all the top councilors attended...Buckingham, Northumberland, Queen Marguerite, King Henry's doctor..."

She clasped her hands as if in prayer. "I was born in 'fifty-seven. Can you remember the babe's parents?"

He shook his head. "I am sorry, child, there were so many in those chambers that Christmas, and it were so long ago."

She placed her hand on his sleeve. "Please, Father, I need to know. That infant may have been I."

He gave her a smile and an encouraging nod. "I shall sequester in chapel and pray God I remember. If so, I shall summon you back."

"Oh, thank you, Father!" She kissed his ring as if he were the Pope and tiptoed out as not to interrupt his train of thought.

Her heart pounded as she pranced over the uneven slabs out of the Abbey. If God's servant could not help, then nobody could.

*   *   *

Handing her mount's reins to her groom, she walked back home, alone. Oblivious to the mongers' shouts and rumbling carts, she stared straight ahead, intent on thoughts close to her heart. She didn't relive the despair, the red herrings. Her family was within reach. Had they spent the last twenty years searching for her, wondering if she was dead or alive?

Walking through the orchard reminded her of Christoforo. Where was he now? Was he as close to his dream as she was to hers?

"Good afternoon, darling wife." She turned to see Valentine. She opened her arms to welcome an embrace as he strode up, his forced half-smile telling her everything.

Their embrace was brief. "I met and talked with a dozen priests who had fond and not-so-fond remembrances of King Henry, but none knew the John who held an infant in 1457. I'm so sorry." His lips quivered, as if he were about to cry.

"Don't be." She grasped his hands.

"You found something, love?" His tone brightened as his eyes lit up. "Do you want to sit?" He motioned to her favorite bench facing the river.

"I cannot sit. Father Welde gave Mass in King Henry's chambers, saw a baby and remembered baptizing me. That is, if it was me," she gushed in one breath.

"Slow down," Valentine's voice soothed her as he stroked her arms. "Did he say who else attended?"

"Everyone, king, queen, King Henry's doctor, many folk..." She ran out of breath and gulped air. "He promised to try to remember who held me ... er, the child. He believes he will remember correctly by giving it thought and prayer."

Valentine's eyes caught the glow of the setting sun behind them. His rings sparkled as he smoothed his chin, a faraway look in his eyes. She never dared interrupt him whilst searching that perfect passage in a missive or plotting battle lines.

After a moment of silence, he turned and headed for the door. "Do not hold supper. I'll be in chapel. This may take a while," he called over his shoulder.

* * *

Valentine entered their dark empty chapel. He lit a single candle and sat in his pew. Elbows on knees, head in hands, he searched the far reaches of his childhood memories...

As he closed his eyes in earnest intention, fragments began to fit together.

King Henry was never in sound mind, even in childhood. Valentine remembered Richard's mother and brothers discussing 'King Henry's curse' or 'King Henry's affliction' or 'King Henry's incontinence.' The king always had doctors at his side, examining him, spewing cures, each more outlandish than the last. One doctor he remembered now was also a priest. The Plantagenets brought Valentine on visits to court as a child. King Henry, old and infirm even then, always leaned on this doctor-priest's arm. Valentine pictured his face as a smudge in a foggy corner of his memory ... this preacher had proclaimed King Henry's title to the throne all those years ago. He never left the king's side. Valentine now gleaned the man's face more clearly, because he saw him again not long ago...

At the first privy council meeting Valentine attended, that same preacher accompanied George to King Edward's council chamber. George and the preacher burst into the chamber. George babbled about usurping Edward and that strife led to George's destruction.

He slapped the bench with his open palm. "That's him! Father Goddard! Father *John* Goddard."

Chapter Fourteen

King Richard sat in his Nottingham Castle solar engrossed in a chess game with the earl of Devonshire's son. The door burst open and Thomas Stanley stormed in, a glaring breach of custom. "Your highness!" The guards seized his arms and started to drag him out.

Richard looked up and waved the guards away with a nod of dismissal. "Leave him, he is Constable of England, he excites easily."

They bowed out, bumping into each other along the way.

Red and panting, Stanley approached Richard and doubled over in a deep bow.

"Rise, Stanley." Richard pushed back his chair and stood. "God's truth, what is it?"

"My liege, Henry Tudor and two thousand Welshmen under his colors are at Shrewsbury." He gulped for breath. "Sir Gilbert Talbot has declared for him with several hundred retainers at the ready."

All this strengthening of the Tudor army made Richard wonder what side Stanley would take. But he kept that to himself. He drank from his tankard and wiped the ring it left on the table. "Very well then. At dawn we depart for yet another battle with Lancastrians, their destriers, and that horse's ass, Harry Tudor." He gave Stanley a casual wave. "You are dismissed." He sat back down and studied the chessboard, to his opponent's stunned surprise.

"Will you not prepare with all haste, your highness?" The boy's voice quivered.

He moved his bishop three squares. "Nay, Taffy Harry can wait. He can't fight a battle without me, now, can he?"

Gulping, the youngster nodded and made his move, confusing pieces and putting Richard in check with his own knight by mistake.

Richard responded with a smile: "'Tis hard enough to win a battle without my own knights turning against me." He grasped the lad's trembling hand. "Worry not about Tudor. When he runs from this battle, the only way to tell him from those ugly French whores is that he'll be wearing my broadsword for a codpiece."

* * *

Richard and his generals arrived in Leicester two days afore the intended battle and roomed at the White Boar Inn. As grooms assembled the king's bed in the largest chamber, Valentine and Richard set their tankards down on a table to flatten the drawing of the battle lines.

"Remember Dr. John Goddard, the preacher who took care of King Henry?" Valentine asked the king.

Richard pulled bags of coin from his satchel and began secreting them in a drawer in the bed frame. "Aye, he accompanied George the day he burst into privy council. I could hear Edward's blood boil clear across the chamber."

"He's the one. Denys told me a certain Father Welde was present when an infant was presented unto King Henry by a physician. I have the strangest feeling." He paced back and forth. "The physician may have been John Goddard. Do you know his whereabouts?"

Richard nodded. "Aye, he dwells in Chelsea, not far from my townhome."

Valentine's eyes grew wide. "Are you sure? I don't want her hopes shattered again."

"I saw him but a few days ago." Richard sat and began to polish his war helmet.

"Grand!" Valentine clapped his palms together. "I shall send a message to Denys and have her call on him. I shall not be a minute in composing it. 'Twill give her something to do while we're at battle."

Richard polished his helmet. "That should keep her busy, but it will not take any more effort to repel Tudor than it'll take her to journey to London. At least it won't snow," he added.

Valentine took parchment, quill and an ink horn, and began to write. "I want this as much as she does, for her to find her family."

"You mean in case we don't win this battle and she loses a husband." Richard attempted a smile.

"I know we will rout Tudor's army," Valentine assured him. "But we both know the seriousness of this challenge. Some of our followers may turn on us with a change in wind direction—and Thomas Stanley is the most volatile of all. You know how desperate Denys is to find her family. She lives for it."

Richard placed his helmet down and spread the polishing rag over it. "Whoever they are, if they love her half as much as you do, she will be most fortunate."

* * *

Denys entered London's Aldgate far ahead of her retinue, Valentine's note tucked in her bodice. As the guards at the gate bowed and offered polite greetings, one thought stayed on her mind: Father John Goddard was her last hope.

In Chelsea, she inquired of a villager where to find John Goddard's residence. As she knocked on the door of his townhome with trembling hand, her grooms caught up to her and remained mounted. She held her breath as the door opened to a young maid. "Good day, I am here to see Father Goddard."

The maid gaped at the regal figure adorned in the finest silks. Then she glanced over Denys's shoulder at her retinue in their equally fine attire. Backing off and bumping the door, she bowed her head and rushed inside. "Father! Father! Royalty is here, I know not if she be the queen or the Princess Elizabeth or … she stands here at your doorstep!" Her shrill cries echoed through the narrow foyer. "Me lord! Me lord!"

Denys hid a smile in her palm as John Goddard appeared and gave a polite bow. "Please, Father, I am neither queen nor princess. I am Denys Starbury, duchess of Norwich. I have a few questions about my past."

"Surely, duchess, come to the great hall." He ushered Denys into a room with a simple table, hardback chairs and hearth. "Please forgive Jane, my lady. We never see such as your grace in these parts."

Valentine had mentioned Goddard's coal-black hair, sturdy stature and clear eyes. He retained all this, long after attending King Henry.

She smiled. "Tis quite all right, Father Goddard. I should have sent notice. But I am in far too much haste. I need your help desperately."

"Oh, please. If you will, my lady. Do ask. I am at your service." He bade her sit but she declined.

"You were in service to King Henry the Sixth as his physician, were you not, Father?" She began to ask the vital questions.

He reddened and grasped the back of a chair. "Ah … aye," he stammered, "but that was long ago, my allegiance to the House of Lancaster ended with King Henry's demise, then I served the duke of Clarence—"

"Do be calm, this is nowt to do with allegiance," Denys's composed tone put the doctor at ease, for Goddard loosened his white-knuckled grip on the chair. "It concerns an infant child, a ward of King Henry. You were there at her first Christmas in 1457 during the Mass in the king's chambers, do you recall?"

"Fifty-seven, Christmas, that was…" Eyes closed, he tapped his forehead. "Aye!" He opened his eyes and nodded. "The silver-haired child."

Silver-haired. Her heart took a tumble.

"Where did the king get her? Do you know her parentage?" she goaded, all in one breath.

"You will not sit, my lady?" He pulled a chair out.

"I am too taut to sit. Pray go on." She motioned with her hands.

"King Henry became her warden, after her young mother handed her to me. She carries royal blood, but I know not how thick. I baptized her and gave her to King Henry, saying 'take good care of her, sire, she may be of value someday.' Then the king, with the blankest of looks on his face, knowing not what to do, looked round, then handed her off to a nurse."

"Was the baptism recorded in the parish records at Westminster?" she asked.

"Aye." He nodded. "But under what name, I know not."

"Woodville?" she prompted. "Elizabeth Woodville took me in after my mother died. That child may be me."

"Oh, I doubt it, lass." He shook his head. "'Twould likely be your father's name. But I've no way to know who he was."

"Do you not know my mother's name?" Her voice broke. By now she could hardly breathe.

"My memory betrays me." He pressed his hand to his eyes. "For the love of God, what is the lady's name? Oh, Jesu, let it come to me!"

"Please," she begged, her breaths ragged.

"My memory fails me as my eyes fail me. How my wits delude me. But I shall try, lass. No other thought will enter my silly head till I remember her name."

Oh, let him see this face and remember! She slipped the small locket out and held it before him. "Father, is this the lady?" He opened his eyes and blinked, took the picture and held it closer, then farther, trying to see it clearly. Recognition lit up his eyes and he nodded. "Aye, 'tis she, as if she stands before me and breathes. This locket—she wore it that very day in the chapel."

Denys gazed at the locket as if for the first time. Now she knew for certes. By the grace of God, her mother's eyes looked back at her. "Ma mere." She'd never spoken those words in her life.

She looked at Father Goddard. "You cannot remember her name, Father?" She stepped into a beam of sunlight shining through the window. "Please remember," she beseeched and held out her hand. "Come here to this sunbeam, so warm and bright, straight from God. Perhaps the answer is here. Stand here and hear God speak."

He approached the sunbeam and looked up at the sky. She backed out of his way, studying him as he stood in the light pouring from heaven, encircling him.

"Let me think on my own, lass," he spoke without moving. "I promise when you come back, God will have given me the answer."

She thanked him and left him standing in the sunbeam, waiting ... waiting to change her life.

* * *

Leaving her traveling party at her London townhome to rest, she had a groom saddle a fresh mount and accompany her to Westminster Hall. Her mother's locket rested next to her heart. Its pounding kept her alert. She'd already rehearsed her words to Elizabeth Woodville a thousand times over.

* * *

"Tell the queen her niece waits without," she told the page who opened the door. She pictured Elizabeth studying her book of hours, in expiation for a lifetime.

Elizabeth and her children lived sequestered behind locked doors and armed guards. The page led Denys into a damp antechamber. Elizabeth's youngest daughters gathered in the corner singing softly.

Elizabeth appeared, unable to sweep down the corridor in a rustle of satins and gauze, for she wore but a simple black cloak, devoid of jewels. Her appearance shocked Denys. She recoiled at a sudden stab of pity. No anger. No hatred. Denys knew this woman no longer had the capacity for cruelty.

I am grown now; she can no longer oppress me.

The doorway dwarfed the former queen's figure. The willful spark in her eye had dulled to the tiredness of worn-out pewter. Her face was drawn and bony. Loose skin hung from her chin.

She rushed up to Denys and embraced her like a long-lost daughter. "What a lovely surprise! I've been so alone, how I long for company, and here you are."

Denys no longer felt the contempt that filled her heart all those years. She would never walk through this door again.

She searched Elizabeth's eyes for some hint of transparency, but the broken woman wallowed in the mire of self-defeat. Years of baiting and destroying victims had finally taken their toll. Empty and resigned, the deposed queen's fate had dealt her a final blow she no longer had strength to resist.

"Aunt Bess—" She struggled to steady her voice. Years of memories washed over her all at once. She no longer even know who Elizabeth Woodville was. "I am so sorry about Uncle Ned. I loved him so and miss him. A part of me died along with him."

"I know how much you loved your uncle. 'Tis a pity you and I could never share such closeness." She showed no remorse or grief. She seemed devoid of all feeling.

You never wanted to share, she ached to say. *You shoved me aside and sent me away. You never wanted me. Now, twenty years later, 'tis a pity?*

Aye, a pity it is. "But look how it worked out, Aunt Bess. I have Valentine whom I love dearly and I believe I carry his child."

"I'm to have a grandniece or nephew? That is marvelous!" After the briefest glance at Denys's middle, Elizabeth clasped her hands together. For the first time, a hint of color appeared in those stormy eyes.

Denys fought back tears with all her strength. To acknowledge Denys's child as her grandniece or nephew was the farthest Elizabeth ever reached out to her. But it was too late. If she'd treated Denys like a niece instead of an outcast, Denys would have believed herself a Woodville. But that seven-year-old forever cried out, *Aunt Bess, who are my Lord Father and ma mere?* And now, with God's help, Denys could finally tell her. Now that lost little girl inside her could rest in contentment.

"I see Prince Richard has joined his brother Prince Edward in the Tower. I am glad for Edward. He was so alone there," Denys said.

"Twas a fatal mistake to let him go join his brother." Elizabeth turned and looked at her daughters. "I mistrust Gloucester."

Of course she hadn't expected Elizabeth to refer to Richard as king or even by title . "He has no reason to trust you either. You should pledge a truce."

"I'll have no truce with Gloucester." She turned to Denys once more, her lips a thin line.

"The princes will be fine," Denys spoke the truth.

"At least I still have my girls." She once again gazed at her youngest offspring.

"Aunt Bess, I've come to show you something." Denys swept the beads out from under her chemise and held them up to Elizabeth. As the locket swung to and fro, Denys gestured for her to take it.

Elizabeth grasped the locket and studied the picture, then looked at Denys. "Where did you get this?"

"It matters not where I got it. But is she not lovely? She's someone I'm sure you know well. She looks so regal, as if born to the throne." She snatched it away afore Elizabeth could tighten her grip.

"So that is why you are here. You would never just visit me, would you?" Elizabeth's eyes narrowed. Now she was her old self.

Denys knew the answer to that: "Possibly in time, after the pain eases. But that is not the issue." This matter was of utmost import. She was closer to the truth than ever in her life. "This lady resembles me, does she not?" She didn't await a reply. "Amazing. I can see myself in her eyes." She kept her voice steady, though tears pressed to burst forth.

Elizabeth jerked her head with a snort. "Oh, cease. Now I know why Thomas Stanley rides into battle. He'd rather better see two thousand horses' asses than that beastly countenance." She flicked a hand at the locket.

Denys gasped. Thomas Stanley?

Her mind reeled back through the documents, she matched names and faces from court, pictured every person walking through their door.

Thomas Stanley was married to Margaret Beaufort!

"Margaret Beaufort is my mother?" she breathed in an anguished whisper. Hearing it from her own lips made her heart stop.

Elizabeth's eyes ceased their careless wandering and pinned her. Two pairs of eyes locked, two wills clashed, ever circling each other, but neither one succumbing to defeat. Until now.

Victory! She'd lost every battle, but finally won the war. It had taken a lifetime to defeat Elizabeth Woodville. She had nowt more to say to this woman, now a stranger in every sense.

The beads fell to the floor. Denys reached them before Elizabeth's foot came down, intent on crushing them. She swept them up and thrust them down her bodice.

"At last I know who I am. Farewell—your *highness*," she added, deliberately and mockingly.

"You mean you didn't know? You—you tricked me?" Elizabeth shrilled, as if anyone could best England's once-formidable queen.

Denys shut her eyes to black out the sight of this woman from her mind forever. Without another word, she turned and quit the chamber.

Margaret Beaufort—the Lancastrian spy who financed her son Henry Tudor against Richard and provided intelligence to the enemy, the enemy herself—her own mother. Imprisoned in the Tower for treason, awaiting execution after this latest battle.

"Ma Mere," she whispered.

Denys rounded the corner, exited the chambers and closed the outer door behind her, shutting out her past. Once outside, she looked straight ahead, into her future.

* * *

At the small Westminster chapel, she asked the chaplain for the 1457 birth records.

Margaret Beaufort was thrice wed. Was one of those husbands her father?

Denys slowly turned each page of the thick book until she found the leaf headed '1457' in ornate script. Taking a deep breath, eyes forced wide open, she traced her finger down the list of names...

...and found it.

A girl...and a boy...twins...born January 28, 1457 to Margaret Beaufort and her husband Edmund Tudor.

"My father was Edmund Tudor? Oh, God Jesus," she cried. "Oh, no."

Denys bowed her head, made a fist, pounded the book in anguish. Henry Tudor, at this moment fighting to seize Richard's crown, battling her beloved Valentine, was her own twin brother.

The long-lost family she'd longed for was now the enemy—the dreaded Lancastrians.

She fled the chapel, mounted her horse, and ordered her groom, "To the Tower of London," where her mother languished, awaiting death.

* * *

The guard stationed at the White Tower regarded her with awe and confusion. It was plain she was no commoner, but with tangled hair and muddied gown, she hardly looked noble.

"Tell me where to find Lady Margaret Beaufort," she demanded.

"The Beauchamp Tower, my lady." He waved in that direction. "But why—"

"I am her daughter!" Saying it for the first time to this stranger seemed to ruin the magic of the revelation. Somehow she'd pictured it differently. She wanted to tell Valentine or write it in her journal, not spout it to a stranger.

"Lead me to her, please," she requested politely.

She followed him across the outer court, knowing she could go back home and alter the course of history, but she didn't dare. Swallowing her misgivings, she climbed the winding stone steps and strode down the dank passageway. They halted before a wooden door.

Now only this door separated her from her heritage, her own flesh and blood, Beaufort blood.

The guard unlocked the door with an iron key and swung it open. Denys took a deep breath. He backed away.

A woman sat with her back to Denys at a small desk, writing. With its pallet of straw and open window, it hardly resembled a dungeon. No mold clung to the walls. No rats scuttled past. No piles of waste lay about. No dreadful shroud of doom hung in the air. She smelled no fear, sensed no impending death.

The woman turned and looked at her. She saw that same face from the locket, but aged. Their eyes met in instant recognition.

A scene flashed before her: a young mother handing her baby to an older woman. "You must raise her as your niece," she told the woman. "She is royal and a daughter of our enemy. Never let her know who she is."

Denys trembled, her breath catching in her throat. She stepped forward into her mother's outstretched arms.

"I prayed you would come, my child." She embraced Denys. "After all these years, I can finally hold you. Oh, how much precious time we've lost."

"Ma mere," Denys spoke to her mother for the first time. "I'm here now so let us not look back. We will start anew from this moment."

Their tears mingled, tears of feelings that words could never convey, in English, French or any language. Their tears and embrace said everything.

Her fear of warring enemies and slaughter vanished. Her twin brother, her husband, and her king were not fighting to the death for England's crown. In the face of this miracle, that couldn't be happening on a field near Leicester.

"You're with child." Her mother surprised her with that observance. She held Denys's chin twixt her strong fingers.

"How do you know?"

"I see it in your face. You glow." She smiled.

"Aye, I am." She placed her hands on her middle. "I'm having your grand-child."

"I prayed all your life for this moment." She clasped Denys's hands over the life within. "But at the same time, I feared you'd hate me for giving you away."

Denys looked into her mother's eyes, so like her own. "I knew you didn't give me up because you didn't want me. I knew that as much as I knew I was no Woodville. Now that I know who you are, I know why you gave me away. You were afraid."

"Oh, my child." Her eyes spilled over with tears. "I was so fiercely defensive of you, you'll never know. I had to do what was best for you."

"Please start at the beginning, ma mere," she requested.

"I was King Henry's ward and when I was twelve, he married me to his half-brother Edmund Tudor. He was King Henry's heir. Along with my right to the throne through my ancestors, we were to reign together as king and queen. He went to fight in the Battle of St. Albans. Yorkists seized him and he died of plague two months later. I birthed you and your brother Henry at Pembroke Castle six months later." As she spoke, she led Denys to the pallet, for she had but one chair. Denys gathered her skirts and sat cross-legged on the horsehair blanket. She sank into the straw.

Her mother knelt beside her. "The king married me to Henry Stafford, and we went to live in Lincolnshire, on the edge of the Fens. I sent you and Henry away separately to ensure the greatest safety. I knew Henry would be safest with your uncle Jasper in Wales, because of the endless war between Yorkists and Lancastrians here in England. I had big dreams for Henry. I wanted him on the throne, so I had his uncle train him as a warrior as soon as he could lift a sword. With his royal heritage, he deserves the throne, if not through blood, by battle. So I helped finance his armies. But you—my daughter, my princess—" She faltered. "I had to make a much greater sacrifice for you. I told King Henry you died, and delivered you unto Elizabeth Woodville. Because I feared for your life even more than Henry's, I asked Elizabeth to change your name and keep it secret."

Denys tensed at the Woodville name. "Why give me to her?"

"I had good reason to give you to her, and she had good reason to take you in. She had a mad fancy for Edward Plantagenet and thought him destined for greatness, perhaps even the throne. I knew Edward quite well. Our families are kindred and we spent much of our childhood at Maxey Castle in Northampton-shire. Elizabeth promised me she'd protect you if I made match twixt her and Edward. But if Edward didn't fall under her spell, she wanted something else in the bargain—the manor house and its lands that I inherited, Foxley Manor."

"Was she always so greedy?" Speaking of her left a sour taste in Denys's mouth.

Her mother shook her head. "Nay, not till she knew she had the upper hand. As for Edward, I told him he should court Elizabeth. I always teased him about his wenching and urged him to take a wife. I told him of a beauteous widow with a burning desire to meet him. I arranged for him to court her under an oak tree in Grafton. It's become legend. The superstitious folk brand it witchcraft, but it really happened that way. He fell for Elizabeth at once. Belief held that she'd cast a spell, but it was nowt more than simple attraction. He was smitten."

Denys knew all too well how hard Uncle Ned had fallen. "It may as well have been witchcraft. He was always under her spell."

Her mother went on, "Then Edward seized the throne, overthrowing King Henry. As a Lancastrian in line for the throne, you were in terrible danger if your claim were known. All this while I had a beauteous daughter I couldn't acknowledge. It tore my heart to shreds."

"That is way Bess did not tell me who I was when Uncle Ned became king. To ensure I'd never claim the throne." Denys's chest tightened as she clenched her fists.

"Of course. When Elizabeth knew she was to be queen, she had more reason than ever to keep you secret. The fewer claimants to her husband's throne, the better. If an enemy learned who you were, they could put you on the throne and oust her husband King Edward. After birthing Edward's heir, she knew anyone with a claim to the throne was a threat to her princes."

"Did Uncle Ned know who I am?" Denys asked.

She shook her head. "Nay. He believed you to be Elizabeth's niece."

"He would have told me the truth had he known." A stab of grief for Uncle Ned pierced her heart.

"He may well have, my dear, with no regard for his crown or his life. He was too honest and noble. That is why I could not tell him. 'Tis one thing to have a son in the thick of battle for the crown, but not my daughter."

Restless, Denys stood, paced in circles, and stopped at the window overlooking the deserted outer court.

Her mother got to her feet and stood at her side. "As for my life," she said over a sigh, "After Henry Stafford died, I married my third husband, Thomas Stanley. He wavered 'tween the Yorkists and Lancastrians. Finally I moved him to support my son, which he agreed to do in this latest battle."

Digesting these hard truths, Denys closed her eyes and reopened them as if waking from a dream.

They stood side by side in silence and wound their arms round each other.

"I know you do not want to hear it, Denys, being raised Yorkist, but your brother does have a rightful claim to the throne. And so do you," her mother stated the truth.

"Oh, Jesu, no." Denys clasped her trembling hands together. "I do not want it! Bess's two princes are declared bastards. Now the crown belongs to Richard."

"That all depends on how hard he fights for it." Her tone sharpened. "This time Henry will win."

"You know my husband fights at Richard's side." Denys looked her mother in the eye.

"I know, my dear. But God willing, he shan't perish. He and Henry may even become friends." With a thoughtful sigh, she gazed out the window.

"Valentine is not your husband. His loyalties are unwavering." Denys no longer wanted to discuss court affairs or battles or claims to the throne. This moment was too precious, it would not be so again—until she met her twin brother.

Her mother changed the subject for her. "I hope to meet my little granddaughter."

Denys's jaw dropped. "How do you know 'twill be a girl?"

"You want a girl?"

"Aye." She nodded. "I've always wanted a girl!"

"Then you shall have a girl."

* * *

At dusk, Denys left her mother and returned to Rockingham, their home in Leicester. When she next gazed into her mirror, someone else looked back at her. Denys Beaufort Tudor. With a claim to the throne of England.

At this moment, her brother battled her husband and her king. But she did not fear Henry Tudor and his unstable support. She had faith in King Richard and his first general, no matter who betrayed them.

But Henry was her brother, and every battle ended with but one winner.

And one loser.

"Please, God," she prayed, still stunned beyond belief. "Please keep them all safe." For some strange reason, she felt trapped—with nowhere to turn.

Chapter Fifteen

Valentine charged up the hill, leading his men, his face pale and unsmiling. Denys tore across the outer court. Her heart pounded as if it would burst.

He unhorsed and she embraced him. "Are you hurt?"

"I am not hurt, but…" His voice broke. He could not look her in the eye. "There is something I must tell you…"

"Wh—what happened? What happened?" she stammered, her thoughts in fragments, her mind addled by the torment of waiting.

Placing a finger over her lips, he finally made eye contact. "Denys—" A sob escaped his throat. "Richard was killed in the battle."

Her breath halted. "W—what?" She couldn't have heard right.

He paused and took a deep breath. "Richard is dead. Tudor has won."

"No. No, Valentine." She shook her head, stunned by this outlandish revelation. He had to be wrong.

"Please listen to me!" He clasped her shoulders. "He was so close to slaughtering Tudor himself when Thomas Stanley turned on him."

"No," came out in a whisper, her voice gone.

"Richard held Stanley's son hostage to force fealty, but Stanley refused Richard's order to join the fray. When Northumberland saw Stanley go to Tudor's side, he stood by and watched as all hope vanished." He took a ragged breath. "Richard was unhorsed and Stanley's men surrounded him. He was offered a fresh horse, but refused, insisting to continue the battle, to either live or die as king."

She clung to him, shattered with grief. "Oh, dear God…"

"Once Stanley's army swarmed over him, Richard had no chance. With his last words, 'Treason! Treason!' he fell and they beat him lifeless." Valentine broke down into shuddering sobs. He turned away, leant against his horse and dragged his hands through its mane. "We lost him," he muttered, his muffled voice ragged and strained.

Her knees gave out, she pitched forward and hit the ground, tasting dirt.

He helped her up and led her to the stone wall. The scorching August sun seared her. She did not want to hear any more, it was all too much to bear.

"Thomas Stanley." Hugging her arms to her sides, she walked in circles. "My mother's husband. She told me he would betray Richard so Henry would win." If her mother and Stanley had not betrayed Richard, he would still be alive.

The unbearable weight of guilt crushed her. "I could have stopped it."

She couldn't tell Valentine. Not yet.

Still pacing in circles, she clutched her skirts in clenched fists. She stopped and faced him. Their eyes met, misted with tears, each a blur in the other's vision. "Where is Richard? I must go to him."

"His body is at the Gray Friars chapel in Leicester on public view. He is to be buried tomorrow."

She leaned into him. "Please take me there. I need to say goodbye."

* * *

They arrived long after the moon sank below the horizon. He opened the door to the chapel. Flickering candle flames cast eerie shadows on the walls.

She stepped inside. Valentine left her alone and the door groaned shut. Her shoes scuffed over the paving stones as she took small steps up the center aisle, dreading what she was about to see. Before the altar lay a coffin, no bier, no cloth of gold hangings, no sprays of flowers. She peered inside at a lean figure in the flickering shadows, the face drained of color, a patch of cloth carelessly tossed over his loins. Wounds slashed his chest and arms, blackened with dried blood and dust, gouges that emptied his life's blood in that final battle for his crown. Kneeling before him, she swept off her riding cloak and covered his battered body. "Valentine will carry on your work as best he can," she promised. "Henry Tudor may be my brother by blood, but you will always be my brother in my heart." She kissed her fingertips and touched them to his cold lips. "Farewell, King Richard." As she stood, her legs trembled from kneeling upon the stone floor. She turned and retreated down the aisle, shrouded in silence.

* * *

243

She found Valentine asleep on a stone bench outside, their mounts tied to a tree.

He ran a hand over his eyes and stood. "Where is your cloak?"

"I covered him with it. Do you want to say goodbye?" She tried to wet her lips, her mouth dry, her throat scratchy.

"I said goodbye yesterday. He knows I am here." Valentine gazed at the chapel as if willing Richard to walk out the door.

"He looks as if he sleeps." She grasped her husband's hand. It comforted her. Yet she shivered as if an icy wind froze her blood.

"He is." Valentine led her to her mount. "Finally, he will get some rest."

Chapter Sixteen

She turned, led him back to the bench, and sat. "My search ended yesterday."

"Dear God...how?" Eyes wide with wonder, brows knitted in disbelief, he sat beside her.

She took a deep breath, suppressing a shiver at the memory of her encounter and the stunning facts she learned. "I found my mother."

His mouth opened but he did not speak. His heartfelt smile broke her heart.

"You will not like it, not at all." She lowered her head, unable to look him in the eye.

"How can I not like it? This is what you've always wanted." He held her hands in a tight grip.

"Not quite this way." A flood of mixed emotions choked her—sadness, relief, joy, confusion, even loathing. "I've held this in too long. Valentine, my mother is Margaret Beaufort. Thomas Stanley's wife. Henry Tudor is my twin brother." Her words rushed out in one breath.

"Oh, Denys..." His eyes looked pained as if he held back tears.

"She married Edmund Tudor when she was twelve years old. He was King Henry's half-brother and heir. She gave me up in fear for my life, with my royal lineage on both sides. She gave me to Bess as part of a bargain," she repeated her life story, reduced to four brief sentences. "I am Henry Tudor's twin sister. We took our first breaths together." Her voice shook. "Henry Tudor, the mortal enemy who usurped Richard's crown, with finance from my mother, as my stepfather led an army of traitors."

"My God, I don't believe it..." Valentine's reaction was the same as when she looked in the mirror at Denys Beaufort Tudor.

He drew her to him. "But now you know."

His embrace helped comfort her. "All these years of frustration, contempt, torment, pain…leading to this cruel irony of fate…oh, why must it end this way?"

"It is hardly the end, my darling." He stroked her cheek. "This is a new beginning. You had to know who you are and I wanted it just as badly. Tell me, would you rather go to your grave not knowing? Would you live the rest of your life as a lost soul?"

She shook her head without pause. "Nay. I now know who I am, and I am relieved for it."

"So Tudor pardoned me because I am your husband. He knew all along that he is my brother-in-law," Valentine said.

"How?" She drew back, out of his embrace.

"Your mother must have told him. He would not pardon me out of the kindness of his heart. I was the king's first general. The others fled or were arrested."

Her breathing finally calmed. "I will meet with my brother and find out."

"Shall I accompany you?" he asked.

"Nay, I must do this myself."

"I know this is nearly impossible." His eyes met hers. "But forgive him as Richard forgave his enemies and you will know peace within your heart. Go to your brother and let your hearts enjoin."

* * *

At home, she sat down to write the most difficult letter of her life. She began with the truth: *I found our mother, and now I would meet you. Expect me on the morrow and do not think to avoid me.*

Tragic news reached London two days later: The two young princes, Edward and Richard, sequestered in the Tower during Richard's reign, vanished without a trace.

* * *

Westminster Palace bustled in chaos, squires and men-at-arms milling around everywhere, swords at their hips.

"I am here to see Henry Tudor," she told the guard at the front gate. She could not bring herself to refer to him as his highness the king.

He looked her up and down. "Who is calling?"

"The duchess of Norwich."

He clucked and dragged his feet, but before he spoke another word, she thrust Valentine's badge into his face. "I am also his sister." He gulped, bowed, and waved her on.

The sight of the palace saddened her. It was a different place altogether. It now bore a gloom, the guards menacing. No one spoke. A pall of starkness cloyed it.

Two men-at-arms led her through the gates. A page led her to the king's audience chamber. Neither Uncle Ned nor Richard had ever surrounded themselves with such a retinue of armed guards. What did Henry Tudor fear?

Until today, she planned to storm into Henry's chamber and scream at him for his slaying and dethroning her beloved friend. But she was drained of all feeling, all cried out, her sadness and rage spent. She would be unimpressed with any words in defense of his seizing the crown. But he was her brother, and a strange communion alerted her, a feeling she couldn't define.

The men-at-arms threw open the doors to Henry's audience chamber and there he stood. He regarded her with curiosity in green eyes that mirrored her own.

Her eyes wandered over his thinning hair, abundant at the sides but a scant tangle of strands on top, the same silvern shade as her own. His muscles bulged under his threadbare velvet robe. She noted an absence of gems, gold or other adornment. As her scrutiny met his, Valentine's words echoed in her mind: "Forgive him as Richard forgave his enemies and you will know peace within your heart. Go to your brother and let your hearts enjoin." At that instant, she felt a fiercely powerful bond.

His eyes betrayed a spark of recognition. The arched brows contained that sense of determination, echoing her desire for truth and the pain she bore to find it.

"Denys, dear sister, how lovely you are." His speech flowed in French eloquence, yet with an underlying Welsh harshness.

"Your grace." *Why do I treat him with reverence?* she wondered as she addressed him. *It is a betrayal of Richard's memory.* Yet he was her brother, flesh of her flesh. "In private I shall call you Henry." If he disliked it, she did not care.

"As you will." He grinned, displaying a row of rotted teeth. As he bowed his head, strands of thin hair fell out of place.

He held out both hands to her, so like Richard had. She took them and stepped closer. His arms encircled her awkwardly at first, then closed tighter. She rested her head on his shoulder, loving him, hating him, refusing to recognize him as king, yet overjoyed to finally hold her brother, even if he was Henry Tudor.

"My first order as king was for grapes, I craved for grapes so badly!" As he laughed she looked away from those eyes so much like hers, now bright with a mischievous spark she couldn't behold. She wanted to bellow at this heartless sod why his first order wasn't to treat Richard's slain body with dignity.

"Did our mother ever tell you about me?" she asked evenly.

"Nay, Denys, never." He shook his head. "But I learned I had a twin sister quite some time ago."

She had to know. "How did you find out, if not from our mother?"

"Elizabeth Woodville."

"Oh, Jesu." She gritted her teeth. That name she hoped never to hear again.

"She wrote me before my first invasion," he explained. "When Gloucester took the throne, Elizabeth knew her sons would never reign. She thought the next best thing would be to have her grandsons rule instead."

"Grandsons?" Denys raised her brows, confounded.

He nodded. "I am in troth to wed her daughter Elizabeth."

She gasped, her hand flying to her mouth. "You … are marrying Elizabeth? She's so young." She hoped the poor girl was aware of this scheme and her role as an innocent pawn.

"'Tis most practical. I shall unite the houses of York and Lancaster, and Elizabeth Woodville will get her royal descendants." He scratched his scalp. "I did not want to come forth and tell you who you were. 'Twas I who had you watched and people done away with who could've helped you. I bribed priests not to tell you the truth about Foxley Manor. I also had your genealogy taken from your house. All to thwart you. I thought that if you knew you of your claim to the throne, your husband would renounce Gloucester, with a potential queen as wife. He would be right there to place you on the throne, forcing me to fight my own sister."

"How dare you!" She clenched her fists and slammed them against her thighs. "Valentine would die for Richard. He never would betray him. They were closer than brothers."

His eyes narrowed. "One never knows what one will do when one's wife is of royal lineage and a few steps from the throne."

"So here I am." She raised her arms and let them fall to her sides. "Are you still afraid we will take the throne from you?"

"Nay, I pardoned him, didn't I?" His lips spread in a smirk. "But I will be doubly pleased if you accept what I am about to offer."

"What can you offer that I want?" She broke eye contact with him, suppressing a shudder of disgust.

"Denys, as children of Edmund Tudor and Margaret Beaufort, our claims to the throne are equal. I have no heirs yet, you are my only sibling, and I would like you to be my heir, until Elizabeth brings forth a prince."

She let out a bitter laugh. "Is that supposed to be a boon?" Would Richard have wanted her to take the throne as sister of Henry Tudor? Never! To succeed Henry Tudor would take the crown further from the Plantagenet line, which she refused to do. "I have never aspired to the throne, I do not aspire to the throne, I have no interest in the throne. Do you understand me, Henry? Should you die without issue, I advise you to name George Plantagenet's son Edward as successor. He should be next in line."

"The days of House of York rule are over. I won the crown by conquest with the support of Stanley and many others. It is evidently what the people wish." His voice rose to a level that grated on her nerves.

"You have not visited the north, Henry," she corrected. "The north is Yorkist country, and subjects there will always swear allegiance to the House of York. I know, having spent almost my entire life there."

"But the Yorkists are no more. Richard is gone and I am king." His voice took on a whining tone. She wanted to knock him off his lofty perch. Here he was king of England, behaving like a spoilt child. "The north is in the same realm as the south."

"We do not talk of chessmen, Henry," she deliberately spoke down to him, as his arrogance began to stick in her craw. "If you would rule like a caliph, you have conquered the wrong part of the world."

Two sets of eyes blazed. Beaufort stubbornness set sister against brother for the first time ever.

"Then I will progress north and win the hearts of my countrymen there. They will grow to trust me." His voice wavered, as if he didn't believe himself.

"Don't count on it, brother. Leave the north to my husband and the lords up there. Put your house in order first. Then sire heirs of your own, for I have no desire to rule. Or usurp. You have nowt to worry about over me or my husband."

"As you wish, Denys." He held up his right hand in truce. "And to prove that I harbor no ill will towards you or your fallen king, I will reverse the attainder against George Plantagenet and name his son Edward heir to the throne until I sire my own. Keep in mind that is unlikely to be, as he is an addleheaded dolt, hardly fit to rule."

"He has daughters," she stated.

"They are but babes," he countered.

"Richard the Second was eleven when he ascended the throne and Henry the Sixth was but nine months," she argued.

"Aye, and having a sovereign barely weaned lends itself to endless strife." He cast her a sly glance and raised a brow. "Look what happened when King Edward died. His young son was proclaimed king, but Gloucester moved in as if he had divine right. That proves my point."

"You bloody well do not prove your point!" She forgot he was king; he was simply her upstart brother showing the ugly side of his character. "King Edward made Richard Lord Protector. Then the princes and all Edward's children were declared bastard. That includes Elizabeth, your betrothed."

He gave her a half-smirk. "I shall rectify that. I tell you I will make Edward Plantagenet my successor as you proposed. Now let us cease argument. All I want is to make amends for having caused you such misery."

"Nowt you can ever do will make amends. Not only did you kill my dearest friend, you seized the crown from him—quite undeservedly." She raised her chin and stared him down.

He railed. "I spared and pardoned the duke of Norwich, unlike many of Gloucester's other supporters, only because he is your husband. Had I the cruel heart you believe I have, I'd send him to the dungeons with the other traitors."

"He is no traitor."

"We shall see," he retorted.

"What do you mean?"

"I need keep close eye on him lest the northern rabble arise and give me trouble." He glanced over his shoulder as if some enemy lurked behind his back.

"You will not have trouble from us, Henry. Let us be."

"Very well." He nodded. "Just remember, you have a brother now, who is king. I want to make it all up to you, your emptyhanded searches, your tragedies. Should you change your mind and be my successor lest I not sire a male heir, then the kingdom will be yours, as queen." He held out an imaginary crown. "However if you will not succeed me, I understand. But if there is anything I can do for you, not only as your king, but as your brother, just say the word. Your husband will retain his titles and lands, they will not be taken from you."

She waved away his offer. "I am happy up north serving my husband and our subjects there. My plate is full."

"Then so be it." He smiled. "But let me know if there is anything else I can grant you."

"Aye, there is. I would like a family painting. As of now, this is all I have." She reached into her satchel and pulled out the beads. The locket swung to and fro. She held it up to him.

"The eyes." He squinted, studying it. "You have her eyes. Beaufort eyes. And the chain round her neck in the portrait, she gave to me. I have it here." He went to his desk and returned with a gold "B" hung with two pearls suspended on a gold chain. Before Denys could utter a word, he slipped it over her head. "She gave it to me last time I came upon these shores. I was going to give it to my daughter someday, but I think you should have it. Besides, I intend to sire sons," he added with a superior smirk. "And now that Foxley Manor is back in the crown's hands, I want you to have that, too."

That hauntingly beauteous abandoned house that she'd wished to pretty up was now hers. "I would like that, Henry. Our mother's legacy."

He nodded. "Besides us, of course. She would like you to have it."

"Why was Foxley Manor empty when I went?"

"Elizabeth Woodville had tenants there, but when she learnt you'd go seek it out, she ousted them and their chattels to leave you no clew," he said.

"Except they missed this little clew." She clasped her fingers round the beads. "Oh, what a wasted life, living as a Woodville."

"Don't dwell on the past. Think of what you have now. A brother who is king, a husband who was spared. Go back to him now ... and enjoy life in the north."

"I will," she vowed.

"Now then ... you must attend my coronation, of course, you and your duke. I hope to be crowned by mid-October."

She shook her head. "Nay. Do not expect us at your coronation, Henry. It is too painful. Even you can understand that."

"Then this is farewell, dear sister. For now." He held out his hand and she grasped it. It was hot and sweaty.

"Godspeed, Henry." She exited the palace and began her journey home. "My quest is ended."

Chapter Seventeen

Denys sat in her favorite window seat overlooking Dovebury's outer court. As she rocked her baby son Richard to sleep, a fierce and abundant love filled her heart. Certain she was breeding with their second child, she intended to give Valentine a shire full of sons.

A horse draped in Tudor's banner, the red dragon, entered the outer court. Denys froze. *Dear God, what did he want?* She summoned the nurse to hold Richard and hastened outside.

"A message for the duke of Norwich from his highness the king." The messenger bowed and handed her a parchment embossed with the royal seal.

Valentine, tending to business at Middleham College, would not return til the morrow. Unable to wait, she broke the seal as the messenger departed and that dreadful dragon faded from her sight.

She unfolded the parchment and read a summons to court. "Why does he want Valentine at court?" she wondered out loud. His queen, Elizabeth, just birthed their first son, so he had his precious heir, the future King Arthur. But what did he want from her husband?

Henry Tudor had not gained in popularity, especially in the north, which remained Yorkist with a staunch loyalty to Valentine.

She fetched her cloak, rounded up a retinue to load a pack-horse with supplies, spurred her mount on and took the road to Middleham College. This could not wait.

* * *

A week later, Valentine stood in the outer council chamber at Westminster Palace. During his time as chancellor, good humor and fellowship filled the air.

Now the chamber sat enshrouded in gloom. The king's grooms and footmen wore peevish faces as they carried out their duties. Armed guards stood everywhere. That bloody red dragon repeated on dozens of banners made the whole place a Yorkist hell.

The king's guard swept through the doorway and strode up to Valentine. "His highness the king wishes your service, Sir Starbury."

He shook his head in perplexity. "In what capacity?"

"He has assigned you the office of Great Chamberlain."

"I am governor of Yorkshire. I have no desire to serve in the royal court. Please relay that to his highness." Valentine turned to leave.

The guard clapped a hand on Valentine's shoulder. "You may not return to Yorkshire. You will serve your king..." He paused and swallowed. "...or die a traitor."

Two more guards appeared from the shadows and seized Valentine. By nightfall, he sat in the Tower of London with one week to ponder his decision. He sent a message to Denys, urging her to stay calm.

* * *

His message outraged her. "How could he! How dare he!" She clenched her teeth as fury heated her blood. Her heart pounding, she flung the message to the floor and shredded it with her shoes.

"Please saddle my mount," she ordered her groom and collected her retinue. "We leave for London—now." The servants exchanged looks of utter bewhape. "Make haste!" she demanded and they scrambled about to prepare for the journey.

As her maid packed a satchel for her, she held her baby in her arms and rocked him to sleep in a teary farewell. Blowing him one more kiss as he lay in his cradle, she set out for London.

* * *

The guard opened the door to Valentine's cell in the Byward Tower and Denys hurled herself into his arms. "Are you all right? What have they done to you?"

"I am quite comfortable." He gestured to the featherbed and the window open to a soft breeze and streaming sunlight. "Henry paid me a personal visit. He turned the key in the lock and entered alone. Rather a humble entrance for a usurper."

"What did he say?" She clutched his arms, unable to let go.

"He gave me a week to decide, which, I must admit, is quite liberal. So I must take my leave shortly and give him my decision." He led her to the two overstuffed chairs by the window.

"I didn't want to return to court." She sat next to him.

"Listen to me." He grasped her jaw twixt his thumb and fingers just as he did when he delivered the dreadful news of the lost battle. Fear kicked her in the stomach. "I have chosen to die."

She screamed, sprang to her feet and locked her arms round his neck. "God, no, you know not what you say!"

"I cannot serve him, Denys. I yield myself up freely. I said I would die a noble death and now I will prove it." He pushed her arms away as two guards strode in, pulled him to his feet and clamped their hands to his arms.

"But you have too much to live for! What of our children? You'd leave us all alone?" In her frenzy, she tried to pry the guards' hands off him.

"You shan't be alone, Denys. You have your mother and your brother. For me to serve Henry Tudor under threat of death is the most cowardly act I can conceive. You would come to loathe me. I will not have you live with a coward and a traitor to Richard's memory. Death is the most noble choice." The guards led him out of the cell.

"Then I am going with you! We die together, I will not live without you!" Frantic, unable to breathe, she followed on their heels.

"We will not die together," he spoke over his shoulder as the guards pushed him onward. "You are his sister, you are royalty. I am a bloody thorn in his side from the white rose of York. You must understand. There is no other choice for me or Henry."

One guard clutched her elbow and guided them both down the Byward Tower's circular stone stairs.

She could do nothing more here. "Nay, I shan't let you do this alone, Valentine. I know what must be done. I must go to my brother."

As she descended the dizzying steps, she decided to depart this world knowing she'd accomplished what she'd set out to do.

She fought a pang of regret that she would never see her children grow up. She hoped Henry would not take her life until the birth of their second child. But there was no time for regrets: the door to the king's receiving chamber opened and Henry stood before them. As Valentine bowed, Denys bobbed her head.

"Denys. Sir Starbury." Henry gestured them to enter and they followed him into the chamber. He invited them to sit. "How nice to see you, dear sister."

She did not acknowledge his offer, and Valentine also remained standing. "We have come to give you our decision."

"I will speak for myself, Denys." She blanched at Valentine's harsh tone.

"Ah, then you will serve me." A superior smirk spread Henry's thin lips.

Denys shook her head. "Nay. I come to die."

Henry blinked. "You do?"

Husband and brother stared at her with equally startled eyes. Valentine clutched her shoulder. "N—nay, she does not mean that, sire—"

"Valentine, cease!" She shook his hand off and turned to her brother. "Loyalty does not end with death, as anyone in Yorkshire will bear witness." Denys kept her voice steady. "Spare Valentine and take me. He's worth much more to you alive than his estates will be after he's dead. Don't you see that executing Valentine only leads to rebellion? He is more loved in the north than Richard ever was. Slay him and northerners will swarm like angry wasps. Wars will begin again. Tis better that you take your wrath out on me. Are you too ignorant in the ways of state and moreover, the hearts of your subjects, to grasp that?"

The king stood speechless, assessing her words. Denys couldn't stand to look at him. All feeling drained to numbness.

Valentine grasped her sleeve again and this time she did not resist, but took his hand in hers.

"Denys, I am impressed." Henry nodded. "Doubly impressed that you would die in place of your husband rather than live a royal life here. I cannot undermine your loyalty to your dead king. I know you consider me no ally, but I cannot kill my only living sister. Valentine, your sway in the north is formidable. I cannot expect everyone to like me. Not everyone liked Richard either." The corner of his mouth twitched in a weak smile. He cleared his throat and carried on. "If you were to rebel, you would have already. I no longer consider you a threat. You may go."

Valentine bowed and began to back out. But Denys stayed rooted to the spot, forcing herself to look into her brother's eyes. She found her voice, uttered a short "Farewell, Henry," and eschewing further custom, joined her husband.

"Denys," the king's voice reached her as they neared the stairs.

She turned to face him.

"Would you not like to see your new nephew, Prince Arthur?"

"I'm an aunt." She nodded and smiled. "Aye, Henry, I would indeed."

He personally ushered them into the nursery where Elizabeth sat rocking the infant. She was no longer the child that harbored fancies about Valentine. She was a woman and a queen. Her new-found regal airs brought an amused smile to Denys's lips.

The queen greeted Denys and Valentine warmly. "Let bygones be bygones, Denys." She let Denys hold her nephew. "If you can find it in your heart to forgive Henry's affronts and how my mother treated you ill, I welcome you as our sister."

"'Tis past and done now, Elizabeth. Let us look forward to making a better world for our children." Denys gazed into Prince Arthur's young eyes, so much like hers, her brother's and their mother's. His lips had the same heart-shaped pout. He was Beaufort through and through, nowt of Woodville in sight.

"He is lovely, Elizabeth, so very lovely." Joy lightened her heart, knowing that her and Valentine's surpassing love had created a miracle of their own.

"But why did you not name him Henry?" Denys asked her brother. "Would you not have your own Henry grow before you?"

"Welsh bards tell me the Breton version of King Arthur's legend, and I made them tell it over and over. I dreamed of living that legend, and having a son I would name Arthur. An apt name for a boy born to be king." Henry patted the top of Arthur's head. "Our next son will be Henry. And who knows, someday Henry the Eighth."

So he dreamed of Arthur's legend, too; he longed to live it, just as she had.

"Legends are compelling, Henry, but they are just that, legends. Being king will show you that you cannot live in a legend. However, I wish Arthur a long and propitious reign as our king."

Before they took their leave, Henry spoke a few last words to his sister. "Loyalty takes many forms. Do not forget you have family here."

"It gives me great joy that I finally found my family, Henry. But I've also found my life, which is in the north with my husband." She nodded her final farewell.

The king watched with renewed pride as his sister and brother-in-law walked down the corridor, arm in arm.

Chapter Eighteen

The Tower of London

The guards led Denys to a small chamber. The earl of Warwick, son of the slain George, duke of Clarence, greeted her with a confused expression clouding his gray eyes.

"Hello, Edward. I am Denys. I was a dear friend of your Uncle Richard, and I knew your father. We had some wonderful times together." Now that Henry had his first son, Edward's days were numbered. She knew Henry would remove Edward, the last Plantagenet. She feared he would also banish Edward's wife Sabine and their daughters into obscurity. Edward was Denys's last link to her past, and she needed to call on him.

Edward's eyes lit up. His father's mischievous twinkle lurked behind the darkness of a lifetime of imprisonment. His wife Sabine joined them, followed by their two daughters, Topaz and Amethyst.

The little girls chased each other, pulled each other's hair and shrilled with delight, blissfully oblivious of the pain and suffering to be endured because of who they were. Topaz sat straight and tall in the window seat and placed a gold circlet atop her head, looking every bit the child queen.

"Topaz, you are a jewel, and so are you, Amethyst!" Denys marveled at the tyke's confidence, the small yet proud figure. Topaz bowed her head with dignity. "Topaz is all ready to sit on a throne." Denys smiled. "She looks a queen already."

"We shall never know." Sabine stroked Topaz's golden mane of hair. "Who knows which way the fickle crown will go after we're gone."

Denys bid her farewells and headed home.

Her mount glided over the fields in the late summer twilight. "I am on my way home to you, Valentine. I do not want the crown of England, as long as I am crowned by your love!"

THE END

Dear reader,

We hope you enjoyed reading *Crowned By Love*. Please take a moment to leave a review in Amazon, even if it's a short one. Your opinion is important to us.

Discover more books by Diana Rubino at
https://www.nextchapter.pub/authors/diana-rubino

Want to know when one of our books is free or discounted for Kindle? Join the newsletter at http://eepurl.com/bqqB3H

Best regards,
Diana Rubino and the Next Chapter Team

The story continues in:

To Love A King by Diana Rubino

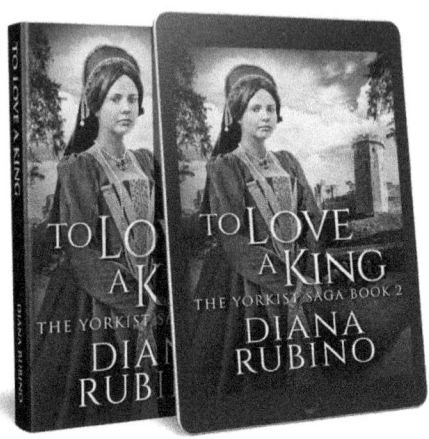

To read first chapter for free, head to:
https://www.nextchapter.pub/book/to-love-a-king

Epilogue

Cristoforo Colombo didn't forget Denys and Valentine; on his fourth voyage to the New World, after finally securing finance from King Ferdinand and Queen Isabella of Spain, he named one of the islands LaHuerta, which means "The Orchard."

Acknowledgments

I would like to extend my sincerest thanks to the Richard III Society, notably Peter and Carolyn Hammond in London, for their assistance with my research. The Barton Library documents were especially helpful.

Author's Note

Anne Neville's father, the earl of Warwick, was slain at the Battle of Barnet, not Tewkesbury. To accommodate my story, I kept him alive a bit longer than he actually was.

About the Author

My passion for history has taken me to every setting of my historicals. The "Yorkist Saga" and two time travels are set in England. My contemporary fantasy "Fakin' It", set in Manhattan, won a Romantic Times Top Pick award. My Italian vampire romance "A Bloody Good Cruise" is set on a cruise ship in the Mediterranean.

When I'm not writing, I'm running my engineering business, CostPro Inc., with my husband Chris. I'm a golfer, racquetballer, work out with weights, enjoy bicycling and playing my piano.

I spend as much time as possible just livin' the dream on my beloved Cape Cod.

Visit me at www.dianarubino.com.
My blog is www.dianarubinoauthor.blogspot.com.
My author Facebook page is DianaRubinoAuthor.

Lightning Source UK Ltd.
Milton Keynes UK
UKHW041851020720
365951UK00007B/277